LOST
IN
THE OFFBEAT

A NOVEL

PATRICIA HOPKINS

Lost In The Offbeat

Visit my website at **http://www.wanderlustbooksllc.com**

Copyright © 2015 Patricia Hopkins

Cover Image Shutterstock/Vitalliy/177078881

ISBN-10: 0991449118

ISBN-13: 978-0-9914491-1-8

Dedications

My love... The journey is more important than the destination. Let's make lots of pit stops along the way.

My wonderful children... Never give up on your dreams. You are just one idea away from making them come true.

My friends and family... Thank you all for your continued support.

* * *

Sometimes you must lose everything you once had before you can appreciate the importance of what you still have.

ALSO BY PATRICIA HOPKINS

~~~ NOVELS ~~~

LOVING IN THE OFFBEAT

LIVING IN THE OFFBEAT

MORE THAN A NOTION

~~~SHORT STORIES COLLECTION~~~

I AM THE SHADOWMAN (AND OTHER SUPERNATURAL TALES)

OLD GRACIOLA YOUNG

~~~ CHILDREN'S BOOKS ~~~

INVASION OF THE GLOBOTS

Space with no Air

The story of my life rewrites itself with each passing moment
Fueled by an urgent restlessness I cannot ignore.
Infinite patience arrives to replace the weariness,
In this quest to define my dreams;
To bypass this struggle that never seems to end.

I pause to reflect...

Words sent adrift on the winds of an impromptu spring storm
Blow seamlessly through tender green leaves,
Sending hopeful wishes to the graceful treetop;
Questions with no answers abound
For a life that is yet to be fulfilled.

An unfinished story...

Wayward thoughts now have a destination,
Towards the infinite sky where heaven resides
On the wings of birds that soar without limits,
To a place high above the clouds where my sight cannot reach;
One word at a time, the story of my life is slowly revealed.

In this space where there is no air, a quiet whisper reminds me to
strap on my oxygen mask first,

And breathe...

~Patricia Hopkins~

LOST IN THE OFFBEAT

Chapter One

Joie straggled behind Cedric trying her best to keep up as her husband hurried towards the hotel reception area.

Cedric explained his situation to a patient concierge, gesturing angrily towards his pleading wife who stood near a huge indoor palm tree with her arms crossed. This was not the first time the concierge had dealt with a couple whose trip did not turn out the way they planned. So it took all of five minutes for the gentleman to arrange transportation from the remote beachside resort to the Santo Domingo airport. The earliest flight was scheduled for six in the morning. Cedric planned to be on it—with or without his wife.

While Cedric made plans to depart the island, Joie continued to ask, plead, and beg for his forgiveness—all to no avail. And listening to his wife's incessant apologies only managed to aggravate him, leaving his head aching with a kind of misery he couldn't shake. He tried to ignore her chatter and headed to the checkout counter to settle their tab.

"*Lo siento, Señor* Parker," said the hotel clerk, while rifling through stacks of paper on the counter. "I found *Señora* Parker's *pasaporte,* but unfortunately someone has misplaced yours."

"What do you mean, 'someone has misplaced my passport'?" Cedric asked through clenched teeth. "How in the hell does a hotel misplace a guest's passport?"

Joie hung back near the concierge station secretly thanking the gods for this small delay. Now maybe she could talk some sense into her husband.

"*Señor,* I will call your room as soon as we locate your *pasaporte. Entretanto,* here is a coupon for *cena gratis para dos* in *un restaurante* of your choice. *Por favor.*"

"I don't want no damn free dinner," he shouted. "I just want you to find my passport so I can get the hell outta here."

The clerk took notice of Cedric's bloody hand and disheveled appearance. The last thing he needed was a guest dripping blood all over the lobby floor. The man pursed his lips together and continued searching through stacks of passports experiencing anxiety that was impossible to hide. He motioned for an employee to give the man a towel. "You should go to your room and take care of your hand. I promise I will call you when I find them."

"No thanks. I'll wait," Cedric stubbornly replied in a loud voice.

Several other guests were now starting to notice the scene.

"*Señor* Parker," the clerk said, appearing as if he were about to faint. "*Por favor.* Your hand…"

A young, attractive woman came from behind the counter, sidestepped Joie, and began to carefully wrap a towel around Cedric's hand. At first he flinched, but her calm demeanor and gentle touch gradually comforted him. She whispered in Spanish phrases meant to soothe.

"All right." He calmly acquiesced. "I'll go to my room. But I want you to call me as soon as you find it."

"Do not worry. We will find it. It has to be here somewhere," the clerk replied in relief.

Joie didn't appreciate the concern shown by the young woman as much as her husband did so she took the towel from the young woman and told her, "Thanks. I got this."

The woman backed away and returned behind the counter, but not before throwing Joie a sideways glance.

"C'mon, baby. Let's go to *our* room," Joie said loud enough for everyone within earshot to hear, just in case anyone had any doubt about her status.

Back in their suite, Cedric lowered his bruised hand into the ice bucket supplied by the hotel staff as Joie looked on from across the spacious room. The cold water numbed the pain only slightly, causing him to grimace when his swollen knuckles brushed against the sides of the stainless steel container. It had been many years since he felt the need to punch a man. And despite the pain he now endured, punching Tomas in the jaw was worth it.

"Well?" Joie asked nervously. "Do you believe me or not?"

He swirled his hand in the icy water leaving flecks of blood in the cold liquid while contemplating his response. After finding their way back to town after leaving the Duarte's villa, the only thing on his mind was getting as far away from his wife as possible. Only problem was, nothing in the Dominican Republic was done quickly.

"Cedric? Answer me, baby." She wrung her hands together in desperation because despite her nonstop apologies, her husband had not spoken a word to her since getting out of the car. Their honeymoon was not supposed to end with Ced leaving her ass behind because of a little misunderstanding.

He heard the hurting in her voice, but tried in vain to ignore it. Although she had no apparent bruises, he felt the pain ooze from her body as if it were an open wound. Joie's pleading didn't work, but the way she chewed on her bottom lip, causing the little dimple in her left cheek to appear, did. The anger enveloping his heart began to thaw, much like the ice cubes in the water where his hand was immersed.

"I'm sorry... Please forgive me..." she continued to beg. "I had no idea Tomas was going to be at the wedding."

Gradually, the more he listened to Joie's incessant apologies, he allowed his vision to clear as he pushed the painful anger aside. Finally he spoke. "Do you love me?"

The sound of Cedric's voice was music to her ears because nothing is as deafening as the silence which comes from someone you have hurt. She slowly closed the gap between them, stepping over suitcases pulled out in haste, and over clothing carelessly strewn across the floor, until she was inches from her husband's face. And in a voice just barely above a whisper, she said, "Yes, I love you. Until the end of time, I will always love you and only you."

He exhaled his relief, lifted his hand from the melted ice cubes, and dried it on a towel. The pain had finally subsided. From his hand and his heart.

"And will you forgive me for hooking up with Tomas while we were dating?"

Cedric stared at his wife. He had forgiven Joie for many things most men would never have let their wives get away with. Forgiveness is what marriage was all about, is what he firmly believed, so it is what he practiced. In fact, when it came to his wife, and much to his own detriment, turning the other cheek had become something he had done so often, it had almost become second nature. In spite of everything, he still loved her.

Joie planted a juicy kiss on his lips. Then his neck. She took his bruised hand in hers and gently kissed each knuckle one by one. She placed his hand against her chest and rested her head on his shoulder. Then she exhaled in relief.

After several moments had elapsed, he enveloped his wife in his arms and quietly whispered, "Yes, Joie, I forgive you."

Chapter Two

Several days later…

Two hours after departing Miami International, the airplane skirted the southeastern coast of the United States heading towards Virginia. In direct contrast to Cedric and Joie Parker's honeymoon paradise in the Dominican Republic, the newlyweds were treated to a very rough ride home. Had either of the couple been superstitious, they might have seen the bumpy ride home through more ominous lenses, rather than as a result of weather-related turbulence.

Minutes earlier, the pilot announced in a garbled, barely decipherable voice that they were beginning their descent. He also thanked his passengers for choosing their airline, finishing up with hoping everyone had enjoyed their flight.

The pilot's remark prior to landing never made much sense to Cedric because as far as he was concerned, as long as the plane was in the air, they were still flying. Thus, he wouldn't know whether or not he had enjoyed his flight until after they landed. Landing safely would make a huge difference in his enjoyment level, as far as he was concerned.

While the incessant drone of engine noise blocked out the mundane conversations of his fellow passengers, Cedric thought about his honeymoon. For the briefest of moments, he allowed himself to fantasize about the possibility of finally having planted his seed into his wife who lay with her head propped against his shoulder. From their first go-round of marriage, Cedric understood that Joie had a lot to be desired in the wife department, but knew for a fact that she was one helluva mother. He reasoned that the last thing needed to permanently bind them together as a family, and more importantly to keep his wife from wandering was for Joie to bear his child.

~ ~ ~

"Ladies and gentlemen, please return your seatbacks and tray tables to the upright position. All electronic devices should now be powered off. Carry on items need to be stowed securely underneath the seat in front of you. We will be arriving in Norfolk on time this afternoon to a chilly temperature of twenty-six degrees. If you are catching a connecting flight…" The male flight attendant's voice boomed loudly over the plane's intercom. Speaking with a proper British accent, he carefully pronounced every syllable of each city as if he were reciting the lines of an acclaimed Shakespearian play.

Joie began to stir releasing a deeply satisfying moan. Remnants of a sensual dream swirled around her mind, slowly dissipating into that strange space where sleep and wakefulness collided. She tried with all her might to hold on to the fleeting images, but all that remained once her eyelids parted was the delicious feeling of making love to a man who oddly enough was not her husband. Upon hearing Cedric's voice, her dream lover retreated completely to the hidden recesses of her mind to await the moment she summoned him once again. She yawned loudly into a full body stretch with both arms lifted high above her head.

"Hey sleepyhead. You were really out of it," Cedric remarked with amusement.

"Was I?" Joie responded. With her eyes still partially closed, she watched the male flight attendant, who resembled a clean-shaven George Michael from the 1980's boy group, *Wham*; rattle off the list of connecting flights.

"Excuse me," interrupted another flight attendant. "Is there anything else I can get you before we land?"

"Yeah, I'll take another refill of champagne," Cedric replied.

Joie shook her head, no.

"I'll have that right out," replied the flight attendant.

"You have slept practically the entire time since we took off from Miami." He returned the *Skymall* magazine to the seat pocket for the next passenger's reading pleasure. "You that tired?"

"Yeah, I'm that tired." She yawned again. "It's not like we spent much time sleeping while we were in the DR."

Cedric smiled a deliciously wicked grin at Joie as the flight attendant refilled his glass.

"What is so funny?"

"Baby, this is our first time flying first class and you missed all the special attention." Cedric drained his glass of champagne with a smile of satisfaction pasted across his face. "What a shame..."

"Looks like you enjoyed it enough for both of us."

"I sure did. Got to drink as much of the bubbly as I wanted. And they even gave me a hot towel to clean my hands."

"Well, I wouldn't be so damn tired had you let me sleep last night."

"Did you really expect to get any rest? I thought you'd be happy for the attention instead of complaining…"

"I'm not complaining."

"Are you all right? You seem a little out of it."

"I'm good. I was just having this amazing dream."

"So that explains all the moaning…" He grinned slyly while running his hand along her thigh. "Was I in it?"

"Not this time." Joie twirled the wedding band around her finger, having yet to become accustomed to wearing it again. "I actually forgot exactly what I was dreaming, but it must have been good if you say I was moaning."

"You were probably dreaming about all the freaky stuff we did in the airport bathroom. I know it's still fresh in my mind. And on my fingers." He slowly slid his finger first under his nose; then hers.

"Ugh! Stop being so damn nasty!" She playfully pushed his hand away.

"What are you *ughing* about? That's all you, baby. Your sweet nectar."

"Whatever…" Joie blushed in embarrassment.

"That's all right. As long as we're together, I forgive you for not dreaming about me."

"You do know I don't have a whole lot of control over my dreams, right? According to an article I read, dreaming is done at the subconscious level."

"Is that right?" He signaled the flight attendant requesting another refill of champagne before landing. "Maybe you were subconsciously dreaming about how much fun we had on our honeymoon, huh?"

"We did have a good time, didn't we, Ced? Despite the fact that we *were* married for almost six years, you'd think we wouldn't need another honeymoon."

"Actually, *this* was our first honeymoon."

Joie smiled as she recalled memories from their first marriage. "I guess so… Remember we spent our first night as husband and wife at the old *Holiday Inn* over on Mercury Boulevard?"

"Yes. And you convinced the manager to give us a fifty percent discount because you lied and told him you saw a cockroach in the bathtub."

"I had to do something. We barely had enough cash to pay the hotel room bill…"

"We really knew how to have a good time with barely nothing, didn't we?"

"Sure did," she agreed. "We walked across the parking lot to the *Waffle House* where we could both eat breakfast for less than ten dollars."

Cedric smiled as they reminisced. "Even though we didn't have the money to take a real honeymoon when we got married the first time, we made the most of what we had."

"Those were the days, but I prefer living like this much more," she sighed happily. "And flying first class is the bomb! I don't think I'll ever fly coach again."

"I agree. Over all, the trip turned out better than I expected."

"A week at a luxury resort in Punta Cana? Right after Christmas? And for only a few hundred dollars? Talk about a bargain!"

"Even if I had to pay ten times what I paid for this trip, you are worth it, baby."

Joie snuck a peek at the flight attendant who was now occupied with his pre-landing flight checklist. She quickly plucked a miniature salt and pepper shaker set, along with several miniature bottles of complimentary liquor from the serving cart and tucked them into her bag.

"Joie, what are you doing?"

"I'm taking a few souvenirs from the plane home. Why?"

"Because its kinda ghetto, that's why."

"No, it's not. All they're going to do is throw this stuff away. They can't serve other passengers anything we have already touched. Anyway, they want us to take this stuff home. Why else would they put the airline's logo on it if they didn't?"

Cedric knew that when Joie's mind was set on an idea—ridiculous or not, it was better to just let her have her way. "Can I ask you something?"

"Sure. What is it?"

"Baby, since you seem to love the DR so much, maybe it should become our vacation spot. You know... make it our own special place. What do you think?"

There was one tidbit of information Joie still hadn't told her husband. She took a deep breath and said, "Ced, there's something I need to tell you because we promised no more secrets."

"You gonna tell me about that dream you were having?" he asked again. This time his hand cupped her breast.

She swatted at his hand again. "No, I'm not gonna tell you about my dream..."

"Fine. So what's up?"

"Well, I didn't want to say anything earlier..."

"But?"

"But, this wasn't my first time vacationing in the DR."

He leaned his head back into the headrest, allowing the drone of the engines to mask the growling noises building in the base of his throat. It was obvious his previously relaxed and happy mood was now gone. "Is that right?"

She nodded.

"So when were you there?"

Joie winced at the painful memory because this was not a topic she ever wished to revisit again. But just like a bad meal, the betrayal to her marriage seemed to keep coming up.

"Was it before, after, or *during* our marriage?" he asked.

Joie crossed her arms tightly across her chest as if this small action would protect her from the hurt that would surely result from this conversation. "I, uh, I'm only telling you about this now because I don't want us to have anymore secrets between us."

"Go on. I'm listening."

"I flew down there before the twins were born. I told you I was going on a business trip to Miami, but instead I went to Punta Cana."

"Was Ronnie's husband with you?"

"What?"

"I asked you if Derek Jordan was with you."

She replied without hesitation, "I ain't gonna lie to you no more. Yeah, me and Derek was together."

Cedric shook his head from side to side in an attempt to rid himself of the images threatening to creep into his mind. He gripped the metal part of the seat divider and squeezed tightly. Finally, after several minutes had passed, he visibly relaxed and stated matter-of-factly, "Look, I know we got a lot of stuff we need to work on. I appreciate you telling me the truth."

"What? That's it?"

This time, he nodded.

"That's all you got to say?"

"Joie, the past is the past and there ain't a damn thing I can do about any of what happened back then. When I asked you to be my wife again I accepted you and all the bullshit that came with it."

"I appreciate your understanding, but you don't have to be so blunt about it."

"Maybe I am being a little blunt, but I'm just saying that we've got a lot of stuff to work on in our marriage. Honesty is the first issue we must tackle. Trust is the second. I can have all the love in the world for you, but if we can't be honest with each other, we might as well part ways now."

Joie twisted her mouth sideways, glancing at her husband from the corner of her eyes in disbelief. This wasn't the Cedric she knew. The old Ced would have cursed her out after hearing about her cheating on him. Didn't matter if they were on an airplane full of people or not. She whispered, "You're serious, huh?"

"As a heart attack," he replied.

"I thought you would be pissed off at me."

"I am. I mean, I was, but thankfully, I have had a couple of years to get over it. I forgave you a long time ago."

"I know you forgave me. I guess I'm surprised that you're not more upset, that's all."

"Joie, I couldn't hold on to that anger and ask you to be my wife again, could I?"

"I guess not," she replied.

"I'm glad you told me. Now we can move past it."

"Hey, since we're being so honest, don't you think it's about time you told me about that woman you married?"

Cedric's left eye twitched at the mention of an event he so wanted to forget.

"I mean, after all, I didn't even find out you had married somebody else until *after* you proposed. And even then it was only because you slipped up when you said I was the last woman you ever planned on marrying…"

"Are you sure you want to hear about this?"

"We're married now. No more secrets, right?"

"Joie, it wasn't a real marriage. It only lasted a few months."

"Did you have to get a marriage license?"

"Yes."

"And did you get a divorce?"

"Fine. I was married. But like I said it was very brief and turned out to be a very bad decision on my part."

"So why did you do it?"

"I was stupid. After I found out about your affair and the truth about the kids... Well, I guess I temporarily lost my mind. I ran into this pretty young thing at the club, she rocked my world for a minute, and I proposed after just a couple of weeks. Right after she moved into the house I realized I had made a huge mistake."

"How old was she?"

"She was old enough."

Joie snorted. "Humph! I bet she was barely twenty."

"If you must know, she was twenty-two."

"Damn! Still wet behind the ears." Joie shook her head. "What was her name?"

Cedric lowered his head and quietly whispered, "Lovely September Rose."

She laughed out loud. "What?! For real?! You actually married somebody named *Lovely September Rose*? What was she? A stripper?"

"No, but since you asked, she was a swimsuit model. And that is her real name."

Joie snickered. "I will never understand why you old-ass men fool yourselves into thinking these little young girls want to hook up with you. Most of 'em are only after what you can do for them."

Cedric held his tongue. He refused to allow Joie to pull him into a conversation that resulted in his having to explain the benefits of having a much younger woman. And he had enough sense to not mention all the amazing things his young ex-wife did in bed—things Joie would never do in a million years. For those few short weeks he was married, he and Lovely had sex in every position imaginable, sometimes three times a day. But it turned out that the fine Lovely September Rose *was* only after one thing. She wanted a financially secure man to take care of her while she completed school and pursued her fledgling modeling career. When she discovered Cedric couldn't support the lifestyle she wanted, things quickly fell apart.

"Like I said, it was a mistake. She and I had totally different ideas of what we wanted in life. Besides, I didn't love her and she obviously didn't love me."

"When did you know it was a mistake?"

"After a month or so in, I had my suspicions. I knew for sure the day I came home to find her in bed with a guy she normally studied with."

"She cheated on you? In your bed?" Joie wrinkled her nose in disgust. "Ugh! I hope it ain't the same bed we've been sleeping in."

"No, I tossed that mattress out along with her. Anyway, she told me they were just *fuck buddies*. Can you imagine that? Fuck buddies!"

Joie could only shake her head in disbelief. "Kids these days…"

"I couldn't even get mad. I just told her to pack her shit and get out."

"Serves your old ass right…" she said more to herself than to him.

"Baby, can we please talk about something else? I don't want to end our honeymoon reliving my lapse in judgment."

"Fine," she replied. "I just wanted to know because you always changed the subject when I tried to get you to talk about it before."

"I hope you can understand why I didn't want to talk about my ex-wife. Shoot…I was trying to get you back; not push you further away."

Joie averted her eyes as she continued to play with her rings. Cedric was right. She did not want to talk about his younger ex-wife who also just happened to be a swimsuit model. Lord knows the girl must have been absolutely beautiful, not to mention she must have also had a killer body and 38DD breasts.

The older female flight attendant passed by their row, visually checking passengers—tapping the seats of those who were still in the reclined position. Joie tightened her seat belt when the woman looked her way.

Cedric noted his wife's sudden discomfort. He glanced out the window at the waters of the Chesapeake Bay peeking between the clouds scattered below. Most of the ground remained covered in snow thanks to an unexpected Nor'easter that had recently pummeled the east coast for days.

Joie closed her eyes trying to hold on to the happy feelings from the last week, unfortunately the realities of life continued to surface threatening to disrupt it all. Even though Ced had declared his mistake by marrying that chick, she still felt hurt by how quickly he had wanted to replace her.

"What's up, baby?" he asked. "You having second thoughts about us getting remarried?"

"No, of course I'm not having second thoughts. What about you, Ced? Are you happy to call me your wife again?"

"Yeah, I'm very happy we're back together."

"I hope you don't think this was a huge mistake after a few months have passed. You know...with me and the kids being back in the house again."

"Not a chance. I love you and I love our kids. *Our* kids. You hear me?"

"I hear you. I love you, too."

"What else is bothering you?"

She shook her head. "Nothing else," she lied not wanting to admit being hurt. "I just want us to be a family again."

He took her hand in his. "Then let's be one. The only people who can stop us from being a family are us."

"I never stopped loving you," Joie admitted.

"I know," he replied.

"I just want us to be happy, Ced. We both messed up, so let's just forgive and forget."

"Already done."

"Because if we continue bringin' up shit from the past, we will never be a family again. At least not a happy one."

Cedric leaned back in his seat. Wanting to change the subject to a lighter topic, he said, "You know what? That was a very nice ceremony that Luis and Ronnie had. I'm glad they invited us."

"Me too. It was just as beautiful as their wedding in Santa Elena, but the recommitment ceremony was extra special because they had both families there."

"I know one thing," Cedric joked. "Your friend sure does know how to finish a wedding with a bang. I thought she was gonna drop those babies poolside."

"Ronnie ain't the only one who knows how to end a party with a bang."

"What do you mean?"

"I just knew you had broken Tomas' jaw with how hard you punched him." She plucked a breath mint from her purse and popped it into her mouth to freshen her breath. "You want one?"

"Thanks." Cedric accepted the mint. "That brotha deserved it. Don't no man be kissing on my wife."

"You got that right..."

"Fake-assed Spanish accent, pretty boy muthafucka," he muttered under his breath. "Niggah probably working on getting a green card."

"Actually, he is Dominican so he really *does* speak Spanish. French too... and he already has an American passport."

Cedric slammed his fist on the armrest causing several passengers to look his way. The passenger across the aisle shot him a disapproving look before returning his attention to his paperback novel.

"What's wrong with you, Ced?"

"Damn, Joie! Why in the hell are you trying to explain this dude to me? I don't give a fuck where he is from or how many languages he speaks. On top of everything else, do you really think I want to hear specifics about that niggah?"

"I'm sorry, baby. No need for you to get so upset."

It was bad enough for Joie to bring up her adulterous relationship with Derek, but the absolute last person Cedric wanted to hear about was Tomas de la Cruz. She and Cedric had already beaten that horse to death on the way back to the hotel from Luis and Ronnie's villa. The only thing that stopped him, other than the hotel losing his passport, was the good loving she put on him when they returned to their hotel room.

Joie promptly changed the subject. The set of Cedric's jaw let her know she was this close to really pissing him off again. The sweat popping out on his forehead had nothing to do with nervousness from the plane descending through turbulence, but had everything to do with Joie about to get on his last nerve.

"I'm cool," he uttered.

Not wanting to add fuel to the fire, Joie backed off by returning the subject to a more neutral one. "Anyway... I am so happy for Ronnie and Luis. Like you said, it was a beautiful ceremony."

The anger management group Cedric joined after their divorce a couple of years ago had really paid off. He relaxed the anger away through a series of deep breathing exercises, so he was now better able to control his temper. Most of the time. In a much calmer voice, he replied, "They do seem to make a nice couple. And it's about time Veronica found somebody who could deal with her bougie ass."

"I thought you had let go of how you felt about Ronnie."

He shrugged. "She awright. But she's still the most bougie woman I know."

"Whatever."

"The woman is bougie, Joie. Admit it. Always pretending to have more than what she got. Thinking she better than everybody else."

"That's your opinion."

"On the other hand, their villa on the hillside with those nice views of Santo Domingo below was slammin.'"

"Well, I'm happy for her and Luis. For all of them, especially Kiara. She's so excited to be a big sister."

"Is Kiara planning to live with them?"

"Naw, I don't think so. Ronnie told me Kiara moved back to California to finish her last year of school. Afterwards she's planning to work in Luis' office in Santa Elena because she wants to live close to Travis, and his new wife, Monique."

"Good for her. She seems like a really intelligent young lady."

"She is..." Joie smiled because she was truly happy for her friend. "Can you believe it? Ronnie went and had two beautiful twins. A baby boy *and* a girl... Just like us, huh?"

"Yeah, just like our Trey and Maya." He brought her hand to his lips.

Joie had put Cedric through hell by giving birth to another man's children. Because of this, she never imagined that he would ever accept Derek's kids as his own. Her parents advised Joie to give him time, because time is supposed to heal all wounds. So she did. And while she dated lots of other men, including Tomas, she could never get over the fact that she was still in love with Cedric.

"Sweetheart, you and I belong together." Joie placed her index finger besides his. "See that little scar we both have on the same finger?"

"Yeah, I see it..."

"That means we are destined to live the rest of our lives as one."

"Is that right?"

"That's right. And I plan on keeping this honeymoon going for the rest of our lives."

Cedric smiled at his wife, happy to have the love of his life back. "I love you, Joie."

"I love you more."

The male passenger across the aisle looked their way again, only this time the look on his face was one of relief. He looked first at Joie then turned his attention to Cedric, before shaking his head.

When Joie noticed the man staring, she shifted her head to the side and said, "I hope you found our conversation entertaining. That must be one boring ass book because I noticed you haven't turned the page over the last fifteen minutes."

The man turned nine shades of red, and then looked away in embarrassment of having being caught eavesdropping. The subject of the book the man pretended to read suddenly became the most interesting subject in his world as he buried his nose in it.

"Baby, leave that man alone."

"His ass shouldn't be so damn nosey," she replied. "Sitting over there with a stick up his ass judging us..."

Chapter Three

The plane touched down at Norfolk International Airport. As soon as the fasten seat belt sign went off, passengers started gathering their personal items. Cell phones were turned on with calls made to loved ones informing them that they had arrived safely.

Cedric turned to Joie and said, "I just want you to know that in spite of everything that went down, I really like the DR. I think we should find our special place there and make it our own."

"That's fine with me, baby. That's fine with me..."

~ ~ ~

Because they had already cleared customs in Miami, the couple proceeded directly to the baggage claim area for their luggage. During the short walk to the long-term parking lot to retrieve their car, the windy conditions resulting from the nor'easter whipped up the kind of damp cold that gave people pneumonia if they stayed out in it too long. Cedric noted that the blanket of snow he observed from five thousand feet was at least 3 inches on the ground.

The traffic on I-64 was fairly heavy as they headed north to Hampton. It was slow going because most drivers chose to drive overly cautious on the slippery road.

While Cedric focused on the car in front of him that kept hitting its brakes, Joie stared out the window at the wintry landscape as she listened to WHOV 88.1, Hampton University's, *Lessons in Jazz*. The DJ was involved in an interesting commentary about how the youth of today no longer appreciates jazz.

It wasn't often the Tidewater region got snow at all, but when it did, the area was literally shut down. Still, Joie thought the snow covered ground was beautiful.

Just before they reached the bridge leading inside the Hampton Roads Bridge Tunnel, Cedric looked over towards the Norfolk Naval Base to where several ships were docked. An enormous grey battleship that seemed to defy the logic of something that heavy being able to float, dwarfed the other ships, making them appear like tugboats in comparison. The battleship must have recently returned to port because it wasn't there when they left.

The brisk wind sent sprays of water from the choppy waves of the bay below, over the sides of the bridge, and unto the windshields of surprised drivers. For the I-64 traveler not used to the tunnel, a wave of water coming over the bridge as they descended into the darkness was quite unsettling, and only caused them to hit their brakes a bit earlier than they otherwise would have. This accordion effect caused traffic to back up for miles as drivers more experienced with the region tailgated those just passing through. Perhaps it was the fear of getting trapped inside a tunnel filled with water that caused drivers to react so erratically. But as far as Joie recalled, the HRBT had only flooded a few times when the main pumps had malfunctioned, but never while traffic was inside.

Two hours after leaving the airport they finally arrived in Hampton, stopping by Joie's place to pick up a few items for the twins who were staying with her parents over the winter break.

While Joie flitted between Trey and Maya's rooms selecting outfits for the week, Cedric waited inside the foyer patiently thumbing through a stack of magazines. He noted Joie had put her personal touch on Ronnie's old house by repainting the previous warm earthy tones with bright vibrant colors making the house uniquely hers. She had also taken down all traces of Ronnie's expensive silk taffeta drapes and replaced them with custom made plantation shutters.

"Joie? How's it going?" Cedric called out patiently.

"I'll be there in a minute. I just need to find Maya's boots," she shouted from the back bedroom.

"Take your time," Cedric replied. "I'm sure your parents ain't ready to get rid of their grandkids yet, especially since this is the last weekend they'll have them for a while."

Joie joined Cedric in the hallway. She carried a tote bag filled with clothes for the twins. "I can't believe Mom and Daddy are moving to Florida in a few weeks."

"Your father has been talking about retiring to Florida for as long as I've known him."

"I know, but I never thought he was serious." She exhaled loudly. "Virginia is their home. Our home. What am I going to do when they leave?" She dropped the bags to the floor.

"Tampa ain't that far, baby. You can fly down to see them whenever you want."

"It may as well be the other side of the world because I've always had my parents nearby." She lowered her head. "The kids are really gonna miss their grandparents..."

"You got me.... I'm right here."

"You're right. I guess I'll just have to get used to not seeing them as often. Still, it's going to feel strange knowing some other family will be living in their house."

Cedric surveyed the house that used to belong to Ronnie. "Speaking of houses... Baby, I've been thinking."

"About what?"

"This house. Don't you think it is time to sell? After all, you and the kids have moved back home with me."

Joie cocked her head to one side considering Cedric's question. "Know what? As much as I love this house, you do have a point. We don't need to be paying two mortgages."

"After all, we are married again, so we should be living under one roof. Don't you think?"

"You're right," she said again. "Tell you what. I'll contact a realtor first thing tomorrow. I doubt if I'll make any money on it, considering I've only lived here a little over two years. Might even lose money..."

"You don't ever have to worry about money again. We are gonna be just fine now that we're back together." Instead of picking up the twins' suitcases, Cedric shut the front door.

"I thought we were about to leave," Joie said.

"How about we make good use of our last few minutes without the kids?"

"Oooo... What do you have in mind?"

"Something that's been on my mind since we were on the airplane."

"What are you up to, Cedric?"

"How about you just play along?"

Joie smiled coyly before stepping out of her high-heeled shoes and into one of her favorite roles.

Cedric jumped right into character. He extended his hand and said, "Thank you for inviting me in, ma'am."

"My pleasure. What can I do for you today?"

His lustful eyes took in Joie's voluptuous figure. "I'm selling vacuums for two g's each. Are you interested?"

"I'm sorry, sir, but I don't have two thousand dollars to spend on a vacuum cleaner."

"Beautiful lady, this revolutionary vacuum is very special and worth every penny. The suction is twice as good as any you may have experienced before."

"My husband would have a fit if I spent that kind of money without discussing it with him first."

"If you don't mind me asking, where is your husband?"

"He's at work, but he should be arriving home at any minute. Anyway, like I said, I can't spend that kind of money without his input."

"So don't tell him."

"Okay... What if it's not the right size?"

"No worries in that department. This customized attachment has been carefully designed to be one-size-fits-all. Especially for those tight spaces." Cedric stepped closer as his breath quickened.

"Is that right?" Joie went to the stereo where she popped in a CD. "Well, my husband usually takes care of the vacuuming around this house. What makes you think yours is better than what I have now?"

"Because I guarantee satisfaction. Once you've experienced the pulsating action of this magnificent device, you will never need nor want another vacuum cleaner." He unzipped his pants. "Ever."

Joie bit her bottom lip. She was enjoying this immensely. "Oh my goodness! What are you doing?"

"I am going to provide you with a demonstration of its power. Once you see what it can do, I guarantee it will change your life."

Joie crouched down on her hands and knees as if examining the floor. She rubbed her hand over the fabric of the area rug. "I don't think my husband would mind if you just showed me how well your hose works."

Cedric joined Joie on the floor. "The first thing I need to do is examine your rug."

"Yeah," she replied, breathlessly. "My rug really needs attention in one particular area."

He maneuvered her back to the floor, placing his hand between her thighs. "You're right. I can feel a wet spot developing there."

"Do you think you can do something about it before my husband gets home? He always told me not to let salesmen in the house when he's not here. Says y'all only want one thing."

Cedric grinned. "Ma'am, your husband is correct. And at the rate I'm going, I'll be finished in less than five minutes."

"So what are you waiting for? Let's try this thing out to see how well it works. That spot is getting moister by the moment."

"Okay ma'am, I am going to give you the deluxe treatment. Now just lay back and let me do my magic." He pulled off his pants.

"Oh my goodness!" Joie's eyes bugged out in surprise. "Sir, I didn't know you were going to use an industrial sized hose!"

"For you pretty lady, only the best." He knelt down, placing his face between her trembling thighs.

"What? Are? You? Doing?" She moaned passionately.

"Spot treatments." Cedric moistened his lips with his tongue. "I always like to get the rug nice and wet before I begin. Makes it much easier to slip my hose into those tight spaces."

Joie arched her back and thrust her hips forward, rocking in time to her husband's motion, allowing him to fill her every desire with his lovemaking. She called out Cedric's name over and over until they had both reached the peak of orgasm. Afterwards, they both lay on the rug spent.

"I thought you were playing when you said you'd be finished in five minutes..."

"Not to worry, my love. That was only round one. Lean back because there is much more where that come from," he stammered with sweat pouring down his face. He flicked her erect nipple with his tongue. "How do you like this?"

"Ummm." She purred. "I like..."

"I thought you would," he whispered. "Now tell daddy what you want. And take your time."

"Oh Ced..." Joie laid back while he worked his magical tongue all over her body. "You make me feel so good. I don't want this to ever end."

He lifted his head and whispered, "Neither do I, baby. And it won't have to end because we have our entire lives to look forward to. Now let me get back to this delicious honey pot you got going on here. Damn! You taste good..."

"Oooh baby. This is all yours... Forever and always."

Cedric slid his penis inside Joie and released his load after several strong climatic thrusts. As the last bit of his semen made its way from his body, he shuddered involuntarily.

Joie simultaneously reached orgasm, gazing deeply into Cedric's eyes, feeling his love shine through.

"Baby, you know how to make me feel so good!" She closed her eyes to revel in the sensation of good lovemaking. Lost in the throes of passion, Joie caught herself before another man's name made it to her lips.

"That's right baby. Say my name!"

Oh my God! Did I really almost call out Tomas' name?! What the hell am I thinking? Why am I making love to my husband and thinking about another man? She closed her eyes even tighter. Unable to contain the tears of confusion welling up inside, they spilt forth down her face.

Cedric's loving gaze indicated that he was totally unaware of the Freudian slip that had almost occurred. Pleased that they could still make love at the drop of a hat, he knew Joie had also reached orgasm when he saw the tears of joy roll down her face.

They both so wanted to believe that their love would conquer all. That love would be enough to sustain them for a lifetime and see them through till death do they part. Yet still, as their bodies were locked together as one, both Cedric and Joie struggled to silence a nagging doubt each had about the other.

As he watched his wife, he wondered, *will I ever be enough man for Joie? Can I trust her? After all, she cheated on me with Derek Jordan, and was involved with that Tomas de la Cruz dude just a few months ago. But she says she loves me so I guess I should believe her.*

Chapter Four

Joie's father stood outside the family home sweeping snow from atop the *For Sale* sign planted in the front yard, with his gloved hand. After being on the market for less than a month, they already had received multiple offers on the well cared for house.

"Hi Daddy! I just stopped by to see how things are going," Joie said upon exiting her car. She frowned at the realtor's smiling face on the sign. "You sure didn't waste any time putting the house on the market."

"I told you that we were selling the house before you went on your honeymoon. I guess you were just too excited to have paid attention."

"You've been talking about selling the house for as long as I can remember. I just didn't think you were actually going to do it."

"We had to wait for the right time." He straightened the sign. "And now is the right time."

"Daddy, I can't believe you and Mom are actually moving," Joie said. "Why didn't you guys wait until it was summer so we could drive down with you?"

"C'mon, now baby girl. Your mother and I have been planning this move to Tampa for years. It's time for us to enjoy our retirement."

"I know. But I'm going to miss you. And so will your grandkids."

"We're going to miss you, too. But you can visit whenever you want. Just give us a few hours notice so me and your mother can make sure we're decent..." He cleared his throat several times. "Never know what us old folks can get into without kids around. Know what I mean?"

"Daddy! Please stop. I do not want to have an image inside my head of you and Mom getting your freak on."

"Sorry, honey. I didn't mean to embarrass you." He laughed. "Now that you and Cedric have gotten back together, you both need to focus on your family. Make that your priority."

"What about the house?" She scanned the contents of her parent's lives packed up in cardboard boxes awaiting the arrival of the movers. "Do you have enough money saved?"

"As a matter of fact, the realtor just called with a solid offer at our asking price. We're gonna use the proceeds to fund our retirement." He tossed the suitcases into the trunk. "Besides, this house was too big for us after you and the kids moved out."

"What am I going to do without you? Who will I call when I need someone to talk to? Daddy, you have always been here for me."

"Joie, you know I will always be here for you. We're moving to Florida, not the moon. And you can always talk to your husband if you need someone to talk to."

Joie stared at the house she had grown up in. Memories flooded back of riding her tricycle for the first time down the driveway. The tree she had accidently backed the car into still bore the evidence of a "lack of focus" as her daddy described it. For as long as she could remember, when Spring rolled around, she helped her mother plant vegetables in their backyard garden that they would harvest in the summer. Now, after forty years of calling this house home, someone else's family would reside in it. It was almost too much to bear.

"You guys won't like Florida. It's hot, humid, and they have cockroaches the size of compact cars. The only people who live there are retirees and foreigners who can't speak a lick of English..."

"How do you know so much about a place you've never been?" he teased.

"I've heard things. And I'm not even gonna mention all the tourist traps they have there."

"Tampa is a nice city. You'll see when you come down for a visit."

"Daddy, you know how Mom fusses over her hair. She's going to hate the weather."

"That's why we're moving during the winter. Before it gets too hot. This way, we'll have several months to become acclimated to the heat and humidity."

"I'm telling you... You're going to miss the four seasons. No more watching the leaves turn fall colors. No more snowstorms. Just endless days of summer with the threat of hurricanes." In spite of her rough exterior, Joie always turned into a little girl around her father.

"Come here." He pulled Joie close, wiping her tears away.

"Daddy, you just don't know how hard this is..." She sniffled. "I feel like I'm losing you..."

"Honey, I know our moving is difficult for you, but it will only be hard for the first few weeks. In time, you and the kids will regain your routine with Cedric and pretty soon you won't miss us as much."

Joie's mother burst through the front door with her cell phone plastered to her ear. She called out to her husband, "Honey, the movers are on their way. They should be here in less than ten minutes so I need you to move the car."

"All right, Slim," he shouted back to his wife. "I'll park the car over in Reggie's driveway. He's at work so I know he won't mind."

She ended her cell phone conversation. "Hi Joie. I didn't know you were out here."

Joie dried her eyes and pulled back from her father's embrace. "Hi Mom. I just stopped by to see if I could help out anywhere. Don't want you guys to pull a muscle or anything."

"Oh baby, we're fine. The movers are doing all the work." She looked to Joie's car. "Where are my grandchildren?"

"They're at basketball practice. I dropped them off at the Y on the west side before I came over."

"That's fine, but I want to see those lil' rascals before we leave tomorrow."

"Why don't you guys stop by the house later to say goodbye? I can make dinner."

"That sounds like a good idea." Her father added, "Well, I've got to go move the car. I'll be right back."

Her mother went to where Joie stood. She looked at her daughter as if seeing her for the first time, noticing several grey hairs that seemed to have magically appeared overnight. The dark circles under her eyes did not bode well.

"Are you all right, baby?" she asked with concern.

"Yeah, Mom. I'm fine."

"Are you sure? You don't look all right. You seem a little...out of it."

"I'm just thinking about you guys moving so far away. You've always been right around the corner. Now look what's going on. You're selling the house I grew up in."

"Joie, stop being so melodramatic."

"I ain't being melodramatic." She pouted knowing she had never been able to pull the wool over her mother's eyes, as she did with everyone else. "I'm really going to miss me and Daddy's late night porch talks."

"I know how close you guys are, but there is such a thing as the telephone. You can call your daddy every night if you want to." She took in Joie's disheveled appearance more closely. "You sure everything is okay? You don't look so good."

"I'm all right. I just haven't been sleeping very well."

"How are you and Cedric getting along?"

"We're taking it day-by-day."

"What does that mean? Day-by-day?"

"Well, it hasn't been as easy as I thought it would be getting back together with Cedric. It's only been a few months, but sometimes the way he looks at me makes me wonder if he regrets getting us remarried."

"What about you? Did *you* make the right decision?"

"For the most part I think I made the right decision, but like I said, there are those times I can imagine his anger brewing beneath the surface. He doesn't say anything; it's just the way he looks at me."

She pressed her lips tightly together trying to not be irritated by Joie's attitude. "Cedric is a good man. And you did give him a lot to handle. It can't be easy raising another man's children when he thought for years that they were his own. That is a large burden to place on anyone."

"Can you please be on my side for once?"

"I'm your mother, child. I will always be on your side."

"Then why do I feel like you're taking Ced's side in this?"

"Joie, you know I love you, but you can be a tough cookie once you set your mind to something. You have a sharp tongue like me and you have no problem stepping on other people to get what you want."

"What are you talking about?"

"You are your mother's child."

"I know that…"

"What I mean is I see so much of myself in you. I have watched you over the years and you have grown into a beautiful woman. But like me, you have a mean streak and if you're not careful, you will alienate everyone you come in contact with."

"You think I'm like you?" Joie didn't know whether to feel proud or be ashamed. Her mother had been a shrewd businesswoman in the workplace. But she had her moments of being spiteful, especially with her daddy.

She nodded. "Your quick wit can alienate folks. Might even offend a few… Because I recognize this in myself, I allow your father to rein me in when I start to lean in that direction. You need somebody who will do that with you."

Joie contemplated her mother's words. What she said was true. Her mother was never one to mince words with anyone. Never had been. She said exactly what was on her mind, never sparing anyone her wrath when she was angry. As a result, very few people ever stuck around long enough to call themselves her friend. And as much as she hated to admit it, her mother was right about her.

"I think it is time you started taking responsibility for your actions. Now that you and Cedric have gotten back together, there are going to be times and situations that remind him of what you done. You lied and cheated. Had another man's children and then lied to him about it. He don't seem like the type to hold grudges, but he is just a man. A little anger is bound to come up every now and then."

"I know what I did was wrong because I am reminded of it every day."

"Is that right?"

"I guess it is a lot for Cedric to handle because the kids aren't biologically his."

"Has Cedric mistreated the children?"

"No, Mom. It's nothing like that. Cedric loves Maya and Trey."

"Then what's the problem?"

"Sometimes, he makes hurtful insensitive comments."

"Like what?"

"Take for instance what he did this morning. Trey was in the bathroom watching Cedric shave. He imitated Ced's every movement by putting shaving cream all over his face and pretending to shave."

"What's wrong with that? Sounds like they were bonding."

"I thought so too until Trey asked Cedric if he was going to grow up to look like him."

Her mother shook her head from side to side. "That must have been hard to answer."

"Ced didn't know I was listening. Mom, I was so pissed off by his response."

"What did he say?"

"He told Trey that he was going to grow up to look exactly like his father because he already had his eyebrows and his nose. Well, my baby ain't no dummy. Trey compared his nose to Cedric's, and then asked him why his own nose was so pointy while Ced's was flat. He said he didn't think their noses looked alike at all. And then he asked him why he had a thick unibrow when Ced's eyebrows were barely visible."

"Oh Lord…"

"Trey kept asking so Ced told him that he looked just like his father. Then he told him to be quiet."

Joie's mother crossed her arms. "I suppose he answered best as he could without outright lying."

"I guess." Joie pulled a twig from the snow-covered ground. She bent it until it snapped in two. "He also wants us to have a baby."

"Whaaaaat? Honey, I think that is a wonderful idea. You know I'd love to have more grandkids."

Joie turned to watch her father back his car into the neighbor's driveway. "Mom, he says he wants to have his *own* children."

"Oh…"

"Yeah. Although he says he loves and accepts the twins, he doesn't really consider them as his. Not really."

"Do *you* want more kids?"

"Actually, I always thought the twins were more than enough for both of us. At least they were until he found out they're not his biological children."

"Child, even if Cedric raises the twins as his own, the fact is that most men want children who have their bloodline. Someone to carry on the family genes."

"That's exactly what he says. He wants a son to carry on his family name."

"You can't blame him for wanting that, dear."

"Mom, this situation is so complicated," she explained. "The twins already carry his name, but I'm worried about Trey and Maya. What if I have another baby and Ced prefers it to them? I don't want him giving preferential treatment to one child over the others."

"Well, there's probably not much you can do to prevent that. Most parents have a favorite child even if they don't admit it."

Joie stared at her mother. "Did you ever want more than one child? And if you did have other children, would you have treated my siblings better than you treated me?"

"You know that is a question I can't answer because The Lord didn't choose to bless me and your daddy with more children. But if we had more, I would have treated you all the same."

"I'm glad you didn't have more kids, because if you did, I probably wouldn't have gotten any of your attention."

"That's not fair, Joie. I know you and your daddy have a close relationship, but that don't mean I didn't also love you," she replied, offended by Joie's insensitivity.

"I'm sorry, Mom. I didn't mean anything by that remark. I know you love me. Besides, even if I did want to get pregnant, physically, I might not be able to have more children anyway."

"Why not? Is something wrong, sweetie?" she asked with deep concern.

"Yeah. I got fibroids. Lots of fibroids. My gynecologist told me some have grown so big that they're taking over my uterus. She said it would be a miracle if I can get pregnant at all. And my chance of carrying full term is almost nonexistent."

"Oh baby... I'm sorry. Is there anything you can do about it?"

Joie shrugged. "She described a few different procedures that may save my uterus. She also told me that if they continue to grow, I will most likely have to get a hysterectomy. I'm tried so many different medications to shrink these fibroids. So far, nothing is working."

"What a shame..."

"I may eventually lose both my uterus and my husband." Joie kicked at the snow covered grass. "Ain't life ironic? I finally get my husband back only to lose him again because I can't give him his own children."

"Look Joie, Cedric will come around. And if I were you, I'd look into a few alternate treatments. Look for a doctor who offers a holistic approach to treating fibroids."

"How do I do that? All the doctors and specialists I've seen all say the same thing."

"Sweetie, I've been listening to that radio show from the university. On Friday mornings, they have a show dedicated to natural holistic healing. I don't remember the man's name that hosts the show, but one of his favorite sayings is, 'God gives us every plant and herb in the garden'. So instead of taking all this medicine, why don't you try using an alternate therapy? It can't hurt, can it?"

"At this point I'm willing to try anything. When Ced and I rededicated ourselves to one another last month, we both promised we would love and support one another to grow stronger as a family. I think the problem is that neither of us really understood how difficult this was going to be."

"Joie, you have to realize that Cedric may have forgiven you, but he will never forget. I know that man pretty well. He would never hurt you intentionally. He loves you too much. Just give him some time."

"I'm trying, but…"

"But what?"

"You know I love Ced with all my heart, right?"

"Well, that's what you keep telling me. So what is this *really* about?"

"I keep feeling like maybe I missed out on something by getting back together with Cedric."

"You mean someone better might come along?" Her mother shielded her eyes from the sun as she looked across the street at her husband. "I know what you're thinking. You're wondering whether you settled when you remarried Cedric."

"Not exactly, *settled*. It's just that I dated somebody very special before Cedric and I got back together. This man took my breath away. He was handsome, successful, and we had so much fun together."

"Okay, but did you love this other man?"

"I don't know whether I loved him or not. Ced came back into the picture when I was seeing this other man. He told me how much he loved me and that he wanted us to be a family again. I guess I wanted the same thing. For the twins' sake. So when he asked me to remarry him, I said yes."

"That must have been a difficult decision for you."

"You have no idea how difficult it was."

"Why did you say yes if you weren't sure?"

"I kept remembering how good things were between me and Ced before everything fell apart. We were pretty happy and very comfortable for the most part. I hoped we could get back what we had then. Become a family again…"

"Neither one of you is the same person you were before the secret came out. I imagine he changed just as much as you did." She watched her husband lock the car and head back towards them. "Can you imagine how your daddy would feel if I all of a sudden told him you weren't his?"

"Mom? Are you trying to tell me…?" Joie's face immediately registered a look of horror.

"Girl, don't be silly. Your daddy is your father. Of that I am one hundred percent certain. But what I'm trying to say is that Cedric took you back knowing that you perpetrated one of the worst lies a woman can tell a man."

"Dang, Mom… Do you have to go there again?"

"I know you don't want to hear it, but it's true. Not many men would have forgiven a woman for not only cheating on him, but also giving birth to another man's children. And lying to him on top of it."

"You're right… Maybe that's why I was willing to remarry Ced. He forgave me and part of me felt like I owed him."

"You must know that a sense of obligation ain't strong enough to keep your marriage together." She carefully studied her daughter wondering where her head was really at. "So you decided to remarry Cedric because he was a sure thing?"

"That's only partially the reason." She paused and exhaled. "The truth is, I was afraid of being alone and being a single mother. I didn't want to chance this other man walking away if things didn't work out."

"You say you love Cedric. Are you *in* love him?"

"I think so… I really do love Ced. He is so good to me and the kids…well, he used to be. I just want us to get back to where we were. Do you think that's possible?"

"That ain't what I asked you."

Instead of answering her mother, Joie looked at the ground as if the solution could be discovered in the snow.

"It is only possible if both of you put in a hundred percent. Marriage ain't easy, but when you have a man who is honest, hardworking, and dependable, often times that is more important than a man who puts butterflies in your stomach."

"That doesn't sound romantic at all." Joie looked at her mother perplexed. "Does daddy still give you butterflies?"

"Yes, he does. That man is the love of my life. My world. My rock. I don't know what I'd do without him. But I'm not talking about me. I'm talking about you. And you just remember that all that fluttering around in your stomach can make you nauseous. I think that you are better off with Cedric whether you believe it or not."

"Why do you say that? You don't know anything about this other man I'm talking about."

"I know that everybody comes with baggage. I'll bet that other man who kept your head in the clouds ain't as wonderful as you think he is. Anyway, what I do know is that it's easier to clean up your own shit than it is to clean up someone else's. Yours may stink like it ain't nobody's business, but at least it's yours. You ever tried cleaning up a grown person's shit? I have. It ain't for the faint of heart."

Joie gasped in surprise. "Mom, I don't think I've ever heard you curse."

"I only curse when it's appropriate. And in this case, it was appropriate to get my point across. My advice to you is to stop being so damn evil and hold on to that man of yours."

"Why you calling me evil?"

"I raised you, remember? I know how you are when you don't get what you want, so I can only imagine the drama you keep going in your house. You should stop questioning everything and be grateful Cedric took you back at all. And you need to get rid of that doggone chip on your shoulder… Everybody is not out to get you, Joie."

"I can't help I'm a high maintenance woman who knows what she wants." She rolled her neck. "Anyhow, if I have a chip on my shoulder, it's because my life hasn't turned out the way I want it to."

"I blame your daddy for spoiling you. You had him so wrapped around your little finger that he ruined you so that no man will ever be good enough."

As if on cue, Joie's father approached his daughter from behind. In his hand, he carried a red *Macy's* shopping bag, which he thrust in her direction.

Joie squealed like a little girl. "Ooooh daddy, what is this?"

"Just a little something for my beautiful daughter," he said before joining his wife at her side. "It's a going away gift from the both of us."

Joie peeked inside the shopping bag. "Oh my goodness! It's the *Coach* handbag I was looking at the other day! I had to put it back because it was way too expensive."

Her mother said, "I remember you mentioning it. I told your daddy about it when we were in *Macy's* picking up a few items for the move. He thought it would be nice to get it for you."

She opened the handbag with a puzzled expression. "An umbrella? What's this for?"

Her mother said, "That is my gift to you so you will always feel protected. I chose the color yellow to lift your spirits when you're feeling a little down."

"Awwww… that's so thoughtful. Like a little sunshine in the rain."

"It's just my little way of saying I will always be with you when you're feeling all alone."

"Thank you both so much!" She kissed both parents on their cheeks. "I should be the one giving y'all a going away gift, not the other way around. But I'm glad y'all did!"

"Like I said," her mother said with a good-natured laugh. "Spoiled."

Her father looked from his daughter to his wife, confused. "Slim, did I miss something?"

"No dear, you didn't miss anything. We were just having a mother-daughter private moment, that's all. Everything is fine."

"Thanks for the advice on everything, Mom." Joie hugged her mother. "See, I may be a grown woman, but I still need you. And as soon as I get home, I'm going to start my own research on curing my body. And I'm gonna try to start appreciating my husband more."

"That's good dear, because no matter if you decide to have more kids, you only have one body so you need to take good care of it." She looked at her husband. "And if you're lucky, you marry a man who puts God first and you next over everyone else."

"I love you." She embraced both parents at once. "I'm really going to miss you…"

"There's just one more thing I need to tell you, sweetie."

"Yeah, Mom. What is it?"

"All kinds of people are going to come into your life, but not all are meant to stick around. They will bring good and bad with them, but it's up to you to choose who gets to stay. What I've learned over the years is that I can learn something from everyone I meet."

Joie reflected on her mother's words of wisdom, mentally running through the list of people in her life.

"Some of them jokers showed up just to teach me what I should avoid." She chuckled. "Others have changed my life with a single word or a simple act of kindness."

Her father agreed with Slim, "That's right. I have met some folks that I should have crossed the street when I seen them coming. But I'm not as perceptive as your mother. She has always been a better judge of character than I am."

"All we're saying is for you to be careful out here, Joie. I know some people, including your father, think I am a bit jaded, but there is nothing wrong with having a little cynicism every now and then. It keeps you on your toes."

Chapter Five

Ever since that Sunday morning two months ago when Joie watched her parent's drive away out of her life and into their retirement to Tampa, her weekends were no longer her own. It wasn't until Joie's parent's had moved away, did they realize how much they relied upon them to babysit.

Thus, another Monday morning rolled around quickly after another jam-packed weekend filled with shuffling the kids from one activity to another. Cedric was usually tied up with work-related events on the weekend, so he wasn't much help at all. Joie arrived at work exhausted, but was still expected to put in a full day of work.

The weekly staff meeting thankfully went by quickly. Afterwards, Joie retreated to her office to make a private call to her husband. Seemed lately that her coworkers had way too much time on their hands, because every time she turned around someone was coming into her office to gossip about one thing or another. She used the office phone to call because it had better reception.

"Hey Ced. You busy?" she said into the phone, ignoring an incoming call on another line.

"Not really. I'm sending out emails because I'm trying to arrange a trip to the city jail for my youth group next week. I need permission from all their parents first. It's my version of *Scared Straight.*"

"Oh, that's a good idea. Those knucklehead kids need to know what a real jail looks like before they get the wrong impression from those glamorized TV prison shows."

"What's up, baby?" he asked as he continued to jot down email addresses.

"I have some good news!" She plopped down in the chair opposite her desk.

"What's going on?"

"My realtor called earlier. I just got an offer on my house."

"That was fast. You just put the house on the market a month ago."

"The realtor says the market is hot right now. Apparently April is the beginning of the season when sales take off. The buyer made a cash offer for the house "as is"."

"Are you going to accept it?"

"That's what I wanted to talk to you about. The offer is just enough to pay off the bank and the realtor's commission. I'll be lucky if I walk away with a few thousand dollars after all is said and done."

"Do you think you'll get a better offer if you wait?"

"Maybe... I think we can afford to pay two mortgages for a while, but what if this is the only offer I get?"

"Well, I guess you can factor in that they are accepting the house as is, which means you won't have to fork out any money for repairs. That alone may end up saving a few thousand."

"Yeah, I guess you're right."

"I think you should take it. Even though we can swing it, I really don't want to be paying two mortgages, especially on an empty house."

"Right... There are lots more ways we could be using this money."

"Yeah, we can fix up our house. Starting with that bathroom you've been on me to remodel for years..."

She laughed good-naturedly. "That damn bathroom has had that same ugly wallpaper from when we first bought the house. Ain't you tired of looking at it?"

"To tell you the truth, I never thought about it one way or the other."

"Men!" she exclaimed. "Y'all could live in a cardboard box and not notice."

"Baby, however you want to decorate the house, I'm cool with it." He chuckled.

"So anyway, I'm going to call her back and say that I accept."

"Sounds good."

"Now that that's settled, do you want to do anything special after work? I can arrange for a babysitter."

"Not today, baby. I forgot to tell you that I'm working late."

"Again?"

"I'm sorry. The center is having a program this evening so I'm staying late to assist."

Joie exhaled slowly before she spoke. "You told me that since they promoted you to manager, you wouldn't have to be so hands on with those kids. It seems that you're working more overtime now than you ever did."

"I know, but it takes a lot to keep this program running smoothly. Most of my new youth counselors lack the experience working with troubled teens so I need to remain closely involved."

"Fine. What time do you think you'll be home?"

"No later than ten o'clock, which means I won't be able to pick up Trey and Maya from school."

"Really, Ced? You haven't picked up the kids since last Monday."

"Joie, it can't be helped. The awards ceremony starts at six. We're going to recognize several of our kids for their outstanding support in the community. The mayor is even going to present an award to the teen volunteer of the year."

"Good for them," she replied sarcastically. "They see you more than our kids do..."

"Hold on a minute, baby." Cedric placed the phone to his chest to speak with one of his coworkers.

Joie heard a woman's muffled voice followed by a round of laughter on the other end. Listening to Cedric yuck it up with another woman pissed her off. She felt her anger quickly soar high on the wings of jealousy.

"Okay, I'm back," he replied.

"Who was that?"

"Who was who?"

"The woman you were giggling with."

"I don't giggle. And that was Sheila. She's one of the other senior counselors."

"Right..."

"Joie, don't start."

"I'm not starting anything. You're the one laughing it up with your coworker while we're in the middle of an important conversation. Can't she see you're on the phone?"

"She didn't know I was on the phone..."

"Is *Sheila* going to be working late also?"

"Yes, she is." Cedric sighed wearily. Ever since they got remarried, Joie turned a jealous eye towards every woman he came in contact with. Her insecurity was tiresome, annoying, and so very unnecessary. "Baby, like I have told you a million times before, I love you and you alone. It is part of my job to interact with women—all kinds of women, so please know that you have nothing to worry about."

"Ced, you are around single women *and* single mothers all day who want nothing more than to have a man around the house to help with their bad-ass kids. I know how women operate."

"Joie..." he sighed. "Let's not do this. We have this same conversation over and over again and frankly, I'm starting to get a little tired of it."

"We wouldn't be having this conversation if you came home on time more often. I'm starting to think you got some trick on the side..."

Cedric responded to Joie's accusation with silence.

"You need to be spending more time with your own kids. And your wife."

"Well, you also know *me*, so you have nothing to be concerned about. Okay?"

"Okay..." she reluctantly replied.

"Now get on the phone and call your realtor back before that buyer decides to change his mind."

"I'll call her as soon as we hang up," she replied, returning to the chair behind her desk. Despite what Ced had told her, she knew women all too well, especially those in a certain age group. As soon as they achieved a level of comfort with a man, especially an unsuspecting married man, they would swoop right in for the kill.

"Okay, baby. You do that."

"I love you."

"Love you back. Bye."

Before ending the call, Joie overheard another burst of laughter in the background. She thought *something is up with that Sheila person. Girlfriend was giggling way too much for that to have been an innocent conversation. Sounded like she was flirting to me. Well, there's only one way to find out. I guess I will also be attending this little ceremony this evening.*

A soft knocking at the door interrupted her thoughts.

"Come in," she called out.

In walked Rufus, her boss's assistant. Joie knew from the moment she laid eyes on Rufus a few years ago, when he first started working for the agency, that he was a closet homosexual. Although she always suspected Rufus was gay, the fact was confirmed when he showed up at her hair salon one Saturday morning with his boyfriend. She was getting her weave tightened and they were getting their chests "manscaped". After the initial shock of recognizing his coworker at what he thought was an out-of-the-way salon wore off, he confided in Joie that his biggest fear was having his chauvinistic and very homophobic boss discover his secret. Even though gays were a protected class, his boss could come up with a myriad of other excuses to fire him. Once Joie agreed to keep his secret, the two of them quickly became close, sharing secrets like good friends.

"Joie, you got a minute?" he asked.

"I was just about to call my realtor, but I guess it can wait a minute. What's going on?"

"I just heard they hired a new branch manager. And he's African."

"They hired an *African*? When did this happen?"

"He's supposed to start next week. Rumor is he was hired to get this office back into shape because we have lost several of our large accounts."

"I knew we weren't as busy as usual, but they're bringing in a new branch manager?" She shrugged. "Oh well, hope he does a better job than the one we got now."

"I'm really worried," he stated.

"Why?"

"Because most Africans don't like homosexuals. I may lose my job if he finds out I'm gay."

"But wasn't that always the case?" Joie said, trying not to make light of his concerns. "You don't want anyone to know you're gay because you were worried about being fired?"

"I think everyone knows, but they haven't said anything. And I really don't try to hide it anymore." He smiled. "I even have an adorable picture of my partner sitting on my desk."

Joie was fascinated by the abrupt change in Rufus' speech pattern whenever they met behind closed doors or away from the office. When it was just the two of them talking, he subconsciously began speaking with a pronounced lisp. Even his mannerisms became more feminine. She said to him, "Yeah, I was meaning to ask you about that."

"Ever since the LGBT community started fighting for equal rights, I haven't been as afraid of anyone discovering my sexual orientation. But this African guy may be a different story."

"Well, Rufus, I wouldn't be too concerned if I were you. Just because this man is from Africa don't mean he's anti-gay. Besides, practically everybody knows someone who is gay nowadays."

"Let you tell it, girlfriend," he responded. "So anyway, what's up with you?"

"I think I sold my house today-y-y-y," she sang out.

Rufus wrinkled his nose. "That's a shame. I know how much you really liked your little house. Are you sad?"

"A little. That house held some good memories, mostly because my girlfriend owned it before she sold it to me. But I do feel relieved to not have to pay that mortgage anymore."

"In that case, congratulations!"

"Thank you." She opened *Outlook* to check for emails from her boss. "Me and Cedric are going to take the money I was putting paying on that mortgage to start fixing up our own house. I was just about to call my realtor before you walked in."

Rufus stood up to leave. "I'll let you get back to your business. I just wanted you to know about the changes coming down."

"Thanks for the info. And don't you worry about this African, Rufus. He is just another man."

Joie dismissed the conversation with Rufus as nothing more than his usual paranoia. She had more important things to tend to, including getting her house sold. As soon as Rufus left, she dialed her realtor's number.

"Hi Joie," her realtor answered excitedly. "Talk to me. Do you want to accept the offer?"

"Yep. Tell the buyer I accept their offer."

"That's wonderful!" the realtor exclaimed. "This has got to one of the quickest sales I've made in a long time. I'll be in touch with the details."

Joie disconnected the call, leaned back in her chair, and stared blankly at the computer screen displaying several spreadsheets of a company's financial records she was auditing. The millions of dollars she worked with everyday were just numbers on the screen that didn't mean much of anything. "If only I had a fraction of what this company made in profits last year, I wouldn't have any worries at all. Less than one percent would make all the difference in the world to my family. Oh well, back to work."

Chapter Six

Joie stopped by the YMCA to pick up the kids from their afterschool care program. She and Cedric had an agreement to only use the Y as a last resort because Maya, and very rarely Trey, ever finished their homework while there. 'Too many noisy distractions', was how Maya explained it. After the twins were buckled up in the backseat, Joie told them, "Daddy had to work late again so we're going to eat out. Where do you want to go?"

"I want McDonald's!" Trey shouted with glee.

"Not McDonalds, again. Let's go to a real restaurant like Applebee's or Red Lobster," Maya suggested.

"I don't like Red Lobster, Mommy," Trey stated. "Those lobsters in that tank remind me of ones I saw at the zoo. Instead of being trapped inside that tank waiting to become dinner, they should be crawling around the bottom of the ocean."

Joie smiled at her thoughtful child. "How about Applebee's?"

"I guess so. Do they have kid's meals?" he asked.

"Yes, dummy. Every restaurant has kid's meals," said Maya.

"Maya, don't call your brother dummy," she reprimanded. "Now apologize to him."

"I'm sorry for calling you a dummy." Maya rolled her eyes at her brother. "But you know Applebee's has kid's meals because you always order the same thing. Chicken tenders, French fries, and applesauce..."

"Oh yeah...that's right. Okay, Mommy. Let's go to Applebee's."

Joie was not going to let Maya work her last nerve. She was always picking on Trey about one thing or another. But what Maya didn't understand was that in a few years when they became teens, the tables would turn and Trey would become the ultimate instigator to make up for all the years she taunted him. Until then, Trey would just have to suffer through his sister's antagonistic behavior. Funny thing was, most times Trey didn't seem to mind Maya at all. Come to think of it, Maya's behavior bothered her more than it did her son.

Joie glanced at her children in the rear view mirror. They both had their heads down focused on their *iPads* completing their homework.

The phone rang. It was her realtor.

"Hello," Joie answered. "I hope you have good news for me."

"I actually have great news. The buyers want to do a quick close in a couple of weeks."

"That is great news. I just wish I was getting a little bit more after the sale," said Joie. *At least as much as your ass is getting on a commission that you barely had to work for*, she wanted to add.

"Joie, look at it this way. Because they accepted the house "as is", there are no contingencies, no repairs to be made, no extra money you'll need for fork over at closing."

"You're right. Do you know much I will eventually make from the sale?"

"I only have a rough estimate, but for now it looks like you will leave with between three to five thousand dollars."

"That's it?!"

"Unfortunately, it is... That's what's left over after closing costs and my commission, of course."

"That ain't much money at all. But I guess it's better to just sell the house and not have to worry about paying two house notes."

"I'll set everything up. All you have to do now is show up at closing."

"Well, thanks for everything. This is one less thing I have to worry about. I guess..."

"What's wrong? You don't sound happy," the realtor said.

"Me and the kids was just getting used to living in that house." She added, "I didn't expect to be selling it so quickly, that's all."

The realtor didn't know how to respond so she said, "I will contact you with the closing information. If you have any questions, please give me a call."

"I'll do that." Joie clicked off.

"Mommy, you sold our house?" Maya asked.

"Yes, baby. It's done. No more purple bedroom for you."

"Maybe daddy can paint my bedroom in our house purple. I kinda liked that color Auntie Ronnie chose because every other room in the house was painted brown or beige."

"Don't be sad, Mommy. I like the house we live in now much better because it feels like home," Trey added in his two cents.

"That's good baby, because it's the only house we have to live in now."

~ ~ ~

Joie whipped into the parking lot at Applebee's, noting the lot was almost empty. It was barely five-thirty and since it was only Monday, she figured they could grab a quick bite to eat, swing by Ced's office to check out that Sheila person, and be back home by seven so the kids could complete their homework.

The waitress seated the trio in a booth near the door. She handed out menus and asked, "What can I get you to drink?"

"We're ready to order," Joie said before the waitress had a chance to leave and not come back for another fifteen minutes. "I think they already know what they want."

"Ready when you are," the waitress said, holding unto a pencil poised to take their orders.

Trey pretended to study the menu. "I think I'll have the kid's meal with chicken tenders, French fries, applesauce, and raspberry lemonade."

Maya glanced sideways at her annoying brother. "I want macaroni and cheese, a side salad with ranch dressing, and a glass of chocolate milk."

"I'll have a chef's salad and water," Joie said. "With vinaigrette on the side, please."

"Okay, it'll be right out," the waitress replied.

While the kids busied themselves coloring the placemat using the small boxes of crayons the waitress gave them, Joie excused herself to the restroom.

"Call me!" she texted Cedric. Just as she hit send, she noticed a missed a call from her father. "Hmmm, I wonder what Daddy wants. Usually it's Mom who calls. Oh well, I'll call him back after I talk to Ced."

There were three stalls in the restroom. The lock was missing on one stall. Of the remaining two, one was for handicapped patrons. She pushed the door of the remaining stall open with her hip, and closed it with her elbow. Using only one fingertip of her right hand, she slid the metal latch until it firmly clicked into place.

After Joie carefully lined the toilet seat with toilet paper, she finished using the restroom, using her foot to flush. Afterwards, she went to the sink and turned on the faucet only to discover there was no hot water. She checked the soap dispenser mounted on the wall. It was also empty. A wad of paper towels dangled from the dispenser above the sink. It looked like someone had taken out too many and stuffed the rest back into the dispenser.

"No hot water. No soap... Used paper towels... If there's no soap for the customers to use, I know these kids working in the kitchen ain't using none either. Gross." She rinsed her hands under the cold water and then wiped them dry on her dress. Using her elbows to avoid touching the doorknob, she managed to open the door, and tried to not think about the cleanliness of the employees' hands.

After her hands had air dried sufficiently, she scrolled down to Cedric's number and dialed. The call went directly to voicemail. She tried calling again. He still didn't answer. "Fine. Don't answer your damn phone. Probably somewhere with Sheila giggling like a bitch."

Just as she was about to begin typing a long message to her husband about not answering his phone, her phone rang again. It was her father.

"Hey Daddy! I was just about to call you."

"Hi baby," her father replied in a tired voice. "Where are you?"

"Me and the kids are having dinner at Applebee's. Why?"

"Cedric's not with you?" he asked.

"No, he had to work late again..." After checking on the twins who were sitting in the booth happily immersed in coloring, Joie stepped back into the bathroom so she could better hear. "What's wrong Daddy? You don't sound like yourself."

"I really wish Cedric were there with you or you were already home. Listen, I can call back later..."

"Daddy, what is it? Are you okay?" Joie felt her heartbeat quicken. Whatever it was, it couldn't be good news She had never heard her father sound like this before.

"Honey..." her father said before breaking out into heart wrenching sobs. "Your mother..."

Joie backed against the wall, holding unto the sink as she attempted to stop the room from spinning. "Did something happen to Mom?" she asked, already knowing the answer.

"I got bad news, baby. Slim passed this afternoon."

"What?"

"Doctor said it was an aneurysm."

"What? Mommy's gone," she whispered in a voice that sounded like the little girl she felt inside. "Nooooooo!" she cried out loud.

"Baby girl, listen to me. I didn't mean to tell you this right now, especially since you're out by yourself with the kids, but you have got to pull yourself together."

Joie felt as if she were going to faint. The walls of the bathroom began to close in as her vision faded to black. Her father's sobs bounced off the walls while faint strains of an unfamiliar song became the backdrop to the sad realization that her mother was no longer alive. She sank to the cold tile floor on her knees and rested her head on the sink. It was cold. It felt good. Her cell phone slipped from her hand and landed on the floor, sliding effortlessly until it came to rest against the toilet in the empty handicapped stall.

"Joie! Joie!" screamed her father through the phone. "Baby girl, talk to me! Joie!!!"

Joie shut her eyes tightly, yet a steady stream of tears poured through her closed eyelids. *It can't be! My mother can't be dead! I didn't even have a chance to say good-bye. Didn't even get to see the house they lived in. And the last time we spoke, I didn't even tell my mother that I loved her. Now it's too late. She's gone forever.*

The restroom door burst open allowing loud chatter, interspersed with happy laughter from the Applebee's crowd, to enter into the small space. An unsuspecting woman, with nothing more on her mind that using the restroom, encountered a distraught, professionally dressed woman kneeling on the floor sobbing uncontrollably. The woman carefully took in the situation. She noticed the cell phone lying at the base of the toilet and heard a man's voice screaming out someone's name. The woman knelt down to Joie and tenderly asked, "Sweetheart, what's wrong?"

Joie barely opened her eyes. And when she did, all she could see was a pair of tortoise shell glasses and a head full of blonde curly hair surrounding a very kind face. She didn't know, nor did she care who the woman was. Joie just needed someone to hold her close.

The blonde-haired woman pulled Joie to her breast, rocking her gently as if she were just a child. She had no idea what was happening, just that this woman was in a world of hurt. "What is it? What's wrong, honey?"

In a sorrowful voice filled with so much anguish and grief that it brought tears to the woman's eyes, Joie whispered, "I-I-I just lost my mother. She's gone…"

Chapter Seven

Cedric had intentionally ignored the calls and texts from Joie. If he was ever going to finish putting the final touches on this evening's program, which began in less than an hour, he couldn't afford to go round in circles with Joie arguing about why he needed to work late. Tonight was important. They would be presenting awards to young people who made a difference in their community.

Joie can be a pain in the ass when she wants to be. Always complaining about me working overtime. Asking all kinds of questions about my female coworkers and wanting to know who is married and who ain't. She actually had the nerve to accuse me of cheating with several mothers of kids who attend the center. On top of everything else, when either twin misbehaves at school, she blames me for not spending enough time with them. No explanation seems to satisfy her and only pisses her off further. As he swiped the ignore call switch he told himself. *No need for me to stoke the fire with excuses she won't hear, because there ain't nothin' that I can say to dissuade her frustration with me for not spending enough time with her and the kids.*

Though she was mad at him, she would be even more so if she were discover that Lovely would be one of their presenters. Actually, it was all Sheila's idea to include Lovely in their program. She thought that Lovely's story on how she overcame numerous obstacles—dyslexia, being overweight, and coming from a single parent home—to become a model would inspire other young ladies to continue reaching for their dreams. Too bad Sheila refused to hear the real story of how Lovely gained her success as a model.

After being married to Lovely, he knew her achievements were gained mostly on her back, and by manipulating men, including himself, to make her way to the top.

Cedric considered himself to be a fool in love when he married Lovely after knowing her only a short time. He learned the hard way how foolish he was when he took out a second mortgage on the house to buy her an expensive diamond engagement ring and pay for the many trips and cruises.

When things fell apart, he took another home equity loan to pay his divorce settlement to the tune of fifty-thousand dollars. In less than one year, all the equity he and Joie had built up in their home was gone. That one financial blunder was the reason he worked so hard. Joie didn't know about the second mortgage, but he desperately needed to get them out of the red.

Being married to Lovely had proven to him that the road to success for some women was simple. All they needed to get ahead was a beautiful face framed by long hair—real or fake, shapely legs, big titties, an apple shaped ass, and then throw in some street smarts… Put it all together and there would be no limit to a woman's success. And one look at any television reality show proved him correct on a daily basis.

He didn't despise Lovely; he just didn't like her. In fact, if he ever laid eyes on her again, it would be too soon. So when Sheila broached the subject of including her daughter as one of their presenters, Cedric balked. As far as she was concerned, Lovely was the last woman any girl should emulate unless she wanted to be a spoiled, manipulative, lying bitch with an extraordinary sense of entitlement. But in the end, after Sheila convinced their director that Lovely's story was truly inspirational, he had no choice but to include her.

Sheila walked in just as he was finishing up his review of the presentation. He wanted to make sure the names of the children receiving awards were spelled correctly, considering that most of their first names were uniquely created by their parents.

"Hey, Sheila. How does it look out there?"

"All the kids are excited about this evening." She reviewed the list of names over his shoulder. "And most of the presenters are already here reviewing their part of the program."

"*Most?* Who are we waiting for?" he asked, as if he didn't already know.

"Lovely should be here any minute. She texted me and said she was running a little late."

"Figures…" Cedric said as he silenced another incoming call from Joie.

"It's going to be alright. I briefed her on what she's supposed to do."

"This is important, Sheila. I don't want Lovely fucking this up tonight."

Sheila cringed at Cedric's tainted perception of her daughter. It was she who had introduced them to one another when Cedric's marriage fell apart. Since Lovely missed out on having a father in her life, she hoped it would be good for Lovely to have an older man as a husband. And Cedric was just about the nicest, most intelligent man she knew.

Hell, if she were younger, she'd have taken him for herself. Unfortunately, Lovely had other aspirations for herself which didn't include playing housemaid to any man. So throughout their short lived marriage, she ended up using Cedric primarily for money and gifts. Sheila knew all this which is why she gave Cedric a pass on dissing her child.

"I'm serious." He narrowed his eyes thinking about his ex. "Remember, I never agreed to any of this, so if she fucks this up, it is on you."

"My daughter knows her responsibilities for this evening. It's going to be fine. I promise."

Cedric's phone rang twice more, followed by several text messages. He ignored them all.

Sheila gave him a reassuring smile. "Lovely stopped by last night and gave me a dry run of her speech. It was wonderful. Very inspirational."

"I'll take your word for it. Just call her again and tell her to get her ass down here."

"I'm on it." Sheila pulled out her cell phone to make the call.

His phone vibrated again. He knew who it was without glancing down. The call went to voicemail along with the others.

"You gonna get your phone. Obviously somebody wants to talk to you really bad."

"Nope. I've got more important things to worry about. You just make sure your daughter makes it here on time."

Sheila spoke into her cell, "Hi Lovely, it's your mother. I'm just reminding you that the program starts at six so I need you to get right away. Give me a call when you get this message."

He shook his head upon hearing Sheila's message. "If she's not here in twenty minutes, we're cutting her from the line-up."

"She'll be here. I promise." Sheila backed out of the office. "I'm going to make sure the sound system is working. I'll see you out there."

Cedric leaned back in his chair listening to the happy sounds of children playing. He smiled momentarily before pangs of guilt tugged at his heart. Joie was correct in saying that he spent more time with these kids at work than he did with Maya and Trey. Truth be told, those children running around the center were as much his as the twins were.

Lately, he seemed to be battling with repressed anger about the twins' biological father. Ever since he and Joie had gotten back together, the bond that he used to have with the children, especially with Trey, was no longer there. Every time he looked at the boy, he saw that asshole Derek. And dragging them back and forth to Tequitta's house to visit Laila and her brother had become more than tiresome, considering Joie's insistence on keeping the charade of them being cousins in place. He had grown weary of constantly being in the middle. Of keeping their little secret. As much as he loved the children, they would never be truly his. He could raise them as his own, love them like they were his, but he would always be referred to as *the man who raised them*. Not their real father. He'd heard this line from too many children to look at it any other way.

His wife didn't help matters either because she refused to understand his point of view. He wanted to have another child—their own child—but Joie was adamant that two was enough. Told him that he already had children and didn't need more.

The marriage he once knew to the woman he adored was over. Everything had changed. Nothing was the same. Whereas he and Joie used to fuck like rabbits, Cedric couldn't remember the last time he had made love to his wife. Despite having financial troubles, disagreements over having more children, and the issues with the twins not being his biologically, their most pressing problem was a lack of intimacy. Now that was a huge problem. Something would have to give.

Noting the time, he pushed thoughts about his marriage aside and refocused on tonight's events. In less than an hour, he would be standing in front of hundreds of people from the community to recognize a dozen outstanding teens. This was no time to be reflective on his personal life. As usual, that would have to wait.

~ ~ ~

Joie slowly regained control of her emotions while the woman soothingly stroked her hair. After a few moments of taking stock of her current situation, she crawled over to the toilet to retrieve her cell phone, seeing that the call to her father was still connected. Still on her hands and knees, she picked up the phone, bringing it to her chest.

"Honey, I know you must be hurting something awful about now, but you've got to get yourself up off this nasty floor," said the woman. She reached high to pull several paper towels from the holder and handed the wad to Joie.

"Thank you for your kindness," Joie replied as her weeping finally began to subside.

"Don't mention it." The woman stood with her hand reaching towards Joie. "Here, let me help you up."

Joie accepted the woman's assistance. "I'm sorry...."

"No need for you to apologize."

"I don't know what to do." Joie said, shaking her head from side to side. "What am I supposed to do?"

"First thing you have to do is breathe," the woman told her. "Then you take each day one moment at a time."

As the woman looked on, Joie stood in front of the sink and stared at the face that so closely resembled her mother's. With one hand, she turned the faucet on hoping this tiny act of normalcy would shock her back to reality. A stream of water slowly filled the basin. She placed the cell phone down, still listening to her father's voice on the other end calling out her name. She turned to the woman who stood patiently at her side and whispered, "Thank you."

"I'm real sorry to hear about your mother," the woman said before going into the stall to take care of the business that brought her into the bathroom in the first place.

Joie used a paper towel to wipe the phone clean before turning on the speaker. She took a deep breath to calm her nerves before asking, "Daddy? Are you still there?"

"Yes, I'm still here." He breathed an audible sigh of relief. "I'm glad that nice woman is there with you."

"Me too," she replied. "I'm gonna be okay. I promise."

"That's good baby," he said unable to keep the weariness from entering his own voice. "Why don't you call me back when you get home?"

"I'll do that, daddy." She wiped away the last of her tears. "I love you."

"I love you, too. Now be careful driving home and call me when you get there. Okay?"

"I will Daddy. Bye..."

The woman exited the stall to wash her hands. "Is there anything else I can do to help? Is there someone in the restaurant I can get for you?"

Joie gasped in dismay. "My children! I left my kids alone at the table."

"You want me to go check on them while you get yourself together?" the woman asked.

"No, I've got to go check on them now." Joie started for the door. "They're probably scared to death wondering where I am."

The woman gently gripped Joie's arm. "Honey, if you go out there looking like this, you are going to scare your kids to death."

Joie stared at her reflection in the mirror seeing what the woman saw. Her eyes were ringed black with smeared mascara, the ruby red lipstick she wore to accentuate her full lips was smudged sideways across her mouth, and her hair was a total mess. The woman was right. She couldn't go out there looking like this. "My kids are twins. A boy and a girl. Eight years old. They're sitting in a booth near the entrance."

"How about I take a quick look on them?" the woman offered.

"Thank you."

The woman was back in less than ten seconds. "They're doing fine. Looks like they're already eating their dinner."

"Can I ask you just one more favor?"

"Sure. What is it?"

"Please tell my kids that I'll be right there."

The woman smiled warmly. "Yes, I am more than happy to do that for you."

Joie reached out to hug the stranger who had just shared one of her most intimate moments. "Thank you so much for helping me. I probably would have lost my mind right here on this bathroom floor if you hadn't come in."

The woman replied, "I'm sure you would have done the same for me. Roles reversed."

Joie nodded and said, "Of course, I would."

"You take care now," she said before closing the door.

Joie watched the kind stranger leave. As she looked in the mirror, trying to correct the damage sorrow had done to her face, she wondered if she would have stopped to help a stranger who was in her current situation. As much as she would like to think she would, Joie knew that if she had encountered a devastated stranger sobbing uncontrollably on a restaurant's filthy bathroom floor, she would have simply ignored the person and gone on with her business.

"I see you have your dinner," Joie said trying to sound normal.

"Mommy, what took you so long? Trey and I are almost finished eating," Maya informed her mother in her best grown up voice.

Joie slid in the booth beside Trey who was busily mopping up the last remnants of ketchup with a handful of fries. She pushed the chef's salad she ordered towards the edge of the table because the thought of eating anything after spending fifteen minutes on a bathroom floor turned her stomach.

"Are you okay? Your eyes look puffy," Maya said, studying her mother's face.

"I'm fine," she said, signaling for the waitress.

"Are you sad because you sold the house?" Trey asked innocently.

"Yeah, baby, that's it. Mommy's sad about the house, but I'm gonna be fine."

"Would you like to look at the desert menu? We have a pretty delicious chocolate lava cake? Or do you wanna try our special ice cream sundae treat? Both are my absolute favs!" the waitress said making a lame attempt at up selling.

"No desert. Check please."

"Would you like a box for your salad?" the young woman asked cheerfully.

"No. Just the check."

"Okay, be right back."

Joie opened her purse and pulled out a small bottle of hand sanitizer. She emptied a huge dollop on a cloth napkin then proceeded to wipe every crevice of her cell phone until it was literally dripping with the clear gel.

"That stuff stinks," Trey noted. "Why are you cleaning your cell phone at the table?"

"Because I dropped it on the bathroom floor."

"Is that what took you so long? You were looking for your cell phone?" asked Maya.

"Something like that." She checked her messages to see if Cedric had called or left a text. He hadn't done either, so she dialed his number several more times.

The perky waitress returned with the check. Joie pulled enough money from her wallet to cover the bill and the tip. "You kids ready?" she asked trying her best to put on a happy face.

"Yep, I'm ready," Trey said, licking his fingers.

"Use a napkin," Joie admonished her son.

"I'm done," Maya said as she daintily dabbed the corners of her mouth with a napkin.

"Okay, let's go." As Joie herded the kids from the booth, her eyes momentarily locked with those of the woman who had so graciously consoled her in the bathroom.

The helpful woman sat at the head of a large table with over a dozen people, who Joie assumed were family and friends, gathered around her. A single lit candle flickered atop the small cake placed before her. It was the woman's birthday.

Joie paused to watch. The woman looked her way giving a small wave as a cadre of waiters and waitresses gathered at the table to sing Happy Birthday. After they sang the last note, the woman blew out the candle. When Joie returned the greeting, it wasn't until that very moment that Joie realized she didn't even know the woman's name

"Do either of you have to use the restroom before we leave?" she asked. "We need to make quick stop to see your daddy."

Both twins shook their heads.

"Mommy, I thought you said we were going home," whined Maya. "I have to finish my homework."

"I finished mine in the restaurant while you were coloring," Trey said proudly.

"Maya, I need to speak to your daddy. He's not answering his phone so I'm going to stop by his job."

Joie drove the few short miles to where Cedric worked. The parking lot of the center was overflowing with cars and people were still coming. *Damn! That's right...they're having some special presentation this evening. Well, this is much more important than someone's award.*

"I need you guys to help me find a parking spot, okay?"

"Over there, Mommy! That car is leaving," Trey said pointing to a parking space near the front entrance.

"Way to go, Trey!" Joie quickly rounded the aisle and turned on her blinker.

While they patiently waited for the car leaving to back out, another car approached the space from the opposite direction. Before the driver could completely straighten the wheels to pull forward, the other car swooped into the spot, stealing it from Joie. And while Joie sat behind the wheel fuming, a young, beautiful woman with legs that went on forever exited the vehicle.

"Wait a minute! I know you seen me sitting here!"

The young woman shrugged and said, "Snooze you lose!"

"What?!"

"I said, You snooze, you lose! You shouldn't have been so damn slow."

Joie leaned halfway out the window and yelled, "I should get outta my car and whup that ass!"

"Mommy! Language..." Trey covered his ears.

"Sorry, I was here first," the young woman casually called out before walking off as if she had not a care in the world.

"Bitch! I ought to run your little skinny ass over! You better be glad I got my kids in the car with me!"

The young woman laughed as she shouted over her shoulder, "Whatever! But I still got that parking spot didn't I?"

Joie counted to ten trying to send those little devils that kept popping up on her shoulders back to hell. She glanced in the rearview mirror at the frightened looks on the face of her kids, when suddenly thoughts of her mother surfaced removing all traces of anger. She forced a smile to push the sadness away, turned to look at her kids, and told them, "Sorry guys. Mommy is okay. I just got a little upset, but I'm fine now."

Finally after circling the parking lot for another few minutes, she got lucky when a car pulled out. This time, there was no was no one waiting to steal her parking spot. Joie tried Cedric's cell phone once more, but still no answer.

Upon entering the center, they bypassed the busy auditorium where the majority of people had gathered, and headed straight for Cedric's office. Joie heard a woman's laughter as she approached the office. She stopped outside in the hall, reached into her purse and pulled out a five dollar bill, handing it to Trey.

"Go to the arcade and play a few games. I need to talk to your daddy in private. Okay?"

"Why did you give the money to Trey?"

"Because he won't lose it, that's why. Now go play."

"Can we buy a candy bar?" Maya asked.

"I don't care how you spend it. Just don't leave that arcade," she warned.

"Yes ma'am," they both replied, happily.

Joie waited until the twins were out of sight before she gathered what little remained of her courage. With feet feeling as if they were encased in heavy cement, she steadied her nerves for whatever she was about to encounter. As she got closer to her husband's office, she recognized the high-pitched laughter from the phone call. She recognized Cedric's voice, as well. Joie stood outside Cedric's door and took another deep breath before taking that final step into his office.

Cedric failed to contain his surprise at seeing his wife standing in the doorway of his office. In all the years they were married, counting their first marriage, he could count the number of times she had visited the center on one hand. She always told him it was because she didn't like being around all those bad assed teenagers.

"Joie, what are you doing here?" he asked, surprised.

"I've been trying to reach you for the past few hours," Joie replied, staring at the unattractive, slightly overweight, fiftyish year old woman sitting in the chair next to his desk.

He reached into his desk drawer for his cell phone. "I'm sorry, baby. I had the ringer turned off. Sheila and I have been working all day on this ceremony that's about to begin in a few minutes."

"*You're* Sheila?" Joie asked, hoping neither of them heard the sigh of relief escaping her throat.

The woman stood with her hand extended. "You must be Joie. I've heard so much about you. I'm Sheila. Sheila Rose."

"Your last name is Rose?" Joie placed a finger at her temple in deep thought. "Where have I heard that name before?"

Sheila glanced uncomfortably from Cedric to Joie before answering, "I'm, uh... I'm... Didn't Cedric tell you?"

Cedric chimed in interrupting their brief conversation, changing the subject before Sheila could say more. "So, uh, Joie, what brings you down here? And where are the twins?"

"The twins are in the arcade playing games. I just needed to speak to you. You got a minute?"

"Of course," he replied. "Sheila, will you give me a minute?"

"Sure. What do you want me to tell Lovely when she arrives?" she asked Cedric.

As if on cue, in walked the attractive woman who had stolen the parking spot from Joie. "Tell Lovely, what?" she asked strutting into the office, tossing her mane of hair across her shoulder. She perched atop Cedric's desk as if she owned it.

Joie stared at the woman. Then at Sheila. And then her eyes rested on Cedric. Finally all the pieces fell into place. The pretty young swimsuit model with the DD breasts and shapely legs that went on forever, with the perfect skin, who rocked her husband's world, during their "in the meantime", stood before her in the flesh. Joie pointed at the woman and shouted, "You're Lovely?!"

"Well, thank you," Lovely smirked. "And you're the crazy woman from the parking lot, right?"

"What the hell is she doing here?" Joie shouted at Cedric.

"I'm presenting an award this evening. But for now, I'm saying hello to my mother and my ex-husband. Why? Who are you?" Lovely asked, becoming annoyed with the woman who appeared to be on the verge of an emotional breakdown.

"Mother?! Ced? Sheila is this bitch's mother?!" Joie yelled.

"Joie, calm down," Cedric said. "Ladies, can you please give me a moment with my wife?"

Lovely raised her eyebrows. "Oh, so this is the famous Joie? I should have known by the way you behaved in the parking lot. Cedric always said you were a crazy-assed bitch."

Joie swung her *Coach* handbag, the one her parents gave her as a going away gift, at Lovely before Cedric stepped in between the two women. "I'll show you who is a crazy-assed bitch!"

"Whatever..." she replied. "C'mon, Mom. Let's leave these two alone before this heifer does something really crazy."

"Uh, nice to meet you, Joie," Sheila said before escorting her daughter from the room.

"You want to see crazy?! I'll show your ass crazy..." Joie bent down, took off her shoes, and threw one at Lovely. The first one missed, but the next one found its mark.

Lovely screamed more out of surprise than pain when the shoe connected with her backside.

"Gotcha!" Joie shouted in victory.

Cedric angrily gripped his wife by both arms. "Joie! What the hell is wrong with you?! Why are you coming here starting all kinds of drama?"

Joie stared at Cedric with a look of desperation in her eyes. Feeling the anger emanating from her husband's strong hands, her knees buckled as she suddenly went limp, allowing all the fight to drain from her body.

"What has gotten into you? Have you lost your damn mind?!"

She sank to her knees, pulling Cedric down with her. Once she felt secure in his embrace, Joie finally released the emotions she managed to keep in check since first learning of her mother's passing. A new flood of tears erupted, pouring from her eyes so heavily that she could no longer see. Her body became wracked with such uncontrollable weeping that it took all her remaining strength to whisper through a voice colored with an indescribable pain. She wailed, "No, I haven't lost my mind, Ced. I lost my mom. My mother is dead."

"What?" he asked.

"Daddy called about an hour ago. My mother died this afternoon."

"Oh no! Baby, I'm sorry. I am sooooo sorry." He fully embraced his wife trying to take some of the pain away.

And out in the hallway, after hearing Joie's sorrowful cry, Sheila led Lovely September Rose away from Cedric's office to allow him the privacy to properly console his grieving wife.

"What happened?"

"I'm not sure. Daddy told me... I think it was a stroke or something." Joie rested her head against her husband's chest, forgetting all about Sheila and Lovely. "Me and the kids were at Applebee's. He called. I went into the bathroom so I could hear him better. The next thing I know is some frizzy haired woman was helping me up off the floor."

"I don't believe it... Your mother always took such good care of herself. She's such a strong woman."

Joie felt her nose run. She tried to wipe it with her arm.

He pulled out a handful of tissues and gently began wiping her face.

"Ced, I feel so lost now. My mom was my dad's rock. Mine too. I didn't even get to say good-bye." Another wave of emotion caused her to cry so hard, she developed hiccups.

"Shhhh.... It's going to be alright." Cedric held unto his wife until the crying subsided again.

"My poor daddy is all alone down there. I've got to go see him."

"First things first. Let's get you home."

"What about your program?" she asked between sobs.

Cedric was torn. His responsibility to the kids would have to take backseat, because tonight, he needed to be there for his wife. "Sheila can take over. It will just have to go on without me."

"Thank you," she whispered.

After her tears began to subside, Cedric helped his wife to her feet left bare after she used both shoes to take aim at Lovely. Joie's mother was the one who taught her to always remove her wig, earrings, and shoes before getting into a scuffle with another woman since those items were within easy grasp. Her reasoning was it was better you pull them off than have someone else do it for you.

Joie leaned against Cedric's strong shoulder, staggering down the narrow hallway towards the entrance, burdened by the weight of an unimaginable grief that still had yet to fully sink in. The concrete floor the director insisted on installing due to its purported durability was cold to her bare feet, yet the chill was just enough to keep her grounded in the presence. For at any moment, the clutches of grief threatened to pull her down and refuse to let her back up. And as they made their way towards the door, she felt stares from hundreds of inquiring eyes of those gathered for that evening's ceremony. Each wondering what could have caused the woman to be in such a state.

Maya and Trey stood in line trying to buy sweets before their mother changed her mind. They both knew something was amiss because it was a rare moon when mom allowed them to have candy. However, kids being kids, rather than question their mother's decision, they decided to take full advantage of the situation.

Joie spied her children at the concession stand. Without anyone having to tell her that she looked a hot mess, she already knew. She gripped Ced's arm and whispered, "Can you take me home before we get the kids? I don't want them seeing me like this."

"You haven't told them?"

"I couldn't… I don't think I would have been able to drive here if I had."

That was probably a good decision, he thought, taking stock of Joie's condition. "I can ask Sheila to keep an eye on the kids until I get back."

She nodded okay.

"You think you can make it to the car alone?"

"I'll be fine," she said wiping at her eyes, trying her best to stop the flow of tears.

"Here, take my keys. My car is parked around the back.

"You sure?"

"Yes, it'll be fine here. We'll come back for it tomorrow."

Joie felt as if she were slogging through a vat of mud. Every movement felt exaggerated, as if she were moving in slow motion. She thought, *Funny how tragedy can place a person outside themselves, forcing them to be on the outside looking in. I don't feel like myself at all.*

"Hey, wait a minute. Don't forget your shoes," Cedric said with a hint of a smile. "I wouldn't want you hurting those pretty little feet of yours."

"One thing my feet have never been is *pretty* or *little*. But thank you for making me smile."

Cedric leaned over to plant a kiss on Joie's cheek before backing away to get the twins. He gave her a brief wave before slipping into the crowd.

Joie clutched the ring of keys in her hand and headed towards the door. She managed to locate Cedric's car fairly quick. It was strictly old school. The kind of car that still required a key to be placed in the ignition before it would start. As Ced loved to remind her, his hoopty wasn't the nicest car or the latest model, but it was reliable, safe, and most of all, it was fully paid for.

Chapter Eight

"You sure you don't want me to go to Florida with you?" Cedric asked. "It won't hurt the kids to miss a couple of days out of school."

Joie stuffed the last outfit into an already over packed suitcase. "No, I don't want to pull them out of school to go to a memorial service that they probably wouldn't understand. Anyway, I already explained to the twins that Meemaw had passed on. They seemed to handle it fine."

"Well, I would like to be there with you."

"Baby, I'll be okay. I'm just gonna go down there to Tampa, see about my daddy, make whatever arrangements my mom needed done to have her ashes scattered, and then come back home. I won't be gone longer than a few days."

"We can all drive down together," he offered.

"Ced, it's okay. Really. Anyway, I need you to be in town in case that realtor needs something. I had my office draw up a power-of-attorney this morning so you can act on my behalf to get this house sold. With so much going on at once, the last thing I want is this house deal to fall through."

"Fine, I'll stay." Cedric sighed wearily.

"I'll be alright. I think I'm over the initial shock. Now I just have to deal with it."

"You know, I never took your mother as one who wanted to be cremated."

"My mother gave my dad firm instructions that she if she went first, she did not want to have a funeral. She told him the thought of a bunch of people she hadn't seen in years looking at her dead body, making all kinds of comments about how good she looked, kinda creeped her out."

"But what about her family? Do you want to have a funeral for your mom?"

"It was her last wish. She really didn't want to be buried in the ground. She told daddy that she wanted her ashes scattered in the wind so she would always be free."

"Did you know about this?"

"She and my dad only talked about it recently. Who would have thought she would die from a blood clot."

"I hear blood clots are more common than you think."

"Yeah, I guess." Joie turned to face her husband. "Daddy said she was out planting flowers in the flowerbed. Apparently, she was down on her knees long enough for a blood clot to form. When she stood up, the clot traveled up to her brain. She probably didn't feel a thing. At least, I pray she didn't."

"In the Florida sunshine, planting pretty flowers in her garden… Your mother went doing something she loved."

"I suppose."

"When I last spoke to him, your father sounded like he's handling it pretty well. What do you think?"

"About what? About how well my dad is dealing with losing the love of his life?"

"Well, when you put it that way… I guess he can only handle it the best way he can."

"Tell you something else…"

"What's that?"

"I think my dad is running low on cash."

"Really? I thought they were loaded, as stingy as your parents always were with their money." He laughed. "Remember how the kids always complained because Meemaw only put a dollar in their birthday card?"

"My mother did have a good head for business. Said they would never have anything if she gave it all away."

Cedric remained quiet, pushing thoughts of his own foolishness handling money aside.

"Mom didn't have life insurance. My father always told her that he didn't take a life insurance policy on her because if she died, there was no way he could touch that money. Shoot, she barely had health insurance. Neither one worked so their costs were out of this world. And she was too young for Medicare. Guess it's a good thing she wasn't hospitalized."

"What about the Obamacare insurance? That's supposed to be affordable…"

Joie guffawed. "Have you taken a look at the premiums for a couple of sixty year old retirees too young to qualify for Medicare? Even with the tax credit, they didn't have that kind of money to get a good policy. Instead they got one with minimal coverage and high deductibles."

"But they sold their house. Didn't they make a killing from that because they didn't have a mortgage?"

Joie exhaled loudly before her eyes clouded with tears. "There's something I didn't tell you about my parents."

Cedric took Joie by the wrist and pulled her towards him. "Sit down. Let's talk. You can finish packing later."

"Okay. Remember how surprised I was when it seemed like my parents just up and moved?"

He nodded.

"Well, I spoke to my mother a couple weeks after they moved to Tampa. She told me why my dad was so enthusiastic about moving to Florida. It had nothing to do with fishing."

"What's going on?"

"One of my father's friends moved down there a couple of years ago. This so-called friend started up a business. Apparently my dad wanted to get in on the ground floor of this supposed huge opportunity. He wanted to invest in his friend's business thinking this would solve all their financial worries during retirement."

Cedric dropped his head. "Don't tell me he gave this friend the money he got from selling the house."

"My dad practically handed over everything to that asshole." She shook her head in disbelief. "He is one of the smartest men I know. I can't believe he was taken."

"So what happened?"

"Nothing. The guy left town with all my parent's money."

"Didn't your mother try to stop him from doing the deal?"

Joie chuckled. "You don't know my father. There was no talking him out of anything once he puts his mind to it."

"Damn! Does he have any money left? How is he managing?"

"Well, instead of buying their house outright, they rented a little house in a different neighborhood than the one they originally planned to buy in. He has a pension and a few stocks so he'll manage. Other than that, he'll have to wait for social security to kick in."

"I'll bet he's pissed."

"I don't know. We haven't discussed it," she continued, wearily. "As far as I know, he doesn't know that I know what happened."

"Are you going to talk to him about it?"

She shook her head. "No, not yet. I need to take care of Mom's arrangements first."

"Well, this might not be the right time to bring this up, but I've been thinking about starting my own business. Nothing fancy, just something to get my feet wet as an entrepreneur… I'm tired of working for the city. I need to be my own boss."

"Not, now Ced. I've got way too many other things on my mind." *Plus, you don't know the first thing about starting or running a business. I'm not gonna let you drag this family down like my daddy did with that hare-brained scheme of his.*

"You're right. We can discuss this some other time."

"Thank you."

"Baby, if your dad wants to come back to Virginia, he can come live with us."

"I appreciate you saying that. I think my father is way too proud to come live with us, but it's nice to know the offer is out there. I'll be sure to let him know it was your suggestion."

"Is there anything else I can do? Make any phone calls? Notify other family members?"

She shook her head again. "Not much to do. I think I made all the phone calls last night."

"Did you talk to Ronnie?"

"Yeah, she gave her condolences. Of course, she wanted to jump on the first plane out here."

"So why didn't you let her? If I can't help you, at least you have your girl with you."

"Seriously, I'm okay. Me and daddy can handle most of my mother's affairs. My mom's sister, my Aunt Carol, lives in Georgia and she's going to meet me there."

"That's good. This is going to very difficult for both of you. It always helps to have someone else around to lean on." He kissed her cheek. "Just say the word. I'll put the kids in the backseat of the car and we can be down there in a heartbeat."

"You are so good to me," she told him. "What would I do without you?"

"Hopefully, you'll never find out. I'm gonna be on you woman like flies on a horse's ass. You ain't never gonna get rid of me."

"I love you, Cedric Parker."

"I love you more, Joie Parker."

Chapter Nine

Joie stood in her closet trying to decide between three different white outfits to wear to the concert. Her hands rested on a white linen pants suit she had worn to scatter her mother's ashes on the Tampa coastline. Her had father chartered a small yacht for the intimate ceremony because that was what Slim wanted. It was a beautiful homegoing ceremony that included family and several close friends, and only after she had gotten there did she wish she had included her husband and children.

She sighed deeply and moved the white pants suit to the back of the closet. There was no way she would feel comfortable attending a concert wearing the outfit that she had said goodbye to her mother in.

"Joie, c'mon we're running late." Cedric checked his watch as he buttoned up his short-sleeved white shirt over his matching trousers. "You know we are supposed to drop Maya and Trey off at six."

"We're not that late," she shouted back. "I'll be out in a few."

"The jazz festival starts at eight and I am not trying miss any of the concert. You know Frankie Beverly is old school. He don't work on CP time."

Joie casually strode from the bathroom with her hair still up in curlers. She pulled the loose fitting, threadbare terrycloth robe, the one Ced hated with a passion, taut around her body.

"You're not even dressed, yet?"

"What's the rush? Tequila ain't got nowhere to be." She added hatefully, "Nowhere except the food stamp line..."

"Listen Joie. We both agreed that we were going to let the twins spend time with their half siblings. Now if you are having a problem with it, maybe we need to work something else out because after doing this shit for six months, I've had about enough. This is ridiculous!"

"I know I promised Derek's mother that I would let the twins get to know his other kids. But I seriously hate taking them over there to that bitch's house."

"Then let Tequitta bring her kids over to our place. I'm cool with that."

"I'll be damned if I let her bring bay-bay's kids up in my house. They ain't gonna come over here messing up my place and stealing our kids' stuff."

"All right... Then we'll have to continue dropping the twins off over there if that's the way you feel."

"Anyway, Maya always comes home smelling like fried chicken. Ugh!"

"What's wrong with fried chicken? The twins love fried chicken. I do too. For that matter, so do you."

"That ain't the point, Ced. I don't like them being over there in her house. Ain't no telling what she's doing up in there with her triflin' ass. And Trey told me that she was drunk the last time they spent the night."

"Here we go again..." He bent over to tie his shoes. "You don't want the twins in her house, but at the same time, you don't want her kids in ours. So figure out a solution and quit bitchin' about it. Damn! What the hell is wrong with you? Always bitchin' about one thing or another!"

"I think you would be a little more supportive of me, considering these are her and Derek's kids we talkin' about." She rolled her eyes. "Plus, do you want your kids to be around a drunk? I sure as hell don't."

"Know what? I give up..." He held up his hands in defeat. "Ever since you got back from Florida, you have been impossible to live with. Look, I'm sorry your mother died. I'm sorry your father lost his money. I'm sorry I can't give you the champagne and caviar life you want, but I'm doing the best I can, Joie."

She crossed her arms, rolled her eyes, and thought to herself, *if this is your best, I for damn sure hate to see your worst.*

"I have every intention of looking into starting my own business. I just need a few more dollars for start up cash."

"Humph! If you hadn't spent all your money on that *Lovely* bitch, maybe you'd have some money," she murmured under her breath.

"What?!" Cedric's head snapped around in disbelief. "Where did that come from? What the hell does my ex have to do with anything?"

"I'm just saying that if you had more money, maybe we could help my daddy get into a decent house."

"Do you even think about what you're saying before you speak? It is not my fault that your daddy let some thief run off with his money. It is not my responsibility to buy him a house. I'm trying to take care of my own family, in case you didn't notice."

"My daddy *is* family."

"Know what? I am not going to have this conversation." He exhaled slowly in an attempt to return his heart rate back to normal. "Are the kids ready?"

"I suppose so. They're in their rooms watching TV." She retrieved her matching white outfit, a sexy dress cut to accentuate her curves, from the closet. "That bitch ain't got nothing to do anyway. She can wait."

"Why don't you just admit that you don't like Tequitta because she married Derek Jordan?"

"That is not the reason I can't stand that trick."

"Well, that's good to know. Because if that were the case, I would look like a damn fool up in here trying to smooth things out between the two of you, wouldn't I?"

"Cedric, I ain't studying Tequila. It's just that I haven't told the twins that you're not their daddy."

"What the fuck, Joie?! Have you lost your damn mind?!"

She stopped and stared at her husband who managed to turn four shades of red in spite of his dark complexion. "What?" she asked innocently.

"You must be out of your goddamn mind saying some shit like that!"

"What? What did I say?"

"You can be so hateful when you want to," he replied. "For the record, Joie, I *am* their daddy. I just didn't contribute the sperm."

"Baby, I'm sorry. That's not what I meant. I meant to say that Derek was their biological father. Of course you're their daddy."

"Next time, think about what's coming out of your mouth before you say it."

"You're right. I was being insensitive."

"You think?"

"I crossed the line. I apologize."

"Anyway, we need to tell them soon. Hell, they probably already know."

Joie stopped dead in her tracks to consider what he had said. A worried expression crept into the crease that suddenly appeared on her forehead. "You think that heifer Tequila told them already?"

"Or *Tequitta's* kids have..."

"I wish that bitch would say something to my kids. When I made this arrangement with Derek's mother two years ago, we all agreed to let the kids think they're cousins until the time was right to break the news."

"Do you actually think Trey and Maya don't know something is up? You've been dropping them off without saying more than two words at a time to Tequitta. Trey may not have suspicions, but you know how inquisitive Maya is. And she absolutely adores her baby cousin... I mean, baby brother."

"Yeah, you're right. For being only eight years old, she is very perceptive."

"So either we tell the twins or they're going to find out another way. I think it's better if it came from us."

"How about we tell them this weekend? Afterwards, we can have a picnic at Buckroe Beach or something to reinforce that nothing has changed. We are still a family."

"Sounds like a plan," he replied. "Now would you please get dressed so we can go? This might be the last time Frankie comes to town. You know he's getting up there in age. This might be his last tour."

"Okay. Give me five minutes. I'll meet you and the kids in the car."

"We're taking my Caddy tonight. I don't want to be seen riding around in your hooptie."

"Fine. Give me your keys."

"They're in the kitchen. On the counter where they usually are."

Cedric glared at his wife before asking, "Am I driving?"

"Yes." She looked at him as if he had lost his mind. "If you don't mind."

"I know how you are about me driving your new car. Sometimes I think you love it more than me."

"That's ridiculous." She rolled her eyes. "The Caddy is still fairly new. Give me a minute to break it in."

He stormed out the room and headed to round up the twins.

Joie plopped down on the edge of the bed. She freed the plastic rollers from her hair two at a time, thinking about the first time she laid eyes on Tequitta and her daughter, Laila. It was at Derek's funeral. Not knowing anything about the woman Derek had married, she damn near fainted when she saw that Tequitta was pregnant, but more so when she laid eyes on their daughter. The child appeared to be the same age as Maya and Trey with an unmistakable resemblance to Derek.

After it was revealed to everyone that Derek was Trey and Maya's father, and shortly after she and Cedric divorced, Derek's family reached out to Joie to connect with the children. For the longest time, she managed to keep the children's father's identity hidden. Opting instead to pretend that Tequitta's children and hers were cousins. But the time had come to tell the twins the truth about their real father, just like Cedric said.

I just hope I'm doing the right thing. I know my kids are going to find out one day that Cedric ain't their real daddy. How awful would it be if that news came from somebody other than me? As much as I don't want to do this, the time has come to tell the truth. They might hate me for a minute, but thank the Lord Cedric has embraced them and raised them as his own.

Chapter Ten

"Bye Mommy. Bye Daddy!" Maya bolted from the car as soon as Cedric rolled to a stop in Tequitta Jordan's driveway.

Joie waved at Tequitta who stood in the doorway of her spacious townhome holding Derek III in her long, thin arms. She named the baby Derek III because Derek's oldest son was already named junior. Yeah, it was confusing, but no one seemed to really mind. Although Derek had a modest life insurance policy at the time of his death, half of the proceeds went to pay off his medical bills, and a generous amount went to the funeral home. After several monetary gifts were distributed to his mother and a few others, there was left just enough left over to buy a small home for Tequitta and her kids. And if it weren't for Ronnie giving up what Derek had left her to Joie and the kids, they might not have seen any of Derek's insurance money, considering he didn't know the twins were his in the first place.

Joie studied the woman she had come to despise. Half of Tequitta's head was covered in shoulder length micro braids with the remaining hair sticking to and fro. The child of a Filipino mother and a Black father, Tequitta was a very attractive woman. Too bad she was dumb as a box of rocks.

The baby had to be almost three years old, but still wore a diaper because he wasn't potty trained. *I wonder if that baby is retarded. With a crack whore mother like Tequila, there has to be something physically wrong with that poor child. And I hope she ain't still nursing that boy. Big as he is.*

Joie noticed the screen missing from the bottom of the broken storm door. She surveyed the overgrown yard, noting it hadn't been mowed in a month. And Derek's old car, expired plates and all, was still parked in the driveway as if he were merely inside watching television instead of being dead longer than the child had been alive.

Laila rushed towards Maya and wrapped her arms around her sister's neck. *I can't get over how much those two resemble one another. They have similar mannerisms and even sound the same,* Joie thought.

"Mommy, are we spending the night?" asked Trey interrupting his mother's thoughts.

"No, son. We'll be back to pick you up after the concert," Cedric answered for Joie.

"Okay. I'll see you guys later," Trey replied.

"Hey? Don't I get a kiss?" Joie asked.

"Sorry." Trey climbed over the seat and planted a big wet kiss on his mother's cheek.

Tequitta shouted from the doorway, "Y'all going to the Hampton Jazz Festival?"

"Yeah," Joie replied. "It starts in about an hour so we need to get going."

"I wish I was going, but I'm not really into that type of music. Plus, too many of you old school peeps are going to be there," she said jokingly.

Joie rolled her eyes in annoyance.

"What time y'all coming back for the twins?"

"We should be back around midnight," Joie responded.

"They can stay overnight if y'all want them to. We aren't doing anything."

"No, that's awright. We need to pick them up tonight. We have plans for tomorrow," she answered cordially.

"Okay. Well, I'll leave the porch light on. Y'all have fun and don't worry about the kids. They always have a good time over here."

"Thanks," Joie answered. Then she murmured under her breath, "Umh! You need to go inside and put some clothes on your funky ass."

"Joie, the woman *is* wearing clothes," Cedric responded.

"Please don't tell me you're defending that tramp." Joie smacked herself on the forehead. "Oh, damn. I must be crazy! Of course you like what she's wearing."

"Don't start... And what is wrong with how she's dressed? It is over ninety degrees out here."

"It's obvious she ain't wearing a bra because I can see the outline of her nipples through that tight-assed shirt. And her ass is practically hanging out of them shorts... Looking like some stank-ass 'ho slut around my kids."

Cedric tooted the horn at the kids as he backed out the driveway. He merged unto I-64 to head to the Hampton Coliseum. When it was safe to do so, he glanced sideways at his wife.

"How do you manage to do that?" he asked.

"Do what?"

"Go from being sweet and friendly to a hateful witch in a matter of moments," he replied. "If I didn't know you better..."

"What exactly are you referring to?" she asked oozing sarcasm.

"The way you spoke about Tequitta. You called the woman a stank-ass 'ho slut."

"I didn't call her that. I just said she looked like one. Anyway, she didn't hear me." Joie pulled a small flask filled with *Remy* from her purse. "You want a hook before the show?"

Cedric sighed. "Maybe later. But back to my question..."

"You're asking me why I don't like little miss Tequila."

"That was the question."

"As if I have to remind you, I don't like her because she was fuckin' my best friend's husband. He left Ronnie for that home-wrecking heifer."

Joie took a long swig from the flask and passed it to Cedric. He placed it between his legs for later. Cedric contemplated his response with an understanding that whatever was said in the next few moments would probably mess up the remainder of the evening.

"Is that right? So you actually think Derek Jordan left Ronnie for Tequitta?"

"He married the bitch, didn't he?"

Instead of responding immediately, Cedric diverted his anger for the next ten minutes by focusing on driving to the Coliseum. He exited the highway and turned unto the Power Plant Parkway. Afterwards, he followed the parking lot attendant's directions to the nearest empty spot that was about as far from the entrance as he could be. He put the car in park before he spoke.

Joie reached between Cedric's legs for the flask. She popped the top and took another long swig. "Ooo wee! That feels so good going down. You better take a drink before I finish it off."

"Baby, I need say this."

"Damn! Why are you being so serious all of a sudden? Let's go get our party on with Frankie Beverly and Maze."

He sighed heavily. "Joie, you know I love you..."

"I love you, too, Ced."

"I'm trying my best to stay cool about this situation, but..."

"But what? What's going on?"

"You are working my last nerve. You need to let go of how you feel about Tequitta. That woman didn't do a damn thing to you."

"The hell she didn't! She messed up my best friend's marriage."

Cedric stared at Joie as if he no longer knew who she was. "Are you serious?"

"Do I look like I'm playing?"

"Baby, I hate to be the one to remind you, but you did the same thing Tequitta did. You also slept with your best friend's husband and got pregnant on top of it. Maybe you hate her because she reminds you of yourself."

"Fuck you, Cedric! You gonna keep reminding me of my mistakes?! You go to your little anger management classes and now all of a sudden you are the fuckin' expert?! Give me a fuckin' break!"

"Joie, who in hell do you think you're talking to?"

She crossed her arms to ward off the chill emanating from her beloved husband. *After six months of remarriage, he still manages to bring up my past and throw it into my face. I guess he ain't never going to let me forget what I did.*

"And I wish you would say the woman's name correctly for once. Her name is Tequitta. Not Tequila. Not bitch. Not heifer. And not stank ass 'ho slut. The woman's name is Tequitta Jordan," Cedric corrected Joie for the umpteenth time.

She smacked her lips together. "Whatever... Let's just go to this damn concert."

"What's going on with you? Aren't you happy with me?"

Joie had asked herself that question a million times over the past several months. Ever since scattering her mother's ashes in the Gulf of Mexico two months ago, she had fallen into a deep funk that she couldn't climb out of. Everything and everybody, especially Cedric, got on her last nerve. Nothing made sense anymore. Her mother and father had worked hard all their lives to have a successful retirement. And just when they were just starting to enjoy their new life, her mother died and left her father alone, trying to etch out some kind of existence. Why should anybody work so hard if this is how they would eventually end up? Instead of being happy to have gotten her family back together, she pondered how her life would have turned out had she remained single. Or taken up with that fine ass, very successful Tomas de la Cruz.

He tried to take the flask from Joie's hands, but she pulled away and turned the flask upwards emptying the contents into her throat. The brown liquor went down easily while soothing the sting left by her husband's accusation. She carefully returned the container to her purse before getting out of the car.

"You need to lay off that liquor, Joie. Aren't we still trying to get pregnant?" Cedric asked trying to smooth things out.

"We are, but since my period just ended yesterday, I know for sure that I'm not pregnant now. Might as well drink while I can, right?" Joie had lied about her period. And she knew she was being a passive-aggressive bitch, but she didn't care.

"That just means we have to work a little harder on making a baby."

"Uh huh," she replied. "If you say so…"

"Not to change the subject, but I enrolled in a course down at the SBA for people interested in starting their own business. You should go with me."

"Ain't nobody thinking about no damn SBA class right now." She rolled her eyes. "You sure picked a weird time to discuss business."

"Well, we haven't had time to talk about his. I just signed up this morning. The class starts next week. You interested?"

"Negro, puh-leeze! You don't know the first thing about starting a business."

"That's why I'm taking the course. To learn. Anyway, we'll talk about it later," he replied in defeat.

"Sure we will," she whispered under her breath.

Cedric's eyes rested on the satiny white material clashing against the soft caramel color of Joie's thigh. He wanted to enjoy his evening. Not wind up in another fight. "Did I mention how sexy you look in that dress tonight? Makes my dick hard just looking at you."

"Umh… Is that right?"

"Joie, it's been several months since we've made love. I'm horny as hell. How about you give me some tonight?" He placed his hand between her legs letting his finger slide beneath the fabric of her panties, making slow circular motions in an attempt to get her aroused.

She pushed his hand away. "Stop it. You're going to mess up my dress."

"Woman, you are really pushing it, you know that." He stared out the window trying to fathom a reason for Joie's recent behavior. Her attitude had turned to shit on a dime and for the life of him, he couldn't figure out why. "What the hell is wrong with you?"

"Me? Not a damn thing is wrong with me. What's wrong with you?" The *Remy* had taken effect causing her words to slur.

"You know what? Never mind…"

They exited the car and walked the short distance from the parking lot to the coliseum's entrance in silence. Every other couple that walked alongside them appeared to be in a good mood, in direct contrast to their own. After they cleared through the security checkpoint entrance, Cedric turned to Joie with anger still flashing in his eyes.

"Here's your ticket. I'm going the bar to get a drink. I'll meet you at our seats."

Joie took the paper from his outstretched hand. She stated, "I'm going to the bathroom first. You gonna wait for me?"

Cedric didn't acknowledge Joie, nor did he accompany her to the restroom as he normally would. He simply walked away, leaving her standing there looking like the fool she felt.

"Forget him! If Cedric wants to act like an asshole, I'm gonna let him." She stomped off to join dozens of other ladies waiting in the restroom line that never seemed to get any shorter no matter how many women passed through the exit door.

"Joie Parker? Is that you?" called out a man's voice from a few feet away.

She turned towards the source of her name, immediately recognizing her new branch manager. From the moment Joie laid eyes on Amir just a couple months ago, she had felt an immediate attraction. He was tall, dark, handsome, very well spoken. According to Amir, he was a true African—not a watered down, faux African-American version who have never stepped foot in Africa, but he proudly proclaimed to all that he was from the Dark Continent itself.

"Amir? What are you doing here? I didn't know you like this kind of music."

The African version of Idris Elba took several steps forward before leaning in to whisper, "Tell you the truth, if it were not for Frankie Beverly and Maze, I would not have come. Too many of *your* people up in here."

"*My* people?" She repeated louder than she expected.

"You know what I mean..." He grinned, revealing teeth so white they didn't seem real.

After engaging in several conversations with Amir at work, Joie quickly discovered his contempt towards black Americans. He referred to them as *mutts*, believing he was somehow superior because of his supposed untainted bloodline.

"*Your* people who mistakenly call themselves African-American despite the fact that most have never stepped foot in Africa."

"Oh, that's right. You don't consider yourself one of *us* because you're from Africa."

"Somalia to be exact."

"Right..."

"You want to know something, Amir? I've never really liked Africans."

"No. Why not?"

"Because y'all Africans are so damn arrogant, that's why. Think you better than us regular Black folks."

Amir stood up straighter, cleared his throat, and replied in a condescending tone, "We are not arrogant. We are what you would have been had you not been slaves."

Joie let that revelation sink in for a moment. Amir was trying to say that Africans didn't have to deal with the legacy of brainwashing passed on by the institution of slavery that Black Americans inherited. He had hit upon a nerve that was a little too close to the truth to ignore. Way too many of her people possessed a slave mentality whereby they relied upon the government for assistance, or manipulated the system to get something for free rather than working hard for it, taking shortcuts and blaming the "white man" for all that was wrong with their lives. It was "easier" to place blame rather than accepting your poor choices was the reason your life turned out the way it did.

Whereas prisons now housed more black men than were in college, in many cases the blame rested more on the individual than society. Joie understood that American had a very long way to go providing equality and civil rights for all its citizens. However, at the same time, women having children by multiple men who refused to raise them, was purely a personal decision and way too rampant in the community. She did not have a response to such a profound observation on the state of Black America. So instead of trying to play tit-for-tat in a conversation she was not well-equipped for, she chose to let it slide.

"So where is your wife? Or are you here on the prowl?" Joie teased, trying her best to not let on that she was teetering on the edge of being drunk.

"For your information, I am not married. A friend of mine had an extra ticket and invited me to accompany him and his wife. What about you? Did you come here alone?"

"I'm with my husband. He's around here. Somewhere." She dismissed the thought of Cedric with a drunken wave of her hand.

"What a fool he must be."

"Why you calling my husband a fool? You don't even know him." Joie let out a loud hiccup. "Um, excuse me. Too much soda pop."

Amir smiled at Joie's behavior, but he did not let on that he was aware of her obvious intoxication. "Because only a fool would leave someone as beautiful as you alone. If you were my wife, I would not let you out of my sight in a place such as this."

The woman standing in line ahead of Joie fanned herself with a program. She stated in a voice loud enough for several other women to hear, "Gurlllllll, if you don't want that African king you can hand him over to me. Umh! This man is too fine!"

A chorus of agreement came from several other women within earshot.

"Well, Amir, it looks like you have a fan club."

He leaned in close and whispered, "I would never go out with a woman who speaks so boldly. I am the hunter, not the hunted."

"Right... Because you're from Africa..."

"Most definitely. In my country, the men are the protectors and providers for the family, unlike America where women have taken over the roles of men."

"Some of us women have no other choice but to be strong." Joie defended her fellow sisters.

"If you were my wife, you would never have to worry about being strong. You would never have to worry about anything. And you would certainly not be in a venue such as this alone."

"My husband is here. Somewhere..."

"I understand." He acquiesced. "If you ever tire of your weak husband, let me know."

"I never said my husband was weak."

He brushed the back of his hand against Joie's cheek tenderly. "You didn't have to say it. Your actions speak louder than words."

Joie stood uncharacteristically flabbergasted by his bold language, as well as his gentle touch.

Amir pulled his cell phone from his jacket pocket. "What is your phone number?"

Joie rattled it off before she could think not to. Within seconds, her phone vibrated inside her purse. *Oh lord... The effect this man has on me! Must be some kind of African voodoo!*

"Now you have my cell number. It is totally up to you whether you choose to use it."

"Uh, excuse me Amir, but I told you I am married. And if I wasn't, I make it a rule to never date coworkers."

"I cannot change the fact that you are married, Joie. But in case you have not heard, I was transferred to the Richmond office as of last week. So you see...we are no longer coworkers."

"Is that right? Well, I suppose that changes everything, huh?"

The woman who spoke earlier turned around and pretended to look for something in her purse, when in fact she was simply being nosey. Every now and then, she tried to strike a sexy pose to gain Amir's attention.

Joie told the nosey woman, "You're next in line to go inside."

"Huh?" the woman asked, grinning at Amir.

"The line for the bathroom..." Joie replied. "You're next."

Amir smiled politely at the woman as she made her way into the restroom. He was used to women, particularly Black American women, throwing their unabashed attention his way. Scarcity breeds desperation. Therefore, the chance of an educated Black woman hooking up with an educated Black man was about as likely as finding a glass of water in a desert. The majority of these women were so hungry to get a taste of a real man that they fawned all over him every chance they could get. And he felt it was his duty to oblige as many of them as possible.

"I hope to hear from you soon. Until then, take care, beautiful lady."

"Uh, okay," Joie murmured.

He raised her hand to touch his lips ever so slightly. "In case no one has told you, you are absolutely ravishing in that dress. *Bonjour.*"

"Yeah, see you later, Amir." Joie remained speechless as Amir walked away leaving a trail of female heads turning in his wake. In spite of Amir's powerful effect on the opposite sex, Joie tried her best to remain immune to his charm.

Joie's thoughts rambled around her head in no particular order as she attempted to sort things out. *Lord, if I wasn't married... Let me stop. I am married. To Cedric. Married him twice, in fact. But Amir is everything I could ever want in a man, but he is so damn conceited. Yet I find that confidence so sexy. He reminds me of Tomas in the way he walks, his mannerisms, his self-assurance. What am I thinking? I made my vows to Cedric and I intend to keep them no matter how messed up we've both been acting lately. I love my husband, so why can't I stop thinking about Tomas de la Cruz? I do love Ced, don't I? Damn! I shouldn't have taken that second hit of Remy...*

The nosey woman stopped Joie on her way to the bathroom stall. "Excuse me, but would you happen to have a spare tampon?"

"Hold on. I think I might have one." Joie fished around in her purse. She unzipped the side pocket and pulled out two. "Take both...just in case."

"Thanks. Wouldn't you know that the night I'm wearing white would be when these damn fibroids start acting up again."

"Yeah, that used to be my problem too. In fact, my periods were so bad, I was afraid to wear light colors at all."

"But you're wearing white tonight."

"That's because I cured my fibroids."

The woman was taken aback. "You cured them? How?"

"Well, I didn't actually cure them, but I did get them to shrink significantly so they're not a nuisance anymore."

"No shit? How?"

Joie explained, "I took control of my body. I stopped taking all those different birth control pills the doctor prescribed because they manipulated my hormones so much that my estrogen levels were all over the place. A few months ago, I eliminated all soy from my diet, cut out hormone treated red meat, switched to almond milk, gave up chicken injected with antibiotics, and I eat mostly organic produce. Instead of coffee and donuts for breakfast, I eat steel cut oatmeal topped with flaxseed and walnuts. And for lunch I have a green salad drizzled with olive oil and apple cider vinegar."

"Isn't it expensive eating that way?"

"Yeah, organic is a little more expensive, but not as expensive as having a non-reversible hysterectomy. I got the added bonus of losing a few pounds, too."

"I hear that!" She laughed. "But I don't know if I can give up my ribs and fried chicken."

"I do have times when I indulge. When I eat out or over at somebody's house, I can't always control the ingredients. I just go back to my way of eating when I can."

"That is a drastic change. I don't know if I can do it."

"You should try it. If nothing else, at least you'll be healthier."

"Thanks. I appreciate the advice." The woman paused before she asked, "Can I ask you one more thing?"

"Sure."

"...about that man you were talking to?"

"Amir?"

"Yeah, the sexy African."

"What about him?"

"Is he single?" she asked.

"As far as I know. Why?"

"Well, I wasn't trying to eavesdrop on your conversation, but I overheard you tell him you were married. So I was hoping that you could hook a sister up with that fine brotha..."

Joie stared at the woman. She wasn't bad looking. Unfortunately, the look of desperation she wore outshone her pretty smile and gorgeous figure by a long shot. If Joie could see it, she could only imagine what men saw when they looked at her.

What Joie really wanted to say was, "*If Amir were interested in you, he had every opportunity to say something, especially the way you were all up in his face trying to get his attention.*" Instead she said, "Sure. Give me your number. I'll see if he's interested."

"Thanks," the woman said. "We sisters got to stick together, right?"

"Yeah. Sure," Joie replied. She tucked the woman's business car inside her purse.

After finally finishing up in the ladies room, Joie went in search of her seat next to Cedric. They had decent seats—not close to the stage, but certainly not in the nosebleed section where the performers weren't recognizable without watching them on the jumbotron, or where the sound system made everyone sound like they was singing inside a tin can.

Just as she sat down, the host, who also happened to be one of the DJ's at Hampton University's radio station, WHOV, introduced Frankie Beverly and Maze. Dressed in white and wearing his signature ball cap, Frankie hit the first note of *Joy and Pain*, sending the crowd into a frenzied, appreciative, roaring cheer.

"Who was that you were talking to out there?" Cedric asked when he caught Joie's eye.

"Just some woman. I don't know her name. Why?"

"Not her. I'm talkin' 'bout that pitch black niggah whispering in your ear." He eyed her closely. "Seemed like you two know each other pretty well."

"Oh! You mean Amir. He's just a coworker..." *Thank God he didn't see Amir kiss my hand.*

"Since when the fuck does a coworker kiss your hand?"

Oh shit! He did see it! "Oh that... Amir's from Africa. That's their custom over there."

Cedric stared at Joie not knowing whether he should believe her or not. In the end, he said, "Well, the next time you see *Amir*, tell that muthafucka that this ain't no goddamn Africa and to keep his black-ass lips to himself."

"Can we please discuss this later?" Joie shouted over the music. "We came here to listen to Frankie sing, not fight about my coworker."

"All right, but this is not the end of this conversation, Joie."

"Don't I know it..." she mumbled quietly under her breath, feeling more annoyed than angry, knowing that uttering just one more word would just lead to an argument. Instead, Joie bit her tongue and focused all her attention on the performance. After several minutes of singing, her mood was as high as the notes springing forth from Frankie's mouth.

~ ~ ~

The concert ended shortly before midnight. With the magic of their music, Frankie and the fellas in *Maze* had managed to lighten the couple's mood allowing them to temporarily put their disagreements aside. Thus, when the last note ended and the overhead lights came one, Joie and Cedric, along with thousands of other concert goers streamed from the venue floating on the words from their own favorite song.

By the time they arrived at Tequitta's house to pick up the kids it was almost one. While Joie waited in the car, because she absolutely refused to step inside, Cedric went to get the kids.

Tequitta and the kids had stayed up late to watch a funny movie, but one-by-one they all fell asleep. Maya was the only one who managed to stay awake the entire time, and it was she who noticed the car's headlights flash in the driveway.

"Wake up, Auntie T. Mommy and Daddy are here." She shook her aunt several times trying to not spill the contents of the drink still in Tequitta's hand.

"Okay, okay, okay... I'm awake," she slurred her speech.

Tequitta tried to pull herself together. She hadn't meant to drink so much, especially since she was watching the kids, but it *was* a Saturday night. She needed something to take the edge off the loneliness that always seemed to creep back, especially on weekends. After peering through the peephole, she opened the door to let Cedric inside. Despite Joie's comments about how nasty she thought Tequitta kept her house, Cedric had never observed it that way. In fact, the house was surprisingly clean every time he was there. He only wished Joie would take the time to see it for herself, but he knew his wife's refusal to see Tequitta as someone good was clouded by a multitude of other issues.

"Hi Daddy," Maya said sleepily.

"What are you doing still awake?"

"Auntie T said I could stay up late." She replied with a big yawn.

"She did, huh?" Cedric gave her a hug. "Go on to the car while I get your brother."

"Okay." Maya gathered her things. "Goodnight Auntie T."

"Goodnight Maya," Tequitta replied trying her best to appear more tired than drunk.

"Thanks again for watching the kids, Tequitta," Cedric said. While he watched his daughter leave, he picked up Trey from the loveseat and propped him against his shoulder.

"You're welcome. They're such good kids that I don't mind watching them at all," she whispered.

"You must be doing something right because they always want to visit..."

"I'll tell you something else."

"Oh yeah? What's that?" Cedric replied, shifting a sleeping Trey in his arms.

"Laila loves playing with her brother and sister." She remarked off-handedly, "but of course she still thinks they're just cousins."

"What?"

"I can't believe how much Maya and Laila look alike. Can you? They even sound the same. And Trey... well, him and Junior are both the spitting image of Derek."

Cedric was caught off guard by Tequitta's remarks. "Uh, right. Well, thanks again."

"Maybe one day Laila can spend the night at your house. She's always asking."

"I'll talk it over with Joie and let you know."

"Yeah. Go home and talk it over with your wife," she slurred. "These kids need to know the truth."

"Are you okay?" Cedric asked. His eyes rested on the cocktail glass situated on the coffee table near a half empty bottle of *Jack Daniels*. He wondered if the bottle was full when she started.

"I'm fine. I just need some rest." She averted her eyes under the scrutiny of his.

Cedric suspected Tequitta had been drinking, not because of her slurred speech, but by her casually discussing the taboo topic of his children's heritage. He would not tell Joie about Tequitta's lack of discretion, because he would never hear the end of it. "We'll see you later. Go get some sleep."

Carefully balancing Trey in his arms, Cedric descended the three steps and returned to his car. Tequitta stood in the doorway watching. She pulled her worn terry cloth housecoat taut at the waist and gave a quick wave at Joie.

He placed Trey in the backseat next to the now sleeping Maya.

Joie waved back. "At least she got sense enough to cover herself up."

"Give it a rest, Joie."

She smacked her lips together and cut her eyes at Cedric, throwing all kinds of shade in his direction. "Me?!"

"Not tonight, please. I'm tired. Let's just go home." Cedric climbed behind the steering wheel and backed into the street. As he turned his head slightly to make sure the street was clear he noticed Trey was crying.

"Trey, what's the matter?" he asked.

Joie also turned to face her son. "Sweetie, what's wrong?"

Tears streamed down the child's face as he tried his best to control his emotions. "Mommy? Daddy? Why did Auntie T say that Maya and Laila are sisters?"

"W-w-hat?" Joie asked, unable to believe her ears.

"And Auntie T said that me and the baby look just alike—that we favor somebody named Derek."

Cedric remained quiet, allowing Joie to provide answers that only she could. He focused on the road ahead as if he hadn't heard a word.

Though Trey had spoken clearly, it took several moments for his words to register and make sense to Joie. "Uh, did she tell you that?"

Trey shook his head. "Unh unh, I heard her say that to daddy."

"Ced? What's going on? Where you talking to her about this?"

Cedric blinked rapidly trying to sort it all out in his own mind. "Hell no! She just blurted it out! We both thought Trey was asleep."

"Mommy? Who is Derek?" Trey asked between tearful hiccups. "Why did she say I look like him?"

"Oh my God..." she whispered. "I can't believe..."

Within the dark confines of the car's back seat, Trey's young mind began to click on all cylinders. He put two and two together recalling a conversation he had with his father several months ago. "Daddy, remember when you told me I was going to look just like my father? But Auntie T said I was the spitting image of somebody named Derek. Aren't you my daddy?"

"Ced, turn this goddamn car around," Joie said with tightly controlled anger brewing. "Right now!"

"No, I am not going to do that. We've got to deal with this amongst ourselves. At home."

"Lord help me! I'm gonna kill that fuckin' bitch!" Joie hissed. "Who the hell does she think she is?"

"Calm down! You're not helping with all that cussin'!"

Maya was awakened by the commotion. "Mommy? What's wrong?" she asked still half asleep. She then noticed Trey. "Why are you crying?"

"Auntie T said that you and Laila are sisters," Trey stammered. "Does that make Laila my sister, too?"

"Trey, you must be crazy. Laila is our cousin. Right, Mommy?"

Joie barely managed to maintain control of her temper. She was so angry she began to cry. "Ced, what do we do now?"

Cedric gripped the steering wheel tightly as the realization that the moment he feared most had finally come. "What we do now is, we tell them the truth..."

Chapter Eleven

The sun had risen by the time they all climbed into their respective beds, exhausted by the kind of fatigue only truth can bring. There were lots of tears, many questions, gentle answers, and an unending supply of hugs, kisses, and reassurances that nothing had changed. They were still a family. And when the Parker family finally settled down, they did so embracing the knowledge of never having to worry about having their family secret exposed only to unravel the fine thread holding their fragile lives together. Or so each had privately hoped.

Maya was the first to awaken a little past ten o'clock. Despite all that her parents told her about her real father, she still had questions that only one person could answer. She stealthily crept down the long hallway to check on Trey. First, she pushed his door open. Then she tiptoed to her parent's bedroom and placed her ear against the door listening to their quiet snores.

"Good, they're all still asleep," Maya whispered to herself.

Tiptoeing with quiet, soft steps she learned in ballet class, she carefully descended the stairs avoiding the noisy spots that creaked loudly whenever pressure were applied. Pretending to be a spy on a mission, she made it downstairs without making a sound. The house phone was in the kitchen, so that's where she headed. She punched the seven digits and waited.

"Hello?" Tequitta's high-pitched voice came through the phone line and into the quiet space of the kitchen as if she were standing there in person.

"Hi, Auntie T. It's me, Maya."

"Oh, hey Maya. I'm sorry, but Laila is still asleep. And I'm surprised you're up so early," she said trying to ignore the throbbing in her temples.

"Uh, I didn't call to speak to Laila. I wanted to talk to you." Maya slid the phone to her chest and listened. The house was still quiet.

"What's the matter, sweetheart?"

"Well, I want to ask you a question..."

"About what?"

"Uh...well...hmmm... I'm not sure how to ask you this."

Tequitta laughed at how similar Maya and Laila were. One moment you couldn't shut them up, and the next it was like pulling teeth getting them to speak. "Baby girl, you can ask me anything. Spit it out."

Maya listened to the quiet of the house. Everything remained peaceful inside with the only noise coming from the hum of the refrigerator. "Okay... Well, last night Trey heard you tell Daddy that me and Laila are sisters."

Tequitta wasn't prepared to have this conversation with Laila, much less Maya. To avoid her daughter's eavesdropping, which she seemed to do more and more of these days, she took her cell phone into the bedroom. "Uh, shouldn't you be talking about this with your momma and daddy?"

"I already did."

"When?"

"Last night. They told us that Laila is our sister. They said we have the same father. That my daddy isn't our real daddy." Maya felt her bottom lip begin to tremble. She bit into it hard, but not so much as to draw blood, because she did not want to start crying again.

"Oh..." Tequitta felt her heart break for Maya. All those years she had grown up believing Cedric was her father only to discover it wasn't true. Derek had mentioned in passing his fling with Joie, but he had no idea Joie had given birth to his children. That secret remained hidden to all until after his death.

"Is it true? Is Laila my sister?" She sniffled her tears in check. "Laila said she saw me at her daddy's funeral a couple years ago. Was that man my father, too?"

"Sweetie, I really think you should be talking about this with your momma." The throbbing in her temples increased with each additional word from Maya's mouth.

"They're still asleep. Anyway, I wanted to ask you. They said my father's name was Derek Jordan. That's Laila's daddy, isn't it?"

Tequitta felt a tug in her heart at the mention of Derek's name. Even though he had been dead for three years, she missed him deeply. "Maya, I can't answer your questions. Well, I can, but not like this. Not over the telephone. Maybe y'all can come over to the house later on today if it's okay with your parents." Plus, she needed to break the news to Laila before she heard it from Maya.

"Okay, Auntie. But can I ask you one more thing. Did you know about me and Trey?"

She would have to ask me that. Even so, I can't lie to the child. "I didn't know about y'all until a couple years ago. Not until after Derek had already passed."

Maya heard the stairs creak in the background. She whispered into phone, "I've gotta go, but I'm going to ask Mommy to bring us over later."

"Okay, sweetie. That's a good idea."

"Bye," Maya said quickly ending the call. She replaced the cordless phone on the base charger perched atop the counter. When she turned around, Joie was standing in the doorway with her arms crossed tightly over her chest.

Tequitta reached into the medicine cabinet for a bottle of aspirin. Even though the directions said to only take two, she popped four of the chalky pills into her mouth and attempted to swallow. It didn't work. All four tablets became lodged at the base of her throat. Simultaneously, she spit the aspirin into the sink while ending the call with Maya. Glancing into the mirror, she admonished the hungover, swollen-eyed face staring back at her, "Damn it! What the hell have I done?"

Meanwhile, back at the Parker's resident, Maya tried to act as if she were doing nothing more than fixing a Sunday morning breakfast which consisted of a bowl of *Fruity Pebbles*.

Joie said, "I didn't expect you to be up so soon. You only went to bed a few hours ago."

"Uh, I wasn't sleepy anymore." Maya turned to leave.

"Wait a minute. Who were you talking to on the phone?"

"Uh...um..."

"Don't you even think about lying to me young lady. Who was that on the phone?"

Maya looked down to her feet. This time she wasn't able to control the tears that welled up in her eyes from overflowing. "Auntie T."

Joie clenched her teeth tightly. "What were you calling miss thang about?"

"Mommy, I had to ask her about my real daddy."

"Cedric *is* your real daddy. We told you that last night, baby." Though angry with Maya for calling *that* woman, Joie went to her daughter and enveloped her arms around her thin shoulders, wiping her tears away. She used her fingers to gather Maya's bushy hair back into the ponytail holder that was barely hanging on.

"I know what you and daddy told me, but you also said my real daddy's name was Derek Jordan. I just wanted to ask Auntie T about him."

"Oh baby..." Joie replied, quelling her anger. "What did she have to say?"

"She kept saying I should ask you."

"Well, at least she does have a little sense rolling around that bobble head," Joie mumbled to herself. "She was right. You should be talking to me and daddy about this."

"She said we can come over later if it's okay with you." Maya looked at her with big old sad eyes that reminded her of Derek. "Can we?"

Joie didn't answer Maya right away because the thoughts in her head refused to form a coherent sentence. To keep her hands from trembling, she went about making a pot of coffee. Cedric always told her the day of reckoning would arrive when she least expected it. As she pushed the button to start the coffee brewing she thought, *I'd rather pour this entire pot of scalding hot coffee over the top of my head than sit across from that skank and have a conversation about Derek. What the hell am I going to say to that heifer? It's bad enough that my kids are spending time over there. This was not part of the plan.*

"Mommy, can we go? Please?" Maya begged.

Joie exhaled slowly. One breath in, one breath out. Another breath in, one more out, until she was certain she would not faint. She calmly walked over to the stereo and tuned it to her favorite jazz station. *Anything to quiet these uncomfortable thoughts swirling around my head. My mother, Ronnie, and even Ced have continually reminded me that this is my bed and I must lie in it. Yes, it was my intention to take this secret to my grave, but obviously God had other plans because very soon everybody and their brother is gonna know all about my past and how bad I messed up.*

"Mommaaaa?" Maya whined. She tugged so hard on Joie's robe that she almost pulled it loose. "Answer me..."

It wasn't like Joie was intentionally trying to ignore her child. She just needed a moment to get her thoughts together before the wrong words came out like they usually did. Her first thought was to tell Maya to leave it alone. Let sleeping dogs lie. Cedric was her daddy now and that was that. But when a song began to play on the radio, her thoughts suddenly changed. Joie laughed out loud because Gerald Albright's saxophone rendition of *We Fall Down* flowed into the kitchen space, filling up the room to remind her to forgive herself. She listened to the words carefully, allowing them to caress her weary mind. *We fall down, but we get up... we fall down, but we get up... for a saint is just a sinner who fell down...*

Joie quickly became lost in the music, allowing the space in the offbeat to speak to her as only music could. After the last words were sung and the music had ended, she turned to Maya and smiled. "Yeah, baby. I'll take you over there. It's about time me and Auntie T got to know each other."

"For real?"

"Didn't I just say I would?"

"Thanks Mommy!" Maya gave her mother a big kiss on the cheek.

"You're welcome. Now get upstairs and go brush your teeth. And wash that dried spit off your face."

"I love you, Mommy. I just wanted to know more about Derek Jordan, that's all."

Joie playfully swatted Maya on her behind. "Girl, you are too grown for your own good. Now get your little behind upstairs before I change my mind," Joie teased.

She watched her eight-year-old child skip out of the kitchen with a little less innocence than she had the day before. Her thick ponytail bobbed up and down as if it were trying to hold her back from growing up too quickly. It wasn't fair to burden Maya or Trey with the sins of their parents, so she had to think of a gentle way to explain her relationship with Derek. Lord knows she couldn't tell her kids the truth. Although the truth can set you free, this type of truth could destroy her precious little angels. Throughout her life, Joie often heard people say that children were resilient, but what most failed to realize is that resiliency often came at a very high price.

The coffee pot beeped three times to signal the coffee was finished brewing. She pulled a packet of bacon from the freezer and placed it on the counter to thaw, and then poured herself a big cup of black java.

Joie stared out the kitchen window lost in her thoughts while she listened to gospel music playing in the background. *It is a beautiful summer morning I refuse to spoil it by worrying about my conversation with "Auntie T". I can't let myself get all worked up about what might happen until it actually happens.* As she sipped her coffee, she glanced outside. *Would you look at that? Two Cardinals chasing each other from treetop to treetop! Now that's a good sign if ever I saw one.*

The house phone rang in the background interrupting the momentary escape from the reality of the conversation she just had with her daughter. First thought was to just let it ring, but hardly anyone ever called on her house phone unless they couldn't reach her on the cell.

"Hello?" she answered, slightly annoyed.

"Joie? It's Ronnie!"

"What?! Is this *the* Mrs. Veronica Duarte?" Joie laughed.

"How many other Ronnies do you know?"

"Girl, I'm still trying to get used to you not being Veronica Pierce anymore."

"Don't worry about it. It still sounds strange when I hear someone call me Veronica Duarte."

"It is so good to hear your voice!"

Ronnie laughed. "I know, right? It's been a minute since we've last talked. These babies keep me so busy that I barely have time to breathe. But I wouldn't have it any other way."

"I know that's right. I can say the same about Maya and Trey. These kids have a social life that I could only have dreamed of when I was their age."

"Gotta keep these little munchkins busy or they'll get bored," Ronnie said. "So how is your father doing?"

"He's doing better. We keep trying to convince him to come back to Virginia, but he ain't having none of it. He said fishing in the Chesapeake Bay is no comparison to what he pulls out of the waters off of Florida."

"Good for your dad. I know he's missing Miss Slim something awful, so it's good he's keeping his mind and body occupied."

"Ya know, I miss my mom too. But my daddy is gonna be just fine."

"And so will you…"

"Thanks girlfriend." She reminisced on the memory of her mother for a moment. "I'll tell daddy you asked about him."

Ronnie took a deep breath before continuing. "So the reason I'm calling is because I wanted to ask if you're free next weekend."

"Hold on a minute. Everybody's still asleep so I'm gonna go outside on the deck." Joie turned off the house security alarm before opening the kitchen door. "Okay, you were saying…"

"I'm sorry, Joie. It's after ten. I thought you'd be up and out shopping by now."

Joie dusted off a thin layer of dust from a lawn chair before taking a seat. "Usually we are up by now, but we had a late night. We went to the Hampton Jazz Festival to hear Frankie do his thang."

"That is the one thing I do miss about not living in the states. We don't get too many artists coming down this way, unless they're at one of the resorts. How was it?"

"You know Frankie, girl. He never disappoints." She sipped her coffee. "So you were asking about next weekend. What's going on?"

"Luis and Tomas are attending a conference in Virginia Beach. I was going to come up for a few days and hang out with you in Hampton. If you're not doing anything."

Joie froze at the mention of Tomas' name. It wasn't as if she sat around thinking about Tomas de la Cruz or missing his presence. What she did miss was the good times they shared. Lately, it seemed that she and Cedric were never on the same page anymore. It felt like they spent more time arguing than making love. A warm breeze stirred through the tree leaves with the memory of the first time she laid eyes on Tomas. She and Ronnie were having drinks at a restaurant on the Santa Elena Pier. At first glance, she was smitten and so was he... She pushed away the different scenarios of what would have happened if she hooked up with Tomas instead of remarrying Ced.

"Joie? You still there?"

"Yeah, yeah, I'm still here." Joie's focus returned to the conversation at hand. "When did you say you're coming through?"

"We're flying in next Friday. Luis and Tomas are staying for the week, but I'll be in town just for the weekend. Luis' mother is watching the kids so I don't want to be gone too long."

"For real?! I can't wait to see you guys." Joie squealed, "We are gonna have so much fun!"

"Yeah, it's been over a year since we had a good old ladies night out."

"You're right. Last time we kicked it, you were still living in California," Joie said.

"That was a while ago."

"Yes indeed. Last time we hung out was right before I hooked up with Tomas."

"How can I forget that? You kicked me to the curb to hang out with him."

"Girl, if you knew what I did with Mr. de la Cruz, you would have kicked yourself to the curb too. Lawd have mercy!"

"Unh, unh, unh… For real though, Joie… You and Tomas as a couple? I can't see how that would have ever worked out. You two are too much alike."

Joie laughed because she knew Ronnie's perception was correct. "How is Tomas, anyway?"

"He's good," Ronnie replied then quickly redirected the conversation to more appropriate territory. "How is Cedric?"

"Cedric is… okay, I suppose."

"I know you two are still on your honeymoon." Ronnie laughed good-naturedly. "You and Cedric are the only couple I know who do all that freaky-deaky role playing."

"We're taking things one day at a time. It hasn't been as easy as I thought it was going to be. Nothing has."

"You want to talk about it?"

Joie hung her head, sighing wearily. "Girl, the kids found out that Cedric isn't their father."

"What?! How did that happen? I thought you were going to wait to tell them."

"Waiting for a better time was the plan, but big mouth Tequitta let it slip last night when Ced was picking up the twins."

"Oh no! How did they take it?"

"Well, we explained to them that Ced is their daddy and he loves them. We told them he will always be their daddy even if not biologically. They took it as well as could be expected."

"Damn… How are you handling it?"

"At first I wanted to go kill that bitch. But now that I've had time to think about it, I guess it's better they found out sooner than later."

"I'm sorry, Joie. This can't be easy, but like you said, its better that they find out now. At least Cedric is there to help explain."

"Regardless, me and Tequitta need to have a conversation about her role in my babies' lives."

"Joie? Are you all right?"

"Yeah, I'm fine. Why?"

"This has got to be the absolute first time that I have ever heard you say that woman's name correctly. Twice."

"Unh unh, I've said her name before."

"Oh no you have not. You have called her every name in the book besides the one her mother gave her."

"Whatever, but like I was saying. Me and *Tequitta* need to sit down and get our stories straight. I am not about to tell my kids the entire story of how they were conceived." Joie shuddered at the thought.

"That's a story no one should ever hear. You and my ex getting busy... Disgusting."

"Shut up, Ronnie. You got Luis and those beautiful babies in your life now, so you don't have nothin' to be disgusted about."

"My marriage to Derek happened a lifetime ago. I'm not even tripping off of it anymore. But as for you, it's about time you and Tequitta talked this mess through. It won't be easy, but life never is."

"Anyway... You were telling me about Tomas?"

"I was not telling you anything about Tomas. Woman, you are seriously trippin'. You and Cedric have only been remarried for six months."

"And?"

"And...technically you're still newlyweds. So why are you asking me about another man?"

"Ronnie, you seem to have forgotten that Cedric and I were married before so *technically* we are not newlyweds. Anyway, I just wanted to know how Tomas has been."

"He's fine."

"I know he's fine," Joie said with a huge grin on her face. "I thought that since we're going to be hanging out that maybe I'd see him too."

"Joie Parker! Girl, you ain't never gonna change."

"I'm just having a little fun, that's all. Things have been too serious around this house."

"Oh yeah? How so?"

"Maya come to me and says she wants to ask her Auntie T about Derek."

"Say what?!"

"Just before you called, Maya practically begged me to take her over there."

"What did you say?"

"Of course, I gave in. Now you tell me if that ain't some mess. Hell, it's barely ten thirty in the morning and I'm trying my best to not start drinking."

"You better hold off on that drink until after that conversation. That's probably when you'll really need it. Is Cedric going with you?"

"He don't know nothin' about it yet. I've got to ask him how he wants to handle this."

"Despite all of Cedric's flaws, that man has always loved you. He will have your back on this."

"You're probably right. But lately he's been acting kinda funny."

"Funny? Like how?"

"Lately, when he comes home from work, he goes straight to his office and shuts the door. He says he needs time to decompress before he can engage with me. What the hell does that mean? Engage with me? And for the past few weeks, it seems like all we do is argue."

"You know, he does have a stressful job working with those troubled kids. It must take a lot out of him to have to deal with that craziness all day."

"I guess so," Joie agreed, preferring to cut the conversation about her marital difficulties short. "Hey girl, I've got to go, but before I hang up, I want to let you know that you're welcome to stay with me while Luis and Tomas are at their meetings in Virginia Beach."

"Thanks. I'll think about it. Luis has already reserved a hotel room for us, but I'll let you know."

"You know, even though I don't live in a sprawling hillside villa like yours, we do have room for you," Joie teased.

Okay, I'm coming! Ronnie shouted in the background. "I'm sorry girl, I've gotta go. Luis needs help with the kids."

"Tell Luis I said '*hola*.'"

"All right, I will." Ronnie added, "I'll call you in a few days and let you know more about when I'm flying in. And keep your chin up. You've been through a lot worse and always manage to land on your feet."

"Thanks, girlfriend. I'll talk you later."

"One more thing before I go..." Ronnie said.

"What's up?"

"I wasn't going to say anything, but Tomas has also been asking about you too."

Joie ended the call with a smile on her face and thoughts of seeing Tomas on her mind. She sipped the remaining coffee that had by now turned cold. Or as cold as a sunny eighty degree morning would allow.

Chapter Twelve

By mid-morning, the air had gone still as the heat of the day began to build to its full weight of oppressive humidity. Summer was in full swing with the sounds of lawn mowers starting up with neighbors trying to get a jump on the yard work before it became too hot. She inhaled the heavy scent of freshly cut grass. A pair of blue jays fluttered near a nest in the tree where she had seen the Cardinals earlier.

"Joie?! Joie, where are you?" Cedric yelled from inside the house before appearing at the kitchen door, dressed in jogging clothes. "Have you seen my earphones?"

"Good morning to you, too," Joie replied sarcastically. "Where are you going?"

"Jogging," he explained. "After last night, I need to run off some of this stress."

"Since when did you start jogging?"

"Actually, I started about a year ago. I've slacked off in the last six months, but now it's time I picked it up again." He pinched the fat surrounding his waist. "I'm trying to get rid of these love handles."

"Good for you."

"Have you seen my earphones?" he asked while he rummaged through the junk drawer.

"For your phone?"

"I'm not taking my phone. I'm using my old IPod because I have my music loaded on it."

"Oh those? I think Maya borrowed them last night. Check the dining room table. That's where she normally leaves her IPod stuff."

He stepped around the corner into the dining room. He shouted out, "You were right. Got 'em."

"I thought so. I keep telling Maya she needs to start cleaning up after herself."

"Maybe if you stopped picking up after them, they would do more of it themselves," he replied through the partially open door. "These kids got to learn we are not their maids. What you need to do is remove those TVs from their bedrooms until they start listening."

"Yeah, yeah, yeah..." she responded, annoyed with Ced's continuous musings about her spoiling the twins. "Speaking of Maya, she asked me to take her to Laila's house later on."

"Why? She was just over there last night."

"Your daughter called Tequitta this morning."

"Really? Why?"

"Maya wants to ask her Auntie T a few questions about Derek."

"Do you think that's a good idea?"

"No, but she's going to ask anyway. Might as well be when we're there." Joie slipped past him to return inside the kitchen. "You want to go with me?"

"Go with you where?"

"To Tequitta's house. I think it'll be better if we put up a united front."

He guffawed. "Are you out of your mind?"

"No, I'm serious. This is a family issue that we should handle together."

"Joie, listening to you two discuss your babies' daddy is the last thing I want to hear. On a scale of one to ten with ten being my doctor telling me I have a week to live, hearing about you and Jordan is a solid thirteen."

"Hmmm, I suppose..."

"But what I do want to talk about is us," he stated matter-of-factly.

"What about us?"

"How about we finish the conversation we started before the concert?"

"Ced, I know we need to talk. Right now, we have to deal with the issue of the kids first."

"You can't keep putting this conversation off. We have some serious shit we need to deal with. Number one being that you have slacked way off in the sex department. Three months without making love don't have nothin' to do with the kids. What's up with that?"

"Has it been that long?" ...*speaking of having sex, when was my last period? Did I even have one this month? I must have... Maybe I missed my period because of all the stress I'm under. Good thing I'm on the pill. Otherwise I'd be panicking about now. Maybe I'm heading into menopause...* Joie's thoughts wandered all over the place.

"Baby, we spend more time fighting than conversing. This is not what I had in mind when we got remarried."

"I didn't realize it has been three months." She shrugged, nonchalantly. "Anyway, I've been so worried about my daddy since mom passed. I've also been preoccupied with what's going on at work.

The kids always seem to need me to take them somewhere... Take your pick."

"I understand you are busy, but don't you desire me anymore? We used to make love twice a day."

She sighed heavily. "I do want you, but..."

"But *what* Joie?" he asked waiting for a response that failed to materialize.

She looked away.

"Look, I'm only going to put up with your excuses for so long. Something's got to give."

"And what does that mean? You gonna go find some bitch to fuck?"

"Please don't go getting overly dramatic on me first thing in the morning. I'm just saying that we need to work on our marriage *if* this is going to work."

"Yeah, yeah, yeah. I hear ya," Joie acquiesced. "We'll talk about us later today. I promise."

Cedric smacked Joie on her ass. "Wanna go running with me? You're getting a little thick back there."

"In your dreams," she said backing away from his reach.

"Unfortunately, in my dreams *is* the only place I've seen your fine ass lately..."

"In other news... Guess what?"

"What?"

"Ronnie and Luis Duarte are coming to town next weekend."

"Seriously? They're coming to Hampton? Why?"

"Not Hampton. Luis is attending some kind of convention in Virginia Beach and Ronnie is coming along. They're leaving the twins with his mother in the DR." *I know I should tell him that Tomas is coming too, but Ced would lose his mind if I mentioned that man's name in this house.*

"Cool. You plan on seeing them?"

"Of course! I can't let my best friend come to Virginia and not see her."

"You should invite them over for dinner."

"I'll see. That will depend on his schedule."

"Oh? *His* schedule? Well, excuse the hell outta me. Guess they don't have time for us regular people, huh?"

"Don't do that. I'm sure that if Luis isn't busy, they will drop by to say hello."

"Sure." He poured himself a glass of water and promptly changed the subject. "So what time are you taking Maya over there?"

"I don't know. I haven't even called Tequitta yet to see if she's gonna be home."

"Why don't you do it now?" he asked, wondering if whatever devil that had chased Tequitta into that bottle of *Jack Daniels* had released her from its grip yet.

"Okay." Joie scrolled down to the S's where she had Tequitta's name filed under Skank-ass 'ho.

Tequitta answered on the first ring. "Hello?"

"Um, hey Tequitta. This is Joie."

"Joie? Well this is a surprise. I don't think you've ever called me directly."

"Yeah, I know."

"What can I do for you?" She asked getting right to the point.

"It's about the twins. Maya told me she called you this morning."

"She sure did. Did she tell you what she wanted?"

"Yeah. She wants to talk to you about Derek. I figure she has questions only you can answer. Considering you were his wife and all."

Tequitta hesitated before answering. She had never spoken to Joie directly. Whenever the subject regarding Joie was broached with Cedric, he always cut the conversation short. "Sure. You can bring her over. If it's alright with you, it's alright with me."

"Sounds good. What are you doing around two this afternoon?"

"I'm getting my nails done at three. Why don't y'all stop by around one?"

"Okay, I'll see you then."

Joie ended the call. She turned to Cedric and asked, "You sure you don't wanna go with me?"

"No, thank you. I want you to handle this."

Trey strolled into the kitchen still half asleep, rubbing his eyes, scratching his stomach. He let out a huge yawn and said, "Morning Mommy. Morning Cedric."

Within that single moment that seemed to last for an eternity, the birds stopped chirping, the wind ceased to blow, and the earth stopped turning on its axis at the very second their eight-year old son lost his ever-loving mind. Both Joie and Cedric spoke at the same time.

Cedric spoke in a much too calm voice when he quietly whispered, "What did you call me?"

Joie's reaction was just the opposite. She screamed out loud for all to hear, "Boy, what did you just call your daddy?!"

Trey snapped wide awake as if he'd been slapped across his face by both parents. In a quiet voice, which trembled when he spoke, he whispered, "I thought since he not my real daddy, that I should call him Cedric."

Cedric clenched his teeth in anger and bit his tongue so hard he tasted blood. "Joie... you... better..."

"Listen here young man. Cedric is your real daddy and the only daddy that you have ever known. So don't you ever let me hear you disrespect your father like that again! Do you hear me, boy?!" Now apologize!"

"Yes, ma'am." Trey turned to Cedric. "I'm sorry daddy. I won't do it again." Trey looked up at Cedric. Sorrow and shame clouded his once innocent eyes. At eight years of age, he understood he would never grow up to be like this man he called daddy. They didn't share the same genes. Hell, they didn't even resemble one another.

Staring down at Trey, Cedric came to the realization that nothing would ever be the same again. The son he had raised from a baby, the boy who used to look up to him, the child who called him daddy, no longer regarded him as his father. And that fact broke his heart. "I've got to get some fresh air," he said.

"Baby, Trey didn't mean anything..."

"I'll be back in a little while." Cedric rushed through the back door as if he couldn't wait to get away.

"I'm sorry, Mommy. Maya said that since he ain't our real daddy that we don't have to call him daddy no more. She said our real daddy was dead."

Joie sighed wearily, sinking down into a kitchen chair. Shaking her head at the entire situation, she told Trey, "Maya don't know everything, baby. While your real father might be dead, Cedric is your real daddy."

"Does that mean Tequitta is our mother?"

"No sweetie. I am your mother. Why do you ask?"

"Well, since daddy ain't our real daddy, I thought you might not be our real momma."

"I gave birth to you and Maya. You don't have to worry about anything because I am your mother," she reassured him while trying her best to maintain her composure feeling her heart beginning to break.

"Okay. I'm glad you're my mommy because I don't want Auntie T to be my mother."

"Why not?" Joie asked just for the hell of it.

"Because the neighborhood kids, especially the older boys, call her a milt."

"A what?"

"They call her a milt. They say she don't look like nobody's momma."

Joie started to laugh in spite of herself.

"What's so funny?" Trey asked innocently.

"You mean a MILF!"

"I don't know what that is but it does not sound good."

"Don't worry about it, sweetie. It's a disrespectful word that bad boys give older women. And I better never hear you repeat it, either."

"Okay." Trey shrugged and went about his business fixing himself a bowl of cereal.

Joie lowered her head to stare at the floor. *This is the exact spot our world fell apart just a few years ago. I wish my parents still lived here so I could just drive over to the house for a quick visit. Maybe if they hadn't moved to Florida, Momma would still be alive. Everything is starting to spin out of control and I don't think I can handle this on my own. The twins know who their biological father is. Trey is calling Cedric by his first name. Maya is acting like she all grown. My marriage is starting to fall apart...I've been working my ass off and don't have hardly nothin' to show for it. I don't know what to do.*

Suddenly Amir's voice popped into her mind. *"I am not arrogant, I am what you would have been had you not been slaves..."* The confident self-assured manner in which Amir uttered those words stuck in her head causing a sudden shift in her thinking. A long, overdue epiphany took hold. *Oh my goodness! I think Amir was right. I don't think I deserve more than what I have. I have allowed my life to become one drama filled moment after another while I sabotage any chance we have of becoming more. Cedric mentioned wanting to go into business, but I seem to be the one killing his dreams, just like he said. Is this why I behave the way I do? Because I have a slave mentality? When the opportunity comes for us to finally step out on our own, I unwittingly sabotage it to maintain this status quo?*

Her eyes scanned the kitchen of the home where she and Cedric had first lost, but then rediscovered their love. The thought of losing him over some bullshit she had created became almost unbearable. *This is ridiculous. I think it's about time I made a change in my life for all our lives. We deserve better than this chaos I have allowed to enter our once peaceful space. It is time I started treating my husband better. Put my support behind Ced. Encourage him when he tells me about his dreams. Take care of this mess with Derek being the twins' biological father so we can become a real family again. I have allowed too much bullshit to grow in this house instead of filling it with love. It's time for me to step up and be the wife Ced deserves and the mother the twins need.*

~ ~ ~

Cedric hit the streets in a slow jog. By the time he picked up the pace, the humidity had increased to an uncomfortable level making even the simple task of breathing a struggle. With each agonizing step, his anger with Trey subsided.

Too bad the anger he held against Joie continued to simmer beneath the surface. He also needed to rid himself of a lingering sexual tension. Jerking off once a day only worked for so long. He needed a real release, and since Joie wasn't putting out, the only way he knew to get his mind off sex without messing up his marriage was to start running again. So that is what he did.

His usual route took him through the neighborhood and into the local park. Listening to rock music blaring into his ears, which by the way was the only place he could listen to this type of music because Joie forbade him to play rock, heavy metal, or anything that resembled it while she was at home, he kept up a steady run. By the time he made it to the basketball court, he was so out of breath that his sides hurt. He spied a group of teenage boys huddling under the basketball hoop even though there was not a basketball in sight. The oldest couldn't have been more than sixteen.

Those boys ain't up to no good. Since I don't see nobody shooting baskets, being out here this early only usually means one thing. Hey wait a minute... Isn't that one of my kids? No, it can't be Bryson Graves because he is much too smart to be involved with this bunch.. He approached the group of teenagers.

"Hey old dude, what you need?" asked the oldest boy in the group. His voice and gestures were filled with an arrogant bravado that only foolish youth could bring, which also made him extremely dangerous. This boy was like a hand grenade with the pin already pulled. Anything could set him off.

"Old dude?" Cedric asked incredulously while using his shirt to wipe the sweat from his eyes.

"Yeah. Whatcha want?" the boy repeated. His hands disappeared to the back of his waistband to where his piece was hidden.

"He look like he need an ambulance," joked one of the other teens. "Hey man, you awright? You look like you 'bout to pass out."

Cedric sighed heavily. "Don't you kids have somewhere you need to be? Have something else to do besides sell drugs?"

"Hey man. You the po po?" asked a fat boy off to the side.

"No, I'm not the police."

"Man, that's just Mr. Parker. He's cool," explained a boy of about twelve. "He works over at the youth center."

"You some kinda probation officer?" asked the oldest boy.

"No, but I know quite a few of them," Cedric replied.

"Hey ole' G. We just out here trying to make a livin'. Don't be sweatin' us." The fat boy swaggered towards him.

"Go home," Cedric told them. "There are a lot of legal ways to make a living. Dealing drugs is only going to get you into trouble. Or worse."

"Whatever old dude," replied the oldest boy.

"Look, if you're smart enough to sell drugs, you're also smart enough to finish school and start your own business. Try doing things the right way...not just take the easy way..."

"Like I said... Whatever, old dude. We gonna leave, but not 'cuz you told us to," explained the oldest.

Cedric stood his ground watching the younger boys listen to the oldest like he was their father. Come to think of it, this teenage man-child was probably the closest thing to a father figure any of these kids had.

"C'mon, y'all. Let's get outta here," said the fat boy.

The boys began to disband one by one. Cedric noted they were all dressed the same way. T-shirts too big, oversized pants they had to hold up with their hands, and unlaced sneakers. If they didn't already call themselves a gang, they didn't have far to go from the looks of it.

Cedric gripped the boy he recognized by his shoulder.

The boy pulled loose. "Man, don't be touchin' me!"

"Bryson, what are you doing out here with these kids?"

"Yo man, you coming with us?" called out the oldest boy.

"Naw man. Y'all go on," Bryson replied, trying to look tough.

"Awright. Don't forget what we told you to do. We'll hook up later and see how you did."

"Right on," Bryson replied.

"Bryson? What in the world do you think you're doing? You're selling drugs now?"

"Naw, I ain't selling no drugs, Mr. Parker."

"Then what are you doing out here?" He placed both his hands on Bryson's shoulders and looked him in the eye. "You are one of the smartest kids at the youth center. Don't go messing your life up by hanging out with them. Those boys are nothing but trouble."

Bryson dropped his head. "Mr. Parker, I hear what you're saying, but I need to help my mother out. That EBT card she get every month don't help pay the rent. We can barely buy food with what my momma gets from the county."

Cedric shook his head. "A twelve year old should not be burdened with adult problems."

"They're not adult problems. They're my family's problems, so that makes them *my* problems."

"What are you selling?"

"Mr. Parker, I don't want to get in no trouble. I just want to help out my momma."

"What did those boys give you?"

Bryson shrugged. "A bag filled with different colored pills. They told me to sell them to the kids around the neighborhood for $5 a piece."

"Give them to me."

"Mr. Parker. I can't do that. I gave them half the money my momma had for rent."

"Does your mother know you stole her rent money?"

Bryson shook his head.

"Shit..."

"I got to sell them. That's the only way to pay her back."

"Bryson, do you want to be a drug dealer?"

"No sir, but I have to help my family."

"How much did you take from your mother?"

"Five hundred dollars."

"You gave those boys that much money?"

"Naw, just half. I kept the rest."

"What in the hell were you thinking?"

"They said I could double it when I sell all the pills. Momma needs one thousand dollars by Monday or we're gonna get put out of our apartment."

"Let me see what you have."

Bryson pulled a ziploc bag filled with hundreds of colorful little pills from his pants pocket. He handed them to Cedric.

"Damn... This is ecstasy." Cedric was dismayed by the seemingly never-ending cycle of desperation these kids faced on a daily basis. "Do you know what could happen if one of your friends had a bad reaction to one of these pills?"

Bryson stared blankly ahead.

"All sorts of bad things. Seizures, brain damage, even death. These innocent little pills can kill your friends. Do you want that to happen?"

"No sir."

Cedric ran both hands wearily over his sweaty face. "I'll tell you what. I'll take the pills and get rid of them."

"What about my momma's rent money?"

"Let me hold on to what you have. And I'll loan the rest to you. You can pay me back by coming to the youth center and working your debt off. I'll stop by the bank after I get home and bring the money by your house by Monday. You still live in those townhomes across the street from the park?"

Bryson nodded. He watched Mr. Parker slide what remained of his mother's rent money into the bag filled with pills.

"We'll talk to your mother together and explain what you did. Okay?"

Bryson appeared deflated. "Mr. Parker, I was just trying to help."

"I know. But sometimes your good intentions just make things that much worse. You go on home and think of some other ways to help your mother out."

"Okay," Bryson said. He added, "Do we have to tell my momma about the money? Can't you just give it back to me and I can give it back to her?"

"No. You've got to learn your actions have consequences." Cedric looked past Bryson at the other teens still gathered in the park. "When you're older, you'll understand. You might even thank me for this."

"Okay," Bryson backed away unsure. "So I'll see you later, Mr. Parker?"

"Give me a couple of hours, Bryson."

Bryson glanced back at Cedric one last time before he turned to run in the opposite direction out of the park. And for just a moment, as Cedric watched him run, he once again resembled the twelve year old boy that he actually was.

"Damn kids," he muttered. "When will they learn?" He tucked the bag of pills inside the waistband of his jogging shorts because he had nowhere else to stash them. Instead of continuing his run, he decided to go home instead.

As he exited the park, he was met with a loud *whoop, whoop, whoop* noise from behind. He turned to see a police cruiser with its lights flashing headed his way.

Filled with certainty that the police weren't pursuing him, Cedric continued on his way ignoring the siren. The *whoop, whoop, whoop* came once more. He glanced back, yet kept walking, unaware that he was the object of their attention.

"Hey, buddy," called out one of the cops over the car's intercom. "You in the blue shorts. I'm talking to you."

The police cruiser slowly pulled up alongside Cedric. He started walking more slowly. "Are you talking to me?" he asked in disbelief. He'd often heard the young men he counseled talk about being pulled over for "walking while black", but until today, he had never personally experienced it.

A black police officer in the passenger seat wearing a stereotypical pair of Ray Ban shades yelled out to him, "Sir, we need you to stop walking."

"Why? I'm on the sidewalk."

"Sir, I'm going to ask you again. Please stop walking."

"Fine, I'll stop."

The white cop who was driving placed the car in park. The black cop got out of the car and approached Cedric. "How are you today?"

"What can I do for you, officer?" Cedric asked politely.

"You been playing a little basketball this morning?" the cop asked.

"No. Actually, I was out for a jog."

"Really? We observed you speaking to a group of teenagers on the basketball court."

Cedric noted the white policeman speaking into the radio. He explained, "Yes, I stopped to talk to those teens for a few minutes..."

"May I see your identification, sir?"

"I didn't bring my ID with me. I told you I was out jogging and really didn't think I needed it."

"I need you to step over here, please." The black cop pointed to the side of the cruiser.

"Officer, can you tell me what's going on?"

"If I can please have your cooperation, this will be over in a few minutes."

"I just stopped by to talk to them..."

"What is your name, sir?"

"Cedric Parker," he answered.

"And your address?" asked the policeman.

Cedric rattled off his address while the police officer took notes.

"Mr. Parker, the reason we stopped you is because we have received several complaints about teenagers dealing drugs in the park."

"Look, I'm a youth counselor. I work with these kids everyday."

"Really? Where do you work?"

"Over at the youth center near downtown."

"Well, then I'm sure you understand our concerns."

"I don't follow... Why did you stop me?"

"This morning we received an anonymous tip that an older man was in the park making a drug deal with a group of teens."

Cedric's mind immediately went to the bag of ecstasy tucked inside his shorts. He started to laugh at the irony of the situation that was unfolding. After all was said and done, Cedric Parker, upstanding citizen with a good job, a loving family, and well-known in the community had unwittingly become the main character in an age-old script written by society hundreds of years before he was even born

"What is so funny, sir?" asked the black cop.

"I was in the park talking to those kids about this very thing. I told them to all go home and to find some other ways to make a living. This is all a misunderstanding, officer."

"Did you observe any drugs while you spoke to them?"

"No, no, that's not what I said. I mean, that's not what I meant. I had the feeling they were up to something so I told them to leave," Cedric explained nervously.

"Wait here," the cop told Cedric.

The black police officer walked to the driver's side and handed the information to the white officer who was speaking on the cruiser's radio, all the while keeping an eye on Cedric.

Shit! Shit! Shit! Cedric thought. "What the fuck have I gotten myself into?" he whispered to himself. He glanced across the street to find Bryson standing there holding a little girl's hand, who was probably his little sister, watching the scenario play out.

After what felt like several minutes, the police officer returned to Cedric's side. "You're free to go, sir. I hope you understand we have to look into any and all suspicious activity to keep our neighborhood safe."

"No problem, officer. I understand." Cedric reached out to shake the officer's hand. When he did so, the slight motion loosened the bag from the waistband of his shorts. In what felt as if it could only be slow motion, the bag slipped free, slid down his leg, and landed on the sidewalk. Dumbfounded, Cedric stared at the drugs lying at his feet, and then watched in disbelief as the officer bent down to retrieve the bag.

"Well, well, well... What do we have here?"

"I can explain that officer," Cedric stuttered. "It's... This... That isn't what it looks like."

"Really? This looks like a bag of ecstasy to me. And there's a wad of cash inside. Care to explain what you're doing with this?"

"This is all a misunderstanding. Those pills aren't mine. I took that bag from one of my kids when he told me he was going to sell them to other kids around the neighborhood."

"You told us that you did not observe any drugs," stated the white cop from inside the car. "If these drugs aren't yours, how did they get inside your shorts?"

Cedric glanced over at Bryson who looked as if he were going to shit a pile of bricks. He told the officer, "I don't know the boy's name. Just that he attends the youth center."

"No name, huh?" asked the white cop from the car.

Cedric shook his head.

"This is unfortunate, Mr. Parker. I'm sorry, but we'll have to take you in." The black officer placed his hand on Cedric's shoulder. "Please turn around and put your hands behind your back."

"Wait a minute! I said those drugs aren't mine!" Cedric backed away from the cruiser. He glanced around to see a small crowd beginning to gather. The teens he encountered earlier looked on with unabashed amusement, high-fiving one another over his misfortune.

The white policeman exited the car. He stood in front of the duo with his hand resting on his gun. "I know you don't want any trouble. Neither do we."

Cedric understood how quickly this situation could go south if he made any further move that even resembled him resisting arrest. With the current atmosphere of police brutality against Black men reverberating across the country, the absolute last thing he wanted was to become another statistic.

"You're right. I don't want any trouble. I will cooperate." Cedric faced the cruiser and placed his hands behind his back as instructed.

The white officer pulled a small card from his front pocked and began to read, "Cedric Parker, I am placing you under arrest for suspicion of drug possession and distributing to minors. You have the right to remain silent..."

"Goddamn it!" Cedric uttered.

"You almost got away with it," the black officer said, as he placed his hand atop Cedric's head easing him into the backseat of the cruiser.

Chapter Thirteen

"Maya? Trey? You guys ready to go?!" Joie yelled up the stairs.

"We're coming!" Trey shouted back.

Joie checked the time. It was almost twelve thirty. "Where in the hell is Cedric?" she wondered aloud. "He's been gone for almost two hours."

Maya and Trey bounded down the stairs, racing each other to see who could get to the front door first.

"I won!" Maya called out. "I get to sit in the front seat."

"I don't care," Trey replied. "More room for me in the back."

"Come on you two, let's go." Joie entered the garage through the kitchen, pulling the door shut behind them.

"Is Daddy coming with us?" asked Maya. "He's the one who usually takes us to see Auntie T."

"No, I'm taking you today." Joie told Trey, "Hit the garage door button for me."

Trey did what he was told and then climbed into the backseat of the SUV.

Although Tequitta's house was only twenty minutes away, every mile seemed to loom before them. This was not a conversation she had planned to have, nor was it one she looked forward to. Joie glanced over at Maya who had her nose buried in her kindle reading the latest addition to whatever novels preteens read these days. Then she snuck a peak in the rearview mirror at Trey. When she saw the expression on his face, her heart nearly broke.

"Trey? Baby what's wrong?" Joie asked.

"Nothing," he answered.

"What's with the long face?"

"He's mad because he doesn't want Derek Jordan to be his daddy," Maya explained. "…because he's dead."

"Shut up fart face!" Trey snapped.

"You shut up!"

"Hey, hey, hey, you two. Stop it!" Joie returned her attention to the road. "Trey, you want to talk about it?"

"No."

"Okay, how about I talk and you listen?"

He sighed wearily.

"Remember when me and Cedric told you that he will always be your daddy? That this changes nothing? Well, that is exactly what we meant. We both love you kids very much and we are so blessed to be your parents. If we could pick any two children out of a million, we'd pick you both every time."

"Yeah, but..."

"But what?" Joie asked.

"I know what you said, but Cedric ain't my daddy. My real daddy is dead and I never even had a chance to meet him."

Maya chimed in. "Uh huh, you did meet him. Remember when we went to that funeral? That man in the casket was Derek Jordan... He was our real daddy. Right Mommy?"

"You're so stupid. You can't meet a dead person." Trey furrowed his brow in deep thought before asking, "Mommy, how come he's our daddy? Did you used to be married to him?"

Joie struggled with trying to figure out how to explain to a couple of eight year olds that their mother had an affair with a married man and got pregnant. She figured the only answer without telling an outright lie was to be intentionally vague. "No, we weren't married. We were just friends."

"Wait a minute," Maya said. "Mommy, didn't he used to be married to Auntie Ronnie? I think I remember them coming over to our house sometimes."

"Yeah," Trey added. "Hey... Now I remember..."

"He used to bring us boxes of animal crackers." Maya looked at her mother with a puzzled expression. "Mommy, if he was married to Auntie Ronnie, don't that make him our uncle instead of our daddy?"

"That's enough you two. You can ask all the questions you want to ask but not about me and Derek. And after today, I don't want to hear another word about Derek Jordan. Cedric Parker is your daddy and that's all there is to it." She gave them both *the look*. "Do you understand me?"

"Yes ma'am," they replied in unison.

"I mean it! No more questions about Derek Jordan after today. Period."

"I don't understand, Mommy. Why is he our daddy instead of daddy?"

"Little girl, did you hear what I just said to you?"

"Yes, ma'am. No more questions about you and Derek Jordan."

~ ~ ~

Joie pulled up to Tequitta's house a little before one o'clock. She noted that sometime between yesterday evening and this afternoon, someone had mowed the yard because it was now nicely manicured instead of looking like a vacant lot.

Laila stood outside waiting eagerly for her newly discovered siblings. The little girl looked much older than Maya as she was dressed head to toe in designer fashions with her hair stylishly cut into the latest hairstyle.

"Hi Laila!" Maya shouted through the car's open window.

"Maya! Trey! Guess what?! I ain't your cousin! I'm your sister!"

"I know. Mommy and Daddy told us yesterday," Maya explained.

"I am so happy! I finally got a brother and sister the same age as me. Y'all not old like the rest of 'em."

"What are you talking about?" Maya asked.

"We got grown up brothers and sisters. Our daddy got a whole bunch of other kids around here," Laila explained matter-of-factly trying to sound like an adult.

"You mean there's more of us?" Trey asked with surprise.

"Yep. And the best part is that sometimes my sister takes me shopping. She bought me the prettiest shoes for school and they cost a whole lot of money," Laila bragged.

"Are they nice?" Maya wondered aloud. "The other kids…"

"Yeah, they nice to me. I don't know how they gonna treat y'all because our daddy wasn't married to your momma…"

"Laila, that's enough!" Joie cut her off.

"Wow! We have a lot of brothers and sisters now, don't we Maya?" asked Trey

"Uh huh, and we even have a couple of nieces and nephews that's older than us," Laila added.

Both twins looked up at their mother in confusion. *Why didn't we know all this?* is what their expressions seemed to ask.

"You kids go on around back and play. I need to talk to Tequitta privately." Joie looked at big mouthed Laila. She asked her, "Where is your mother?"

"She's in the house putting my baby brother down for his nap. She told me to tell you to go inside when you got here."

Joie noted the appearance of the small yard. The grass was recently mown and neatly edged. Even the loose grass clippings had been swept up and stored in one of those paper lawn bags you get from the hardware store. The flowerbed was weeded with new mulch laid around the bushes. Unable to contain her curiosity, she said to Laila, "The yard looks really nice. Did your mother hire a gardener?"

"No, ma'am. My mother does the yard herself ever since my daddy died. Our lawn mower was broken for a few weeks, but they brought it back this morning fixed. Momma got up real early to cut the grass because she say she can't stand to see the yard messed up."

"Well," Joie replied. "So your mother does yard work, huh?"

"She said she can't see paying nobody to do what daddy used to do for free."

Joie was flabbergasted with Tequitta's ability to handle many situations. She called out, "Maya, Trey, I'll see you kids in a bit."

"Okay, Mommy," they both replied.

Joie walked up to the front door and knocked quietly. She waited a few seconds before opening the door. "Hello?" she called out.

When no one answered she let herself in. *Oh my goodness! This place looks nothing like I imagined. Damn... it's spotless!* she thought, looking around the tidy townhome. She went down the hallway towards the kitchen, silently hoping she would find it a mess. But it was also very clean.

"Hey Joie, I see you made it," said Tequitta pulling a door shut. She put her finger to her mouth. "I just got the baby back to sleep after struggling with him most of the morning with potty training. That child absolutely refuses to pee in the toilet. I'm starting to think he's going to wear pull ups when he starts school."

"That's okay. Laila told me to let myself in. I hope it's all right..."

"Yeah girl. It's okay. And it's about time you came inside the house," Tequitta joked. "I was starting to think I had body odor or something."

Joie stared at Tequitta wanting to hate her. She was barely thirty so gravity had yet to wreak havoc on her well-toned body. Her thick shoulder length hair was done in microbraids swept up into a flattering ponytail. Up close, even without makeup, Tequitta possessed flawless skin with a healthy clear complexion. Wearing an easy smile, she was very pretty. Actually, she was beautiful.

"Come on in the kitchen. We can talk there, plus I can hear the baby if he wakes up." Tequitta motioned to a small table. "Can I get you something to drink? Coffee, water, a pop? Something harder?"

"No, I'm fine," Joie replied.

Tequitta took a deep breath. She had no idea what Joie was going to say, or how she was going to react about hearing details about her marriage to Derek. As a means to break the ice, she said, "Cedric mentioned that your mother passed a few months back. I wanted to send my condolences when it happened, but I wasn't sure you would be receptive, so I'm telling you now how sorry I am for your loss."

You got that right. The last person I wanted condolences from was you. "Thank you. It's difficult losing a loved one, but I appreciate your kind words."

"Listen, I apologize for last night. I opened up my big mouth because I thought Trey was asleep." *And I had a little too much liquor in me,* which she decided not to add. "I know y'all probably didn't want to break the news to the twins like that."

"You're right. We wanted to wait a couple more years when they could probably understand this better."

Tequitta busied herself pouring a cup of coffee. "When Maya called me this morning, I was so mad at myself."

"They were pretty upset..."

"Look Joie. I know you probably hate me, but I gotta tell you that I didn't know anything about you and Derek. And I for sure didn't know about the twins."

"But you knew Derek was married when you were with him?" Joie was in no mood to beat around the bush. She felt her old familiar friend, anger, quickly return.

"Yeah, he told me about Veronica. I never met her, but shortly after we met, he told me they were getting divorced. Said they didn't love each other anymore."

"Is that right?" Joie asked. "How long did you know him before you two hooked up?"

"Not that it's any of your business, but I knew Derek about six months before we were married."

"Where did you meet?"

"At work. I'm a paralegal for an attorney who specializes in family law, particularly divorces..."

A paralegal? Humph! I guess she ain't as ditzy as I thought she was.

"...I met him at the attorney's office when he came in to ask about what he needed to do to get a divorce."

"You mean to tell me that he was considering getting divorced *before* the two of you met?"

"Yes. I made it one of my rules to avoid becoming involved with clients because when a man is in the process of getting divorced, well, that's a very bad time to get involved in a relationship. They're usually on the rebound," explained Tequitta.

"But you hooked up with him anyway," Joie snidely remarked. "You know Veronica was my best friend, right?"

This time it was Tequitta who seemed surprised. "Really? Veronica was your best friend, yet you were sleeping with *her* husband?"

"Actually, she and I cleared all that up a long time ago," Joie replied uncomfortably. Anger slipped out the door to let her other familiar friend, Guilt, walk right on in.

"Let me ask you something..."

"Go ahead."

"Why didn't Derek know Maya and Trey were his children? He used to always talk about how much fun he had with them. He was so upset when he couldn't see them anymore once him and Veronica were divorced. Because you were her friend and all..."

"It was complicated."

Tequitta nodded. "Oh, I see... You were married, but you had an affair and ended up getting pregnant by your best friend's husband. You never told anyone because you wanted to keep this a secret, but somehow your husband found out. How am I doing so far?"

"Damn! You really got it figured out, don't you?"

She chuckled. "I work for a divorce attorney, remember? You wouldn't believe half the stories I could tell you. Trust me, Joie, your situation is more common than one would imagine."

Joie studied Tequitta intensely. In spite of how she thought she was going to feel, she found herself beginning to actually like the woman she had despised for years.

"I have a confession to make," Joie said.

"Really? What is it?"

"I used to hate you because Derek married you instead of me."

"*Used* to hate me?"

"Yeah... used to... I don't hate you anymore because I understand that it was me and Derek who did wrong. You didn't have anything to do with it. I now know that if we had gotten married, it would have messed up a whole lot of people's lives."

"I gotta admit Joie that I didn't know anything about you until I saw Maya at Derek's funeral. When I saw how much she looked like Laila, I about had my baby right then and there," she laughed.

"He must have really loved you because he divorced an amazing woman to marry you."

"Joie, you don't get it do you?" Tequitta stopped what she was doing to fully focus her attention on Joie. "Derek was getting a divorce anyway. It had nothing to do with me. He was leaving his wife because he no longer loved her. Get over it. It happens."

"Maybe if you hadn't come into the picture..."

"What? Derek would have left his wife to marry you?" Tequitta chuckled. "Girlfriend, in my line of work, I have learned that the majority of men have affairs as a way to justify leaving their wives. Some men just do it to prove to themselves that they can still pull the honeys. But they rarely marry their sidepieces."

"For your information, I was more than Derek's sidepiece. He told me he loved me."

"I don't mean to be cruel, but if he loved you so much why did he marry me instead?"

Joie remained uncharacteristically silent as she pondered Tequitta's observation. It was a question she had asked herself for months after she learned of Derek's marriage.

"Let me ask you something else," Joie said.

"Go ahead."

"Laila was telling the twins about Derek's older kids..."

"Uh huh?"

"You cool with them hanging around his other children?"

"Of course. Why wouldn't I be? After all, they are related." She took a sip of coffee. "And I don't consider any of them to be children anymore, they're all over eighteen. Why do you ask?"

"Because I never thought about his kids. I mean, I knew he had some 'cuz he would talk about them sometimes, but they weren't real to me because I never interacted with or even saw them until the day of Derek's funeral."

"Well, he does have three other children. Two sons and a daughter." Tequitta took in Joie's shocked expression. "And a couple of them are now married with kids of their own."

"Is that right?" Joie's eyes widened. "I had no idea he was a grandfather."

"Do you have a problem with the twins meeting their older siblings?" Tequitta asked more out of curiosity than anything else.

"Hmmm, let me think about that. I don't want to confuse them anymore than they already are."

For the very first time since admitting Derek was the twins' father, Joie allowed the consequences of her actions to really sink in. Up until now, the thought of her kids having siblings that weren't hers was just an abstract thought. But now that everything was coming out in the open, the realization that her children had several half-siblings hit her like a ton of bricks. Her children's lives as they knew it, was suddenly forever changed. As their mother, it was up to her to determine how much of an impact this would make.

Laila, Maya, and Trey chose that very moment to rush into the kitchen filled with questions just as difficult as the one posed by Tequitta.

"Mommy, can we please ask Auntie T about our daddy now?" Maya asked hopping from one foot to the other.

"Cedric Parker is your daddy, so what you meant to say was can you ask about Derek Jordan," Joie corrected her.

"Yes ma'am. I mean Derek Jordan."

"Okay. Go ahead," Joie stood ready at a moment's notice to abruptly end the question answer session if the kids broached a subject too delicate for a couple of eight-year old ears.

"Can we see a picture of our daddy?" Trey asked excitedly.

This time Joie remained silent allowing her children to revel in learning about this unknown man who had somehow come into their lives uninvited. With the promise of providing the information they both so eagerly wanted about their birth father, she relinquished this chore to Auntie T.

"Yes, I think I might have a few pictures of him around here somewhere." Tequitta said. "Wait right here. I'll bring in our photo albums."

"Yay! We get to show y'all pictures of my daddy!" Laila shouted happily.

So for the next couple of hours as Maya and Trey endlessly questioned their Auntie T about Derek Jordan, Joie politely endured the responses she had waited years to hear herself. Tequitta produced hundreds of pictures they had taken together, talked about wonderful vacations he had taken his family on, and lovingly told the kids about a life with the man she had loved and lost.

Joie had a painful epiphany as the truth slowly dawned on her. Derek Jordan never really loved her. For the twelve months she screwed Ronnie's husband, she had not meant anything to him. She was simply a sidepiece who had gotten pregnant by her best friend's husband. Nothing more and nothing less. A life with Tequitta was what he had cherished most.

Tequitta sat on the couch proudly showing off pictures of her family to the twins who sat perched on either side in total awe. She explained where each photo was taken and who was in it. She even had Derek's pictures from when he was a boy, thanks to his mother. Trey was excited to discover he resembled his father more than he had ever imagined. As Joie sat back, uninterested in fawning over Tequitta's family photos, her phone rang several times in succession. Each time it rang, she dismissed it because it indicated the call was from a private number.

"Damn it! I wish whoever that is would quit calling me," Joie declared.

"Why don't you just answer it?" asked Tequitta.

"Because anybody who knows me also knows that I do not answer private or blocked phone calls." She hit ignore for the third time in five minutes.

"Maybe it's important, Mommy," Maya stated.

"If it is important, they'll leave a message."

The phone rang once again listing a private number.

"Same number?" asked Tequitta.

"Yeah. I might as well answer." She accepted the call. "Hello?"

"Joie?"

"Cedric?"

"Thank goodness you finally answered your phone," Cedric said. "Where are you?"

"Where am I?" She glanced at the private number. "Where are you?"

"Are the kids with you?"

"Yeah. We're over at Tequitta's. Where are you? Why are you calling from a private number?"

The kids looked up with sudden interest. So did Tequitta.

"Hold on. I'm going to step out of the room for a minute so we can talk."

"Hurry up. I only have a few minutes."

Joie excused herself and stepped outside. "I'm back. What's going on?"

"Baby, I was arrested."

"Stop playing with me," she replied exasperated. "I expected you home a few hours ago. Where are you?"

"I'm not playing with you. I am in jail."

"You're where?!"

"I am in the city jail. I need you to contact a lawyer to see about getting me out."

"What happened? Are you all right?"

"Joie, I don't have time to go into detail. Right now I just need you to get me a lawyer so I can get the hell out of here."

"You're in Hampton city jail?"

"Yeah."

"Can't I just come down and bail you out?"

"No, I'm afraid I'll be spending the weekend. The soonest I can see the judge is Monday."

"What happened?"

"It's a long story. Look, I'll call you tomorrow. But what I need you to do today is hire a lawyer."

"How am I supposed to hire a lawyer? Where do I even start looking?"

"Call Jerome from work. You can find his number in my cell phone. I left it on the dresser in the bedroom. He works with teens in trouble so he should know a good lawyer."

"Okay, baby. I'll do it. Just tell me one thing. What did they charge you with?"

"They picked me up for possession of drugs with intent to distribute to minors."

"Drugs?!" She felt her heart skip a beat.

"Yeah," he reluctantly answered. "But it's not what you think."

"What were you doing with drugs, Cedric?"

"Joie, I've got to go. Just call Jerome as soon as you can. I'll call you tomorrow to see who will be representing me."

"I don't understand…"

"Baby, I can't talk about it now. Just do what I said, okay?"

"Okay. I'll get the kids and we'll go home right now. Don't worry. I'll take care of it."

"Thanks, baby. I love you."

"I love you, too. But you have a lot of explaining to do."

She ended the call with a hundred questions rushing through her mind. *What in the world was Cedric doing with drugs? He don't do drugs. Does he? And how am I supposed to find a lawyer on a Saturday afternoon? Wait a minute... Maybe that's why he's been acting so funny. Damn! On top of everything else that's going on, this is the last thing we need to be dealing with. My life was supposed to be better with Ced back in it, but lately all I have is drama and confusion. Now he's in jail. Lord help us!*

Joie rushed back inside the house. All eyes that were engrossed in the photo albums now turned towards her as she entered the room. She manufactured an awkward smile and said, "Come on kids. It's time to go home."

"Is everything okay?" Tequitta asked.

"Yeah, that was Cedric. He needs me to take care of a few things at the house."

"Mommy, can't we stay for a little longer. Auntie T was just telling us about their trip to Disneyworld," whined Maya.

"No, we need to go. Auntie T has an appointment this afternoon and we don't want to make her miss it."

Tequitta chimed in to help Joie out. "It's okay, kids. We can tell you about Disneyworld some other time."

"You guys have got to go to Disneyworld! It is so cool and we had soooo much fun," Laila added. "I just wish my daddy was still alive so he could take all us."

"One day, if Cedric, I mean... my daddy, ever takes us, maybe you can go with us," Trey told her. "You're our sister now."

"For real?" Laila asked wide-eyed.

"Uh huh. He won't mind, will he Mommy?" Maya added.

"Can I come with y'all when you go? Please?" begged Laila.

Joie was in no mood to bargain with anybody. She told the children, "Listen, we can discuss this later. For now I need you two to get your things and get in the car."

"Yes ma'am." Maya tugged at her brother. "C'mon Trey. You heard Mommy. Let's go." The twins hurried outside with Laila trailing behind.

"Thanks for taking the time to talk to the twins about Derek and for clearing the air with me. I don't know if we will ever be friends..." Joie declared with a smile on her face. "...but at least I don't hate you no more."

Tequitta raised her perfectly manicured eyebrows and laughed. "Hey Joie. It is what it is. I don't have no hard feelings towards you one way or the other. Maybe we can get together sometime. You know... while the kids play."

Joie mulled over the scenario of hanging out with Tequitta. *Since my girl Ronnie moved a couple years ago, I haven't made any new friends, so actually it would be nice to have another girlfriend in my life. But me and Tequitta? I don't know about that.*

"Hey, no pressure..."

"I'll let you know, Tequitta," she responded. "By the kids reactions to the news about being siblings, I have a feeling we'll be seeing a lot more of each other."

"Tell that husband of yours that I said, hello. And you can also let him know that me and Paris are getting along pretty good."

"Paris?"

"Yeah, didn't he tell you?"

Joie shook her head.

"Paris is one of Cedric's coworkers. He teaches martial arts down at the youth center."

"Is that right? No, he didn't mention it."

"I ran into them while I was shopping at *Lowe's*. Paris asked me for my number so I gave it to him. After I got over his weird name, I was cool."

"Paris isn't so weird," Joie said. *It's much better than having a made up name like yours,* she thought.

"Paris *is* a weird name for a man," she retorted. "Anyway we've already been on our third date."

"Good for you. Has he met the kids?"

"No, girl. It's much too soon for that. I don't plan on introducing my children to any man until I know when *or* if we're going to go further."

"Good for you, Tequitta. Derek's been gone for several years so I guess it's time you started dating again."

"It was difficult going out, but thankfully Cedric had only good things to say about Paris."

Humph! My husband had been playing matchmaker to Tequitta and one of his partners without me knowing about it. I had no idea... "Well, we've got to go. I'll be in touch." Joie rushed the twins to the car.

"Y'all have a good rest of the weekend," Tequitta called out from her door.

The ride home was filled with the loud chatter of happy children. Joie glanced in the rearview mirror at her kids. She allowed the relief from their excitement to override her mounting anxiety about Cedric being in jail.

Both of the twins seem happy to have Laila as their sister, in spite of the circumstances. At least they've accepted the situation. I just hope they don't freak out when they find out Cedric won't be home this weekend. Hopefully it will be only for the weekend. I remember the last time Cedric left. It took months for the twins to act like themselves again.

Chapter Fourteen

Monday morning rolled around without a hitch. When the twins questioned her about Cedric's whereabouts Sunday morning, Joie lied. To avoid adding any more confusion to their young lives, she simply told them Cedric had to leave town to attend a weekend camp with the kids he counseled. After several minutes of grumbling about how they also wanted to go on a weekend getaway, they finally gave up in favor of popcorn and a movie.

Joie was able to get in touch with Cedric's coworker, Jerome, who put her in contact with an attorney who specialized in criminal drug offenses. The attorney said he would take care of everything, but she had to be prepared to put her hands on a lot of money for bail. He also provided the name of a bail bondsman who was awaiting her call.

After dropping the twins off at summer camp, Joie headed to her favorite Starbucks to get a java fix. She ordered her usual, a *venti Caffè Mocha* with extra whipped cream, found an empty chair and plopped her behind down. After gulping down half of the steaming hot liquid, she felt energized enough to tackle the day.

"See you next time, Mrs. Parker. Have a nice day," called out the barrister.

Joie lifted her coffee cup to signal goodbye. With her other free hand, she pressed the fob to remote start the engine of her recently purchased Cadillac SRX. Distracted by the upcoming events, she let her mind wander. *Okay... I might as well get this phone call over with. I have a million things to do at work and I can't afford to be out another day, but I ain't gonna let Cedric spend another day in jail.*

She scrolled through her contacts to locate her boss's number stored appropriately under the number 420. Her boss possessed a well known fondness for weed of which he tried to convince everyone that it was for medicinal purposes. No one bought his story, neither did they really care. With a flick of her index finger, she hit the speed dial.

"This is Rufus," answered his assistant.

"Hey Rufus. This is Joie."

"Good morning, Joie. What's up?"

"I'm calling because I need to take the day off. Can you cover for me?"

"Of course, I can. Are you all right?"

"Yeah, I'm fine. I just have some personal business I need to take care of. Is the boss in yet?"

"No, he's up in Richmond having a meeting with HR. He should be back this afternoon, though."

"What's he doing up there?"

The line suddenly went silent.

"Rufus? I asked what is the boss doing up in Richmond?" She recalled Saturday's conversation with Amir.

"Joie, I'm not supposed to say anything."

"But it's me you're talking to. You always give me the inside scoop. Plus, don't I always pick up your slack when you need to take a few days off?"

"I hate it when you do that."

She sighed wearily. "Rufus, I am already having a bad day. More bad news ain't gonna make this day any worse."

"If you say so..." He took a deep breath before uttering, "The boss is going to make an announcement tomorrow about restructuring the company."

"Restructuring?"

"It's not official. Not yet, anyway."

"Rufus, you better start talking."

"I'm sorry, Joie. I'm not supposed to give out any more information. The boss doesn't want to start rumors."

"What difference does it make if you tell me today? I'm not coming in, so I don't have anybody to spread rumors to."

Rufus sighed loudly, "Well, okay. But you did not hear this from me."

"Go on, I'm listening."

"They're closing this office and moving it to Richmond."

"What?! What did you just say?" Joie's heart felt as if it were going to jump outside her chest. Though she had backed halfway out the parking spot, she quickly threw the car into park. She was wrong. The day did actually get worse.

"Apparently management has been discussing it for some time. They've already moved a few people up there."

"You're talking about Amir?"

"Yes, Amir was one of those offered a transfer."

"Rufus, I had no idea they were going to shut down the entire office. What are we supposed to do?"

"I heard they're offering a few of us the option to move. The rest of us…well, the rumor is they're going to start handing out pink slips beginning tomorrow."

"Tomorrow?!"

"Uh huh."

"What the hell, Rufus?! I can't move my family to Richmond!" Joie yelled.

"I'm sorry to tell you this, Joie. But at this point, I'm not even sure you're one of the ones who will even be given that option."

"What? You mean I might be fired?"

"Downsized."

"What?"

"Not fired. Management prefers to call it *downsizing.*"

"Whatever they call it, it means the same damn thing. I'm gonna be out of a job!" Joie pounded her dashboard. "Shit!"

"You sure you don't want to come in today? You might stand a better chance of appealing to the bosses' sensibilities if you're standing in his office. Speak to him face-to-face."

"I can't come in today," Joie responded in defeat. "I wish I could, but I can't."

"Well, if I hear anything else, I'll give you a call."

"I appreciate you telling me. I promise I won't say anything to anybody."

"Thanks. So I'll see you tomorrow. I hope," Rufus said before hanging up.

Joie watched numerous people leave *Starbucks* with steaming hot cups of coffee in their hands as if they had not a care in the world, while her world was falling apart all around her. It was funny how quickly life could turn on a dime. Just this past Friday she was sitting in the Hampton Coliseum singing *Happy Feelings* along with thousands of her closest stranger friends. But over the span of a few days she had to deal with telling the kids about their real father, having to deal with Cedric getting arrested, and now the threat of losing her job. It wasn't fair.

"Damn! Damn! Damn! What am I going to do if they tell me I have to move? Or worse, that I'm fired?"

Joie caressed the soft lambskin covering the passenger seat, inhaling the new car scent as though it were some therapeutic aroma with special powers to calm her nerves. She loved her new car no matter what Cedric said.

She allowed the new car scent to remove the troubles of her day for just a moment while she chuckled at thoughts of her sensible husband. While they were at the Cadillac dealer looking for a replacement for Joie's old car last month, Cedric tried his very best to convince his wife that she didn't need the fully loaded luxury edition of their latest model SUV, but Joie insisted that since she was making the eighty-four monthly payments, her car should be her choice. And her choice was the latest, most expensive, most luxurious model on the lot.

"I haven't even made my first payment yet. If I lose my job, I can't afford to keep you." She stroked the steering wheel continuing to speak to the car as if it were a loved one. "You are the best car I have..."

Beep, beep! A man driving a van tooted his horn at Joie interrupting her conversation with her car. The driver stuck his arm through his window and gave a friendly wave.

Joie's meandering thoughts quickly returned to the present when she received a blatant warning that she was blocking the drive.

When Joie didn't respond, the driver tooted his horn three more times.

What *the hell is this man doing? Can't he see I'm already halfway out of this spot?* "Backup asshole!" she yelled through her open window. Instead of pulling back in the spot like any normal person would, Joie ceremoniously shot up her middle finger, threw her car in reverse again, and forced the van to back up. And for good measure, she shouted a few more choice words.

"Non-driving old fart," she uttered to herself. "You saw me trying to back out."

Just as she was about to pull forward, two women, one pushing a baby stroller, walked in front of her car. She mashed on the brake to avoid hitting them.

One of the women holding a cell phone to one ear and gripping a young toddler's hand in the other, glared at Joie.

"Damn!" Joie said through clenched teeth, watching the woman struggle with the child. "You need to be paying attention to your little boy instead of talking on that damn phone."

While she waited for the woman to clear her car, she inadvertently noticed the writing on the side of the van that pulled into the spot next to where she had just left. It read, *The House of Ruth Ministries.*

It was only after she was completely out of the spot, did Joie notice that she had also mistakenly parked in a spot reserved for the handicapped. If the symbol of the little blue man on the wheelchair sign could speak, he would most certainly tell Joie that she was the one who was the asshole. Feeling about this small, Joie watched a group of elderly senior citizens exit the vehicle.

"You have a blessed day!" shouted an elderly man as he made his way past her car. "And remember that God don't like ugly."

An elderly woman, who was dressed impeccably in a stylish pants suit, shook her head in disgust. The woman's platinum white hair was beautifully styled in a short natural that accentuated her still lovely face. She reminded Joie of the late Ruby Dee. The woman used an intricately carved wooden cane to keep her balance. Though she possessed an unsteady gait, it soon became obvious how sharp her mind was still. She approached Joie's window and said, "It is bad enough hearing a woman use that kind of language, but to hear you use it against total strangers is absolutely shameful."

Joie dropped her head. "I'm sorry."

The elderly woman studied Joie before speaking, realizing that something was amiss. "You should be sorry." She pulled back, pursing her thin lips. "Don't make no sense to go around spreading hatred over innocent folks."

"I know this ain't no excuse for my behavior, but I'm going though some things right now. Today has not been a good day."

"Young lady, as long as you have a breath in your body, you have the opportunity to fix whatever it is that's troubling you."

"Thanks. I'll keep that in mind," she replied sarcastically. "Is that it?"

The old woman narrowed her eyes and whispered harshly, "I do not know your mother, child. But I do know she raised you not to sass your elders."

"You're right. I apologize."

"Listen here. I have been on this earth over eighty years. Outlived three husbands and two of my children. Nothing should cause you to lose your humanity for others. I don't care how bad it seems."

Joie took the woman's words to heart. "You're right... It's just that I received some really bad news."

The woman dug around in her purse before finally handing Joie a colorful business flyer. "Here. Take this."

"What is it?"

"I founded *The House of Ruth Ministries* over on the east side of town. It's a shelter for battered and abused women and their children. We can always use dedicated volunteers to help us run the place. Might do you some good to help someone besides yourself. Gives you a healthy perspective on those less fortunate."

Joie accepted the brochure from the old woman's wrinkled hands. The name on the front indicated Leticia Myers was the founder. The inscription on the backside read, *A safe place to go when you have nowhere else to turn...* She had no intention of volunteering anywhere, but the old woman didn't need to know this.

"You go on now and take care of your business."

"Good-bye," Joie replied taking her lumps. She slowly pulled away while holding on to the pearls of wisdom graciously given to her.

~ ~ ~

Next stops were the credit union and then the bank. The bail bondsman she spoke to on Saturday afternoon advised Joie to be prepared to pay a hefty fine and post a high bond due to the amount of drugs Cedric was carrying.

All day yesterday, instead of enjoying Sunday with the kids, she was online checking the balance of their bank accounts to determine how much money she would be able to lay her hands on after Cedric's bail was set.

Joie quickly discovered she and Cedric didn't have as much money saved as she thought they did. He had spent what was left of his money on her engagement ring and their honeymoon. As far as Joie's finances were concerned, her situation wasn't much better. And she had only managed to clear a couple of thousand dollars from the sale of her house. So for all intents and purposes, as a couple, they were nearly broke.

The credit union had just opened its doors when Joie arrived. She approached the customer service desk where she observed a very young woman who looked to be barely eighteen, stuffing cubbyholes with withdrawal slips.

"Good morning, how can I help you?" sang out the woman-child.

"I want to close my Roth IRA," Joie said matter-of-factly.

"Ma'am, if you close your IRA, you will be subject to a ten percent penalty and you'll have to pay taxes on the withdrawal," explained the young woman who smelled like the bubblegum flavored lip gloss covering her thin lips.

"I understand the penalties."

"Are you sure you want to do that? Maybe you can take out a signature loan?"

"No, I want to close the IRA," Joie repeated.

"You know, that is a really bad idea. When you are so close to retiring, you want to have as much money saved as possible. That is why the government makes us charge a penalty for people who tap into their retirement funds. And that is money you can never get back."

Joie did a slow neck roll before cocking her head to one side. Both hands automatically found their homes on her ample hips. "Listen here little girl..."

The woman-child's eyes became as wide as saucers. Her bubblegum flavored, heavily glossed bottom lip slowly disappeared into her mouth.

Joie felt her blood pressure rising in direct proportion to her misplaced anger. The image of the elderly woman from the Starbucks parking lot appeared in her mind as if on cue to calm her down. After a moment has passed, she forced her hands back to her sides, along with a smile across her face. In a calm voice she stated, "Miss, I appreciate your concern, but I did not come here for a lesson on my retirement. I just want to withdraw my money."

"I didn't mean to upset you, ma'am. The bank manager told me to tell customers about the penalties when they want to close their IRAs because they get upset when they see how much money they're going to lose. I just didn't want you to be shocked that you're not receiving all the money you put in."

"Well, thank you for the information. But I still want to make that withdrawal," she replied with an unfamiliar sense of restraint because she refused to let anyone else piss her off today.

"Okay. I'll let one of the consultants know you're here. What did you say your name was?"

"My name is Joie Parker."

Ten minutes later, Joie walked out the bank with a little over six thousand dollars tucked inside her purse. Including the money in their savings and checking accounts, she had just withdrawn the last of their liquid assets.

Chapter Fifteen

Joie parked across the street from the municipal building in the lower level of the parking garage, arriving early enough to secure a good spot.

She momentarily sat in her car watching the parade of people, including city employees, and mothers and girlfriends of the accused, hurry across the street at the pedestrian crossing. Apparently what Jerome told her was true. Once the building was open, if you missed out on the parking garage, you could plan on fifteen minutes of searching for on street parking with several minutes of walking on top of that.

Cedric's court hearing was in an hour, but she was supposed to meet with his attorney in thirty minutes. Everywhere she looked, she saw signs informing customers that cell phones and weapons were not allowed inside the court room.

"I don't know what's worse nowadays. A cell phone is almost as dangerous as a weapon, especially with everybody sending tweets and posting videos all over *YouTube*. What used to be a private matter, ain't private anymore." She reluctantly placed her phone in the glove compartment. "But that ain't my issue today."

The city of Hampton was situated at the mouth of the Chesapeake Bay, the last stop before entering the three and a half mile Hampton Roads Bridge Tunnel south to Norfolk and on to Virginia Beach. On a clear day, you could gaze in the distance to where the Chesapeake Bay Tunnel Bridge extended its almost 20 mile stretch from Virginia Beach to the Eastern Shore. Though a hazardous journey for some vehicles during high winds, for most it was a beautiful drive over the blue green water to the scenic shores on the other side.

The downtown area of Hampton was not as bustling as other cities in the Tidewater Region; though, it still managed to hold its own. Recently, more and more businesses had chosen to locate in the downtown area adding to its unique old world charm. Annual summertime jazz concerts drew crowds from all over the peninsula.

Joie slowly inhaled, allowing the fragrant, salty sea air to penetrate her nostrils. As much as she enjoyed leaving the region to visit other cities, she loved coming back home.

From the historically black Hampton University, to the jets that flew overhead from Langley Air Force Base, to the recently built

Peninsula Town Centre, there was a certain flavor to the city that made it uniquely original. No matter what others said about Hampton—good and bad, there was no other place like it because it was home.

The small French café where the lawyer arranged to meet was tucked between two stores in a quaint shopping center near the municipal building. On one side was a recently opened gelato bar and the other side was an art studio. Both shops had yet to open, but the café was bustling with city workers getting their morning fix of coffee and breakfast sandwiches.

Joie checked the time on her watch for the tenth time. It was almost nine o'clock.

"Pardon me, ma'am," called out a well dressed, middle-aged white man rushing towards her direction.

She focused her attention on the man.

"Are you Mrs. Joie Parker?"

"Yes, I am. Are you Mr. Wylie?" Joie asked nervously. Despite his fast clip, the poised, confident way he carried himself gave her the impression he was a man used to winning. Someone who sank his teeth into a thing and always got what he wanted. *Umph! Even his shoes look expensive.* She noted the old-fashioned, well-worn briefcase he carried. Only a man with nothing to lose would dare carry an old beat up briefcase to meet a client for the first time.

"Yes, but please call me Hunter," he said, extending his right hand.

"Nice to meet you... Hunter." Joie took his soft, sweaty hand in hers, fighting back the urge to pull it back. "I think we should get going. Cedric's court case starts at nine."

"I apologize for being late. There was an accident in the HRBT that caused traffic to back up for miles."

"You live on the other side?"

"Yes. In Virginia Beach."

"Well, c'mon. I don't want to be late."

"We have time. The court opens at nine, but chances are Mr. Parker won't be called in front of the judge until later. I can explain the process while we walk."

"Lead the way," Joie said. "Here is the money you asked me to bring."

"Thank you, Mrs. Parker. This should be enough to get me started." Hunter Wylie stuffed the envelope inside the pocket of his blazer.

The courtroom was filled with people. Young and old, some were professionally dressed, while others were casual in jeans and t-shirts. As was expected, most of the inmates, as well as the majority of the people in the courtroom, with the exception of the judge, a couple of lawyers and several police officers, were black and brown.

Joie spotted Cedric sitting amongst the other inmates, looking surprisingly comfortable as if he were conversing with his peers instead of a bunch of convicts. They all wore bright orange jumpsuits and were seated in a partitioned room behind a bulletproof glass. She gave a small wave when he looked her way. His lips curved into the tiniest of smiles when he saw her, but no other form of acknowledgement was given.

It was almost noon before the judge finally called Cedric forward. Once he did, the process went rather quickly. The judge asked him a few questions and then set bail.

Joie turned to Hunter Wylie and asked, "Is that it? Can he come home now?"

"Let's talk outside the courtroom, Mrs. Parker."

"What's going on Hunter? You told me you would get him out today," she said, following." He led Joie outside the courtroom to a quiet corner away from earshot of others.

"What now?" she asked.

"After I complete the release papers and you pay the bail bond, he can go home to await his court date."

She breathed a sigh of relief. "Whew! I am so glad that's over."

Hunter gripped Joie's arm. "Mrs. Parker, this is only the beginning. Your husband has been charged with a very serious crime. If he is convicted of a drug felony, he can spend years in prison."

"What are you saying?"

"I am telling you to prepare yourself and your family for a fight. Mr. Parker is a first time offender and he is active in the community so the judge may be lenient with him, On the other hand, his job counseling children may work against him."

"I don't understand what happened," Joie fretted. "Cedric is always trying to help keep these kids out of trouble. He don't belong on the other side with those criminals."

"Unfortunately, because of the nature of your husband's job, the judge may choose to sentence him more harshly. Mr. Parker should have known better than to have drugs in his possession."

"Listen here, Mr. Wylie..."

"Please... Hunter..."

"Right... Hunter... Look, my Cedric don't do drugs. And he for damn sure wasn't planning on selling them to no kids."

"You would not believe how many times I have heard that..." He gathered Cedric's file and began stuffing it inside his briefcase.

"Wait just a minute! Just whose side are you on?"

"I am on the side of the truth. If Mr. Parker is innocent, I will do my absolute best to keep your husband from going to prison." He waved at another attorney leaving the courtroom. "On a positive note, he does have a good reputation with the court system."

"My husband ain't no damn drug dealer."

The man who probably wouldn't have given Joie the time of day before today, returned his full attention to her and asked point blank, "You have children, Mrs. Parker?"

"Yeah, we got twins..."

"I also have kids and it scares the hell out of me to think that a trusted adult might offer drugs to my children. And if this goes to trial that is exactly what those jurors will also be thinking."

"Look, the only reason I called you was because Jerome said you could help Ced. He don't need no lawyer who ain't got his best interests at heart."

"Mrs. Parker, personally, I do not believe that your husband is a drug dealer, but the extenuating circumstances certainly do not help his case. The real challenge may be convincing the jury that he is innocent."

"Do you think this will come to that?"

"It's a strong possibility."

"What are you really saying?"

"Mr. Parker will be assigned a court date where the judge will decide if this goes to trial or not. There is a very slight possibility that he may only be fined, but I wouldn't count on it. Virginia is very serious about its drug laws."

"My babies need their father and I need my husband." Joie fought back hot tears as she spoke. "I just want him to come home."

"I'm going to meet with Mr. Parker this afternoon. After he makes bail, they'll release him. If you do not have the bail money on you, now would be a good time to get in touch with the bail bondsman."

"This ain't no Monopoly game, Mr. Wylie. We don't have fifty thousand dollars…"

"You only need ten percent for bail. Payment can be in the form of bank check, money order, or credit card." He offered a tiny joke, "Bail bondsmen will even take the title to your car if you don't have the cash."

"I have enough money on me," she proudly proclaimed. *Even if I didn't, I wouldn't let your smug ass know.*

"In addition to bail, there's also the fine, court costs, and my fees, of course…"

"I already gave you two thousand dollars…"

"That was just my retainer…"

"Damn… How much is this going to cost us?"

"I hate to break it to you, but this is going to be a very expensive case." He handed Joie his card.

"I'm starting to see that," she replied after accepting the card.

"My advice to you is—unless you're willing to entrust your husband's defense to a public defender—is to start putting together a list of family and friends who have money."

Joie considered the probability of just having lost her job. They didn't have the kind of money he was talking. Hell, she had wiped out their savings just to get the retainer and bail money. Yet, she uttered with a false sense of confidence in her voice, "I don't care how much it's gonna cost us. You have to keep him out of prison."

"My track record is pretty good…" He paused upon seeing the despair setting in. "I wish we had met under better circumstances, Mrs. Parker."

Joie gave him the once over taking note of his clothes and manner of speaking. She thought *there are no other circumstances where you and I would have met. Even though we live in the same region, I seriously doubt if our paths would have ever crossed.*

"I will call you in a couple of hours with instructions on where to pick up your husband. For now, please try to get some rest. I expect it will be a rough night for both of you." And just like that, Hunter Wylie spun on the heels of his expensive shoes and headed in the opposite direction.

"Damn…" she whispered to herself watching Cedric's best chance of being freed walk away. "When it rains, it fuckin' pours…"

Chapter Sixteen

Joie followed Hunter Wylie's instructions on what to do in the courthouse. After posting Cedric's bail, she retrieved the car and went to pick him. As she rounded the corner, she spied him waiting outside the city jail wearing the same running clothes he wore when he stormed out of the house that fateful Saturday morning. She was just relieved he wasn't still wearing that awful orange jumpsuit.

"Hey stranger!" she shouted out the window. "Want a ride?"

"Thanks, but I'm waiting for my wife..." Cedric responded, playing along.

"I'm sure she won't mind if I give you a ride. Hop in."

Cedric slid inside, pulling his wife's face towards his for a welcoming kiss as he shut the door behind him. "You have no idea how happy I am to see you, baby."

"Yes I do. I missed you, too." She pulled back for a better look. Her hand brushed against the stubble sprouting from his face. In spite of his not having shaved, nor combing his hair for several days, he was still quite attractive, in a homeless man sort of way.

"With all the times I had to come up here to help somebody get their kid out of jail, I never imagined I'd be in here with them."

"Was it really bad in there?"

"It *was* jail...so yeah, it was pretty bad."

"How are you doing?"

"Better. Now that I'm out."

"Good."

Cedric glanced in the back seat. "Where are the kids?"

"I dropped 'em off at Tequitta's to spend the night. I thought we needed some time alone. Some time to talk."

"That's a good idea." He visibly relaxed for the first time since getting into the car. "Baby, before you say anything more, I need to tell you that I was not selling drugs. This is all just a huge misunderstanding. You believe me?"

"Of course I believe you. You don't even like to take aspirin so I know you wasn't about selling no drugs."

"Thank you, baby." He stared at the police station furious at the situation he allowed himself to be pulled into. "Let's get the hell outta here. I don't want to be anywhere near this place."

"You got it."

Joie did a u-turn in the parking lot and headed home. They rode in an uncomfortable silence for a few miles because neither knew what to say to the other.

"So you two must be getting along?" Cedric asked, breaking the silence.

"Who?"

"You and Tequitta." He closed his eyes while he leaned into the headrest. "I know it must have gone well with you two because you actually said her name correctly."

Joie nodded. "She awright. The girl ain't as dingy as I thought she was."

"Is that right?"

"She also said to tell you that she is getting along with your partner, Paris."

"Yeah, I didn't tell you about that. We ran into Tequitta at *Lowe's* a few weeks ago. She was trying to put a bag of fertilizer in her shopping cart. It was funny as hell watching her trying to lift that bag with those skinny little arms of hers."

"I bet you went over and saved the day, right? Offered to lift the bag for her?" she asked throwing in a sideways glance for good measure.

"No, actually Paris did that. They started talking so I went on about my business. That was the day I came home with the paint you wanted for the hallway bathroom."

"Yeah, I remember because that bathroom still ain't been painted."

Cedric laughed. "I'm going to get to it."

"I hope so. I'm sick and tired of looking at that ugly wallpaper."

"Anyway, I'm glad that Tequitta has found a good man. She's good people when you get to know her." He glanced from the corner of his eye at his wife. "I gotta admit I didn't think she would go out with a white guy."

"Wait... Paris is *white?*"

"Yep. From some small town in Wyoming. Can't get much more white bread than that, can you?"

"Damn... A white man? I didn't see that coming. And she didn't mention it at all."

"Why should she? I just mentioned it because I think it's cool that she's giving my white brother a chance because I know a lot of sisters around here wouldn't. You have a problem with interracial dating?"

"No, I don't have a problem with interracial dating or marriage. If she like it, then I love it. I just prefer black men myself."

"Well, I hope you ain't out there looking. You got yourself a fine, black man sitting right here in this car next to you."

"And now that you've been arrested, you can count yourself as even more black..." she teased. "...because you finally got your 'niggah been in jail card'."

Cedric shot her an angry look. "That shit ain't funny, Joie."

"I'm sorry; I'm just trying to lighten the mood."

"That's what's wrong with us today. We think a black man ain't down until he's been behind bars. Do I need to remind you that not all of us are criminals?!"

Joie did not want to get Cedric started on the ongoing systematic problems occurring in the black and brown community. If he ever had a chance to meet Cornel West, he could give the man a run for his money.

"If our damn government stopped wasting our tax dollars on building prisons and instead focused on increasing educational opportunities for minorities, then maybe the institution of choice for the black man would be *educational* rather than *correctional*."

Joie bite her tongue to avoid any further discussion on the matter. This was not the time, nor the place to debate the failings of the system when it came to African-Americans. "Anyway, did you know Tequitta is a paralegal?"

"No, I didn't know that," he added. "A paralegal, huh?"

"Uh huh."

"Baby, I sure wish I had gone with you and the kids instead of running. Then I wouldn't be in this mess..."

"Well, it's too late to be wishing."

"Maybe Tequitta can provide me with some free legal advice because that man you hired is gonna cost us an arm and a leg."

"Don't I know it! I had to give him a two thousand dollar retainer just to get him to take your case. And that was with Jerome's friendship discount."

"Two grand, huh? Damn! How much does he charge an hour?"

"Baby, we can't worry about money right now. We just need to make sure he keeps you out of prison."

"I really messed up this time..."

Joie pulled into their driveway and parked. The neighborhood looked like it always did at five o'clock on a Monday evening. People were coming home from work; some were out jogging; others walking their dogs. A few who waited until the heat of the day had passed were out mowing the lawn. Kids were riding their bikes down the middle of the street while cars crept slowly around them. Even sitting in the car outside their home appeared normal. Yes, from the outside looking in, it was just another perfect day in their suburban neighborhood. But looks can be deceiving.

"Ced, why don't you go inside and get cleaned up while I pick up something for dinner. I would have cooked, but with everything going on this weekend, I didn't have time to go grocery shopping."

"Baby, are you all right?"

"I'm fine. I just want to get dinner so we can focus on us tonight."

"Okay. You want me to go with you?"

"No. You've been through a lot this weekend. You need to relax. I'll be back in less than an hour."

"What are you going to get?"

"How about Chinese food? I can order takeout."

"That sounds delicious. That mess they served in jail was one step above garbage, so I could really use a good meal about now."

"I heard that."

"I'll see you when you get back. Then we can talk." Cedric kissed Joie once more.

"That's fine, baby."

Joie began backing out the driveway, but was stopped by Cedric pounding on the passenger door. She pressed her foot to the brake and rolled down the window. "What's wrong?"

"I need my cell phone. I didn't take it with me when I went jogging. Have you seen it?"

"You left it on top of the refrigerator," Joie replied, not mentioning that she had already perused through his messages.

"I need to contact the job and let them know why I didn't come in today."

Joie didn't say anything. She gave a quick wave and continued backing out the driveway. On the way to the restaurant, Joie went over the events of the day in her mind. Jerome called earlier and left a message for Cedric. He had been fired from his job as a counselor the day he was arrested. Although he hadn't officially received a pink slip, she was sure Cedric already knew it was coming.

The Chinese restaurant was empty except for the owner's family gathered around a small table near the kitchen having dinner. Joie took a peek at the food they were eating, not recognizing any of it because the food they ate wasn't on the menu. There was nothing fried in any of their dishes, in fact, the vegetables looked much fresher than any she had received in her meals. Despite her suspicion that they kept the freshest, best food for themselves, it was still one of the better Chinese restaurants in the area. She placed her order and stepped outside to wait.

How are we going to pay for a lawyer if I lose my job? The only money we have left is in my 401(k). I can always take a cash advance on my credit cards... This is stupid. I need to find out if I'm going to still have a job come tomorrow.

She took out her cell phone and checked the missed calls from Friday night. There was only one and it was from an unfamiliar Richmond number. It was Amir.

Before she could talk herself out of making the call, she hit dial on the unfamiliar number. The phone rang several times before going to voicemail with a short canned greeting. *"You have reached Amir. I am not available. Leave your name and number. Please."*

"Hi Amir, this is Joie Parker. I'm sorry to bother you after work. Please call when you receive this message. It's urgent." Before she could return the phone to her purse, it rang.

"Hello?" she answered.

"Joie?"

"Yes, this is Joie."

A man with a baritone voice laughed on the other end. "I knew you would call. I am just wondering what took you so long."

"Amir?"

"The one and only... I see you missed me."

"Hey Amir," she responded. "Uh, I hate to burst your bubble, but this ain't that kind of phone call."

"No? Then what kind of call *is* this?"

"Well, I heard they're closing our office and moving most of us to Richmond. I just want to know if it's true."

"Ah, I see... This is business related."

"I told you I'm married, so yeah, this is all business. Is it true? Are they relocating us?"

"I think you should speak to your management about your options. It really is not my place to provide these details."

"If you know something, I'd really appreciate you giving me a head's up. I've got way too much personal stuff I'm dealing with right now. I really don't need to be surprised when I got to the office tomorrow."

"Joie, I can only tell you what I know, but nothing is set in stone yet..."

"I understand," she replied. "What's up?"

"Yes, it is true. The company is closing the Hampton branch and relocating most of the senior staff to Richmond."

"What about the rest of us?"

"About a dozen or so mid-level managers will also be given the option to relocate. If they choose not to, they will receive a generous severance package."

"How about the employees? Are they keeping any of us? Are we getting a severance package? And what about me?"

Amir let out a heavy sigh before responding, "I am sorry, Joie. I did not see your name on the list of employees who will be offered a position in the Richmond office."

Joie sank her weary body against the *Egg Roll's* glass window. "Are you telling me that I don't have a job?"

"This will not happen right away."

"How long?"

"I really think you need to speak to your management."

"Amir? How long do I have?"

"The branch is scheduled for complete downsizing by the end of September."

"September?" She shut her eyes tightly to prevent tears from spilling forth.

"They will begin offering buyouts to eligible employees a bit sooner, but the office downsizing will be complete by September."

"That's just a couple months away."

"I wish I had better news for you. Had I known this is why you were calling, I most likely would not have answered."

"I'm glad you did answer, because there's no telling when they would've finally told us employees that we're going to be without a job soon."

"I am very sorry, Joie." He paused before adding, "If you need anything... I can write a reference letter if you'd like."

"No, Amir. I'll be okay. Thanks for giving me the heads up."

"You sure you don't need anything?"

"Only my job back."

"I sincerely wish there was something more I could do."

"Yeah, well, so do I," she replied. "Hey, I forgot to say congratulations on your transfer."

"Take care, Joie. Stay strong."

Joie tapped the screen to end the phone call before he could say more. Although the call was disconnected, the profound prophetic words uttered by Amir just a few days ago continued to reverberate in her mind. *'I am what you would have been...'*

Deep within Joie's soul, something stirred. *What the hell is going on with my life? Things ain't supposed to be this way. I'm supposed to be happy, but lately everything seems to be falling apart. I need to talk to someone before I lose my ever-lovin' mind.* She picked up her cell phone and dialed her best friend's number. The phone rang twice on the other end before Ronnie picked up.

"Helloooo?" Ronnie's happy voice sang out.

Joie didn't say anything at first. She was too ashamed to tell Ronnie how badly her life was falling apart. Too embarrassed to admit that her husband was arrested for selling drugs, even though she knew in her heart he wasn't guilty. She also didn't want to discuss how badly she screwed everything up—so much that her children were now questioning how they were conceived with a man they both called "uncle". Her inclination was to hang up because the last thing she needed to hear when she was feeling like warmed over doodoo was how happy her friend was.

"Hello?" Ronnie asked again. "Joie? Is that you?"

Joie finally found her sorrowful voice. "Ronnie...hey...girlfriend. Yeah, it's me."

"Are you okay?"

"Yeah... Yeah... I'm fine," she tried her best to project a shred of happiness into her voice.

"You don't sound fine."

"Well, I am."

"Joie, I know you and you don't sound like yourself."

"I'm good, Ronnie. I just have a little summer cold, that's all," she lied. "Anyway, I was calling to see if you're still coming out this weekend."

"Yes, I'm still coming. I was going to call you tonight with the details. Since I have you on the phone, I can tell you now."

The girl who had taken Joie's order poked her head outside and said, "Excuse me, miss. Your order is ready."

"Thanks, I'll be right there."

"Who are you talking to?" Ronnie asked.

"Girl, I'm at the Chinese restaurant picking up dinner." She pulled a twenty from her wallet to pay for the meal. "Go on. I'm listening."

"Oh, okay. But like I was saying, I'll be flying in on Friday afternoon. We'll be checking into the Hilton. Maybe we can get together? Just you and me for dinner while the guys are out taking care of their business?"

"Yeah, I can drive down after I get off work on Friday. That shouldn't be a problem."

"Me and Luis can come up to your house on Saturday. You know…to visit with Cedric and the twins."

There ain't no way in hell I'm going to let you and Luis come up for a visit. Especially not after everything that happened over this weekend is what Joie really wanted to say. Instead she said, "Cool! We can grill out or something. Make it a party."

"That sounds like a plan," Ronnie said.

"Okay. That's all I wanted. Send me a text when you get to the hotel. Okay?"

"Joie, I can't wait to see my "ride or die", again! I love being a mommy and wife, but I need me some girlfriend time!"

"I hear ya. Me too." Joie returned to the register to pay for her order. She grabbed a handful of soy sauce and duck sauce, absentmindedly tossing the plastic packets on top of the food. The aromas of the spicy house fried rice, and the greasy pupu platter wafted into her nostrils sending messages to her stomach, reminding it how empty it was.

"Okay, girlfriend. Whatever is going on with you, we're going to talk about it on Friday."

"I said I'm cool."

"Awright, I will let you slide for now, but we will catch up when I see you."

"Okay girl. I'm looking forward to it. And y'all have a safe flight." Joie clicked off the call, placed the food in her trunk, and got into her car.

Ronnie sounds so happy and excited about her life. I don't know how I'm going to get through a weekend without telling her about all the drama going on in my life. This is my shit to deal with. Well, mine and Ced's, so I might as well get to it. She threw the car in drive and headed home to face the music, in whatever form it would come.

~ ~ ~

Cedric waited for Joie to drive off before going inside the house, figuring he had a good hour to himself before she returned. He made a beeline to the bar, took out a full bottle of *Remy* with the black label that he saved for special occasions, retrieved a cocktail glass from the shelf, grabbed his cell phone from the kitchen counter, and headed for his office. The house was quiet, just like he needed it to be.

After Joie moved back into the house, she convinced Cedric to turn the spare room over the garage into a man cave. She told him every man needs to have a special place where he can escape from the family for a minute. He agreed wholeheartedly to her reasoning. Since it was his room, she didn't even put up a fuss when he found an old wooden door in the junkyard and had it made it into his desk. She had surprised him with a beautiful leather chair, which was also quite comfortable, and even bought a fifty-two inch television and had it mounted. He would jokingly say she just wanted to hide his sports memorabilia away and that's why she was so happy to give up the space she once used as her home office.

Cedric took a seat behind the desk. After he poured two fingers of the amber liquor into the crystal glass, he swirled it around numerous times before inhaling its fragrant aroma. He carefully placed the liquor bottle on the desk and then picked up the drink in his hand. In the other hand, he held his cell phone.

Which one should I choose first? Do I want to indulge in pleasure or experience the pain? From the moment that damn cop placed those fuckin' handcuffs on my wrists and threw me in jail, all my choices were taken away in an instant. They told me when to eat, what I could eat, when I could shower, even if I could take a shit. And no matter how many times I told those muthafuckas I wasn't guilty, no one cared. I was just another niggah in jail as far as they were concerned. Know what? Fuck them. I'm gonna enjoy this drink because I'm in my house now.

Cedric raised his glass to make a toast, "Here's to you, Bryson Graves. May my sacrifice today, be your saving grace tomorrow." He drank the entire drink in one gulp before pouring another.

Even though his cell phone was the latest model and was as light as a feather, it rested in his hand like a heavy brick waiting to smash him upside the head for his stupidity. Using his thumb, he scrolled through the list of missed calls noting the number of voicemail messages. Even though Cedric already knew who the messages were from, it didn't make listening to them any easier. He raised the cocktail glass to his lips again. This time, he sipped slowly while he listened to his messages.

"Cedric, this is Jerome, call me..." was the first voice mail.

"Hey Cedric, this is Jerome again. Look, I heard what happened, man. Your wife told me you need an attorney. Don't worry...we're going to take care of this."

"Mr. Parker, this is Nancy from Human Resources, we need to discuss the events of this weekend. Please call me at your earliest convenience."

"Hey man, its Jerome again. Look, I'm sorry. I tried to talk to the boss and convince him that you ain't guilty of selling no drugs. I guess you haven't gotten any of my messages... Well, call me when you can."

"Hi Daddy. Mommy said you went camping this weekend. Me and Trey are so mad at you for not taking us with you. I love you. Bye." He smiled when he heard his little angel's voice. Leave it up to Maya to make him feel better, if only for the briefest of moments.

"Mr. Parker, this is Nancy from HR again. I'm afraid that we have to dismiss you from your position as a youth counselor. Please contact me at your earliest convenience to complete the paperwork."

"Cedric, this is Nathen Jakes. The police contacted me over the weekend regarding you. I'm sorry, but I cannot keep you on with these allegations against you. I'm sure you understand..."

"Man... Mr. Jakes just told me he had to fire you. If you need anything, you know...just call me. This ain't right. I know you didn't do what they said... Sorry dude..."

Cedric poured another drink after listening to the last message from Jerome. It was official. He no longer had a job. He was now just another statistic. A black man facing drug charges with a possibility of going to prison. And there wasn't a damn thing he could do about it. The cops had arrested him with the drugs on his body, so it wasn't like the charge was circumstantial or anything.

After the third drink, he placed the phone on his desk next to the liquor. He leaned back in his chair as he scanned the room taking in all the awards he had received over the years. The bookcase held too many trophies to count. His job had presented him with numerous plaques for outstanding counselor five years running. Yet, despite the many awards and trophies he had received from all those organizations, the one he was most proud of was presented to him by President Obama. He and several other counselors were invited to the White House to receive recognition for making a difference in teenagers' lives. While he stared at a picture of himself and the president, who presented him with one of the ink pens he used to sign a bill into law, an overwhelming sense of sadness overtook him.

Cedric didn't know if it was the liquor coursing through his veins or the tragic turn his life had taken, but he suddenly felt very lost. Like he didn't know where he had been, or where he was going. Nothing made sense anymore. His life had been dedicated to helping others, and yet ironically, it was because of his need to help someone, in this case twelve-year old Bryson Graves, that he was now in this predicament.

Feeling as if he were on the edge of breaking down, he needed a hot shower. To let the water run over his body and wash away the filth of the past few days. He checked the time, Joie had only been gone for about thirty minutes, but it felt like she had been gone forever. He walked through the house. His house. He was free and he embraced how wonderful it truly felt.

When he passed by Maya's room, he smiled. She was such a beautiful, inquisitive child who would be a handful in a few years. And then there was Trey. Trey was a smart, curious, and very thoughtful little boy. He needed a strong man around to guide him, especially living in a house with two strong-willed women. If Joie wasn't careful with her quick wit, she could unintentionally crush Trey's gentle spirit. With every fiber of his being, Cedric loved these children and would walk a thousand miles over blazing hot coals to protect them. And anyone who tried to say they weren't his kids had better come prepared for a battle.

He made his way to their spacious master bedroom with the adjoining on-suite master bath and walk-in closet. He removed his clothing and tossed the dirty garments into a heap in the corner of the room.

Their king-sized bed looked so inviting compared to the thin excuse for a mattress he had slept on for the past two nights. More than anything else, he wanted to flop down into the comfortable bed.

Knowing his wife, Joie would have a fit if he laid his naked body across her white down comforter, especially considering where he had just come from. If he wasn't showered by the time she returned, Cedric could only imagine her reaction to the possibility of him bringing all those nasty jail germs into her house.

Rather than relax on the bed, he went to the shower and turned the water on as hot as he could stand before getting in. The steam billowed from the shower stall into the coolness of the bathroom where it fogged over the mirror. The hot water stung his skin. Any other time he would have made the water cooler, but this time he embraced the pain.

As he stood in the spacious shower he had always taken for granted, he reflected on his experience of being arrested. The first night was the worst. He was strip searched and fingerprinted. They took his mug shot and added his information into a criminal database. He was tossed into a cell built for ten men, but overflowed with at least twice that many. He spent the first night on a mattress on the floor because there were not enough beds. He did not fall asleep. He didn't dare.

The second night was not much better. Because it was the city jail, all levels of criminals were stuffed into the overcrowded area awaiting an appearance before the judge before being moved. Their crimes ranged from petty misdemeanors to hardcore murderers. It was not a place for the faint of heart. When he proclaimed that he didn't belong in jail, that this was a huge misunderstanding, and that he was innocent, nobody listened. The attendees just nodded their heads and let him speak.

What he said wasn't new. What they knew, and what Cedric didn't realize is that if they released everyone who said they were innocent, the jails would be empty.

He was allowed two showers during his stint in jail. The first shower was provided courtesy of two rough neck attendants who stood back and watched as he scrubbed himself raw with disinfectant soap. The other shower was all of two minutes, and was mandatory because he had to come before the judge. Both times the water was so cold he thought he was going to pass out.

Due to the nature of his job working with troubled teenagers, Cedric recognized several other inmates. Many were astonished to see Mr. Parker in jail. When he told them why he was picked up, some were shocked, but way too many were not. Their lack of surprise spoke volumes, leading him to believe he was nothing more than a statistic, just as Joie had alluded to during the ride home.

Being arrested was unfortunately a rite of passage for far too many brothas who looked like him. He recalled lying in his jail-cell bed listening to a myriad of voices—some pitifully crying over their plights. It was then that he questioned the good he thought he had done, pondered if his efforts had made any difference at all. To anyone. Or was it all in vain?

Cedric let the water run over his body before picking up a bar of Joie's favorite soap to cleanse his skin. He inhaled the honeysuckle fragrance remembering how sweet his wife tasted after using it. Before he recognized what was happening, a single tear fell from his eye, mingling with the warm water. Then another tear fell from the other eye.

The combination of losing his dignity, his freedom, his job—all within the past 72 hours, he succumbed to his emotions. Cedric balled up on the floor of the shower where he cried like a baby releasing all his pent up frustrations. He cried for so long and so hard that he didn't hear Joie enter the bathroom.

"I'm back," she called out as she walked into the steamy bathroom. "Food's nice and hot. Just like you like it."

Cedric didn't hear her. He didn't respond.

Joie opened the shower stall door. "Ced? Are you okay?"

He looked up but his throat was constricted with emotion. He wasn't able to form any words.

Distraught over what she was witnessing, her heart went out to her man. "Baby? What is it?"

Cedric was so overwhelmed that he could not speak.

"What are you doing?" she asked tenderly. "Why are sitting on the shower floor?"

Feeling lost, broken, and utterly alone, he reached for the one person in the world who still believed in him. Without any thought or hesitation, he pulled Joie into the shower. "I need you," he spoke in barely a whisper.

"I'm here, my love." She pushed the water from his face. "What is it?"

"Baby, I lost my job. They fired me." Between sobs he whispered, "I don't know what I'm gonna do..."

Joie stepped into the warm flow of water to encircle her husband in a loving embrace. She brought Cedric's head to her chest and slowly rocked back and forth, making soothing noises while he wept.

"Shhhhh. It's going to be all right my love. Don't you worry. I'm not gonna let them break you. We're going to get through this together. Me and you, baby. Me and you..."

Chapter Seventeen

Life at the Parker residence had returned to some semblance of normalcy by the time Friday morning rolled around. For the past several days, Joie woke up, made breakfast, and got the kids ready for school before heading off to work. After she left, Cedric dropped the twins off at school and then filled his day working on his legal defense.

Neither Joie nor Cedric wanted to discuss the shower scene—each for their own personal reasons. On Joie's part, it was the first time she had ever seen her husband in such a vulnerable state. On one hand, his vulnerability was endearing. Yet, at the same time it was frightening to witness her husband fall apart to that degree. To make matters worse, Joie still hadn't told Cedric about her office closing because she was afraid what he'd do once he heard. It was better to wait before she broke that news.

Cedric was mortified by his own behavior. And to have his wife see him like that was beyond embarrassing. He was the man of the house. The strong one. The rock. And yet, it was Joie who comforted and consoled him when he was on the verge of breaking down. He vowed to never let himself get that close to weakness ever again.

Joie was in the kitchen in the middle of her normal morning routine. She popped a couple of whole grain frozen waffles into the toaster and then rinsed a cup of fresh blueberries in a stream of running water.

"What ever happened to plain old syrup on waffles?" Cedric asked, watching in astonishment at how Joie made smiles in the peanut butter using individual blueberries. "You turnin' our kids into health nuts at such a young age?"

"I stopped feeding the kids syrup a long time ago. Too many carbs. Goes right to their bloodstream and makes them hyper. This is a much better breakfast for them. Protein lasts longer and they really like it." She licked her fingers. "You want one?"

"Uh, no thanks. I'll just have a cup of coffee for now."

"You sure. It won't take but a minute."

"I'll stop by *Hardee's* for a breakfast sandwich after I drop the kids off at school."

Her phone beeped with an incoming text. She opened the tiny envelope. *In VAB. Staying at the Hilton. Text when you're on your way. See you later, girlfriend.*

"Who was that?"

"It was Ronnie."

"Is that right?"

"Don't forget that you need to pickup the twins from school today."

"Why? You have something going on at work?" Cedric measured out two rounded teaspoons of sugar and then poured the steaming coffee into a travel mug.

"Don't you remember last week when I told you that Ronnie is coming to visit? We're going to have a girl's night out. I told you last Saturday morning..." Joie stopped speaking mid-sentence because that was the day Ced was arrested.

He ran his hands over his scruffy face. Ever since getting fired, he had stopped shaving, opting to grow a beard instead. He pinched the space between his eyes with his thumb and forefinger as if warding off a headache. "Yeah, I do remember you mentioning it."

"I was going to drive down to Virginia Beach after work to meet her. But if it's going to be a problem, I can pick up the twins and bring them home."

"No, I can get the kids." He twisted the lid on tight so as to not spill any of the hot liquid. "What time will you be home?"

"I shouldn't be too late. We'll probably just catch up over a couple of drinks."

"I thought they were going to come up here for a visit. Why are you driving down to Virginia Beach?"

"I, uh, well, I thought that since all that happened this weekend..."

"Oh. I get it. You didn't tell your bougie friends about your husband getting arrested, huh?"

"No, that's not it. I just wanted to catch up with Ronnie. Just the two of us." She placed breakfast on the table. "Maya! Trey! Breakfast is ready!" she shouted down the hall.

"So are they coming up tomorrow? I can throw some chicken and vegetables on the grill. I'll get a couple of six packs and we can make it a cook-out. Unless chicken ain't good enough."

Joie didn't say a word.

"Maybe we need to serve filet mignon, instead?"

"There ain't no need for you to be nasty about this. A cookout sounds nice. I'll ask Ronnie how their schedule looks."

"Cool." Cedric checked his wallet. It was empty. "Hey, you got a couple of twenties on you? Looks like I'm all tapped out."

Joie picked up her purse. After emptying out their bank accounts to post Cedric's bail, she barely had fifty dollars to her name until payday. "Naw, I don't. Don't you have any cash on you?"

"If I did, I wouldn't be asking you. Would I?"

"What about your wallet?" She handed it to him. "Didn't you just get paid on Friday?"

"I did get paid, but you cleaned out our account."

"Then I don't have any money." Joie tried to not sound sarcastic, but after all, this was all Cedric's fault. "After what happened on Saturday..."

Cedric's thoughts went back to Saturday morning. "Damn it! Their rent money! I forgot all about that!" He picked up the envelope the police had returned to him, ripped it open, and shook the contents unto the kitchen counter.

Joie stopped what she was doing to watch her husband's erratic behavior. He rummaged through the contents before going to the laundry room. She followed him. "What are you looking for?"

"The money I took from Bryson. It was for their rent."

"What money? And who the hell is Bryson? And why do you keep talking about rent money?"

"Damn it! The police kept the money."

"Cedric! Slow down. What are you talking about?"

"Remember I told you that I took those drugs from one of my youths?"

She nodded.

"Well, he stole his mother's rent money, so I told him that I would lend him the money so he wouldn't have to sell drugs. Damn it! I was supposed to get that money to him by this morning."

"Wait just a doggone minute! You were going to give money to some little hoodlum to help pay his momma's rent?! Who the hell is this woman you were *trying to help*?"

"Joie, it's not what you think. I was doing Bryson a favor. I was trying to keep him out of jail."

"Oh, I see... Your ass was thrown in jail, you got fired from your job, which caused me to drain all our savings to pay your bail, just so you could keep this little drug dealer out of jail?! And now you're worried about paying his momma's rent?! Have you lost your mind?!"

Cedric ignored Joie's ranting. "I promised Bryson I would get him the money. He said they had until today to pay the rent or be evicted. Where am I going to find a thousand dollars?" He looked to his wife for a response.

Joie's response was to laugh. Then she laughed some more. In fact, she laughed so hard she began to cry hysterically.

Maya and Trey stood outside the laundry room watching their parents, wondering what was happening to make them behave so strangely.

Cedric paced the floor while Joie was bent over laughing so hard that tears streamed from her eyes.

The twins looked at one another, shook their heads, and went to the kitchen to have their breakfast. At this point in their lives, they had seen their parents break down so often that what they had just witnessed had almost become their new normal.

Cedric stood over his wife angrily. "I'm glad you think this situation is funny. That boy's family is about to be evicted from their apartment and all you can do is laugh like this is some kind of fuckin' joke!"

His last comment really pissed Joie off. She wiped the hysterical tears from her face, stood up straight, and got all up into Cedric's. "You are worried about the wrong family getting evicted, sweetheart. You need to be worried about your own because we have no money in the bank. You just lost your job. I just found out that my job was transferred, but they aren't going to transfer me with it. So excuse me if I think this little situation with Bryson is so funny. You placed our livelihood in jeopardy trying to help out some little punk? Well, if you want to worry about a family who may get evicted, all you have to do is look no further than your own."

"Whoa... What do you mean? You lost your job?"

She lowered her head in despair, not wanting to break the news this way. "They're closing our office down and moving it to Richmond. I just found out a few days ago. I wasn't offered a transfer."

"Well, are they at least going to give you severance package? What about unemployment?"

"Nope. Nothing. Nada. Zip. After I receive the next few paychecks, that's it." She lowered her gaze to the floor. "Unemployment is out, too."

"Shit! Shit! Shit!" was all Cedric could manage to say. *I hoped at least we could stay afloat on Joie's paycheck until I was able to find another job, but now that isn't even a possibility.* With the weight of the world sitting squarely on his shoulders, Cedric entered the kitchen, picked up his keys from the counter, and then gathered the children to take them to summer camp. But before he closed the door, he took one last look at Joie who remained standing in the laundry room. Motionless. Terrified. Filled with doubt whether her husband was capable of supporting his own family. The worst part of all was the emotions dancing across her face were a direct reflection of how he felt inside.

Chapter Eighteen

Cedric dropped the kids off at summer camp and then drove directly to the youth center. After a quick visit to his office, which now belonged to Sheila Rose who had also been promoted into his previous position, he marched straight into the bosses' office. Joie's unexpected announcement took him by complete surprise and had literally shaken him to the core. In less than two months, unless he found a job, neither one of them would be pulling in a paycheck.

Nathen Jakes was not expecting to see Cedric Parker show up at his office that morning, or any morning for that matter, because for all intents and purposes, he had been fired. So the sight of his former employee standing in his doorway got his full attention. He gave Cedric the once over. Studied the man's unshaven face, his unkempt appearance, and the desperation he wore like an oversized, worn-out wool coat.

"Can I speak to you for a minute?" Cedric asked.

"What can I do for you, Cedric?"

"Mr. Jakes, I realize that you had to let me go under the circumstances, but I was hoping you'd reconsider... Maybe give me a second chance..."

He sighed wearily, not wanting to deal with this situation. But he said, "C'mon in and close the door."

Cedric did as he was asked and took a seat in a chair he had sat in many, many times before.

"I must admit I wasn't expecting you, but I'm glad you decided to stop by."

"Mr. Jakes, I am not a drug dealer, nor have I ever been." Cedric explained, "Those drugs weren't mine. I took them away from a boy to keep him from selling to other kids in the community. You have to believe me..."

His former boss leaned back in his chair and studied Cedric. The man before him was a sad representation of the man he once knew. This version sat at the edge of desperation looking as if he could snap at a moment's notice. Considering recent reports of active shooters in the workplace, he hoped Cedric wasn't carrying a gun.

"In all the years we've known one another, I've never known you to do anything illegal. You were always the guy who kept everyone in line. However, when the police stated the drugs were found on your body…"

"Come on, you know me better than that."

"You're right. I do. And for what it's worth, I don't believe the charges filed against you have any basis."

"I appreciate that…" He took a deep breath and said, "Is there any chance I can get my job back, you know…while this situation is getting cleared up?"

"I wish I could Cedric, but it's not up to me. It is policy that any employee who is arrested, and particularly on drug-related charges, must be dismissed immediately. You know that…"

"Yeah, I know… but I was hoping you could make an exception in my case. Up to now, my performance has been exemplary. I've received numerous awards. I have accolades from the mayor and I was even recognized by the president… Do you think I would throw all that away, not to mention destroying my family in the process, over a few fuckin' pills?!"

"I'm sorry. My hands are tied."

"I understand," Cedric acquiesced, allowing the weight of the situation to sink in. "You can't make an exception… Well, can you tell me if I qualify for unemployment?"

"Honestly, I'm not sure. Because you were arrested on a drug conviction, you may not be eligible. You'll have to check with HR."

"I have a mountain of legal bills piling up while I'm fighting this conviction. I need a job so I can take care of my family." He stared at his boss exasperated.

"I wish there was more I could do…"

"So basically, you're telling me I'm screwed."

"Look man, I hate that you're going through this." He scribbled on a post-it note to remind himself to contact HR after Cedric left. "I'll see if I can pull some strings to get your last bonus check released. It won't be much…"

"I don't care how much it is because every little bit helps."

"I wish we could visit longer…" Mr. Jakes glanced at his watch. "Unfortunately, I have a meeting down at city hall in half an hour."

"I have one more question before I go.

"What is it, Cedric?"

"Sheila moved into my office already?"

"Yes, she moved in this morning. As soon as we learned about your arrest, I had to make some tough decisions because we cannot afford to let that position remain unfilled."

"I see." Cedric didn't know whether to be pissed off or proud of his colleague. But in the end, it was still his job she had taken. "Do you think she can handle running all those different programs?"

"She has a steep learning curve, but yes, I do believe she can handle the job. Don't you?"

"Yeah, sure. If you think she is capable, who am I to say she isn't?"

"Like I said, we needed someone in the position, especially with the summer programs ramping up."

"Well, I've taken up enough of your time." Cedric rose to his feet. "Thank you again. I really appreciate your being in my corner."

"Good luck to you, Cedric. When this situation is straightened up, perhaps we'll be able to work something out for you. You always were one of my best workers."

"Thanks again for your time, Mr. Jakes." And with that, Cedric left the youth center without uttering a word to anyone else, not even Sheila Rose who cowered in the entrance to the office that once belonged to him.

~ ~ ~

The next stop was the local state employment office to meet with a counselor. He spent a couple of hours completing online applications and filling out various forms for unemployment compensation. In the end, he was determined ineligible due to the circumstances surrounding his dismissal.

Discouraged, pissed off, and downright disgusted, Cedric returned to his car and drove absentmindedly around the peninsula for the remainder of the afternoon in an attempt to clear his mind. Tried to think of a way to make things right again. Searched the recesses of his mind for ways to make quick money. Finally, after getting low on gas, he drove up to the gas station and pulled up to the pump only to realize he was out of cash. Luckily, their credit union was across the street.

The same young lady that Joie encountered just a few days ago was working the teller window. When Cedric presented her with a withdrawal slip for a hundred dollars, she frowned. Then she entered the information again, only to frown once more.

"What's wrong?" Cedric asked, noting the woman's pained expression.

"I'm sorry, sir. This withdrawal will put your account in the negative."

He took the slip from her hands to make sure he hadn't accidently added an extra zero. "Try it again.

The teller began to type. While doing so, she proceeded to go through a myriad of facial expressions. "I'm sorry sir, but your account has a balance of only twenty-five dollars."

"What? That can't be right. There should be several thousand dollars in this account."

The young woman started typing again. "No. Just twenty-five dollars."

"There must be some mistake."

"No, there isn't. Our records indicate a substantial withdrawal was made just a few days ago." She scanned through several entries before stating, "...and there remains the matter of the first and second mortgages. I'm showing that the last payment was missed."

Cedric had totally overlooked missing the mortgage payments because they usually came directly out of his pay check. But since he no longer had a job, of course the payments weren't applied. "Yeah, I know about that. I was planning on making the payment next week," he lied.

Joie told him that she had practically wiped out their savings to post his bail. He knew they were low on money, he just never realized how close to the edge they actually were. Swallowing his pride, he filled out a different withdrawal slip and handed it to the teller.

The teller typed on the keyboard for what seemed an eternity before pulling a crisp twenty dollar bill from her cash till. "Here you go, Mr. Parker," she said in an overly cheerful tone. "Is there anything else we can do for you today?"

Cedric lowered his eyes under the teller's scrutiny, embarrassed by the sorry state his life had taken. *A measly twenty-five—now only five— dollars left in our savings account! What the hell?!* "No, that's it." He stuffed the bill into his wallet and headed towards the exit.

"Have a nice day, sir," the teller shouted out.

"Yeah, you too..." he mumbled.

The credit union was right around the corner from the local park where he was arrested, and close to where Bryson Graves and his mother resided. As he drove through the entrance to the townhomes, he spied Bryson outside playing with a little girl. He parked the car and approached the children.

"Mr. Parker?" yelled Bryson. "The police let you go?!"

"Hi Bryson," he replied, without responding to the boy's question. He was already embarrassed to be out on bail, and really didn't feel the need to discuss his situation with a preteen.

"Do you have my mama's rent money?" Bryson asked desperately. "They're about to put our furniture on the curb in a few hours if we don't pay."

Cedric shook his head.

"You don't? Where is it?" Bryson screamed. "My mama has been looking all over the house for that money all weekend. I pretended like I hadn't seen it because I thought you was gonna have it today like you said."

"When the police arrested me, I didn't have time to go to the bank."

"Why can't you go now?"

"Because I don't have it," Cedric admitted.

"None of it?"

"No. It's all gone."

"What am I supposed to do now? That money I took from mama was all the money she had. I know I shoulda never listened to you."

"I'm sorry, Bryson. I didn't know I was going to be arrested."

"I knew it! If I just had left with my homies that morning, none of this woulda happened. Instead of making things better, you just made it worse. I knew I shouldn't have trusted you."

"What you should not have done is use your mother's rent money to buy drugs from those boys. This could have turned out a lot different."

"It turned out the same for me and my mama. We still don't have enough money to stay in our apartment." He watched his little sister run towards the house. "Unless you got a thousand dollars to give us right now."

He shook his head. "I wish I did."

"So why did you come over here if you ain't got the money?"

"I wanted to see if you were okay."

The boy turned his back to Cedric and shouted over his shoulder, "I used to think you was somebody, Mr. Parker, but you ain't nothin'!

And I wish you woulda never said nothin' to me that morning. For real."

"Bryson, don't walk away. Maybe there is another way. Maybe I can talk to the manager..." Cedric grabbed his arm.

He roughly pulled free from Cedric's grip. "Man, get the fuck outta my face and leave me alone."

"I'm sorry, Bryson."

"Whatever, man..."

"I'm gonna see what I can do," he called out, knowing how empty those words rang. Even he didn't have faith that he could help them. Bryson was right, his family probably would have been better off without his help.

Chapter Nineteen

Joie left work promptly at 3 o'clock. Since Cedric was picking up the kids, she decided to head straight to Virginia Beach instead of stopping by the house. The rush hour traffic heading south on I-64 was awful even for a Friday evening. Yet still, considering all the drama that existed in the home, the stressful drive to VB promised to be more peaceful than the thought of having another conversation with her husband.

Finally, after maneuvering around drivers who drove too fast, those who drove too slowly, annoying tailgaters, and distracted people on cell phones, Joie pulled up to the Hilton just before 5 o'clock. She peeled her sweaty legs from the leather seats and left her car with the valet to park.

Just as she was about to approach the front, she recognized her friend's voice coming from inside the lounge.

"Joie! You made it!" Ronnie shrieked from across the room. She pushed away from the bar and ran towards her girlfriend.

"Ronnieeeee!" Joie yelled, meeting her halfway.

The two women held each other in an embrace reserved only for good friends and family. They pulled back, took a long gaze at one another, and then began hugging each other all over again, all the while jumping up and down.

"Damn, girl. You look so good!" Joie exclaimed.

"So do you!"

"You think so? I feel like I've packed on a few more pounds since the last time we were together."

"Well, if you did, it doesn't show."

The two women locked arms and headed towards the outdoor patio bar. A young waiter trailed behind them. Once they were seated at a small table facing the beach, he took out his pad and asked them what they wanted to drink.

"I'll take a *mojito*," Ronnie said as she arranged the umbrella to block out the direct rays of the sun.

"Make that two," Joie added. "And don't skimp on the *jito*."

"Two *mojitos*, no skimping on the *jito*, coming right up," replied the waiter, amused by Joie's request.

"Joie, you look really pretty," Ronnie remarked. "I love the weave."

"Thanks girlfriend. You don't look half bad yourself. And I love how you've styled your hair."

"I thought it was going to be hard taking care of my natural hair in the DR, but actually, it's much easier. I never have a problem finding products or someone to style my hair."

"I guess you wouldn't have a problem finding a hairdresser, considering all those nappy headed women living down there in the Dominican Republic."

"I beg your pardon. Our hair ain't nappy. It's just tightly coiled..." she clarified. "You should try it sometime."

"You go right ahead with your 'tightly coiled' natural hair. I'm doing just fine with my relaxer and weave, thank you very much."

"Anyway, how are the twins?"

"They're fine. Maya is too smart for her own good and Trey is still my sweet little gentleman."

"I can't wait to see them. I'll bet they're growing like weeds."

"You know it."

"How about yours?"

"Wonderful! Girl, I love being a mother. I never knew you could love another person so much. It is a different kind of love than what I have for Kiara because I didn't meet her until she was grown. Watching these little babies grow into people is something else..." Ronnie retrieved a stack of photos from her purse. "Here...I brought these for you."

"Thank you," she said going through the stack. "Awwww, they are so adorable. Your daughter is a mini you and little Luis looks just like his daddy."

"Speaking of daddy... How is Cedric?"

"Oh... He's, uh, he's doing awright."

Noticing the hesitation in her friend's voice, she let the subject of Cedric slide for now. "Anyway, like I was saying earlier, Joie. Your complexion is seriously amazing... You're radiant!" Ronnie reached out to touch Joie's skin. "It's really soft too. You know the only time my skin looked and felt like that was when I was pregnant."

Joie smirked. "Well, I hate to burst your bubble, but there ain't no more babies coming out of this cootchie. I am too damn old to be having babies...."

"Too old to be having kids? You're a year younger than me!"

"What does that have to do with anything?"

"I'm just saying that if you're still getting your monthly visits from Auntie M, then you can still have babies. After all, it happened to me."

"Well, you are different. You always were in better shape than me."

"Fine…if you say so. I'm just saying that your complexion says otherwise."

"Girl, I know you didn't ask me come all the way down here to depress me. I told you that I ain't pregnant."

"Okayyyyyy. You should know better than anyone else how your body operates. I'll drop it."

"Thank you!"

The waiter approached the table balancing a tray holding four drinks. He carefully placed two drinks in front of each woman. The scent of freshly squeezed limes intermingled with crushed mint wafted from the glasses.

"Wait a minute, we didn't order two drinks each," Ronnie protested.

"The second round is courtesy of the two gentlemen at the bar," explained the waiter.

Ronnie and Joie simultaneously turned to look in the direction where the waiter pointed. Joie's jaw dropped open at the sight of Tomas standing beside Luis. Either could have been athletes or models, which was evident by the hungry stares coming from the many women who crossed their path.

"Damnnnnn…. Ronnieeee… Holy shit! Tomas is even finer than I remembered…" Memories of making love to Tomas pushed all images of Cedric, Maya, Trey and even Ronnie to the back of her mind. It was obvious he had continued to work out because his polo shirt fit like it was custom made to display his body. He wore a pair of loose fitting khaki Bermuda shorts and flip-flops on his feet. He looked towards the ladies and waved. The sunglasses perched atop his nose hid his eyes, but not his facial expression. When he smiled, Joie felt her heart melt a little.

Ronnie reached over to push Joie's chin upwards. "Close your mouth, girl. Your fangs are showing."

Joie brushed Ronnie's hand away. "Shut up!" she teased.

"Don't you go getting any ideas in your mind about Tomas. You are a married woman. I want you to remember that."

Just as quickly as Ronnie mentioned her marital status, Cedric's face, along with all their recent troubles quickly returned to the forefront of Joie's mind. "Girlfriend, you sure know how to spoil a wet dream."

Ronnie laughed out loud. "I sure hope you didn't just wet your pants over there."

"Umh! If you had left me alone for about three more minutes, I was well on my way to getting there." She began squirming in her seat making funny faces.

"I missed you, Joie. You and your crazy ass mouth!"

The men grabbed their beers and strolled over towards the ladies' table. Luis leaned over and planted a kiss on his wife's lips. "Hi Joie. I see you made it."

"Hey Luis. You know I had to drive down to see my girl."

"*Hola*, Joie. You're looking lovely as ever," Tomas leaned over to kiss Joie's cheek.

"Hi Tomas. You look pretty good yourself." With the touch of his lips on her skin, she blushed in spite of herself.

"You guys want to join us?" Ronnie asked.

"I wish we could, but we have to prepare for this evening's meeting," Luis explained.

"What time do you think you'll be back?"

"The meeting is at the convention center. But it shouldn't last too long. I expect to be back in the hotel by ten."

"Are you staying at the hotel, Joie?" Tomas asked. "Perhaps we can catch up over a drink later on."

Joie felt her heartbeat speed up at the sound of this man's voice. *The possibility of spending time with Tomas is so tempting. Having just one drink with him won't hurt anything. I won't allow more than that to happen, but if it does, I'll cross that bridge when I get to it. Just being in Tomas's presence, I can lose myself in his voice, his kisses, his touch...* As she opened her mouth to respond, a swift kick at her shin brought her back to reality.

"Sorry Tomas. Joie needs to get back to Hampton tonight. To her family. Isn't that right, Joie?"

"Excuse me Ronnie, but I can answer for myself." She turned to Tomas and said, "Sorry Tomas, I didn't plan on spending the night down here."

"I understand..." he said.

Ronnie interrupted, "Honey, you two should get going."

Luis replied, "You're right. Driving across town in this traffic is a pain in the ass this time of day."

Tomas touched Joie's shoulder tenderly. "Well, it was good seeing you again. Take care of yourself."

"You too, Tomas."

Luis bent down once more to kiss Ronnie's cheek "I love you. See you tonight."

"I love you, too," she replied.

The ladies watched Luis and Tomas exit the bar. And so did several other women whose heads turned when they walked past.

"Damn! These hoes around here don't have no shame, do they? They just saw us talking to Luis and Tomas. For all they know, both of them could be our husbands. Look at all the bitches staring after them." Joie looked over at Ronnie who didn't seem to be at all concerned. "Don't that bother you?"

"What?"

"All these tricks lusting after your man?"

"No, it doesn't bother me. Let them look because as long as Luis loves me, I have nothing to worry about. I trust my man," she replied with confidence.

"You are a better woman than I am." Joie made a sweeping motion with her arm. "Look at all these pretty women lying around the pool with their tits and asses hanging out. Ain't you worried about him straying?"

"Joie, if you saw how many beautiful women there are in Santo Domingo, you wouldn't even be tripping. Luis is around beautiful women all the time. But he loves me. I'm secure with that."

And with that, Joie picked up her *mojito* and downed it in one sip.

Ronnie joined her. "I know what. Let's make a toast."

"Okay, but first I want that waiter to start on another round." She caught the waiter's attention. "Another round, please."

The bartender must have already had two *mojitos* prepared because the waiter took no time returning to their table.

"You good now?" Ronnie asked with amusement. She was glad that Joie was having a good time.

"Yeah, I'm ready."

"To our friendship. May it last forever and let's promise to never let anyone—husbands or whoever—come between us."

"To our friendship," Joie repeated. She clinked her glass to Ronnie's and laughed when half of the liquid spilled down her arm. "Damn, I hope that ain't a bad sign."

"Woman, please! You are the least superstitious person I know." Ronnie used the napkin her drink rested on to help clean up the mess.

The waiter rushed over with a wet towel and proceeded to wipe the spill unto his tray.

Just then, Joie's phone rang displaying Maya's face. She knew this must be urgent because Maya was only allowed to use her cell phone in emergencies. She told Ronnie, "I'll be right back. I gotta take this call." Joie accepted the call with the swipe of her finger.

"Hey Maya. What's wrong, baby?"

"Hi Mommy. When are you coming to pick us up?"

"Your daddy was supposed to pick you up today."

"Well, he's not here."

"Maybe he's running late. Have you heard from him?"

"Nope."

"Are you still at school?"

"No ma'am. We're just hanging out in front of the Y. When daddy didn't come pick us up from summer camp, we walked decided to walk over here. Is that okay?"

Joie held her tongue to avoid having Maya hear her cursing out her father. "Sweetie, let me call you right back. I'm gonna try to reach your daddy."

She dialed Cedric's number. It went straight to voicemail. She tried it twice more with the same results. She dialed the number once more, only this time he picked up.

"Hello?" he answered.

"Cedric?! Why haven't you picked up the kids? You were supposed to get them from summer camp an hour ago?"

"I'm on my way there now."

"They're not at school. They're waiting at the Y."

"Ok. I'll be there in a few minutes."

"Are you serious? What in the world was so important that you're late picking them up?"

"I had to make a few stops that took longer than expected, but I'm on my way over there now. Don't worry."

She slowly counted to ten before speaking to keep from swearing. "You know I don't like to have the kids walking along those busy streets, especially on a Friday with all these can't-drive-a-damn assholes rushing home from work."

"Look, I just spoke to Maya. I told her I'm on my way."

She exhaled loudly, still pissed off. *What in the world could be more important than picking up their children?*

"What time are you getting home tonight?" he asked.

"I'll be home later."

"Oh, so it's like that, huh?"

"Like what?"

"You and your girlfriend gonna hang out all night long drinkin'?"

"Since you mentioned it, I have been drinking. Ronnie offered to put me up in the hotel so I don't have to drive home." *Well, technically she hadn't offered, but it was just a matter of time before she did.* "Is that all right with you?"

"I guess the decision has already been made."

"Would you prefer that I drive home drunk? Take the chance that I won't make it all the way from Virginia Beach to Hampton in one piece?"

"No, Joie. Go on and spend the night." As an afterthought, he asked, "Did that fake-assed Spanish speaking niggah come too?"

"Who are you talking about?"

"So now you're playing dumb, huh? Well, if you do see him, you just remember that you are still my wife."

"I don't know what you're talking about," she replied in frustration, knowing full well who he meant. "I'll see you first thing in the morning. Bye." She clicked off without giving him a chance to say another word and then dialed Maya.

"Hello?" Maya answered in her big girl's voice.

"Baby, your daddy is on his way. He should be there in a few minutes."

"I know. He just called."

"Are you and Trey all right?"

"Yes ma'am. Trey is sitting on the steps finishing a project the counselors gave him. And I'm helping."

"That's good, sweetie."

"Mommy, I see daddy's car," she reported.

Joie breathed a sigh of relief. "Okay, that's good."

"When are you coming home? I want to show you my math test."

"I'm going to spend the night with Auntie Ronnie so I won't see you until tomorrow."

"Oh. Okay. Tell Auntie Ronnie that we said 'hi'".

"I will. Now you be a good girl for me. I love you. And tell Trey I love him, too."

Maya pulled the phone to her chest. She told her brother, 'Mommy said she love you'. She returned to the phone and said, "Daddy's here. I'll see you later, mommy. Bye-bye."

Joie backed against the wall and took several deep breaths to relax. The rum from the *mojitos* made focusing difficult. As she glanced around the hotel lobby, her eyes played tricks on her, causing everyone to look like they were moving in slow motion. In a moment of confusion, she forgot why she was standing in the lobby of the Hilton, or whether she was there with anyone. However, as quickly as the fogginess came, it lifted. She watched couples check-in, some carrying just overnight bags for luggage. They all seemed so happy. Maybe they were checking in for a weekend getaway—like the mini vacations she and Cedric used to take at the drop of a hat.

The bright and airy beach décor of the hotel contrasted sharply with how she felt inside. The joy she experienced at the beginning of the year after she and Cedric returned from the DR had faded, similar to how the sun had bleached pieces of driftwood used to decorate the lobby from a rich brown to an ashy gray.

Sometimes being drunk puts you in a state of reflection. All the losses she had experienced this year—with her parents moving to Florida, her mother dying shortly thereafter, Cedric getting arrested, combined with losing her job... One could say that the threads of Joie's life had not only unraveled, but now laid in a heap of unrecognizable confusion at the soles of her feet. No matter how hard she tried to keep it all together, the only appropriate description that seemed to fit her life lately was *lost*.

A hotel bellhop on his way to returning a luggage cart took one look at Joie and asked, "Are you all right ma'am? Is there anything I can get you?"

"No, I'm fine," she lied. "Just taking a little break."

"I can help you over to that chair, if you'd like."

"Thanks. I'm fine," she reiterated. "Really."

"All right, if you say so..."

The brief conversation with the bellhop was enough of a distraction to snap her out of the funk. She pondered, "It's not like Ced to forget about picking up the kids. He is always the one reminding me to be on time." And then taking one last deep breath, she relinquished the sorrow threatening to overtake what remained of a good evening--one she hadn't had in a very long time. "Well, there ain't a damn thing I can do about it from here, so I might as well enjoy myself the rest of the night. Because when I get back to Hampton, all hell is gonna break lose."

Chapter Twenty

The sun slipped lower on the horizon revealing layers upon layer of wispy, pastel colored clouds against the darkening blue sky. The ladies moved to the hotel restaurant where they ordered soft shell blue crabs and fresh grilled vegetables for dinner. And of course, more *mojitos* for dessert. Feeling relaxed from the liquor, the ladies decided to take a quiet walk on the beach before going inside.

"Joie, can I ask you a question?"

"Sure. What is it?"

"When Maya and Trey were babies, did they learn at different rates? I'm asking because my babies are going on eight months now. LJ is pulling himself up to stand on the side of the crib, but little Isabella seems content to just lay there."

"Just because they're twins don't mean they will learn at the same rate. Maya always seemed to be ahead of Trey in the learning process, but lately, I think he's catching up with her. His grades over the last year have been much better than hers."

Ronnie contemplated Joie's explanation. "Yeah, I guess you're right. After all, they are different people."

"I sometimes wondered if Maya and Trey *were* identical twins would they have matured at the same rate. You know, be more alike than different."

"I really have no idea..."

"Anyway, how are things in the Duarte home?"

"Things are really good." Ronnie gushed. "Did I tell you how much I love living in the Dominican Republic? I'm even learning Spanish so I'll be able to understand the twins when they start talking. Their *abuela* only speaks to them in Spanish, so I want to know what they're saying to each other."

"That shouldn't be too difficult, especially since Spanish is Luis's first language." Joie glanced at her friend, trying hard to not envy her life. "Seems like you'd pick it up in no time at all."

Joie continued on extolling the virtues of living in the DR. "Remember how I used to always complain about the fruits and vegetables not being fresh in the grocery store? Well, I don't have that problem anymore. If I want lemons, bananas, mangoes, pineapples...whatever, I can go out on our land and pick it fresh. Right off the tree! And the meat! Girl, I have never tasted chicken or pork like this before. It makes you wonder what the government does to our food before it reaches us."

"Is that right?"

"Umh huh… Girl, Luis even cooks dinner sometimes. He'll make me a local dish—something that his mama taught him. He doesn't always follow her instructions, but somehow it always turns out delicious." Ronnie shook her head in amazement. "He is such a good husband and a wonderful father. I am truly blessed."

"It sounds like you're really happy."

"I am. Sometimes I'm so happy I feel like I'm going to burst!"

"You deserve it. All that shit you went through before you met Luis… Let's just say your happiness was long overdue."

"So… How are you and Cedric getting along?"

Joie wanted to tell Ronnie the truth about her life spiraling out of control, but after hearing all the great things happening in her friend's life, she wasn't able to form the words in her mouth. It was too depressing. Too pathetic. Too sad. Simply put, her life was fucked up. So, instead she responded, "We're going fine."

Ronnie stopped walking. She stepped in Joie's face and said, "All right Joie, spit it out."

"What are you talking about?"

"I have given you plenty of time to tell me what's going on. You haven't said more than two words about Cedric other than you guys are doing fine. I know you. I can tell when you're holding back. So what's up?"

"Other than going through a few rough patches that most couples experience, we are fine."

"Are you sure?"

Joie responded with a sideways glance. "What did I just say?"

"Fine, I'll stop asking. It's just that you're usually so open about your life, especially your 'sexual escapades'. I used to envy you two because you were the freakiest married couple I knew." Ronnie chuckled.

"Yeah, well, we kinda cut back on the role playing for a while."

"Why? You both seemed to really enjoy it, from what you told me."

"Okay, you're right. I have been holding back some news." Instead of pretending that all was well in the Parker family, she decided to give Ronnie a tidbit of information to make her back off.

"I wasn't going to say anything, but Ced is thinking about quitting his job as a youth counselor to start his own business. Told me he's tired of working with all them bad ass kids." The lies rolled so easily off Joie's tongue that she almost believed them herself. And it didn't hurt that he had mentioned going into business for himself once or twice.

"Seriously?" Ronnie replied in astonishment. "I never imagined he was the entrepreneurial type."

"You don't have to sound so shocked about it."

"No offense, but I always took Cedric to be the type who liked punching a clock. A worker bee—not the boss." Ronnie added, "I know that Cedric is really smart, but not everyone is cut out to run their own company. It takes a different kind of motivation…"

Despite Ronnie's good intentions, Joie *was* offended by her friend's remarks. Even if *she* didn't believe in her husband's ability to run his own business, who the hell was Ronnie to question it. "Cedric has been taking classes held at the Newport News SBA office. He was even accepted into a mentorship program where he could learn the ropes from an entrepreneur firsthand," she lied again. "So don't count him out yet."

"Good for him." Ronnie turned to watch the birds play in the surf. This conversation was turning into a buzz kill. "Well, if he's really serious about this, I'm sure Luis would be happy to provide a few tips since he's owned his own business for decades."

"Thanks, I'll tell him."

"Maybe we can drive up to visit tomorrow. I know Luis has a full schedule with the conference and all, but he should be finished by four."

"What about Tomas? Y'all just gonna leave him here by himself?"

"I think it would be better if Tomas stayed down here considering Cedric nearly broke his jaw last time."

"Yeah, it probably wouldn't be a good idea for him to show up at my house."

"So, what time should we plan on dropping by?"

Truth be told, the last thing Joie wanted was for Ronnie and Luis to visit her home. Ronnie was her best friend and all, but she wasn't ready to discuss her husband's legal troubles, or the general sorry state of their lives with her and Luis over a couple of cold ones.

"Oh shoot. I just remembered…"

"Remembered what?"

"That phone call I got earlier…well, it was Cedric. He called to tell me that he has to work a double shift tomorrow. He's dropping the twins off at Tequitta's first thing in the morning, so I have a kitchen pass to stay overnight down here if I want."

"That's too bad. I really wanted to see my Godchildren again. And Cedric, of course." Ronnie eyed Joie suspiciously. In all the time she had lived in Hampton and had known the Parkers, there was never an instance of Cedric having to pull a double shift at the youth center, especially on a Saturday. She knew something was up, but opted once more to let it slide. For now.

"Well, maybe he can pull a few strings and get out of it," Joie hedged. "But he also said they had to scrape the bottom of the barrel before they got to him. If he can't cover the shifts, they'll have to close the center."

"Girl, it ain't that serious. This is not my last trip to Virginia. I'll see them next time."

"I'm sorry, but it can't be helped." Joie hated lying to her friend, but she couldn't see any other way to keep Ronnie from discovering how truly badly they were doing.

"We have known each other for a long time and I can tell when there's something you're not telling me. But it's cool. I'll respect your privacy."

"I appreciate that."

"We have been through some shit that would tear normal friends apart."

"You're right…"

"But I hope you know that you can tell me anything. After all, you are my ride or die… Understand?"

"Yeah, I got it."

"If you ever need help with anything, I'm right here."

"Thanks, Ronnie. I do appreciate you saying that, but I'm good." *Who knows? One day, I just may have to take you up on it, but not today.*

"I hope you don't have to rush back home tonight."

"Nope. I can stay all night long, but first I need to get a room in the hotel."

"What about a change of clothes?"

Joie started to laugh. "Did you forget that I always travel with a packed overnight bag in my trunk? My mother raised me to always be prepared. Her favorite piece of advice was, 'always keep a pair of clean underwear, a toothbrush, and a jogging suit in the car—just in case.'"

Ronnie joined in her laughter. "How could I forget that? Miss Slim tried to convince me to do the same thing, but I never seemed to get around to buying that jogging suit."

"You won't believe this, but that packed bag in my trunk contains the same jogging suit that I've been carrying around for years. Every time I buy another car, I just toss that same old worn-out overnight bag in the trunk. Come to think of it, that jogging suit is probably ten years old by now."

Both women doubled over in laughter, partially from the intoxication of four additional *mojitos*, but mostly from sharing a memory about someone they both held so dearly.

"I sure do miss my mom," Joie said. "She and I didn't see eye-to-eye on many things, but she always had my back."

"I know what you mean. You don't really appreciate your parents until they're no longer here. I'm happy that me and my mother finally reconnected after all those lost years."

"Good thing you did because you never know how much time you have left. I thought my mom would be around for at least another twenty years."

"Right. Sixty-two was way too young to pass…"

Joie wiped unexpected tears away with the backs of both hands. "Anywayyyyyy…let's talk about something else. I don't want to kill my buzz."

"You got it." Ronnie grinned slyly.

"You look like you're up to something…"

"Well, I wasn't going to tell you this, because I promised I wouldn't say anything. But since I'm drunk, I can blame what I'm about to say on the a-a-a-a-a-alcohol."

"Gurrrrl, I know you did not just quote that Jamie Foxx song!" Joie busted out laughing.

"Oh yes, I did quote Jamie! I love that song!" Feeling totally uninhibited from all the liquor, Ronnie began twerking as if they were the only two on the beach. In an off key drunken voice, she sang out loud, *"Blame it on the goose, gotcha feelin' lose, blame it on the tron… blame it on the a-a-a-a-a-alcohol…"*

"You need to quit trying to twerk because your ass is too old! You look ridiculous!"

"Whose ass is old?!"

"Your ass is old."

"I don't know why you laughing so hard. I'm just one year older than you."

"Will you just tell me whatever it is you have to say?" Joie pleaded. "I'm dying of curiosity!"

"Okay. Soooooo, Tomas just broke up with his girlfriend because he said she was all flash and no substance, just like some of those airhead models he used to date in California."

"Tomas is single?"

Ronnie nodded. "I overheard him telling Luis that he was sorry he let you get away."

"What?!"

"Looks like you made a lasting impression on him, girlfriend. I never knew Tomas to talk about an ex-girlfriend the way he does with you."

"You mean to tell me that Tomas felt some kinda way about me?" She asked incredulously.

"I think he was in loooove with youuuuu," Ronnie slurred.

"Yeah, right! You must be crazy!" Joie ran ahead of Ronnie into the water, jumping up and down in the surf like a kid. She waded in up to her knees, desperately trying to keep the hem of her dress from getting soaked. *Why did Ronnie have to tell me that about Tomas? I can't be getting involved with him again even if me and Ced are having problems. I can't deal with this right now. Probably better if I pretend like she never said anything.*

"Joie! Girl, get out of the water. You know you don't have nothing to change into 'cept that old ass 1995 jogging suit in your trunk," Ronnie shouted. *Damn... I just had to open my big mouth about Tomas. Should have followed Luis's advice to mind my own business when it came to those two. That ship sailed long ago when Joie decided to get remarried to Cedric. Well, hopefully she's too drunk to remember what I told her.*

Joie backed away when the surf came in higher than expected. More drunk than sober, she laughed hysterically when the water almost knocked her down. Then she shouted happily, "C'mon in girl! This water feels so good on my legs!"

Ronnie stood in the sand watching her friend enjoying herself. It had been such a long, long, time since she had shared a good laugh with anyone besides Luis. Though she loved being a mommy, it was great having some adult girlfriend time away from the kids. She was having so much fun that she didn't see the young waiter approach until he was right upon her.

"Excuse me, ma'am," the waiter said, tapping Ronnie on the shoulder.

"Oh!" She jumped, abruptly turning to face the young man.

"I hope I didn't startle you," he said, balancing the tray with the free hand.

"You did. Just a little bit…"

"I'm sorry." He removed one drink from the tray and offered it to her. "Before Mr. Duarte left the bar, he told me to keep the *mojitos* coming until you told me to stop."

"Thank you." She took a sip. "Mmmmm, this is sooooo good."

"He gave me a hundred dollars and said whatever was left over after you finished drinking, I could keep the change as a tip."

"That was generous of my husband." She smiled at the young man's concern. "Don't worry; we aren't going to drink many more. You'll have a nice tip left over."

"Cool! Do you want me to take this one to your friend?"

"Yeah, I think she can handle one more." Ronnie giggled. She watched the waiter tip-toe through the sand to where Joie played in the water.

"Right on time!" Joie told the waiter. She accepted the drink, raised the glass towards Ronnie, and took a long swig. And just as she was about to turn around to face the water, an unexpected wave knocked her on her rear.

The waiter jumped back several feet just in time to miss the wave. When he saw the water pull Joie under, he reached out to help her to her feet, but backed away to avoid being pulled down. After all, he had another six hours to go and couldn't afford to miss out on a profitable Friday night shift.

Ronnie laughed so hard tears welled up in her eyes as she watched Joie struggle to get to her feet. When she did manage to get up on her knees, another wave knocked her right back down, drenching her friend from head to toe.

Joie shouted at Ronnie, "Heifer, stop all that damn laughing and get your ass over here to help me!"

"Ma'am, is there anything I can do to help?" the waiter said to Joie who sat in the water looking like a wet rag. "I can bring you another round of drinks if you'd like."

Despite being tossed around in the surf, Joie somehow managed to hold onto the drink, albeit the glass was now filled with seawater rather than *mojito*. "Naw, that's alright." She pushed the glass towards the waiter. "Take this."

The waiter retrieved the glass and then slowly backed away. "Okay, just let me know if you ladies want another round."

Ronnie inched her way towards Joie, offering an outstretched hand. Between fits of laughter, she said, "Oh my goodness, Joie! You should see yourself." She pulled her cell phone from the cross body bag resting on her hip. "I've got to get a picture of this."

"Bitch, if you don't put that phone away!" Joie yelled. But when she noticed Ronnie was going to take her picture whether she liked it or not, she struck a pose, making a silly face for added effect.

"Now that is going to be an absolutely priceless picture!" Came a man's voice from a few feet away, interrupting their moment of silliness.

It took several moments to register who the man was because Joie saw Tomas through eyes clouded by too much rum. Even though she was drunk off her ass, she screamed out in embarrassment as she tried to smooth her soaking wet, matted hair away from her face. But the effort was futile—she looked a hot mess. And the money she invested in her weave a few days ago was now a total waste.

Ronnie turned to see Tomas standing behind her grinning from ear to ear.

"What are you doing here? I thought you were with Luis at the convention center."

"I was. I just came back because I left my *iPad* in my room. While I was up there, I stepped out on the balcony to watch the sunset. That's when I saw the two of you; you on the beach and Joie in the water. I gotta admit though, seeing Joie soaking wet is better than attending any conference. Be right back." Tomas left Ronnie standing there with her mouth wide open. He swaggered towards the water, leaned over, and helped Joie up by her waist. He used the towel he brought with him to gently remove tiny bits of sand from her face.

Joie was very comfortable playing the role of a damsel in distress. She demurely batted her fake eye lashes, dropped her head, and whispered 'thank you', all the while she making vain attempts to arrange her hair as Tomas patted her dry.

"Let me help you back to your room," Tomas whispered in her ear. "You've got to get out of those wet clothes."

"That's a great idea. Only problem is I don't have a room."

"No? Then where are you staying tonight? I know you are not driving back home in this condition," he stated, noting the difficulty she had standing up straight.

That's when Ronnie decided to butt in to try to fix the mess she started by opening her big mouth. "Why don't you go on back to the convention, Tomas? We were just about to go inside to get her a room."

"Veronica, did you forget what the hotel clerk told that poor couple who was looking for a room when we checked in?"

She frowned trying to remember.

"Because of this convention, anyone without a reservation is out of luck. There isn't a decent hotel room available in all of Virginia Beach."

"Oh yeah, that's right. I do remember him saying that…"

Joie glanced from Ronnie to Tomas and back to Ronnie. "I can spend the night in your room… if it's okay with Luis."

Without hesitation, Ronnie quickly replied, "Sorry girlfriend. You cannot stay in the same room with me and my husband. We'll figure out something. Maybe Luis can bunk with Tomas for tonight."

Tomas interrupted, "Joie can sleep in my bed. I mean, she can sleep in my room and I can sleep on the sofa."

Joie weighed the possibilities. Drive home drunk or spend the night with Tomas and suffer all the consequences associated with that option? "That sounds like it would be all right. I mean, after all, it's not like we'll be sleeping together or anything."

"I promise I will be a gentleman." He crossed his heart innocently.

"Hold up, Joie, I don't think you should be spending the night with Tomas. What would Cedric have to say?"

"Ronnie, the most I'm going to do is change out of these wet clothes and sleep in his room. I'm a big girl. I can take care of myself."

"Right… You're a big girl," Ronnie replied angrily, feeling her high begin to dissipate. "I thought this weekend was about *us* catching up, not hooking up with Tomas."

"*Come esta?* I am only offering Joie a place to sleep. That is all."

"Yeah girl, quit trippin'. I'm not trying to hook up with anybody." She said as she winked at him. "We can continue our party upstairs. If it's alright with you, Tomas."

"Sure it is. I'm in room 924. And help yourself to one of my t-shirts if you need a change of clothing." Tomas reached into his pocket and retrieved the room keycard.

"I hope you know what you're doing," Ronnie addressed Tomas.

He ignored Ronnie and said to Joie, "You can go up anytime you want. And please feel free to make yourself comfortable. If you need to order room service, just tell them to charge it to my room."

"Are you sure?" she asked.

"I would not offer if I were not sincere."

"Thank you," Joie replied.

"My pleasure." He smiled warmly. "I have a late business dinner scheduled so I probably won't be back in the room until late. I will try to not wake you."

Ronnie sneered disapprovingly at Tomas. He continued to ignore her, which only pissed her off more.

"Well, I'd better get going. I promised Luis I would be right back. He's working on a major deal with a client and they need this report I prepared earlier."

"Thanks again, Tomas. I will see you later." Joie tried to pull her weave into a ponytail. Anything to keep from feeling like the wet rat she imagined she resembled.

"Yeah, thanks," Ronnie stated flatly. "Just remember when you get back into your room tonight and see her sleeping in your bed that she is a married woman! With twins!"

He laughed off Veronica's concerns as he walked away. He rationalized that he was merely helping out a friend in need. Problem was he had no idea what he would encounter once he returned to his room. Nor, how he would react.

Chapter Twenty-One

It was almost eight o'clock by the time they stumbled from the beach and into the hotel, but before they did, they arranged for their favorite waiter bring up several more *mojitos.*

"Wow!" Joie exclaimed upon opening the door to Tomas's spacious one bedroom suite. The separate living area was decorated in softly muted beach theme palette. The cream colored leather sofa, two end chairs, a large flat-screen television and a fully stocked bar were all designed to make the guest feel right at home. The curtains were pulled back from the windows to reveal a spectacular view of the Atlantic Ocean. Two Adirondack chairs were situated on the balcony with a wonderful view of the beach.

"You want to sit inside or out?"

"Damn, Ronnie! I forgot that Tomas had it like this!"

Ronnie had become so accustomed to living large that she was no longer dazzled by an opulent hotel suite. However, experiencing the lavish setting through Joie's eyes, she had to remind herself that she didn't always used to live like this. "Yeah, it's pretty nice, huh?"

"Nice?! Girl, this room is the bomb!" Joie wandered into the bedroom and squealed in delight upon seeing the luxurious king-sized bed. "That is a bed just waiting for a good time!"

Ronnie watched in amusement as Joie fluttered around the suite opening up doors and squealing in delight.

"Hey girlfriend!" Joie shouted from the bathroom. "You gotta see this!"

"See what?" she asked following the sound of Joie's excited voice. "What are you doing?"

"Check it out. Is that one of those rain forest showers?" She stood outside the oversized stall admiring the shower fixture. "The kind that makes you feel like you're taking a shower in the rain?"

"Yeah, I think so," Ronnie replied uncomfortably. Her and Luis's suite was actually more luxurious than this one, but she didn't feel right bringing that up.

Joie spied two thick terry-cloth bathrobes on the shelf underneath the cultured marble basin. "Do you think Tomas would mind if I use one?"

"No, he won't mind because those robes come with the room. Just like the bath towels…"

"Oh," Joie replied, suddenly feeling very small. "Well, I think I'm going to take a quick shower. Get out of these wet clothes."

"Okay. I'll be out on the balcony."

Joie stripped bare. The two mirrors carefully arranged on opposite walls reflected her body in an infinite reflection of naked skin. "I may not be what Tomas is used to, but at least my ass is still firm and my titties are perky." She did a spin to get a view from all angles. "Overall, I think I look pretty good."

"Yeah, you look good, but why in hell are you even thinking about Tomas? That man ain't gonna see you naked!" Ronnie shouted.

"Ain't nothin' wrong with wishful thinking!" Joie shouted back.

"Woman, would you please stop admiring yourself and get your ass in the shower!"

Joie adjusted the shower settings and then stepped into the warm water. *Wow! Ronnie didn't even blink an eye at this suite. Here I am going on and on and she didn't even get a little excited. I remember when she would have been as blown away as I was by this amazing place. Has she moved on up that much?*

The waiter placed the tray of drinks on the table, Ronnie gave him a generous tip even though the drinks were already paid for. The young man thanked her profusely and then disappeared back into the elevator.

She docked her iPod in the docking station and tuned in a jazz station. The music blared out from the small speakers to fill the entire suite. She took the tray of drinks to the balcony and took a seat in one of the Adirondack chairs.

Joie used the complimentary toiletries provided by the hotel. Her weave was a total disaster so she used the ribbon holding the bathrobe together and tied her hair into a ponytail. Pulling the robe taut around her naked body, she plodded to the bedroom closet for something to wear. She pulled an oversized t-shirt from the hanger, slipped it on, and then searched through the dresser until she found a pair of his workout shorts.

Checking her reflection the mirror, she remarked, "Good thing my husband can't see me like this 'cause he would lose his mind." Joie walked out on the balcony carrying the bathrobe in one hand and her dress in another. She plopped down on the chair and spread-eagled each leg on either side.

"I'm glad you found something to wear."

"Me too. Otherwise you'd be staring at my cootchie for the rest of the night."

Ronnie laughed good-naturedly. "No offense girlfriend, but the last thing I want to look at is your cootchie."

Joie smiled at their banter. "I need to have my dress cleaned. You think the hotel can have it back to me first thing tomorrow morning?"

"Yeah, I'll take care of it."

"Good, because I cannot go home wearing another man's clothes."

"No, that probably wouldn't be a good idea." Ronnie rose and went to the living area. She picked up the phone. In less time than it took for Joie to get situated in her chair, Ronnie had returned. "All taken care of. They'll be up in a few minutes to get your dress."

"Thanks." Joie shook her head trying to clear the cobwebs. "I think this might be my last drink. I can barely walk."

"I hear ya. Me too. But the good thing is, neither one of us has to go anywhere tonight." Ronnie stared at the changing colors of the night sky. "This view is amazing."

"I'm glad to hear you're impressed by something tonight," Joie remarked.

"What's that supposed to mean?"

"Did you happen to notice my expression when I saw this suite? I was straight up impressed."

"It's just a hotel room, Joie." She shrugged nonchalantly taking in the beauty of the remaining slivers of daylight disappearing into the ocean.

Joie shook her head from side to side. The drink she held in her hand sloshed over the sides. She responded with slurred her speech, "See! That is what I'm talking about. This ain't just no fuckin' hotel room. This is a goddamn suite overlooking the beach! This bitch probably cost a grand a night and you ain't got nothin' to say except 'it's just a hotel room'?!"

"Why are you getting so upset?"

"Because the old Ronnie would have flipped out over this room just like me. Now you acting all brand new. Like this ain't shit..." Joie swept her arm over their surroundings.

"Look Joie, I'm still the same old me. I haven't changed." She paused as she surveyed the hotel suite through the eyes of her friend. "Yeah, this *is* a really nice room, but I don't allow myself to trip off material stuff anymore."

"Hmph! I guess you don't have to when your husband is rich."

"Luis is doing really well with his business, but we are far from rich."

Joie leaned back in her chair considering telling her girlfriend about her family's troubles, but despite what Ronnie said, she *was* out of touch with how her family lived. Ever since Ronnie married Luis, she probably never had a day where she had to worry about money. The question of how they were going to pay their mortgage—or if they had a mortgage at all, was probably never a topic of discussion. And she for damn sure didn't have to worry about a husband who had just lost his job and was about to go to jail.

"Joie? What the hell is wrong with you? You've been acting funny ever since you got here."

"Nothing is wrong. I'm just drunk, that's all." She drained the remainder of the *mojito,* closed her eyes, and listened to the jazz music pouring through the French doors onto the balcony.

"Then stop trippin' because you are seriously killing my buzz."

"Okay," she agreed because her high was also slipping away. "Can I ask you something?"

"Yeah, as long as it don't have nothing to do with this damn hotel room."

Joie sighed and said, "Remember when you used to tell me that you were living your life in the offbeat?"

"I remember."

"Tell me again about that offbeat thing. I've been trying to discover it ever since you told me about it."

"Seriously?"

"Yeah, I'm interested."

Ronnie went inside and turned the volume up on the docking station. She returned to her chair and said, "Close your eyes, open your mind, and just listen to the music. Try to not get caught up in the song."

Joie did as she was told.

A popular Boney James song came on next. He used the melodious sounds of his saxophone to relay a haunting love song that caused even the most jaded person to sit back and think. Even the seagulls on the beach below seemed to get caught up in the harmonious notes.

Several moments later she declared with disappointment, "I don't hear nothin' special. Can't you put on somethin' else besides that jazz mess?"

Ronnie removed the drink from Joie's hands, "Focus. You have to listen to not only each note, but the space between the notes. It's the quiet, minutia space that exists between each beat. Without the offbeat, there would be no music. No song. It would just noise. But if you open your mind, you can hear it."

"How did you find out about this special place?" Joie asked with genuine curiosity. "And how do you know this so-called *offbeat* really exists?"

"Of course it isn't an *actual place*, but more of a state of mind. A place where peace and joy reside. I know it exists because that's where I choose to live my life. Besides, I decide who to bring into it and who to keep out of it."

Joie furrowed her brow. "How do you do that?"

"Easy. I only allow people who bring positive energy to get really close to me. People who are negative and only want to bring drama into my life, I stay away from. Don't allow them to get too close. Luis is the same way."

Joie wanted to ask Ronnie which category she fit into since they now lived very different lives. However, afraid of the answer she might receive, she decided not to chance it.

"Don't worry, I'm not talking about you," Ronnie joked, allaying Joie's concerns. "You bring a special kind of energy to my life that no one else can."

"Whatever..."

They shared several moments of quiet contemplation.

"Were you able to hear the offbeat?"

"Girlfriend, I think you must have been smokin' some of that Dominican weed." Joie broke into laughter.

"Getting high might actually help, but not necessary." Ronnie laughed along with her. "Now that you mention it, I've heard the DR has some really good stuff..."

"You got any smoke on you." Joie winked at her. "If you're game, so am I."

"Puhleeze... I haven't smoked weed since I was in my twenties."

"I sure could use a hit about now. Maybe then I can understand what the fuck you're talkin' about because all I hear is that crazy-ass music."

"Don't worry, girl. Everybody can't hear it, especially if their minds are filled with too much chatter."

Joie murmured, "Well, that explains why I can't hear it. Ain't nothin' going on in my life but noise and drama."

"Why do you say that? What's going on with you?"

And just when Joie had made up her mind to open up to Ronnie about the troubles in her life, a knock at the door interrupted their conversation.

"That must be the bellhop for your dress. Hand it to me. I'll be right back."

Joie handed Ronnie her dress. Then she closed her eyes and once again tried to hear that elusive offbeat where her friend resided, but try as she might, it remained out of her reach. *Living in the offbeat? Whatever... At this point, the only thing I'm feeling is lost, so I guess I can say I am lost in the offbeat—lost in the offbeat of my fucked up life.*

"Now, what were you saying?" Ronnie asked when she returned.

Joie exhaled, shaking her head. The interruption was enough of a distraction to bring her back to her senses. The burdens she carried were between her and Cedric and that's where they should remain. "Nothin' girl, I wasn't talking about nothin'."

~ ~ ~

Tomas returned to his suite shortly after midnight. When he opened the door, he found Veronica splayed out on the sofa amidst a collection of empty miniature liquor bottles and overturned glasses with mint leaves stuck to the sides. Loud music blasted from the speakers. The television was on with the volume muted.

"Veronica? Wake up," Tomas shook Ronnie several times.

Ronnie rolled over on her back and began to quietly snore.

When he was unable to wake her, and after he had a good laugh at her drunken state, he called Luis on his cell. "*Primo*, come to my room and get your drunken wife."

"I was wondering where she is," he replied. "After I got back to the room, I tried calling her cell phone."

"Well, you can stop looking. She is here. On my sofa. Dead to the world."

"Thanks, Tomas. I'll be right there."

Minutes later, Luis entered the suite to find Tomas perched on the edge of the sofa next to his snoring wife. "What and how much do you think she drank?"

"I don't know, but from the looks of this room, it was a lot."

"Where is Joie?"

"I haven't checked, yet, but she's probably in the bedroom."

Luis leaned over Ronnie. He tickled her ear, his special way of waking her, and pulled his wife to her feet.

"What is Tomas doing in our room?" she slurred.

"Sweetheart, we're in Tomas's room."

"Why are we in Tomas's room?"

"Don't worry. I'll explain it all to you in the morning. For now, let me get you in bed."

"Okay..." She leaned against Luis's shoulder and almost fell back asleep while standing.

"C'mon, sleepy head." Luis turned to Tomas and said, "Thanks, cousin. I'll see you in the morning."

After Luis left, Tomas turned off the TV and the stereo and tidied up. He made note of the closed bedroom door, surmising that Joie was sound asleep inside. He had no intention of waking her.

Behind the closed bedroom door, Joie was in the midst of having a wild sex dream thanks to the copious amounts of liquor she drank, and also because her mind had been on Tomas for most of the evening. In the dream, she and Tomas were having their own special freaky-deaky lovefest on a secluded beach somewhere in California.

After the warm shower, Tomas wrapped himself in a bathrobe and headed towards the bedroom for an extra pillow and blanket to prepare for a night on the sofa. When he told Joie he planned on being a gentleman, he meant it. Problem was, Tomas was not prepared for what he was about to see. Or hear.

He turned the doorknob and peered inside. Through the narrow opening of the door, the light from the living room entered the bedroom, found its home, and bounced off a vision of loveliness named Joie. She was on top of the covers. Butt naked. Legs spread wide apart. Her magnificent breasts flopped downwards into her armpits making her nipples stand more erect. Judging by all the moaning, it was obvious she was dreaming.

Tomas experienced an immediate erection at the sight of Joie's nakedness. He surmised if Joie's condition was any reflection of

Veronica's, she could not be easily awakened. He stared at the small patch of pubic hair manicured into an arrow pointing downward to her vagina. She hadn't shaven completely. For that he was glad. When they were dating, Joie had waxed every bit of pubic hair away. She remarked that she thought men wanted it that way because all the girls in the porn films were clean shaven. Tomas didn't like the look because he thought the look was unattractively prepubescent. He preferred his women to look like a woman and not a young girl.

"Joie?" he called out softly. "Are you awake?"

"Ooooh Tomas," she purred.

In spite of himself, he pushed the door open to allow more light inside. He inched his way closer to the bed.

"Joie? I'm just going to come in and pick up a few things," he whispered. It was obvious she was dreaming.

"Oh yeah, baby." She moaned in quiet pleasure when she turned over on her stomach. "Tomas…"

"Cogno!"

For several minutes, he stared at Joie's perfectly round ass highlighted by the soft lamp light which provided him with glimpses of her glistening pot of gold hidden between her partially opened thighs. While she continued her erotic dream, he positioned his hand so it hovered close enough to feel the heat emanating from between her legs. He momentarily contemplated touching her; trailing just one little finger along her flower to hear her delightful moan again.

And if it were possible, his erection grew even stronger. All it would take was a very slight movement, using the tip of his pinkie to gently caress the outer lips of Joie's vagina. He imagined touching her, feeling her wetness. She moaned loudly and shifted slightly in the bed, now turning unto her back again. He thought about gently stroking her mound, making small circles until her clitoris stood at full attention. He gripped his stiff penis in his other hand, unconsciously stroking himself, imaging slipping it into her sleeping, though very wet, vagina.

Before he proceeded any further, he stopped, moved his hand away from Joie's body, and stepped away from the bed. *What the hell am I doing? Standing over Joie like some pervert considering having sex with her while she's asleep? Amounting to what some would call rape?*

"Yeah, baby…that's the spot. Right there…" she moaned quietly, still asleep. Moving her hips to her dream lover. Caught up in the dream she did not want to awaken from.

Tomas quickly retreated to the bathroom, closed the door, and squirted some fragrant complimentary lotion into a wash cloth. He wrapped the rough washcloth around his throbbing penis. With thoughts of Joie lying naked in his bed with her glistening hot pussy exposed, he stroked himself fast and hard until the magnitude of his orgasm brought him to his knees.

Back in the bedroom, Joie stirred in the bed dreaming about Tomas making love to her. Before she reached her dream orgasm, something caused her to awaken. The bedroom door was fully open allowing the light from the lamp in the living area to stream through. Although she was still very drunk, she realized she was on top of the covers and not underneath. She pulled the cover over her nakedness and shouted, "Ronnie? Are you still here? Hey Ronnie? Stop playing girl."

Tomas used the edge of the vanity to pry himself back to his feet when he heard Joie calling for Veronica. He wiped hot cum from his flaccid penis and tightened the robe around his body prior to opening the bathroom door. He sat on the closed toilet to regain his composure.

"Ronnie? Are you out there?"

"Joie, it's me, Tomas. Veronica has already gone," he yelled back trying to gather enough strength to walk.

She froze momentarily at the sound of Tomas's voice. Her eyes went to her nakedness and then to the open door. "Tomas? How long have you been in the room?" she called out. *And why is my pussy so wet?*

He strode into the bedroom with a smile plastered to his face and replied, "Long enough to see that you still have a beautiful body."

Joie blushed, unsure how to respond. The sight of a partially clothed Tomas standing in the bedroom after she had just dreamt of him was a pleasant surprise. "You saw me naked? Ass, tits? Everythang?"

"*Si*," he replied. "*Todo.*"

"And you didn't try to fuck me?" she asked, bluntly, still drunk.

"No, Joie. I did not."

"Really? Why not? Don't you want to fuck me?"

"Are you kidding? Of course, I would like to make love to you!" he replied incredulously.

She squinted trying to decipher what he was really saying. "And…"

"But you were asleep."

She laughed. "I guess you kept your word when you said you were going to be a gentleman. Any other man woulda been all up in here." Joie tossed the covers back to give him an unobstructed view.

"Okay, I admit. I was very tempted when I heard you calling out my name. Even thought about touching you…"

That still don't explain why I am so excited. She tried to focus on Tomas's handsome face which was silhouetted by the light. "What do you mean you thought about touching me?"

"I almost got a little carried away. I just wanted to touch you. That's all."

"What did you do? Tell me everything. I want to know."

Tomas was embarrassed at what he had almost done. But only slightly. After all, he was who he was. "You were moaning in pleasure. I imagined using my fingers to caress you. I wanted to help you orgasm, but I stopped myself."

Joie laughed. "Are you telling me you didn't even try to slip your dick inside? Cause as wet as I am right now, it wouldn't have taken much to get me off."

"Joie, what kind of man do you think I am?" He searched her face for an answer before allowing his eyes to travel over her body again. "As tempting as you appeared lying naked, looking so beautiful, I would never have sex without your consent. I am ashamed that I even considered touching you, Joie."

The intoxication of too many *mojitos* and whatever else she and Ronnie downed that evening pushed away any remaining inhibitions, as well as all thoughts of her husband. She uttered in a sexy voice, "Well, you don't have to sneak, baby. I'm inviting you in. C'mon, Tomas. We are so good together. I want this. Need this. Don't you want me?"

He tightened the robe, thankful that he had jacked off earlier because the sight of her naked body combined with her pleading might have been too irresistible to pass up. "Joie, I am not going to have sex with you. I can't."

"Why not? We've made love many times before," she said, sensuously sucking on her fingers.

"Because you are married now and I have to respect your marriage even if you don't."

She disregarded his comment and continued on, placing her hand between her thighs. She released a sensual moan. "Tomas, you know that I was dreaming we were making love before you walked in. And now I am more than ready to make that dream a reality."

He did not speak. Simply stood there watching the incredible show.

"If I don't care, why should you?"

"Because I care about you, Joie." He stared at the woman he almost fell madly in love with less than a year ago. But tonight, instead of the fiery, self-confident woman who caught his attention, this version of Joie verged on the edge of being pathetic. "Look, you've been drinking. You are not in your right mind."

"I may be drunk, but trust me. I know what I want." She reached out for Tomas trying her best to play the seductress. When he was close enough, Joie leaned over and pulled the belt to his bathrobe loose, causing it to gape open. His limp penis was mere inches from her face. First she laughed and then she began mocking him. "Damn baby! You're not even hard. What's wrong? You can't get it up no more?"

For once in his life, he was grateful to not have an erection. Tomas pulled the robe together, walked to the closet, pulled out the spare blanket, and grabbed one of the extra pillows from the bed. And before he pulled the door shut, he leaned over and kissed Joie's forehead. "Cover yourself Joie. I will not make love to you tonight or any night because you belong to someone else now. Goodnight."

"What do you mean? Goodnight? Where do you think you're going?"

"You're drunk..."

"Damn right, I'm drunk!" Joie's misplaced anger found its mark on Tomas. Then her tone suddenly softened. "Remember when we first met, baby? You couldn't get enough of this fine pussy."

"You're right... I couldn't, but things have changed."

"Why? Because I got a husband?"

"Yes. Exactly. You're married."

"What the hell does my being married have to do with anything? Me and my husband haven't fucked in months. All I think about is you, Tomas. Even when me and my husband were doing it, I'd be thinkin' about you," she confessed with tears in her eyes. "I wish I had stayed with you instead of marrying Ced."

Tomas stared at Joie, unable to comprehend what he was seeing and hearing. This was not the woman he knew. In that moment, he felt sorry for her.

When Joie saw the pity in his eyes, she flipped. "Fuck you, Tomas! I don't need your ass no way! You make me sick!"

"You don't mean that," he replied calmly.

"I sure as hell mean it! You ain't shit, you know that?!"

"Goodnight, Joie."

"I wish I never met your Dominican ass!"

Tomas closed the door just as a pillow whizzed by, narrowly missing his face. He thought he had left that crazy-ass behavior behind him years ago with the last woman he dealt with in California. Thus, he was quite surprised to encounter it in Joie.

Joie watched Tomas pull the door shut, leaving her alone in the darkness of the bedroom feeling like a stone cold fool. Funny how the truth could slap you straight sober when it needed to. She wrapped herself in the comforter, laid her head on the pillow, and pondered how he could just walk away. Eventually, a merciful sleep finally saved her from the cruel thoughts swimming around her mind threatening to spill forth from her mouth.

He stood on the other side of the door musing over the naked woman lying in his bed who had attempted to seduce him minutes earlier, now yelling out obscenities. The desperate, sex-starved, drunken woman wasn't the Joie he remembered. Yet still, he was slightly amused and very relieved at how he was able to keep his cool under Joie's pressure. Any other time, with any other woman, he would have caved immediately at the first glimpse of the cookie hidden between those supple thighs.

Tomas was a changed man. He had made a promise to both Luis and Veronica, before they landed in Virginia, that no matter how tempted he was by Joie, he would not make a move on her. There was a time when he considered sharing his life with Joie because she was the most interesting woman he'd ever dated. But things were different now. She was married. Their short time spent together in California was magical. However, given the option between him and her now husband, Joie had made her choice and it had not been him. Looking back at what could have been was not a trait he possessed and there was no need to pick that trait up now.

He recalled being sucker punched by her husband right after Luis and Veronica's wedding. Had it been any other man who dared hit him, the outcome would have been totally different. But because it was

Joie's husband, he chose to let it go. Anyway, he was more startled than injured when he felt his fist connect with his jaw.

Instead of turning in, he grabbed two miniature bottles of *Remy* from the bar and went out on the balcony for a drink. Listening to the gentle waves of the ocean lapping against the shore, he let his thoughts drift to the events of the evening, rather than Joie lying naked just twenty feet away. He and Luis were so close to making the real estate deal of a lifetime. Not only would this business deal provide them both with a comfortable living for the rest of their lives, but it would also bring in much needed jobs to the people of Santo Domingo. *Too bad about Joie,* he thought. *The two of us together could have been a force to be reckoned with. Que lastima."* He inhaled deeply. The fragrant scent of the ocean somehow seemed heavier at night. It was comforting. It reminded him of home, and all the beautiful women who awaited his return.

Chapter Twenty-Two

Joie awoke early the next morning with an awful hangover. She had no idea where she was, only that she was alone in a king-sized bed. She scanned the contents of the beautifully decorated bedroom searching for clues as to her whereabouts. Florescent green digits glaring from an alarm clock on the nightstand indicated it was a little after seven o'clock. A card propped next to the clock advised guests about the sheet changing policy. The fogginess slowly lifted.

"Oh yeah… That's right. I'm in Tomas's suite at the Hilton." She crawled to the edge of the bed looking for her clothes. Or at least a robe. Unable to locate either, she pulled the top sheet from the mattress, tied it underneath her armpits and climbed out of bed.

"Ronnie? You here?" She kicked away a pillow that was blocking the door. No one answered. She called out again, "Ronnie? Tomas? Anybody here?"

She stumbled out into the brightly lit living area shielding her eyes from the migraine inducing daylight. Empty miniature bottles of both brown and white liquor were scattered around the room. Several empty bottles of gin, most likely the source of her cotton mouth, were neatly arranged in a line on the coffee table like shots. "No wonder my head feels like it's about to explode… I wonder how many of these I drank."

She peered through the French doors confirming that she was indeed alone.

A putrid smell wafting from a half eaten plate of chicken wings and sliders caused her stomach to lurch. "Ugh! I sure don't remember ordering room service." Holding her nose, she pushed the tray of leftover food into the hallway.

"Dang, where is everybody?" She looked inside her purse and checked her cell phone. There were several missed calls from Cedric, but none from Ronnie or Tomas.

"Well, at least they brought my dress back so I can take my ass home." A single sheet of paper fluttered to the floor when she gathered her dress from the sofa. "Hmmm, what's this?"

The note read, *"Dearest Joie, I apologize for not being here when you awakened, but after our conversation last night, I thought it was best if we end our relationship on a friendly note. I wish you and your family all the best,* signed, *Tomas."*

"What the hell?!" Joie read the letter several times. "Tomas was here last night and all he left me was this lame ass note? What the fuck happened?" She sank down on the sofa, feeling the veins throbbing in her temples.

Regardless of what happened last night, she knew she needed to get home. After a quick shower, she pulled on her damp underwear hanging from the shower curtain, and wiggled into her dress. "I look awful," she remarked upon seeing her reflection. "Well, I guess that's the sign of us having a good time."

She shamelessly gathered up the remaining miniature bottles of liquor and stuffed them inside her bag, contemplating leaving Tomas a note of her own. With pen poised in hand, she balled up the blank sheet of paper and casually tossed it in the trash. "On second thought, since I don't know what went down, I should probably just leave it alone."

Releasing a sigh of deep regret for what might have been, she closed the door after taking one last look at the magnificent suite. And as far as Tomas was concerned, something awful must have happened for him to have written that note. Too bad she couldn't remember. In the end, she chose to write him off as just another casualty in her fucked up world.

"It is what it is…"

~ ~ ~

With the trepidation she felt about going home, she might as well have driven into the mouth of an abyss instead of the HRBT. Joie's cell phone rang. She thought it was Cedric calling again because he had already left five messages asking when she was going to get her ass home. Rather than returning his calls, she figured she would deal with him once they were face to face. But it wasn't him.

"Hello?" she answered.

"Hey lady, where are you? I knocked on Tomas's door, but no one answered. I sure hope you two aren't out somewhere together," Ronnie said trying to not sound pissed.

Before Joie could answer, the call dropped. There was no cell phone reception as she traveled deeper into the tunnel beneath the murky waters of the Chesapeake Bay. She hated driving through tunnels, especially the HRBT with its narrow circumference. Normally, claustrophobia was not an issue, but there was something about the possibility of becoming trapped inside the darkness—underneath millions of gallons of water—that left a negative effect on her psyche.

Her throat began to tighten and her heart rate increased the further she went. To thwart an impending panic attack, Joie popped in the first CD within reach. Unfortunately, it was a CD of children's songs she played to keep the twins occupied during the drive to school. She sang along anyway.

Traffic was flowing nicely and she hoped to be out of the tunnel in another couple of minutes. All of a sudden, the brake lights of the car in front of hers illuminated. And then one-by-on, each successive car hit their brakes until the traffic came to a complete stop. After several minutes of not moving, she placed the car in park.

"You have got to be fuckin' kidding me?" she shouted to no one in particular.

She tried to make a call. Talking to someone always helped when this happened. The previous times when she was caught in tunnel traffic, Cedric had always been there and calmed her down with conversation. There was still no reception.

"Fuck! Fuck! Fuck!" Joie shouted. Beads of perspiration gathered on her forehead. Her pulse rate increased. The more she tried to not focus on the walls collapsing giving way to tons of water rushing inside, the more panicked she became. She turned the A/C up high and popped a different CD into the player. When that didn't work, she began talking to herself.

"Calm down. You are not going to die inside this tunnel. Millions of people drive through this tunnel everyday. Damn! Why couldn't I at least been closer to the entrance? If only I could only see outside, I'd be okay."

The fact that she was suffering through a hangover didn't help matters much. She took a deep breath and slowly counted to one hundred. That helped. She casually glanced at the car in the next lane. The driver was an older white man calmly sitting behind the wheel of a newer model Mercedes-Benz smoking a cigarette. His passenger window was partially down.

Joie rolled her own window down and waved her arms to get his attention. Feeling as if she was going to jump from her car and start running up and down the tunnel like a raving lunatic, she desperately needed to talk to somebody. Anybody.

"Excuse me," she called out. "Hey you!"

The man turned his head her way. He lowered his passenger window, smiled, and called out, "Hi there. Nothing like getting stuck down here, huh?"

"Yeah, it kinda sucks." She felt her heartbeat begin to slow down. "You have any idea what's going on?"

"Nope. Maybe construction. Probably an accident. I'm not really sure…"

Joie gathered her nerve and weighed the options of struggling with the quickly debilitating effects of claustrophobia alone against conversing with a total stranger. In the end, the choice was easy. She blurted out, "Do you mind talking to me?"

"Pardon me?" he asked. The confusion on his face was palpable.

"I'm feeling a bit claustrophobic. Talking to someone always seems to help. I wouldn't ask, but I feel like I'm about to totally freak out." She noticed his look of hesitation. "Please. I promise I'm not up to anything."

The man was slightly amused at Joie's admission. "No, I don't mind. You want to join me over here?"

"Okay," Joie quickly unstrapped her seatbelt, switched off the ignition, and joined the stranger in his car. The way she figured, he wasn't going anywhere and neither was she. And the chances of him harming her were nil considering they were surrounded by dozens of other drivers.

He tossed his cigarette out the driver's window when Joie climbed in. Soft classical music played in the background to help pass the time while he waited for traffic to move. "So you're claustrophobic?"

"I haven't always been. But the older I get, it seems like the more things frighten me."

The man extended his hand. It was pink, soft and pudgy. She imagined it was just like the rest of his body. If she had to guess, the man was probably in his early sixties. His head was shaved bald, probably to avoid the dreaded horseshoe that so many middle-aged men acquired later in life. Studying his classic, masculine features, she surmised that he was probably very handsome man in his prime.

"Hi, I'm Larry."

"Joie."

"Nice to meet you, Joie." He studied her appearance, noting the unkempt hair and face void of makeup. The smell of stale liquor was evident with each breath she exhaled. In spite of her current state, she was an attractive woman. "You remind me of my daughter."

"I do? How so?"

"Erica, that's my daughter's name...Well, she's a lawyer. And a good one at that. But she likes to make others think that she's real tough cookie. Truth is she is a marshmallow on the inside."

Joie smiled at his spot on observation. "Larry, we've just met, but you know me already."

"If you don't mind me asking, where are you headed this early on a Saturday morning?"

"I'm on my way home. I was visiting my girlfriend in Virginia Beach." She glanced his way while keeping an eye on the stand-still traffic. "How about you?"

"On my way to work, but now it looks like I'm going to be late. I'm an engineer. I work at the NASA Langley Research Center."

"Cool..." She leaned back in the seat and finally relaxed. "Would you believe that I have lived in Hampton all my life and have never stepped foot on that place? I have always wanted to take a tour, though."

He pulled his wallet from his back pocket, removed a card, and handed it to her. "Call me up. I can arrange it if you'd like. You have children?"

"Eight year old twins." She tucked the card into her purse. "A boy and a girl."

"Well, you can bring them too."

"Thanks. They'll really like that, especially my son."

"My grandkids love visiting the wind tunnels. They think it's the coolest part about where I work." He laughed a hearty laugh. "We also have an old mockup of a space shuttle on the Center. If your twins are anything like my grandchildren, they'll get a kick out of seeing it."

"I think I'm going to take you up on it." She rubbed her temples, trying to quell the throbbing veins.

"You, young lady, appear to have imbibed on one too many. Probably dehydrated." He turned to his backseat and retrieved a bottle of water. "Here. Drink this. Water works wonders for a hangover."

She accepted the bottle, opened it, and drank it down in one gulp. "Thanks. I needed that."

"What was the occasion? If you don't mind my asking."

"My girlfriend and her husband flew into town for the weekend. I haven't seen her in months, so we had a few too many while we caught up."

"I see." He chuckled. "Girl's night out, huh? My wife has those occasionally when she needs to take a break from me."

Joie laughed along with him, despite the painful headache building strength behind her eyes. "Thank you so much for letting me sit with you, Larry. I feel so much better."

"Glad I can help." He glanced at her sideways. "So Joie, what do you do for a living?"

Joie exhaled slowly. "Well... In about a month, I will be doing nothing. I was *downsized*."

"Downsized?" Larry started to light another cigarette, but instead just placed it between his lips. "That must really hurt."

"Hurts like hell, actually. Never thought I'd be in this situation." She felt the tension slip away the more she talked. The man's words were like salve to a wound.

"What are you going to do?"

She shrugged. "Don't know. Me and my husband will figure out something."

"You're married?" Larry asked innocently. "Does your husband work?"

Joie shot Larry a pissed off look. That old familiar chip on her shoulder suddenly became a boulder. "Why do you assume my husband don't have a job?"

"I'm sorry... I didn't mean..."

"You're probably surprised that I even *have* a husband. Right?"

"No, that's not what I meant..."

Joie smacked her lips together and reached for the car handle. All traces of her claustrophobia were suddenly replaced by anger at this man's presumptuousness. "Don't you ever get tired of that view?" she snapped.

"I don't know what you mean," he replied, confused. "To what view are you referring?"

"I'm talkin' about the view that always has you white people on top. Your neck must be tired from all that looking down on everybody else." She hopped from his car and back into hers.

"I'm sorry!" Larry shouted. "I didn't mean to offend you. I was just asking the question because you seem so worried. I didn't mean anything by it... It was just conversation, that's all."

Inside her own car, with the driver's window rolled down, she heard what he said. She replied, "Larry, I appreciate your kindness, but I got this. Anyway, it looks like the traffic is starting to move again."

"Hey, I'm sorry if I offended you," he said. "You have my business card. If you ever need anything... If I can help your family in any way... I don't know what I can do, but give me a call. Okay?"

"Look, I'm the one who should be sorry. I apologize. I've had a really bad week. I'm hung over. I'm claustrophobic..."

"I understand. It's okay."

"Plus, I have a feeling that things will only get worse before they get better."

"Joie, I don't pretend to know what you're going through, but try keeping your chin up."

"Yeah... Sure."

"Guess it's time we get going."

"Guess so... Anyway, thanks again for your kindness." She started up car, raised her window, and put it in gear.

"Good luck to you, Joie!" Larry shouted. His lane began moving before hers. With a wave of his pink, pudgy hand, and a toot of his horn, he continued on his way, ironically rubbing away the kink that had just developed in his neck.

Luckily for Joie, traffic continued on at a steady pace with drivers speeding up once they approached the exit and saw daylight. She always wondered why drivers hit their brakes on the way into the HRBT and stepped on the gas on the way out.

Her cell phone rang as soon as she cleared the exit. It was Ronnie calling again. She hit the accept call button to speak through her car's stereo while she sailed west, well, actually she was heading north, on I-64.

"Hey Ronnie," Joie answered.

"Girl, what happened? After the call dropped, I couldn't get through. The calls went straight to voicemail."

"Sorry about that. I'm on my way home. Got stuck in that damn tunnel..."

"Really? Did you bug out?" Ronnie teased.

"You know I did! That damn claustrophobia hit and I ended up getting into some white man's Mercedes," she joked. "That man probably thought I was crazy.'

"No, you didn't!"

"Oh, yes I did. I had to do something because I was starting to lose it. Anyways, he was cool. Even offered a tour of NASA to me and the kids."

"Girl, you talk to anybody." Ronnie laughed again. "Okay, so now that I know where you are, why did you leave so soon? I wanted to catch breakfast with you."

"I left because Tomas was trippin' last night."

"How?"

"I'm not sure. I only know that he left me a note this morning basically telling me to have a nice life."

"What?! He did that?"

"Yep. Funny thing is I don't even remember seeing him last night because my ass was so drunk."

"Leaving a 'kiss my ass note' does not sound like Tomas…"

"Well, unless somebody else snuck into his suite and wrote me a note, it *was* Tomas. But I ain't mad at him. Not really. I think it's time we both moved on. And besides, I got my hands full at home with my husband."

"Good for you, Joie," Ronnie said. "You're putting your focus on your family where it belongs. Still, I wanted to at least say good-bye. I'm flying out tomorrow morning."

"I hadn't planned on leaving so soon, but I need to get my ass home. Cedric has been blowing up my phone."

"Since we're not coming up, make sure you tell Cedric and the kids we said 'hi'. But, if you change your mind, me and Luis have the evening free. We can jump in the car and be up there in less than an hour."

"Naw girl, that's all right. I really had a good time with you last night—at least the part I remember."

"Yeah, me too." Ronnie said. "I miss hanging out with you."

"Who knows? Maybe me and Cedric will fly down to the DR to visit."

"That sounds real good."

Joie saw the sign for her exit. "Well, I'm almost home. Give me a call to let me know you made it back safe."

"You take care of yourself, Joie. And I hope whatever's going on with you, that you find a solution for it soon. Problems usually don't resolve themselves; they just turn into bigger problems."

"Thanks, Oprah," she replied sarcastically.

"Whatever, heifer... Bye."

"Bye Ronnie. Love you, girlfriend."

"Love you, too." Ronnie hung up with a lingering uneasiness that something was seriously off with Joie. Until her friend invited her in, there was absolutely nothing she could do. Except wait. And pray.

Chapter Twenty-Three

Ever since his lawyer called late Friday night, Cedric replayed those few minutes from that Saturday morning that changed his life, over and over again in his mind. He wondered what would have happened if he'd done something—anything differently.

If only he hadn't taken that particular route through that neighborhood near the park. If only he had minded his own business instead of trying to reach out to those troubled teens. If only he hadn't taken that bag of drugs from Bryson... If only Bryson had stepped up to claim those drugs, he wouldn't be in this mess. If only... Yes, his life had become one big '*If Only*...'. But he had taken that route, he had stopped to talk to those boys, and he had taken those drugs off Bryson. And yes, he had been arrested.

The string of events that followed his arrest was unfortunate, indeed, but just as Hunter Wylie told him, he would have his day in court. He just didn't expect it would be so soon.

Back to that phone call from Friday. Hunter called to tell Cedric that his court date was moved up. Apparently, the city of Hampton was selected by the state of Virginia as a test area to study the outcome of implementing a policy conducting speedy trials involving drugs because so many of their arrests were drug-related.

Cedric Parker was the lucky offender to have his case selected as one of the first in the trial study. Hunter Wylie wasn't sure if this was a good thing or a bad thing. And as he warned Cedric, the outcome of having a speedy trial could go either way.

After Cedric hung up from Wylie, he tried calling Joie several times, but each time his calls either went unanswered or straight to voicemail. He thought about leaving a message or even sending a text, but decided against both. This was the kind of news that you only broke to your wife in person.

In the meantime, while he waited to hear from Joie, he kept the twins up late watching scary movies and eating popcorn. Anything to keep his mind off thinking about the inevitable journey he was about to undertake.

Midnight rolled around and Joie still hadn't called. It was then that he realized she wasn't coming home that night at all. In a way, he was relieved to have the quiet time to think without having to provide answers to her questions that he didn't have.

So after the last movie had played, he put both twins in their respective rooms and crawled into his own bed. He stared up at the dark ceiling wondering where he would be sleeping a week from now since his trial was scheduled for Tuesday morning. And while he waited for sleep to rescue his thoughts from the terror creeping around the edges of his mind, he embraced the darkness, feeling alone but unafraid. He may even have felt a little lost... But considering the numbness he experienced earlier, at least now he felt something.

~ ~ ~

She slipped into the house as quietly as possible to avoid waking her still sleeping family. Or more importantly, she hoped to not wake Cedric. She first went to check on the twins. Both were fast asleep. Next, she tiptoed through her master bedroom, saw that Ced was still in the bed, and went to the walk-in closet to change.

Cedric heard Joie come in because he was not asleep. He had spent the majority of the night tossing and turning, trying to reach some kind of resolution to his family's problems. He threw the covers off the bed and went to find his wife. She was standing in front of the mirror about to brush her teeth.

"I see you finally made it home," he remarked.

Joie jumped, covering her heart with her hand. "You startled me!"

"Sorry. I didn't mean to," he replied calmly.

"I thought you were still asleep."

"That's obvious." His eyes scanned her body from head to toe. "Looks like you had a rough night."

"Yeah... Me and Ronnie...we got a little carried away. Had a few too many drinks."

"Considering you're not getting home until nine o'clock in the morning, I would say so."

"I got stuck in the tunnel. Must have been an accident or somethin'. I almost freaked out."

"Where did you sleep?" he asked point blank.

"Huh?"

"I asked, where did you sleep?"

"In the hotel," she answered, hoping that would put an end to the barrage of questions she knew Cedric held inside. "The Hilton."

"Really? Where did you get the money to get a room at the Hilton?"

"*I* didn't get a room. Um, uh, well, Ronnie had one already arranged for me..." she lied.

"Is that right? Ronnie arranged a room for you?"

"Uh huh," she pulled her dress over her head and hung it on a hanger.

"In whose name?"

"Mine. Why?"

"Because when you didn't answer your cell phone I called the Hilton. They said you weren't registered."

"What was so important anyway? Why were you blowing up my phone?"

"Don't change the subject, Joie. Where were you last night?"

"I told you. I stayed in a hotel room in the Hilton." She pulled a pink two-piece jogging set from the closet shelf and stepped into the bottoms. "Ronnie probably made the reservation in her name instead of mine."

Cedric studied Joie, weighing whether she was telling the truth or not. At this point, he didn't need another fight on his hands. "Fine. I don't want to argue about this."

Joie stopped and stared at her husband. He looked as if he hadn't slept a wink.

"Are you okay?" she asked.

"No, Joie. I got a call from Hunter Wylie last night. That's why I was trying to reach you."

Joie walked into the bedroom and took a seat on the edge of the unmade bed. "What did he want?"

Cedric let out an unimaginably long sigh and joined his wife. "He wanted to tell me that my trial has been pushed up to next week. They have this new program... a trial study in Virginia that promises first time offenders a speedy trial. Instead of waiting around for months, they want to get some of these cases off their dockets fast. Hampton is one of the first cities to implement the program."

"What does that mean?"

He shrugged. "It can go either way, according to Mr. Wylie. I can be acquitted quickly or they'll lock my ass up just as fast and throw away the keys."

"Next week?" Joie asked staring off into space. "That soon?"

"Tuesday morning."

"That's just a few days from now." She leaned her head over onto his shoulder. "I thought the trial was going to be months from now."

"That's what they want to avoid. Clogging up the court system with first time offenders."

"Cedric, I'm scared."

"Me too," he admitted.

"What are we gonna do?"

"I wish I knew, baby. I wish I knew..."

"I love you, Ced."

"I love you, too."

And then Joie did something she hadn't done in months. She got down on her knees and pushed her husband back on the bad. He was wearing only pajama bottoms, so access to his love muscle was easy.

"What are you doing?" he asked, surprised.

"Be quiet." She began stroking his penis lovingly with her warm hands. "I'm doing what I should've been doing all along."

"Uh, okay." He laid back and let his wife have her way with him.

With practiced precision, Joie wiggled Cedric's hips free from the pajamas, tugging the fabric downwards until it rested at his ankles in a heap. She pushed herself up on her hands, leaned over his now erect penis, and placed the tip in her hot mouth. With a flick of her tongue, she almost brought him to climax.

Cedric let out a moan of pleasure.

"You like that, baby?" she asked with a grin.

"Oh yeah... I like that."

She continued to lick, suck, and tease Ced with her tongue until he could hold back no more. Cedric gripped Joie by her arms, pushed her back on the bed, and pulled her pants off in one motion. She then spread her legs wide open in anticipation, willing to give herself freely to her husband.

Cedric found Joie's swollen clit with his tongue, teasing it gently until the first orgasm hit her like a sudden wave. As she revved up for the second wave, he slid his engorged penis into his wife's hot vagina for the first time in months. Joie matched his strokes, pushing her hips into his, until he let his load loose with a loud grunt and an earth shattering shudder. He came so hard that he imagined the neighbors heard him making love to his wife. But he didn't care, because for the first time in a long time, all seemed right with the world.

Joie whispered in her husband's ear, "Welcome home, my love. Your sweet little kitty-cat missed you."

Cedric and Joie spent the next hour in bed, snuggled up and enjoying each other's presence after several rounds of sex. Rather than lamenting over the impending trial, they decided to put the uncertainties of Cedric's arrest behind them and instead focus on making the best of the time they had together. As a family.

"Joie, I hate to spoil the mood with serious talk, but we need to tell the kids what's going on. That I may have to go away for a while."

"You're right. I just hate to tell them anything until we know for sure."

"But what if it turns out that it's not good news? I don't want them to be blindsided."

"You do have a point." She twirled a strand of her hair between two fingers, a sure sign of nervousness. "When do you want to do it?"

"The sooner the better."

"This morning?"

"Sure. How about when we get up?" He released a huge yawn. "That way they'll have all weekend to ask questions."

"I know. Let's do something different today," Joie suggested.

"Like what?"

"How about we take the kids to Buckroe Beach? We haven't been in awhile."

"That's a great idea," Cedric said between yawns. "You know they love the beach. We can talk there."

"Okay. And I'll pack some sandwiches. We can make it a picnic."

"Or we can pickup a bucket of chicken from *Farm Fresh*. Maybe a couple of sides…"

"That sounds good." Joie yawned in response to Cedric's. "The kids love *Farm Fresh's* fried chicken. So do I."

"Me too," he said, as he sank his head into the pillow and closed his eyes.

The noise of the television made its way into their bedroom. It was turned up way too loud.

I guess that's our cue to get up," Joie said upon hearing the twins snickering at Saturday morning cartoons.

"What time is it?"

Cedric glanced at the clock on the nightstand. "Almost eleven."

"The kids must be starved by now." She rolled onto her side. "C'mon. Let's get up."

"You first." Cedric pulled the covers over his head.

"Why me?" she yawned. "I'm still sleepy." Hungover was the more apt description, but she didn't want to add any fuel to the fire that had already been extinguished by making love to her man.

"Baby, I was up with the kids late. I haven't had a good night's sleep in days."

"Fine." She threw the covers off her body and grabbed her robe. "I'll get up with them."

"Thanks. You're the best."

Before Joie could slide her feet into her slippers, Cedric had dropped off into a sound sleep, snoring loudly. She smiled down at her husband. "That's okay, my love. You get your rest now." *Because there's no telling when you're going to sleep this good again. Not after next week.*

She padded into the kitchen, her house slippers making a swooshing noise as she dragged her feet along the floor, and went straight to the drawer where they kept the Tylenol. She opened the childproof bottle and shook two capsules into her hand. Then downed the capsules with a swig of water from the faucet.

The sound of their mother rattling around the kitchen brought the twins into the room. Both Maya and Trey approached their mother. "We're hungry, Mommy."

Joie held her pounding head. "Why didn't you fix yourself a bowl of cereal?"

"There isn't any milk," Maya replied. "We started to eat it dry, but it doesn't taste good without milk."

"Okay. I'll fry some bacon and scramble a few eggs. Give me a minute."

"I like my bacon extra crispy," Trey added. "The last time daddy made us breakfast, the bacon was too soft."

"Extra crispy it is," Joie said, reaching for the bacon from the refrigerator. They were down to the last four slices. She would just have to make her and Ced something else.

"Thanks, Mommy," Maya said.

"You're welcome." Joie began fixing a pot of coffee. As she poured the water into the canister, she asked, "Hey, you guys want to go to the beach later?"

"Buckroe Beach?!" Trey screamed in delight. "We get to play in the water?"

"Yes, you can get in the water."

"Cool!" he exclaimed.

"And what about you?" she asked Maya.

"I don't know. I just had my hair done," Maya replied uncertainly. She flipped her freshly blown-dry locks away from her face. "I don't want to mess it up."

"Little girl. Don't worry about your hair. I'll braid it up afterwards."

"Okay. I want to go," she responded enthusiastically. "I love getting in the water."

"We'll go after your father wakes up," she told them. "Go pack your things. I'll call you when breakfast is ready."

The beach was packed, even for a Saturday afternoon. It seemed that everybody was taking advantage of the nice weather. They set up their chairs, coolers, and beach towels underneath a large beach umbrella, alongside many other families. Usually, Joie was the parent who took advantage of the umbrella's shade while Cedric spent time in the water with the twins.

Like most black women who wore their hair relaxed, salty beach water was not her friend. But today, since her weave was already jacked up from yesterday's romp in the water, she decided to join in the family fun. They left their belongings in the sand and then played in the surf before walking out on the long pier, where dozens of people extended long fishing poles on either side.

Trey and Maya ran ahead of their parents to the farthest end of the pier and peered over the side into the murky water below. Each one trying to be the first to spot a fish.

"When do you want to talk to the kids?" Joie asked.

"They are having such a good time. I'd hate to spoil it with talk about me and jail." Cedric stared at the backs of his children leaning over the heavy wood beams of the pier. "But I guess now is as good a time as any."

"You're right. No time is a good time," she agreed.

"Well then. Let's do it."

Cedric and Joie pulled the kids to an area away from others so they could have a little bit of privacy. They motioned for them to sit on the bench.

"What's wrong, Mommy?" Maya asked upon seeing the serious expression on her parents' faces.

"We need to tell you something," Joie said.

"What?" Trey asked.

"Well, remember those few days when your daddy didn't come?"

They both nodded.

"I told you he went out of town with some of his youth center kids..."

They nodded again.

"Well, that wasn't exactly the entire truth."

Cedric interrupted, "What your mother is trying to explain is that daddy got into some trouble that kept him from coming home."

"What kind of trouble?" Maya asked.

"Do you remember me talking to you kids about how I visited certain boys who were sent to jail?"

Trey nodded. "You told me that jail is a place I never want to end up at."

"That's right." Cedric closed his eyes and then reopened them. This wasn't as easy as he hoped it would be. "Jail is a place I never want you to end up in. Either of you."

Joie squeezed her husband's hand for support.

"Unfortunately, I got into some trouble and was sent to jail. And I might have to go back."

"For how long," Maya asked, looking as if her world were falling apart.

"Hopefully for not too long. I will find out for sure next week."

"Daddy, I don't want you to go to jail," Trey whined.

"Neither do I," Cedric said. "But if I do go away, I need you both to be strong for each other. And for your mother."

"Listen to me. No matter what, me and your daddy will be here for you. We both love you very much," Joie explained. "We are going to get through this."

"If I do get sent away to jail, it is going to be tough. On all of us. I won't lie to you. But you mother will make sure you guys are taken care of."

"That's right," Joie added with a smile. "We will get through this no matter what."

"Will we get to visit you?" asked Maya.

"Sure you will."

Trey didn't say anything. He simply stared at Cedric until tears fell from his big brown eyes.

Cedric pulled his son to him and held him close. He reached for Maya as well. Joie rested her hand on Ced's back to let him know that she had his back. Through thick and thin.

Eventually, after several minutes had passed, Trey pulled away. He wiped his nose on his arm and tried to manage a smile. "I love you daddy."

"I love you too, son," Cedric replied with tears in his own eyes.

"Can we go back and play in the water now?" asked Maya. "I want today to be our special family day. Just us four."

Cedric appreciated his daughter's attempt to diffuse the seriousness of the moment. "That is a great idea. I would like that very much."

"C'mon Trey. I'll race you to the bottom," she said. "Loser has to clean the other's room for a week."

Trey stood to his feet. "Get ready to be beaten, sis."

"On your mark, get ready. Set..." Maya began to count down.

Joie jumped in and said, "You kids be careful. I don't want you running into anyone."

"We will," Trey replied. He looked at Maya and finished her countdown. "Ready. Set. Go!" And then he took off.

Maya stood in surprise watching her brother run through a crowd of people. She screamed out loud, "Trey! I wasn't ready. Come back here! You cheated!"

"Maya, you'd better get going," Joie laughed. "Your brother has a pretty good head start."

Cedric and Joie watched their children run down the pier with the carefree attitude that all eight-year olds should possess. At first, they hadn't taken the news very well, but at least they were now aware of what was happening in their little family. For better or worse, the Parker family would face this crisis head on. Just like they did every other time a crisis arose.

Chapter Twenty-Four

Joie slammed the phone down so hard on its base that a piece of the hard plastic casing shot across the room, hit the side of the refrigerator, and landed underneath the table where everyone was gathered for breakfast.

"Who was that?" Cedric said.

Startled by his mother's reaction, Trey returned the forkful of pancakes he was about to stuff into his mouth to his plate. He had never witnessed his mother behave like that even when she got really angry. He looked to Maya for reassurance. Unfortunately, this time, she had none.

Rather than provide an immediate answer that would probably be filled with a few choice words her children should not hear, especially on a Sunday morning, Joie opened the backdoor and stepped outside. The walls felt as if they were closing in and she needed a quiet space to breathe. It had just begun to rain, but that didn't matter because it would wash away the hot, angry tears streaming from her eyes. She hugged her own self and lifted her face to the sky hoping for a miracle to appear.

Cedric got up from the table and followed his wife outside. "Stay here and finish your breakfast," he told the twins before either one entertained any thoughts about following him.

Joie saw Cedric coming through the back door. She didn't say a word, just stood there shaking her head.

"What is it?" he asked tenderly. "What has gotten you so upset?"

"That was Rufus."

"Rufus?"

"One of my coworkers. He called to give me the heads up before I go to work tomorrow."

"What did he say?"

She took a deep breath and blew it out slowly. "Well, it looks like they are officially going to close the office early."

"What?!" Cedric quelled his rising panic. "How soon?"

"Tomorrow."

"I thought this wasn't going to happen until the end of September."

"That's what they told us." She shook her head from side-to-side. "But according to Rufus, they're going to begin handing out pink slips to employees who weren't offered a transfer."

"Are you sure? Is *he* sure?"

"Rufus is the bosses' assistant. So, yeah, he's pretty sure. The only reason he called me is because we're good friends."

Cedric looked at Joie sideways.

"He's not *that* kind of a friend. Rufus is gay," she replied exasperated. "Anyway, I don't care that he's gay, that is why we became good friends."

"Now that you mention it, I do remember your mentioning his name once or twice."

Several moments passed before she said, "That's what's going on... So, uh, what happened with that job you applied for the other day? Have you heard back on it?"

"No. Haven't heard a damn thing from them or any of the other jobs I've applied for." He wiped the moisture from his face. "Guess what they say is true... When it rains, it pours."

Joie bit her lip trying to hold down the panic that threatened to overtake her. She was this close to losing it. "We are almost broke, Ced."

"I made hundreds of calls looking for work, but just as soon as they found out I was arrested, they lost all interest."

"Baby, one of us needs a job." She dropped her head, trying to push back the waves of defeat. "We're gonna need some money coming into this house."

"I know. I was able to make a little money here and there doing odd jobs around the neighborhood, but most of that went to pay that damn Hunter Wylie for my legal fees. And now that my trial has been pushed to the day after tomorrow, I'm not sure what we're gonna do."

"Hopefully, I can find another job soon. With all my experience, it shouldn't take too long."

Cedric embraced Joie in his arms and allowed the warm, gentle rain to soothe them both. "We'll be all right, baby. Trust me. I'm not gonna let nothing tear us apart."

Joie felt the hollowness of his words echo inside her spirit, as clearly as the rain that fell from the sky soaking them both from head to toe. In spite of what he told her, she knew Cedric did not believe they were going to be all right and truth be told, neither did she.

Chapter Twenty-Five

After spending less than a week in jail, Cedric stood before the judge, proud and defiant, unwavering in the knowledge of his own innocence as he awaited punishment for a crime he hadn't committed. There was no way the judge would sentence him to anything but probation. After all, he was innocent.

The trial was quick—only lasted a day, in fact. When the Commonwealth of Virginia made the determination to lean towards implementing speedy trials, neither he nor his attorney expected the short trial would result in a verdict of guilty. He was immediately reprimanded and placed in jail to await his sentencing. During his time in jail, Cedric used the time alone to mentally prepare himself mentally for this moment. So whatever happened in the next few seconds, he knew in the end truth would prevail. It always had and it always would.

Joie sat on the bench behind her husband waiting for someone to awaken her from this cruel twist of fate. She wanted someone to tell her that this entire ordeal had been a huge mistake and that her man would soon be released. But that is not what happened.

"Cedric Parker, you are hereby reprimanded to the Commonwealth of Virginia for a sentence of not less than twenty years." The judge struck his gavel down forcefully as he made his proclamation. "Bailiff, please place Mr. Parker in custody."

Cedric felt his knees momentarily buckle. "Twenty years?! I'm going to prison?!" he questioned Hunter Wylie in disbelief. "Man, I can't do twenty years for something I didn't do."

"Don't worry," Hunter said, just as surprised as his client was. "I am going to appeal this."

"No!" Joie yelled at the top of her lungs to the judge as he walked from the courtroom to his private chambers. "He's innocent! My husband don't belong in no prison!" She struggled to reach Cedric, elbowing the guards who tried to restrain her.

The judge ignored her outburst. Every mother, wife, and daughter of those he recently sentenced all seemed to somehow share the same sentiment. Sure would make his job easier if they were all telling the truth.

Hunter Wylie nodded to the guards to let Joie through. They did.

"Joie, baby, it's gonna be all right," he told her calmly. He wrapped his arms around her in a loving embrace, not wanting his wife to see how distraught he really was.

"I love you, Ced." She kissed him with a desperation she didn't realize she had. "I'm gonna do everything I can to get you out of here."

"I love you, too." The only way he could handle this without falling apart was to totally shut down his emotions. Step outside of himself as if this wasn't happening.

"This ain't over, Ced. We're gonna get you out of this. I promise."

"Take care of the twins," he told Joie.

"Sorry, ma'am, but you'll have to step back," the bailiff told Joie before placing the handcuffs around Cedric's wrists.

After she watched Cedric being hauled off by the bailiff, Joie directed her anger towards his attorney. "How could you let this happen?! You were supposed to keep Cedric out of jail, but all you've done is take our money!"

"I'm sorry, Mrs. Parker." Hunter Wylie stuffed the paperwork into his briefcase in preparation for his next court appearance that afternoon.

"What do you mean, 'you're sorry?' Ced didn't even have a real jury. What the hell can three people decide in a couple of hours?"

"We do plan to appeal..." Hunter told her. "This was Cedric's first offense, all this business about a speedy trial...he shouldn't have received such a harsh sentence."

"My husband is not a drug dealer, Mr. Wylie. He should not be going to prison at all."

"Look, Mrs. Parker..." He pulled her aside for a private conversation. "...I'll do everything in my power to get your husband's sentence reduced, but I cannot make any guarantees. Virginia has chosen to make Cedric's case an example. His being a first-time offender didn't seem to matter because that judge did not differentiate between Cedric being a first-time offender or a habitual criminal. That sentencing was very unusual."

"You've got to do something," Joie pleaded.

Hunter Wylie's attention was directed to his assistant who had waited patiently in the hallway until Cedric's sentencing was complete. He casually told Joie, "I'll be in touch. Try not to worry."

Joie stood outside the courtroom, fully distraught, and feeling totally alone. She plopped down on a bench next to a man she saw in the courtroom earlier. He was also there witnessing the sentencing of a family member.

"That there judge don't mess around when it comes to drug dealers."

Joie rolled her eyes, choosing not to respond to the man's comment.

"If you're a praying woman, right about now would be the best time to start," the man advised her. "This is the second son I've lost to jail, but at least they're both alive. I lost my oldest son to the streets a few years ago…"

"Sorry to hear that," she replied. "Unfortunately, I have never been a praying woman and I'm not about to start now."

"I will wish you good luck, then." The man stood up and left Joie to dwell in her own miserable existence.

~ ~ ~

That following Saturday, in spite of her maternal instincts kicking in and telling Joie that bringing her kids to see their father locked up was not a good idea, she did it anyway.

The visit to the city jail was more difficult than anyone had anticipated. After Joie signed in on the visitor log, she went through a metal detector, had her purse searched for contraband, and was physically patted down before being allowed inside the facility.

Because the occasional ratchet parent had the audacity to try to smuggle in illegal items on their children, Maya and Trey also received a pat down, although not as vigorous as the one Joie received. Whereas Maya was mortified when the blue-gloved woman told her to raise her arms and turn around while she ran over hands up and down her small body, Trey was in a playful mood. He ended up giggling when the young man performed his pat down.

Two guards led the small group of visitors, consisting primarily of wives, girlfriends, and young children, into a room where they were presented with a laundry list of do's and don'ts for their visit to the jail.

A female guard began rattling off the rules. "You will have thirty minutes to visit with your loved one. While you are here, there will be no touching—that includes kissing, hugging, and holding hands." She looked over the group and warned, "If you want to give the inmate something, you need to hand it to the guard first. Are there any questions?"

After the briefing, the families were led into a cafeteria sized room. Each family selected a table and took a seat. The windowless room was bleak, illuminated by overhead florescent lighting that hissed and crackled. The walls were painted a stark white. The tiled floor was well worn, but kept meticulously clean. The only adornment to the walls was a huge clock which loudly ticked off each precious visitation minute.

Several guards were posted throughout the visiting room, poised and ready to pounce at the first sign of trouble.

Cedric shuffled through the double doors into the visiting area decked out in an orange jumpsuit with the initials HCJ emblazoned across the back. His wrists were shackled to a chain connected to his ankles which made walking difficult. He took a seat on the opposite side of the table where Joie, Maya, and Trey nervously waited.

"You guys look so grown up," he told the kids. "I wish I could give you a hug but…" he glanced down at the handcuffs.

"How are you doing?" Joie asked turning his focus off the obvious.

"As well as I can, considering where I am," Cedric replied. "How 'bout you?"

"Ya know… I'm hanging in…Just trying to handle this situation the best way I can."

"What about your job? Have you heard anything more?"

"As of last week, the office is closed, so I am officially unemployed."

"Any leads on other jobs?"

She shook her head. "I've updated my resume and posted it on all the job websites. Got my fingers crossed that something will come up soon."

"How you doing on money?"

"Better now that your last check hit the checking account."

"Good." He furrowed his brow in deep thought. "You'll need to call the bank. Explain that the mortgage is overdue, but you're going to pay it."

"Wait a minute… I thought you paid it last month."

"Just make sure that you pay the mortgage before any other bills. Okay?"

"Daddy, look what me and Trey made you." Maya pulled a card from her pocket and tried handing it to her father.

Before Maya's small hand could make contact with Cedric's, the guard shouted, "Little girl! You are not allowed to hand any item directly to the inmate!"

Joie shot an angry look towards the guard. "You don't have to yell at my child."

"It's all right," Cedric told Joie. He had heard from other prisoners about family members being escorted out for the smallest infractions. He did not want to waste any time arguing with the guard.

"Those are the rules, miss. Either you and your children follow them, or you have to leave."

Cedric said, "Maya, just hand it to the guard."

The guard approached the family. She took the card from Maya's hand and examined it. After passing inspection, the guard handed it to Cedric.

"This is really nice." He smiled at the handmade card that contained a photo of their family inside. The outside was decorated in colorful scribbles. "Did you guys make this yourself?"

"Mom helped a little," Trey admitted. "But me and Maya did the most."

"I love it." Cedric stared to tear up. "Thank you."

Neither Maya nor Trey were accustomed to seeing their daddy become emotional. Both were taken aback by his reaction. He was always the strong parent—the light-hearted one who always seemed to be happy.

Joie noticed the twins' shocked reactions. She quickly jumped in to shift the focus from their father to hers. "Hey, guess what? I spoke to my dad."

"Oh yeah," Cedric replied, thankful for the change of subject. "How is he?"

"He's doing okay. He moved out of that rental house because it reminded him too much of my mom. He found a one-bedroom apartment in a senior's community. Told me he's actually making a few friends to go fishin' with."

"Good for him." Cedric glanced around the room at the other families. With the exception of one inmate who was white, all the remaining inmates were black or brown and also sentenced on drug charges, primarily marijuana related.

"He asked about you…"

"What did you tell him?"

"Let's not talk about this now." She dropped her gaze. "I don't want to upset you."

"You didn't tell him, did you?"

Joie turned her head.

"Are you ashamed of me?" Cedric asked incredulously. "You think I did what they accused me of?"

"Baby, let's not do this now. Not in front of the kids."

Cedric observed the frightened eyes of his children, comparing Maya and Trey's discomfort against the other kids who were disturbingly relaxed in an atmosphere where children did not belong. *This* was no place for children.

"You're right. I just can't believe you didn't tell your father that I'm in jail."

"He's been through so much. I just couldn't have him worrying about me. About us."

"Daddy, when are you coming home?" Trey asked. His bottom lip began to quiver. "I don't like it in here."

"I don't know. But until I do come home, you are the man of the house. I need you to be brave for your mom and Maya. Can you do that for me?"

Trey lifted his head, wiped the tears from his eyes, and while his bottom lip continued to quiver, he replied in a scared voice, "I think so."

"Well, I know you're scared, but do you think you can be brave. For me?"

The little boy stopped crying upon realizing the momentous task his father had given to him. "Yes, sir. I can be the man of the house until you come home. I'll take care of Mommy. And Maya."

He reached over to touch Trey's hand, but pulled back when the guard shot him a stern look.

"Five minutes until visiting hours are over!" announced the guard.

"Already?" said Joie. "Seems like we just got here."

"I miss you all so much," Cedric said. "If I didn't have you guys, I don't know how I would make it in here."

"We miss you too." Joie's eyes went to the clock. "Have you heard anything else about your appeal?"

"Nothing. I guess since we're out of money, Mr. Wylie has pushed my case to the bottom of his pile."

"Damn!" She shook her head from side to side. "There must be something I can do to help. Maybe I can look into the legal aid defense..."

"There's something else I need to tell you." It was his time to avert his eyes. "I didn't want to say anything until I was sure."

"What is it?"

"They're moving me to a facility in northern Virginia. A real prison for the duration of my sentence."

"Oh no...When?"

"Sometime next week."

"I hoped it wouldn't happen, but I expected as much. After all, this is the city jail. Only supposed to be a temporary spot..."

"One minute!" shouted the guard.

Cedric leaned in towards Joie and whispered so only she could hear, "I don't want you bringing the kids to see me up there. I don't want them getting used to visiting me in prison."

"But how will they see you? Twenty years is a long time, Ced. The kids will be grown by the time you get out."

He stood up and smiled for the first time since he walked in. "Have a little faith, Joie. I am not going to be in prison for twenty years. I can promise you that."

"Visiting time is up. All inmates must now line up to depart!"

"I love you, Ced."

"I love you, too. All of you."

"Bye daddy," the twins said in unison as they watched their daddy shuffle through the double doors.

Joie sighed wearily feeling the weight of the world resting on her shoulders. Her thoughts belied what she wanted to believe. *Have faith? Ha! That's a joke. The only thing that's going to help you now Cedric is a goddamn miracle.*

Chapter Twenty-Six

Six weeks after being downsized, and despite being contacted by several headhunters from major corporations within the Hampton Roads region, Joie remained unemployed. There was a myriad of reasons why she couldn't find a job. The positions didn't meet her high standards, the pay was too low, or she felt she was overqualified—there was always some reason she turned down those persistent corporate headhunters.

Consequently, after weeks had passed with her telling those people where they could get off by insulting her with an offer of an abysmal position, the calls eventually dried up. In fact, ever since the word had gotten out regarding Joie's horrible attitude, she had been blacklisted due to a hot-headed temper.

~ ~ ~

As the trees began to shed their leaves in preparation for the upcoming winter, Joie's ability to hold her financial life had all but unraveled. She had come to dread the mailman's arrival. The mail delivery that used to consist of junk mail, advertisement flyers, and letters to occupants, were now delinquent bills with threats of service interruption specifically addressed to Cedric and or Joie Parker.

She used to be pretty good with juggling money, but with no money coming in to replace the money going out, paying the minimum only took her so far. Not wanting to deal with any of it, the mail went into a rapidly accumulating pile on the kitchen counter.

One morning after returning home from dropping the kids off at school, Joie decided to use Cedric's computer for her daily job search. And after not seeing her husband for what felt like an eternity, being in his office made her feel that much closer to him.

She had just booted up the computer in his man-cave when a loud noise coming from outside the house caught her attention. She peered out the window. Two burly white men stood in her driveway. And parked directly behind her Cadillac SRX was a tow truck. One of the two was in the process of loading her vehicle aboard the flatbed.

"Hey!" Joie tried getting their attention by pounding on the window. When that didn't work, she hustled down the steps, taking two at a time, and ran outside.

"What the hell are you doing to my car?!" she shouted at the men.

"We're towing it," answered one man, while continuing his task of loading.

"Are you Miss Parker?" asked the other man who was punching numbers into a small handheld device.

"Yes, I'm Joie Parker!" she screamed. "Now take my car off your truck before I call the police!"

"Sorry, ma'am. But I have an order of repossession from your bank." The man retrieved a letter from his pocket and handed it to Joie.

"What the hell is this?!"

"That gives me permission to tow your vehicle. If you have questions, I suggest you contact your bank."

The other man did a quick walk around to make sure the SRX was securely attached. Then he shouted to his partner, "That's it! Let's go."

In less than five minutes from first hearing the noise, Joie stood in the now empty spot where her beloved Caddie was parked just a moment ago. She stared at the paper given to her and screamed at the top of her lungs, "Fuck!"

Joie marched back inside the house, located the loan paperwork for her vehicle, and immediately called the bank. She selected the option for car loans and was put on hold. Several minutes passed before someone answered.

"Car loans. How can I assist you today?"

"Two men just came by my house and loaded my SRX on their tow truck. They gave me a letter saying my vehicle was being repossessed."

"What is your name and loan number, ma'am?"

Joie rattled off both.

"Mrs. Parker, I see that your car loan hasn't been paid for two months. We sent you several notices. Our notes indicate we even tried to call you regarding the status of your car loan."

"You're telling me I'm two months behind?" Joie's eyes went to the stack of bills sitting on the counter. "Are you sure? I thought my husband had that taken care of."

"Our records indicate the loan wasn't paid for the months of August or September. Per the terms of the loan, once an account is delinquent for 60 days or more, and unless the party makes certain arrangements, it is our policy to repossess the vehicle."

"And what does that mean?"

"It means that you will no longer have use of the car, but you are still responsible for the balance of the loan."

"What? You take my car and still expect me to pay for it? Y'all must be crazy!" She ended the call and tossed the phone to the side.

Joie walked to the stack of unopened mail, scooped them into a pile, and carried them to the kitchen table. After pouring a cup of coffee, she sat down and methodically opened each letter, arranging the bills into separate stacks according to payment date. When she was finished, the stack of bills that were thirty days late was the highest. And just as the lady at the bank told her, there were several delinquent payment notices from the bank.

"How in hell am I going to pay all these bills? The electric company is threatening to shut off the electricity... So is the gas company. Damn... my cell phone bill is due today. The cable bill is late." She picked up another stack. "We have six credit cards between us and all are behind. I even got a letter from the kids' school about their lunch account being delinquent."

The one envelope that caught her immediate attention was from the mortgage company. The envelope had the words 'time sensitive material' stamped across the outside.

"Cedric told me to pay the mortgage. I guess this bill must have slipped past me." She laughed at the absurdity of the entire situation. "Who am I kidding? All these damn bills slipped past me 'cause I don't have no money to pay them." She ripped the envelope open and quickly scanned the letter. Certain words jumped out, like *past due, delinquent, eviction... October 15th*.

"Damn it! The bank is threatening to evict us on October 15th unless I come up with four thousand dollars!" She glanced at the calendar stuck to the refrigerator door with magnets. "Hell, that's only five days from now. Where the fuck am I going to get that kind of money?"

Her thoughts went to a handful of people who could possibly help. Of course, there was her father. Then there was Ronnie. Possibly Tomas, if she apologized for whatever it was she did that night. And Amir was a distant fourth. No, scratch Amir. There was no way she was going to ask that man for anything other than a job.

She picked up the phone and dialed her father's number. He answered on the first ring. "Joie, how is my baby girl?"

"Hey Daddy, you sound like you're in a good mood."

"For the first time in many months, I feel so much better. Of course, I miss Slim as much as ever. That woman was the love of my life, but I know she wouldn't want me to lie down and give up."

"No, she wouldn't." Joie reminisced. "Momma's favorite saying was, 'I'll quit fighting when I'm dead. Until that time comes, watch out!'"

"Yes Lord! That was my Slim... God rest her soul."

"So, what have you been up to?"

"Been meeting a few folks. Even found a few fellas to go fishin' with." He chuckled. "Never imagined myself living in a retirement community, but it suits me better than I expected."

"You sound like you really like living there."

"I gotta admit, it's not bad. Expensive as all get out, but I'm managing just fine as long as I carefully budget my money."

Joie's heart tugged listening to her father speak about his finances, especially considering her parents should have been set for life, instead of having to 'budget his money'. She couldn't ask him for the money he needed to live on. She would have to find the money some other way.

"Is everything all right, angel? Why are you calling me in the middle of the day?"

Not wanting to worry her father, she had forgotten that she hadn't told him about her job being transferred. Nor had she mentioned anything about Cedric going to prison. In fact, she hadn't told her dad much about anything happening in her life lately.

"I just wanted to give you a call. See how you are..."

"I'm fine, love. No need to worry about your old man." He shouted to someone in the background that he'd be right there.

"Well, I'll let you go, daddy. Sounds like you've got your hands full."

"They need a fourth person to play poker."

"I didn't know you played poker."

"Never used to. Slim didn't like me gambling, so I never bothered to learn. But since so many of these old folks sit around playing cards all day, I figured it would be fun to join in."

"I love you, daddy."

"I love you, too. Give my grandkids a kiss for me. And tell that husband of yours he's going to have to bring you down pretty soon to visit your old man."

"Okay, I'll tell him. I'll talk to you later. Bye-bye."

One down, two to go… There was no way she could ask her father for money. Sounded like he barely had enough to live off of himself.

She then dialed her best friend, knowing full well how Cedric would feel if he knew she was even considering asking Ronnie for a loan. After that weekend when she returned from visiting Ronnie in Virginia Beach, she brought up the subject of borrowing money from the Duarte's with him. He nearly had a fit until she convinced him she wouldn't do it. But today, with no one else to turn to, asking her best friend for money seemed to be the lesser of two evils.

"*Hola?*" Ronnie answered.

"*Hola?* Girl, you are too much," Joie teased. "Sounds like you're really picking up that Spanish."

Ronnie laughed good-naturedly. "What's up, girlfriend? I haven't talked to you since I was in Virginia. Every time I call, I get your voicemail."

Joie knew what Ronnie said was exactly true. She hadn't wanted to talk to Ronnie, afraid she'd give away too much about her crappy life. But truth-be-told, she was jealous of Ronnie's easy life. Envied how her friend seemed to want for nothing. Love. Money. Happiness. Joy. All the things she needed, but never seemed to fully grasp came to Ronnie so easily.

"I'm fine. I just wanted to give you a call. You know, see how things are. With the Duarte's."

"I've got no complaints. Hey, Joie. Hold on a minute." Ronnie shouted something in Spanish. "Okay, I'm back."

"What's all that noise in the background?"

"We're having some work done in the house. I'm having the kitchen remodeled and Luis is having some new equipment installed in his exercise room. I'll be glad when they're finished."

"That must cost a small fortune…"

"I guess so, but most of these workers are Luis's family so we get a break on labor."

"Must be nice…"

"How are Cedric and the twins?"

"We're all good."

Ronnie waited for Joie to state the purpose behind her call. Her friend did many things, but engage in small talk just for the sake of talking, wasn't one of them. "So how's the job?"

"Actually, that's one of the reasons I'm calling. I lost my job a couple months ago."

"What?"

"Yeah, I found out about it the weekend you were up visiting."

"Really? Why didn't you tell me?"

"Because I didn't want to believe it myself. I hoped it wasn't true."

"I'm sorry, girlfriend."

"Yeah, it took most of us by surprise. But I should've known once they started making all those personnel changes."

"Well, with all your experience, it shouldn't be too difficult finding another position."

"That's what I thought. Turns out, I think these damn recruiters are racist. As soon as they hear my voice and find out I'm a strong, proud, black woman, I don't get any return calls."

Ronnie took that comment with a grain of salt because she knew her friend too well. "Joie, don't take this the wrong way, but have you ever thought the reason you're not getting return calls is because of your attitude? And not because you're black?"

"What do you mean? My *attitude*?"

"Girlfriend, I'm not trying to be insensitive, but sometimes you tend to come off a little...well, you can be a bit rough around the edges. Overly aggressive, if you know what I mean."

"Oh? So now you're calling me ghetto?" Joie, already on this side of blowing up, took great offense at Ronnie's privileged observation.

"Wait a minute, Joie. Don't get pissed off at me. You've always said how much you appreciate me telling you the whole truth. I'm not gonna start lying to you now."

"Whatever... Look, I might not have everything you and Luis got, but I'm far from being ghetto."

"I didn't call you ghetto, Joie. Those were your words. I just said that your attitude might have something to do with you not getting return calls, that's all."

"As if you would know anything about my life. You sitting up there on the top of that hill, living in your *villa* with maids tending to your every want. You ain't got nothing to worry about, do you Ronnie?

Things always just seemed to fall into your lap. Hell, even the daughter you gave up turned out to be good."

Ronnie pulled the phone from her face. She frowned at the barrage of backhanded insults coming through the phone. "Joie, what the fuck is going on?"

"Know what, Ronnie. I'm sorry I even called you." Joie felt the hot tears of frustration running down her face. "This call was a fuckin' mistake."

"What did I do? Why are you so angry with me?"

"Cedric was right when he said you were bougie. You've probably never known a hard time in your life. Got everything you ever wanted..."

"Look, Joie. I know you're upset about losing your job, but don't take it out on me. I've been nothing but your friend. I have stuck by your side even when I shouldn't have. Not many women would have continued to be your friend, considering what you did to me."

"See, that's what I mean. At the first chance you get, you throw the shit from the past in my face. Like you've never made any mistakes."

"I know you are upset, so I'm going to let you slide. This time. But if you think you are the only person who has been through some shit, well, I could write a book for you."

"Yeah, yeah, yeah, Ronnie. You're always right about everything." Joie hated herself for the words that poured from her mouth. It was if a faucet of self-pity had been turned on and she couldn't stop lashing out.

"You and Luis don't know how good you got it. Always telling everybody how *happy* y'all are. Well, I know better. And I know you are full of shit because ain't nobody that *happy*."

"Joie, I don't know what is wrong with you, but I suggest you lay off the liquor considering its not even noon yet." She pulled the phone to her chest and once again shouted to the workers in perfect Spanish.

"I'm not drunk." Joie overheard Ronnie giving orders to those workers, which only annoyed her more.

"Obviously, something is wrong."

"Know what, there ain't nothing wrong with me. I'm just finally seeing the real Veronica Pierce. The one whose husband walked out on his wife because she was so concerned with herself that she couldn't see nobody else's problems."

"Watch it, Joie. You are getting this close..." warned Ronnie.

On a roll, she decided to dig even deeper. "I'll bet when you don't feel like fuckin', your perfect little husband takes his little-bitty dick in his hands and jerks off like a good little boy. Like it ain't no big deal."

"That's enough, Joie! If you stopped insulting me for a minute and told me what's the matter then maybe I *could* focus on your problems."

"Know what, Ronnie. I got this. I don't need your fake wanna-be-Dominican ass trying to help me with my problems. Go on back to your perfect little life fixing up your precious little *villa* where you and your husband exploit those poor Haitians for their cheap labor."

Ronnie had had enough of Joie. She told her in plain English, "I'll tell you what. Until you can speak to me civilly, don't ever bother calling me again. Got it?"

"Yeah, I got it."

Both ladies clicked off simultaneously. Ronnie knew something was up, but she was too angry to care. She had given Joie more than enough second chances over the lifetime of their friendship to last a dozen lifetimes. Joie was wrong in saying how charmed her life had been. In fact, only after meeting Luis did it make a turn for the better. And now that her life was finally going well, she'd be damned if she allowed someone else's negativity, even if it was Joie's, to destroy it. When people keep bringing shit to your door and you keep inviting them in, you shouldn't get mad when your house starts smelling like shit.

Joie hung up the phone and backed up against the wall until she could not move a muscle. Her current position was a perfect metaphor for her life—backed up against the wall with nowhere to turn.

She allowed the tears to fall, crumbling her spirit and her body until she dropped down to her knees. With her sharp tongue, she had just pushed away the last person who gave a damn about her. There would be no one who could rescue her this time. No knight in shining armor was going to swoop down and ride off with her into the sunset. And no matter how much she pleaded, *Calgon* was not going to take her away from this situation. Continuing with the metaphor theme, she had made her bed and would have to lie in it. All alone.

Her thoughts went to her mother's untimely death. As much as they differed on matters of significance, she knew her mother did not go lightly. Her mother was a fighter who passed to her daughter the principles of life. There are times in your life when the only way through a battle is to pick up a sword and fight your way through. Joie knew fighting was her only escape. She would have to walk this path, taking every painful step along the way, until she either perished, or made it through to the other side.

Chapter Twenty-Seven

On far too many times to count, Cedric had stood on the other side of the correctional institution fence watching young men being carted off to prison, hoping his presence provided them some tiny morsel of support.

The men who now resided behind these walls were once little boys whose mothers carted them to the center to keep them off the streets. He watched boys grow into teenagers, and then into young men. A few lucky ones joined the military, got accepted into college, or defied the odds and found steady jobs and led normal lives. Unfortunately, they were the exception. Today, he was no longer on the outside looking in. Today, he was one of them. An inmate. A prisoner. A convict. A felon.

He and about thirty other prisoners traveled to the Correctional Facility in a non-descript, retrofitted, white security bus. All the windows were redesigned to allow just a small opening for the prisoners to look through. From the outside, you couldn't see inside the bus. It was almost as if they wanted the men to see their last slice of freedom on their ride to prison. Make them realize what they had given up. Armed guards were posted in front, in the middle and at the rear of the bus, each keeping a close eye for any unusual activity. Before he boarded, he noted that two extra vehicles, each with four armed guards, both led and trailed the bus. Anyone who attempted to stop the bus, or make some sort of crazy attempt at escape wouldn't make it very far.

Cedric sat with his feet shackled to a chain extending from his waist and wrists bound by handcuffs. On occasion, he would glance down at other drivers passing by, oblivious to the dozens of inmates who shared their sacred space on that highway. He wondered how those drivers would react if they only knew they were just a few feet away from convicted murderers and drug dealers.

A nondescript minivan driven by a man with a woman in the passenger seat, and three children in the row of seats behind them rode alongside the bus for several miles. A family. Though both vehicles existed in the same space, the worlds of its occupants were drastically different. Cedric closed his eyes to avoid seeing what he no longer had. Freedom.

He watched the minivan take the exit ramp as the family went merrily along their way. The thought occurred to him, from this day forward, the moment he stepped inside the Correctional Facility, he would no longer be Mr. Cedric Parker. He would forever be relegated to a number.

The first day in prison was a blur. Cedric was strip searched as if he were an animal going down an assembly line. The guards, both men and women, loudly barked out orders without any hint of emotion. "Remove all your clothing! Raise your hands above your head! Open your mouth! Stick out your tongue! Turn around! Bend over! Spread 'em! Next!"

"Does she have to be in here?" asked a young man modestly covering his genitals.

"Boy, I have seen more dicks in this place than I care to count. So unless you hiding something new under your hands, I'd advise you to get your narrow ass over here," stated the female guard.

The young man didn't move.

"Get your narrow ass over there and bend over!" she yelled.

The boy reluctantly complied with the help of a muscular male correctional officer.

A different female correctional officer used her gloved hands to search through inmates' hair. She discovered several nits clinging to Cedric's hair, whereupon his head was shaven and his body was doused in some sort of detergent to remove any lice that may have lingered in other hairy regions of his body. After the sterilization process was completed, he was issued two sets of clothing, two pairs of underwear, and a pair of shoes.

Further on down the line, a guard rattled off instructions on how to receive money from relatives, when and where they could make phone calls, and then provided the daily schedule of breakfast, lunch, outside time and dinner. Lights out was nine o'clock.

Cedric was escorted to his cell by a brooding guard who looked like he would have preferred to be anywhere but there. He had watched a lot of movies about prisons, but nothing prepared him for what he would actually encounter inside. The smell was what hit him first. Urine, shit, sweat and other indescribable odors permeated the air. The next thing that hit him was the filth. And lastly, what affected him mostly was the utter sense of despair. It hung in the air like a thick layer of impenetrable smog.

"This is you," the guard said, stopping in front of a small cell that looked impossible for two men to share. He swiped his card, entered a code, and opened the steel barred door. He told the inmate inside. "Got a newbie here. Play nice."

Cedric stepped inside the cramped cell. It was noon, although you couldn't really tell by the darkness of the cell. Someone had taken a black sharpie and colored over the small window removing any chance of sunlight making its way inside. The cell was lit only by a small lamp.

A bespectacled man stood propped up in the corner holding a tattered paperback book in his hands. A knitted beanie cap held a massive tangle of dreadlocks under control, yet one thick rope of scraggly grey hair had found its way out, trailing down past his shoulders. His bare feet were crossed at the ankles. He motioned to the bed and without even looking he said, "Last guy died a couple of days ago. You get his bunk. The top one."

"Thanks." Cedric walked to the bunk and was about to place his extra set of clothing there. His hands stopped midair. One look at the mattress nearly turned his stomach. A large stain of bodily fluid practically covered the entire mattress. "What the fuck? I'm supposed to sleep on this?"

The other inmate peered over the top of his glasses at Cedric. "They were supposed to bring a new mattress a few days ago. But, yeah, that's your bed."

"Shit!"

"That's exactly what it is," the other inmate said. "And piss and vomit."

Cedric stared at the man. He imagined had Bob Marley lived to be sixty, this is how he would have looked. One glance around the cell let him know that this man was an avid reader. Practically every free space was taken up by books.

"They call me Kicks," he introduced himself. "On account of I will kick the shit out of any muthafucka who fucks with me."

"I'm Cedric. Cedric Parker."

"What are you in for?"

"Drug trafficking," he replied. "And you?"

"First degree murder. I have a black belt in karate. I killed a muthafucka with my bare feet because he disrespected my woman. That's why they call me Kicks."

"I see," Cedric replied hesitantly.

"You and I will be cool as long as you respect my space. Respect my books. Respect me. I will do the same for you. And I ain't no sissy, if you're into that."

"Sissy?"

"Yeah. I don't let no niggahs fuck me in the ass. I love pussy too much, even though I haven't had any in twenty-five years."

"Okay."

"So what's your deal? Are you a punk or not?"

"Naw, man, I'm not into that."

"Then we gonna be alright." Kicks extended his hand. "Welcome to hell, Cedric Parker. Welcome to hell."

Cedric accepted the man's strong handshake. His hands were calloused and strong, meaning he probably worked out. "Thanks, I think."

Chapter Twenty-Eight

Cedric always told Joie that he preferred his old beater over her shiny new car any day of the week. Said his hoopty wasn't pretty, but it was reliable. And most importantly it was his—no monthly car payments to worry about. So today when she took the kids to school in Ced's car, she was thankful for her husband's frugality because it meant she still had a vehicle to drive after hers was repossessed. It wasn't the newest, cleanest, or prettiest car she'd ever driven, but at least it ran well.

"I'll see you both after school. And don't be late because we're going to have dinner with Tequitta and her kids," Joie told the twins.

"We're going to have dinner with Auntie T? I thought you didn't like her," Maya said.

"I don't care who we're having dinner with. I'm just happy I get to eat something besides chicken," Trey added, tucking his hands under his armpits like a chicken clucking.

"Yes, we're going to visit with Tequitta." Joie replied, ignoring Trey. "I thought it would be nice for you guys to see Laila and her brother." *Plus, I need to ask her for a huge favor…*

Maya rubbed her hands along the torn leather of the front passenger seat. She glanced upwards at the loose fabric hanging from the roof and then at the missing window handle. "Mommy, what happened to your new car?"

"Uh, I sent it back."

"Why? Didn't you like it?" Trey asked.

"Yes, but it cost too much. Since I lost my job, I had to send it back to the car dealer."

"Are they going to give it back?" Maya asked. "Daddy's car is okay, but I like yours better."

"No, we're going to keep daddy's car because it works just fine."

"Oh. Okay," Maya said, willing to accept her mother's explanation. "Daddy always said he liked his car better too."

Thanks to carefully budgeting what remained of her dwindling funds, meant she could treat the twins to dinner at McDonald's. Instead of getting her usual meal, she would have just a drink while the kids ate whatever they wanted. They had been so good throughout this entire ordeal and did very little whining regarding the many cutbacks she implemented to save money. The way she figured, they were almost broke anyway so splurging on burgers and fries wouldn't make that much of a difference.

"Oh yeah..." Maya pulled an envelope from her backpack. "Mommy, I forgot to tell you that we need money for our school pictures."

Joie frowned at the ordering form. "Pictures? I don't have money to spend on school pictures."

"Don't forget mine," Trey added.

"Fifty dollars each? You kids must think I'm made out of money."

"Mommieeee...we gotta have school pictures," Maya whined. "I don't know about Trey, but I don't want to be the only one in my class who doesn't order any. Ple-e-e-ease..."

The ringing of the second warning bell resulted in a flurry of activity outside the school. Children who were previously chasing each other around the playground quickly lined up with their designated classes in preparation to enter the building. Joie observed the happy faces of the students in her children's classes, lamenting over how she would come up with the money. She didn't want to disappoint her kids. Not again.

Trey shrugged his shoulders. "That's okay, Mommy. I don't care if I don't get pictures anyway."

"Well, I do!" Maya shouted.

"All right," Joie said, giving in. "When do you need the money?"

"Tomorrow is the last day to turn in our orders." Maya leaned over and planted a big kiss on her mother's cheek. "Thanks, Mommy!"

"You're welcome. Now get going before you're late."

"Bye, Mommy!" Trey said as he slammed the door shut. "See you later."

Joie fretted, "Where in the hell am I going to get a hundred dollars by tomorrow?" She opened her purse and pulled out her wallet. All it contained was twenty-three dollars and some change. Barely enough for a trip to McDonald's and a half tank of gas.

Despite having delinquent bills stacking up faster than she could keep track of, Joie's thoughts raced with ways to get her hands on some cash for the kids' school pictures. At the end of the day, when faced with a mountain of increasing debt of which there was no simple solution to get from under, one hundred dollars didn't seem to be asking for too much.

Her gaze dropped to her hands and settled upon the diamond-encrusted wedding ring resting on her finger. Before she could talk herself out of her intended action, she quickly twisted the band off and tucked it securely inside her wallet. *Screw it! This ring ain't doing me no good just sitting on my finger looking pretty. Might as well put it to use.*

"Bye guys!" she called out watching the twins join their respective class. "I love you!"

Joie's route home took her by several different pawn shops. Lately, it seemed they were popping up on every corner, all promising to offer the best prices for your merchandise. One even touted *Cheap Designer Handbags* on its marquee. It was barely after eight, a time of the morning one wouldn't normally think a pawn shop would be open, but with the cost of living rising faster than wages, pawn shops had become almost as important to the community as banks were.

The marquee for the *Last Chance* pawn shop beckoned her with its red, white, and blue flags flapping in the wind. She turned the steering wheel of the car so quickly that the tires, worn bald by years of usage, squealed on the pavement as if announcing her arrival.

Joie went to the door and pushed the door bell to gain admittance. After she was buzzed inside, she marched into the pawn shop with her head held high, daring the sketchy looking man behind the counter to give her grief. She'd watched enough episodes of *Pawn Stars* to know that owners gave unsuspecting customers next to nothing for valuables in order to keep their own profit margins high. Yet, she was not deterred. Business was business.

"Can I help you?" asked the clerk. The man's voice was graveled hoarse by years of smoking; his fingertips stained yellow by nicotine.

"Yeah, I want to pawn a ring." Joie scanned the store, noting that she was the lone customer.

"Okay. Can I see it?"

Joie pulled the ring from her wallet and carefully set it on the counter. She crossed her arms uncomfortably while she watched the clerk. The man picked up her wedding ring—the one she swore she would never remove from her finger—and held it up to the light, examining it with one tightly squinted eye. Next, he used a special piece of testing equipment to determine if it the gold was real, and the number of carats. Finally, he placed the ring under a machine resembling a microscope, turning it in every conceivable angle to gauge the clarity of the diamonds.

She tapped her foot impatiently on the floor watching his exaggerated, slow-as-molasses movements. Every cell in her body wanted to scream for him to 'hurry the fuck up!' because his methodical examination seemed to take forever.

"You wanna sell it?" he finally asked.

"I hadn't thought about selling it…" She frowned with indecision. "What's the difference?"

"Difference is you pay back the pawned amount plus a whole lot of interest. I can give you four hundred if you want to pawn it. Three if you want to sell."

"That's it?!" She shouted in disbelief. "That ring is worth thousands…"

"Not to me, it ain't." He pointed to the glass jewelry case separating them. "I can't even get rid of the ones I already got."

Joie stared at literally hundreds of rings in the glass display case. Diamond engagement rings. Expensive wedding bands—for men and women. Rings with precious stones in intricate settings were the rule and not the exception. And dozens upon dozens of simple gold bands were arranged according to size. The case also held a dazzling display of diamond earrings, necklaces, bracelets, and expensive watches. This collection rivaled any jewelry store. Looking at the jewelry, she wondered how many other people who'd fallen on hard times had pawned the precious jewels they were once thrilled to receive, just to be able to afford life's basic necessities.

"You know, I never thought I'd have to sell my wedding ring." She rubbed the pale circle left by the missing ring.

"Is that right?" he asked with a smirk.

"I promised my husband I would never take it off. Took months for me to get used to wearing a ring again… It was our second marriage…" she explained.

The man looked on with disinterest. He had heard the same sad story whenever some wife came in to pawn her wedding ring. Occasionally, he encountered women who were thrilled just to get rid of anything that reminded them of an ex, but more often than not, these ladies desperately needed the cash.

When she noticed the man wasn't affected by nostalgia, she quickly shifted to business mode. "How about three hundred and fifty?"

"I'll give you three twenty-five and not a nickel more."

"Fine. I'll take it."

The man placed the ring behind the counter and immersed it in a florescent blue cleaning solution. After he had Joie complete the necessary paperwork and made a copy of her driver's license, just in case she happened to have stolen the ring he wanted to be able to locate her easily, he opened the register and pulled out exactly three hundred and twenty-five dollars.

When she reached the line to enter the date, she paused. "Damn it. That's right… Today is October 14th."

"And yesterday was October 13th. What's your point?"

"Never mind. It's not important," she replied. *I'm about to be evicted from my home. Me and my kids won't have a place to live after tomorrow. That's my point!* But there was no need to share this information with the man. Her family's problems were not his concern.

The money she retrieved off the counter grew heavy in her hand. That ring was a symbol representing love, faith, and trust. Selling it for a few hundred dollars felt like a betrayal of her wedding vows. On the other hand, if Cedric hadn't put her in this position, she would never have to make such a difficult decision in the first place. Joie quickly stuffed the money into her purse lest she change her mind.

The man glanced appreciatively at Joie, eyeing her from head to toe. "Hey, if you need to make some quick money, maybe I can help."

"You offering me a job? In this place?" She turned up her nose as her eyes took in the jumbled mish-mash of items pawned by desperate people in desperate situations. She wanted no part of it.

"Not a job… An opportunity." He raised his eyebrows and grinned mischievously, revealing two missing front teeth. A wicked glint in his eye removed any doubt of his true intent. "If you know what I mean…"

The meaning of the man's words slowly sank in. Realizing that she had just been propositioned, tiny prickles of anger began to grow in the pit of her belly and then slowly crept upwards into her throat where they threatened to spew forth into a vile torrent of words. Her eyes narrowed, both hands went to her hips, and she did a deliberate neck roll. The corners of her mouth turned downwards to put form to the words gathering in her mind. "Excuu-u-u-use me?! You must be…"

"Hold on… Hold on… Before you say no, give it some thought. Beautiful woman like you can easily pull in a couple hundred an hour."

As quickly as the anger came, it was replaced with a sense of desperation about her situation. Basic survival mode kicked in so she listened. "A couple hundred an hour? Seriously?"

He nodded, maintaining that devilish grin. "When you have time to think, and if you're still interested, stop by this weekend. I'll make the introductions…"

The implications of her actions would haunt her forever if she made the wrong decision. Any other time, she would have went off and told the man to go fuck himself. But today… this morning… standing in a pawn shop after selling her wedding ring… she actually considered taking him up on his offer.

"If you don't want to wait 'til then, maybe we can work a little something out right now…" He nodded his head towards the closed door behind the counter leading to the storage room. "Might even let you have that there wedding ring back if you're really nice… And you don't bite."

Before she responded, she took a long hard look at the man standing before her unzipping his pants revealing a patch of dark pubic hair upon pale skin. For a second, she imagined a line of drool had escaped the corner of his mouth. The tight white t-shirt he sported showed several layers of dried sweat stains underneath the armpits. It had been years since she spotted a shirt with ring-around-the-collar, and yet here it was being worn by a disgusting little man who wanted to get busy with her in the backroom of his dirty pawn shop. The gap in the man's mouth, his greasy combed over hair, the bulbous, red-veined nose, and those beady little eyes set inside a head that was too big for his body, slapped her dead across her face. It was clear. He was a snake waiting to sink his fangs into her flesh.

Joie returned to her senses and backed away without uttering a single word. Getting away was the sole thought inside her mind. Thankfully, the door opened without him needing to engage the buzzer.

The scent of the morning air rushing through the open door welcomed Joie back to reality. With a backwards glance at the pawn shop, she whispered to herself, "I must be out of my damn mind. What the hell was I thinking even considering doing something like that? I may look desperate, but there ain't no way in hell I would ever prostitute myself. Fool must think I'm a goddamn crack 'ho."

The sight of her husband's car parked below the *Last Chance* pawn shop's marquee boasting a Columbus Day clearance sale was a ridiculous sight to behold. In many ways, the name of the store was prophetic. But since she didn't embrace the particular notion of prophecy, just thinking about the old snaggled-toothed man asking her to perform oral sex for cash was almost laughable. If it wasn't so pathetic.

~ ~ ~

Several years ago, when Ronnie still lived in Hampton, they often visited the old Fort Monroe Army Post when they wanted some undisturbed time to hang out. So this morning, instead of heading west on I-64 to go home, she headed east. After the week she was having, a little serenity would be nice.

It was a beautiful morning with just enough warmth remaining in the air to not need a jacket. Joie parked in one of the many empty spots located near the fishing piers. This time of day, Fort Monroe was a virtual ghost town as most of its residents were retirees. The only activity came from a half dozen dedicated fishermen standing on the pier holding long poles extended into the choppy water below.

She found an empty park bench facing the water. A gentle steady breeze provided a pleasant jogging experience for two joggers making their way along the concrete walkway bordering the bay. Several large brownish-grey pelicans dove into the murky water, scooping up small fish gliding just under the surface, into their huge mouths. And the sound of seagulls calling out to each other resulted in a surprisingly calming effect.

"I've got to do something. But what? How can I make money when I can't even get hired for a minimum wage job?" She leafed through the small stack of bills she received from selling her wedding ring. "A hundred dollars for the kids' pictures, dinner at McDonalds, and after filling up the tank with gas… I got about a hundred in loose change in my milk jug that I can cash in. Maybe I can pawn a few more pieces of jewelry…" Thoughts of returning to the pawn shop to fulfill that nasty man's request sent chills down her spine, but the thought of being broke chilled her even more. "After all is said and done, we have a few hundred dollars to live on."

Not including the sixty day delinquency on their mortgage, the overdue utility bills amounted to over two thousand dollars. They still owed almost fifteen thousand dollars in credit card debt she and Cedric had racked up trying to get their house together. Then there was the money she still owed on her repossessed Caddie.

At this point, the chance of losing the house was pretty high considering Cedric had taken out a second mortgage a couple years ago. She was still pissed about that, but that anger was for another day. Today she had to focus on fixing the damage. Missing two mortgage payments and having negative equity was all the more reason for the bank to evict her family. Bottom line was, no matter how many delinquent notices and threatening phone calls from creditors she received, if she didn't have the money and no way to pay them, they might as well be pissing in the wind. Because as far as she was concerned, air and piss were the only things they would be getting from Joie Parker.

She wasn't running out of options; she had no options left. At her wit's end, she picked up her phone and scrolled through her contacts, hoping someone, anyone's name, would jump out as a potential avenue to getting a job. One thing that she noticed was that the few acquaintances she had quickly disappeared when she lost her job. As if losing a job was contagious or something.

Her day was wide open. The only thing on her agenda after picking up the kids from school was meeting Tequitta hours from now. She took another deep breath to clear her head.

The very first name in her contact list was Amir, who she hadn't spoken to in months. With a flick of her finger, she dialed Amir's number wondering what his reaction would be to receiving a call totally out of the blue. The phone on the other end began to ring. "Well, here goes nothing."

~ ~ ~

Tequitta and Joie rested in the hard plastic chairs while the girls played with baby Derek in the McDonald's indoors playground. Both Laila and Maya were the perfect big sisters to the toddler, fussing over him as if he were one of their fragile dolls. Trey, on the other hand, had found a couple friends to play with.

"What's going on, Joie? Why'd you want to meet here?" Tequitta asked.

Joie swallowed her pride ten times over by calling Tequitta. With the cruel way she had treated Tequitta for all those years because of her marrying Derek, she knew full well that Tequitta had every right to tell Joie to fuck off.

"Uh, well, it's been a while since we got the kids together. To play. And, I just wanted to catch up with you. See how you're doing."

"I'm doing fine." Tequitta took a sip of her cappuccino frappe eyeing Joie suspiciously. After that visit to her house a couple months ago, she hadn't seen nor heard from any of the Parkers. Yet, because she harbored no ill will towards any of them, she would go along to see what Joie really wanted. She responded, "Actually, things couldn't be better."

"That sounds mysterious."

"For the last couple of months I've been dating Paris—the guy Cedric introduced to me in *Lowe's* a while back. He is so wonderful."

"Good for you! I'm happy to hear you found somebody again."

Tequitta grinned from ear-to-ear, showing off her beautiful smile. "What about you guys? I haven't seen Cedric in months. What's he been up to lately?"

"That's why I wanted to talk to you."

"Is he okay?"

"He's fine. Well, actually he's not, fine." Joie glanced about making sure their conversation remained private. "He's in prison."

"What?! What happened?!"

"Long story short, he got arrested because he was accused of trying to sell illegal drugs. He lost his job right after that."

"Wait a minute... I just saw you guys few months ago. When did all this happen?!"

"The judge sentenced him to twenty years after having some new speedy-trial process. With good behavior, maybe he can be paroled after ten."

Tequitta sat back in her chair. Stunned was the only adequate word to describe her expression. "I never imagined Cedric to be the kind of person to use drugs, much less sell them."

"He didn't. It was all a mistake." She glanced around the fast food joint filled with other parents just like her. She wondered how many other mothers were in similar financial dire straits and splurging at McDonald's. "His lawyer is going to file an appeal..."

"How is he handling prison?" She shook her head. "From the stories I hear from some of our clients, I know it can't be easy seeing your husband locked up."

Joie shrugged. "After they transferred him to the state penitentiary up north, I haven't seen him. He didn't want me bringing the kids up there. And since I don't have nobody to leave the kids with, I haven't been up there to see him either. We talk on the phone once a week."

"The kids must be devastated. *You* must be devastated…"

"Devastated doesn't even begin to describe how I feel."

"Is there anything I can do to help?"

Joie lowered her head, released a deep sigh, and then looked to where her children played with nary a care in the world. Despite all they'd been through, their innocence remained intact. For now.

"Yeah, as a matter of fact, there is. But what I'm about to ask is a huge favor. I don't want you to feel obligated to help because you don't owe us—me, anything."

"I'll help however I can. What do you need? I have a few dollars I can give you right now—" She reached for her purse, sitting in an empty chair.

"I don't need your money, Tequitta." She took another breath. This wasn't going to be easy so she just spit it out. "We need a place to stay. Temporarily, of course. Just until I can save enough money to rent an apartment."

Tequitta paused momentarily. She let go of her purse and returned to her original position leaning back in the uncomfortable chair. "You want to stay with me? You and the kids?"

Joie nodded.

"I don't understand. What happened to your house?"

"That's a good question," Joie replied. "Shortly after Cedric was sent to prison, I lost my job…"

"You lost your job, too?" Tequitta asked.

"Yeah. I sure did." Joie figured she might as well lay all her cards on the table. "We got behind on the mortgage. Pretty soon all the bills starting piling up."

"I-I-I'm sorry, Joie. I didn't realize things had gotten so…"

"Messed up?" she completed Tequitta's sentence for her. "Yeah, things went south pretty quick."

"Does Cedric know you're losing the house?"

She shook her head. "No, but there's nothing he can do about it anyway. We're getting evicted tomorrow. I found some guys willing to move our stuff into a storage unit in exchange for Cedric's album collection, but I'm not even sure how I'm going to be able to afford storage costs. I tried everything I could think of to stay in the house, to make money to pay the mortgage, but with nothing coming in, I've gotten myself into a hole so deep I can't see the way out."

Tequitta furrowed her brow in deep thought before responding. "Yeah, of course, you guys can stay with us."

"Are you sure?" Joie visibly relaxed. "I know I'm asking a lot, but I promise we won't get in the way."

"Don't worry, Joie. That's what friends are for." Tequitta began mentally rearranging her home to accommodate her guests. "I can move the baby in with me. You can take his room. Maya can bunk in Laila's room. Trey will have to sleep on the living room couch."

"Thank you so much, Tequitta. I didn't have anywhere else to go. No one else to turn to since my parents moved away. With our kids being related, you're the closest thing I have to family here."

"I'm sorry you're going through these tough times, but I'm glad I'm here to help."

"Me too." Joie sighed in relief. "Me too…"

Chapter Twenty-Nine

Tequitta pulled up in her driveway and took a deep breath. For the past week, Joie had promised she would move her things out of the living room and into the closet. But as of this morning, the boxes still sat where Joie had first dropped them. Blocking the kitchen door. Although she appreciated her picking up little Derek from the daycare center, something had to change. The house that used to be sufficient for three people now seemed way too small.

"Hi Joie," Tequitta said, gritting her teeth together upon seeing those boxes were still in the hallway.

"You're home late," Joie replied. She was sitting on the living room sofa watching another episode of *Wheel of Fortune.*

"I had a doctor's appointment." She turned her head to listen. The house was quiet. "Where are the kids?"

"I just laid the baby down for his nap. The rest of the kids are in Laila's room watching TV."

"So what do you have going on today?" Tequitta asked, noting Joie wasn't wearing her usual sweats. She poured a glass of wine and headed to her bedroom to change out of her work clothes.

"I'm meeting Amir in about thirty minutes." Joie switched off the TV. "I thought you wouldn't mind watching the kids for a little while so I can get outta the house for a minute."

"What time will you be back?" Tequitta shouted from her bedroom. "I'm having dinner with Paris tonight. Our reservation is for eight."

"I should be back by seven. I'm just meeting for a cup of coffee," Joie shouted back.

"Sure, I can keep the kids as long as you make it back on time."

"Y'all been out every day this week." *In fact, you been out every night since I moved in.*

"Well, what can I say? We like each other's company."

She walked into the kitchen and poured her second glass of wine. "So how did the job search go today? You find anything promising?"

"Not good. I'm either overqualified, under qualified, or the pay is damn near nothin'."

Tequitta glanced around the kitchen at the dirty dishes piled in the sink. Several pop-tart wrappers remaining after the kids had their afterschool snack were strewn across the table. Even though it was almost five o'clock, no signs of dinner were evident. She set her glass down and proceeded to clean up the mess.

"Can you please ask your kids to clean up after themselves? The trash can is just two feet away from the table."

"*All* the kids left a mess. But okay, I'll talk to Maya and Trey."

Tequitta opened the refrigerator and peered inside. Now that there was an additional three mouths to feed, her groceries didn't last quite as long as before. "I thought you were going to cook dinner tonight, Joie."

"It's Friday."

"So? The kids still have to eat."

"Nobody cooks on Friday, Tequitta." Joie snickered. "Anyway, I was planning on ordering a couple pizzas."

"Okay.... You think that's a good idea, considering you don't have any money?"

"C'mon. Pizza don't cost that much. Not when you use a coupon."

"Fine. Order pizza for the kids. I'll pay." She sighed in frustration, pulling a couple of twenties from her stash.

"Thanks, girl. I'm gonna pay you back just as soon as I get a job."

"Sure you will," Tequitta murmured under her breath. She looked at Joie sideways. "You think you should be dating another man while your husband is locked up?"

"I'm not going on a date with Amir. I'm just trying to get my job back. Maybe they can transfer me up to Richmond."

"By the way you're dressed, it looks like you plan on having more than coffee," Tequitta said. "I haven't seen you wear a dress that tight. Ever."

"What is wrong with my dress?"

"Nothing, if you're going for the hoochie mama look. And don't bend over because your girls may jump out and put that man's eye out." Tequitta teased. "But hey, I ain't mad at you. You have to get it where you can."

Joie switched off the television. She stood up and smoothed down her form fitting dress.

"Your hair looks nice," she said to Joie. "Where did you get it done?"

"I did it myself earlier. I picked up a box relaxer and a ponytail from the beauty supply store. Cost me less than twenty dollars," she proudly proclaimed.

"Umh!" Tequitta uttered. "You should have bought us some food instead of buying that fake hair."

For the past week since she and the kids moved in, Joie had kept her mouth shut. But today, she could no longer hold her tongue. The angst she felt over tonight's meeting with Amir and the half pint of gin she had downed fifteen minutes earlier, clouded her judgment and caused her to unintentionally lash out.

"Look Tequitta, I have had just about enough of your judgmental ass talkin' about how I dress, the way I style my hair, and what I do with my time when my kids are in school. You need to mind your own damn business *and* lay off all that damn wine. You don't have no room to be judging me."

"Excuse me?"

"I ain't the damn babysitter, either. Every night since I've been here, you leave me here with these kids and don't bring your ass home until damn near the morning. Stay out all night drinkin' with *Paris.*" She made sure to say 'Paris' in a patronizing tone.

"Okay..." Tequitta pursed her lips tightly. She picked up the bottle of wine and poured another glass. She turned to Joie and quietly said, "If you don't like it here, you are more than welcome to leave."

Joie inhaled sharply. When she spoke, it was more out of anger than anything else. "You know what? That's a good idea. I've been picking up funky vibes from you ever since we moved in. And I've seen you giving me the side-eye whenever you ask me what I did all day. So if you want us to leave, just say so."

"Listen, when you and your kids moved in, I was willing to try to make this work. But you treat me like I'm the damn maid. You haven't washed a single dish or cooked a single meal the entire week you've been here even though I'm the one who bought all the food. None of y'all clean up after yourselves. Plus, I haven't seen you look for a job at all."

Joie raised her chin defiantly and said, "You don't have a clue what I'm going through. I have lost my husband, lost my job, and I've lost my house. I have looked for jobs, but ain't nothin' out there except those that pay minimum wage. I can't support these kids on that!"

"I know that, Joie. That's why I was willing to help you guys out. But if you choose to not respect me in my house or go out and get a job—any kind of job—then I have no choice but to ask you to leave. I can't support three more mouths on what I make."

"Fine. Me and the kids will leave tomorrow. I don't need to be judged by you or nobody else."

"Your choice. You don't have to move out. Just take care of your business. Go out and get a job."

Joie smacked her lips together and rolled her eyes.

"If you do leave my house, that's it. You can't come back."

"Cool." And with that, Joie grabbed her purse and headed for the door.

"If you need to leave the kids here 'til you get yourself together…"

Joie cut her off quickly. "We'll be out of your hair first thing tomorrow morning."

Tequitta was not expecting that response because she knew she was Joie's last resort. "Aren't you even going to say bye to your kids."

"My kids know I'm gonna be back for them. No need to say bye."

Chapter Thirty

Joie sat at the hotel bar, sipping on a dry martini, nervously waiting for Amir to arrive. She *had* lied to Tequitta when she said she was only meeting Amir for coffee. When she called him a week earlier, she had all but promised she would do anything he asked for the right amount of money. And when all was said and done, she settled upon five hundred dollars for two hours of unadulterated fun.

"Oh my, you are a vision of loveliness, Joie." Amir appeared as if he had materialized out of thin air. He leaned over and gently kissed her cheek.

"Hey, Amir. Good to see you again."

He sat on the empty barstool beside her and signaled for the bartender. "I'll have what the lady is having. And bring another one for her."

"Joie, how have you been?" His gaze glided over her voluptuous body; settling upon breasts held back only by the clingy, thin fabric of her dress. He licked his lips in anticipation.

"Considering I agreed to have sex with you for money, I guess I'm not doing so well," she joked.

"Look, if you have changed your mind, I totally understand."

She stared at the handsome African sitting with her. With a puzzled expression, she asked, "Why do you need to buy sex? You probably have woman falling all over themselves trying to get with you."

"That is true. They are. But I am not interested in becoming involved. Getting tied up in a complicated relationship is not part of my immediate plan."

"So do you do this often?"

"What? Meet beautiful women in hotel bars for a drink?"

"Yes…amongst other *things*."

He nodded. "Occasionally, I call up a 'friend' when I need a physical release. So when you called me and said you were interested in getting to know me better, I was very flattered."

"What did you think when I said you'd have to pay?"

The bartender placed a martini in front of them both and discretely left them to their private conversation.

"At first I wasn't sure how to take it, but considering you just lost your job, I guess I understand. You need the money. You feel comfortable with me so I consider this transaction an even exchange. I receive pleasure from you and I provide you with adequate compensation."

"You make this all sound so, so… businesslike."

He sipped his drink slowly. Savoring it. "This is strictly business, my dear. Nothing more."

There it is again. Him and that damn African arrogance! "Just so you know, this is my first time doing this."

"Does your husband know what you are up to?"

"Hell no! And as far as I'm concerned, he never will."

"I understand." He nibbled on his olive. "The details of this arrangement will go no further than you and I."

"Thank you," she replied with relief. From what little she knew about Amir, his privacy was one thing he cherished.

"Well, since this is my first time, can you please tell me if I asked for enough?" Her thoughts went to the pawn shop guy who gave her the idea in the first place. "Is two hundred and fifty dollars an hour the going rate for 'ho's?"

He laughed. "Please do not refer to yourself as a whore. You are performing a valuable service for an important client. And yes, what you have asked is a very reasonable rate. Unless you want to perform specialized services?"

"I don't know what you mean by that…"

"You will soon find out, depending upon how well we, shall I say, *fit together*."

Something about the way he said that last line made her slightly uncomfortable. She almost got up to leave, but the thought of earning five hundred dollars for two hours of work kept her butt firmly planted on the barstool. Amir portrayed an air of confidence that made Joie appear weak in comparison. He knew he was totally in control and it pissed her off to no end.

He leaned slightly forward until his face was inches from hers. With one finger, he discretely traced her cleavage caressing the top of one breast and then the other. "Your skin is so soft," he whispered breathlessly. "You remind me of the women in my country."

"Well, they say we all originated in Africa."

"That is true. But not everyone originates from kings." He kissed her hand. "You, my dear, have the blood of royalty running through your veins. I can tell by the way you carry yourself."

Joie laughed at the irony of his comments. "If my ancestors were African kings and queens, then what the hell am I doing here with you?"

"You are looking at this all wrong. This is a business transaction because you have fallen on difficult times. *This* is not your life. It is only a temporary setback." He winked at her. "Always remember that, okay?"

"I like the way you think, Amir." She wasn't totally lying to Tequitta because she did want to ask about getting her old job back. "So, if you don't mind me changing the subject, I have a question for you."

"Go on..."

"What are the chances of me getting up there in Richmond? In my old position or even a different one?"

Amir leaned forward, placing his elbows on the counter. He raised the glass to his lips and drank down the liquid in one smooth swallow. Afterwards, he turned to look directly at Joie when he spoke. "The positions have already been filled. After you called me last week, I spoke to your supervisor about the possibility of bringing you back on..."

"What did he say?" she asked excitedly.

Amir placed his hand over hers. "I don't know what you did to your boss, but he told the director there was no way he would ever consider bringing you onboard again. I'm sorry, Joie."

"Asshole never did like me!" She removed the olive from her drink and gulped it down. "I'm not surprised that kept the little brown noser on."

"Brown noser?"

"Never mind..." She hopped down from the barstool. "C'mon. Let's do this."

"Aren't you the enthusiastic one?" He grinned. "I like that."

Amir paid the bartender, leaving him a hefty tip. This particular hotel was one he frequented with other ladies for hourly escapades. Because he was a big tipper, as well as a regular, the hotel staff did their best to turn their heads the other way whenever he visited. Today was no exception.

Joie followed Amir up to the hotel room. She shifted from foot to foot while he took his time opening the door. He pushed the door opened and she walked inside. It was a basic hotel room. Nothing fancy. Just a bed, a nightstand, a small chair, and a dresser with a flat screen television sitting atop.

Amir was in charge now. He loosened his tie, carefully unbuttoned his shirt, and placed both pieces of clothing on the back of the chair. Next he sat on the bed and removed his shoes.

Joie stood with her back to the door. Now that she was actually in the room with Amir, the brave front she put on downstairs had all but disappeared. She watched him get undressed. A bead of sweat trickled down between her breasts as her nervousness grew.

"Do you need to freshen up first?" Amir asked while he casually removed his pants and then his underwear.

The sight of Amir's muscular body was a delightful surprise. As far as she was concerned, if she was going to have sex for money, she should at least get some pleasure out of it. Not an inch of fat was visible anywhere. It was obvious he worked out. When she saw Amir's penis, she gasped. The shaft was a beautiful shade of a velvety black she had never seen before on a human. And though it was still flaccid, his manhood hung several inches below his testicles.

"Uh, yeah, I'll be right back," she said nervously.

He stood in the middle of the room, butt naked, and began to stroke his penis. "Don't make me wait too long."

Joie wiggled out of her dress and hung it on a hook on the bathroom door. She sat down on the toilet to empty her bladder. Afterwards, she used one of the washcloths and the tiny bar of complimentary soap to clean up. To her reflection she repeated, *I can do this. I can do this. I can do this. I'm not cheating, I'm just fuckin'. Just need a few dollars, that's all.* When she finally gathered up her nerves, she took a deep breath and opened the door.

Amir was sprawled on his back. His penis was now fully erect and waiting for Joie to put it to good use. He smiled in delight when he saw Joie's beautiful body.

She slowly crept over to the bed, wearing the sexy lingerie she used to wear for Cedric. To make this easier, she pretended she was role playing with her husband, instead of being Amir's 'ho. Her eyes went to his penis; it wasn't just long, it was also thick.

"Damn, Amir! Anybody ever tell you that you got a huge dick?!"

He laughed. "Yes, now that you mention it." He sat up and pulled Joie down to the bed. "I want you to relax."

Joie followed Amir's lead and lay down on her back. When he gently kissed her, it felt nice. She was also thankful she had several martinis to loosen up first. He stuck his tongue in her mouth, teasing hers until she kissed him back.

He rubbed his penis between her legs against her panties. Not wanting to rush, he intended to savor every magical moment. His hands went to the thin fabric of her bra. He cupped one of her breasts, massaged, it and then leaned down to tease her nipples with his hot tongue. Somehow, he managed to release her bra without her even knowing. Then he guided her hand to his erection. A low moan of pleasure escaped his throat when her hand finally touched him.

As Joie gripped Amir's engorged penis in her hand, images of Cedric crept into her mind's eye. And each time she tried to push them away they only came back with more fervor. While her body responded to Amir's expert caresses, her vagina growing wet in anticipation of what was coming, she also felt like screaming.

He carefully pulled her panties down and smiled, revealing his overly white teeth. "I love that you shaved all your hair for me. What a pretty pussy," he said with a thick accent.

She felt his hot breath on her freshly waxed pubic area, that she had waxed bare per his request. His tongue flicked her sensitive skin sending shivers throughout her body. He slid one finger inside while his tongue played with her clitoris. Before she realized what Amir was doing, he had switched positions and now straddled her face. She looked up to see his massive penis dangling above her forehead.

"Put it in your mouth," he ordered, breathlessly.

She tried to push Ced's face out of her mind when she put the tip of Amir's penis into her mouth. She heard him let out a load moan, before he started to pump his buttocks. Up and down, up and down, until Joie almost choked. And it wasn't even halfway in her mouth.

Amir continued to lick, suck, tease and tug until he felt Joie's first wave of orgasm hit. She moaned loudly in undeniable pleasure. He smiled, lapping up her nectar, feeling her thrust her hips upwards into his face.

Having Amir go down on her felt wonderful. It had been so long since she had sex that coming was fairly quick. Joie felt Amir's thrusting become stronger, so she wrapped her hand around his penis to prevent him from shoving it down her throat. In that position, all he needed to do was give one good pump and she would probably choke.

Amir got caught up in the moment. He began thrusting his penis into Joie's mouth. And despite how much she protested while they are at the bar, she looked like the type to engage in anal sex. Or at least he hoped she would. He would even throw in a couple more hundred if she at least tried it.

Joie felt herself gag involuntarily as Amir pumped his penis into her mouth touching the back of her throat. He continued to pump faster and faster, pushing his penis deeper and deeper into her mouth. She felt her teeth scrape his delicate skin, but even that wasn't enough to deter him. When she felt the vile taste of vomit threaten to come up, it was enough to end this before it went any further.

"Stop!" she struggled to say.

He was still so engrossed between her thighs, that he hadn't heard Joie's muffled voice.

"Amir! Stop!" she repeated.

"Am I hurting you?" he asked lifting up and repositioning himself. His chin glistening with her juices.

"No, you're not hurting me," she replied quietly. "I can't do this."

"You can't do what?"

"I can't have sex with you. I'm sorry," she said, getting up off the bed.

"What do you mean you can't have sex with me?!"

"I'm sorry," she apologized.

"You have got to be joking!" he yelled revealing an accent that sounded more African than ever.

"This was a mistake."

"A mistake?!" He stared at her like he wanted to kill her. "You have me drive all the way down here from Richmond, and now you're telling me this was a mistake?!"

"I'm sorry. I thought I could do this, but I can't cheat on my husband."

"So you pick *now* to start feeling guilty about cheating on your fucking husband?!"

"I hope you understand, Amir. I just can't go through with letting you put that..." Her eyes widened in amazement at his penis. "...letting you fuck me."

"Unbelievable!" He stroked his massive hard-on. "What the fuck am I supposed to do about this?!"

She shrugged while gathering up her underwear from the floor. "I dunno. Play a porn movie?"

"I just ate *your* pussy, made *you* come, and now you're leaving me alone to masturbate?! Are you out of your mind, woman?"

She backed away from the bed keeping a watchful eye on Amir. He was furious. Even though she had worked with Amir, she didn't know him well enough to trust he wouldn't knock the shit out of her. Or, forcefully finish what she had started.

"Do I still get my money?" she asked, uncomfortably.

"What?!"

"You said you would pay me. I should at least get half."

"Get the fuck out!" he screamed in English and then started swearing in his native tongue.

Joie hurried towards the bathroom, stepping into her panties along the way. She quickly wiggled into her bra, and retrieved her dress from behind the door. She rushed out of the room and finished getting dressed in the hallway, which was thankfully void of other hotel guests.

There was one thing she knew for certain. No matter what country a man was from, when a woman left him half-cocked and ready to explode, there was no telling what he would do.

Stepping into the elevator, she held her head high; thankful that their little rendezvous did not go any further than it already had. *Okay, so I cheated on my husband. I ain't proud of that, but I am proud that I didn't let that man stick that foot long dick into me. But he did get one thing right. I am a queen and it's about time I started acting like one.*

~ ~ ~

Still reeling from what had almost happened in that hotel room with Amir, Joie was an absolute wreck. She couldn't believe that she had actually considered selling her body for money. Had it not been for an instinctual gag reflex, there's no telling how far down that rabbit hole she would have gone.

Instead of driving home, she allowed Cedric's old hoopty to take her wherever it wanted. Having no destination in mind, she drove aimlessly on the highway until she reached an exit leading to a state park. Luckily, there were just a few other cars around.

She closed her eyes and listened to the quiet stillness of the forest, reliving all that had transpired over the past several months. Went over mistakes and the roles she played in them. She missed her mother, and despite their not-so-loving relationship, Slim had always been there for her with an intelligent and thoughtful word.

She thought about all the people she had pushed away with her sharp tongue and quick wit. Regretted how she had alienated her best friend Ronnie because she was the only who could force her to look in the mirror. And the hateful remarks she made to Tequitta, who was kind enough to offer her and her kids a place to stay, played over and over in her mind.

She thought about Cedric, wondering if she would ever feel her husband's arms around her. If they would ever live a normal life as a family, have a place to call home again. If her children would turn out okay. She questioned what tomorrow would bring, or if there would even be a tomorrow.

Finally, when she was filled with more questions than answers, she closed her eyes tightly to thwart the tears. And when the sun began to slip under the horizon to signify the end of the day, she wept.

Chapter Thirty-One

"Mommy, do we really have to live here?" Maya asked, staring at the gloomy entrance to the three-story building. "It looks so... ugly and decrepit."

She had to admit she agreed with her child. The building was depressing. The façade was finished in dreary, dirty brown stucco. Two large trees, devoid of all their leaves, bordered either side of the building. There was no grass, only dirt and pavement surrounding the exterior. The walkway leading to the entrance was cracked, uneven and discolored from wear and age.

"Sweetie, I wish we didn't have to live here, but it's getting too cold to continue living in this car. I've got to put a roof over our heads."

"That motel wasn't so bad." Maya furiously scratched her scalp, which meant her hair was badly in need of a good shampoo. "Why can't we go back there?"

"We don't have enough money to stay in a motel. I wish I did, but this is going to have to do for now."

Joie parked in the tiny parking lot adjacent to the nondescript *House of Ruth Ministries, Home for Women and Children.* The nice woman on the phone provided detailed instructions on how to find the building, which she described as being "situated off the beaten path". There were no signs or plaques advertising the nature of the building, nor who its occupants were. If you didn't know where you were going, you would never be able to find it.

The anonymity of the location was purely intentional, as many of the women who resided in the small apartments with their children were victims of violence suffered at the hands of their boyfriends, husbands, or significant others. For some women, being homeless in the streets was preferential to abiding by the strict rules associated with living in the apartments. But for the majority, the apartments were a Godsend for them and their children—a refuge from the chaotic, violent lives they would otherwise have to deal with.

Trey was stretched out in the back seat huddling underneath his favorite blanket trying to keep warm; his poor body wracked by another uncontrollable fit of coughing resulting from a cold he wasn't able to shake. Ever since the car's heater had died, staying warm had become an impossible task once the day's temperature dipped below sixty, which was pretty average for October.

"Why can't we go back to Auntie T's house? I liked sharing a room with Laila."

"Yeah, Mommy. It wasn't so bad sleeping on the couch. At least I had first dibs on the television," Trey added.

"I don't want to live here. I want to go home," Maya pouted.

"I wish we could go back home, but we can't."

"Maybe if you were nicer to Auntie T, she would let us move back in…"

Joie cut Maya off with a quick retort. "Listen to me and listen good. We are not going back to live with Tequitta and that is all I have to say about it. I'm doing the best I can, so I need you guys to behave for me. Okay?"

"Yes ma'am…" the twins replied.

"C'mon, kids." She turned off the ignition. "It's starting to rain again so we might as well go inside."

Maya tried to be a big girl by helping her mom with unloading the car. She placed her overstuffed backpack on her small body and pulled the little suitcase, trailing behind her mother.

"Mommy, I don't feel good," Trey whined. Poor Trey had broken the wheel on his suitcase. And between fits of coughing and struggling with his suitcase, he was a pitiful sight indeed.

"Just a little bit further, son. We're almost there…"

"I have your umbrella if you need it," Maya said.

"What umbrella?"

"The pretty yellow one. You used to keep it in the backseat of your car. I borrowed it one day for school. I accidently forgot to put it back."

"*You* have my yellow umbrella?" Joie stopped in her tracks. A huge smile spread across her face. "I thought I lost it when they took my car…"

"Mommy, you didn't lose it. It's in my backpack if you want it."

"Did you know your Meemaw gave that to me before your grandparents moved to Florida?" She started to get a little misty-eyed at the memory. "I thought it was gone for good."

Maya shook her head 'no'.

"She told me that I should use it whenever I started to miss her."

"You want me to open it for you."

"Know what, Maya? I think that is just what we need right now."

Maya reached into her backpack and pulled out the compact umbrella. She undid the Velcro strap holding the slick fabric together and pushed the tiny silver button. With a soft whooshing sound, the umbrella unfolded. "Look! It's big enough for all us to get under!"

Joie laughed in delight watching Maya hold up the beautiful yellow umbrella. The vibrant yellow color was in direct contrast to the dreariness of the day and helped to brighten all their moods. Joie's mother's words from months ago resonated with her. ...*so that you'll never feel alone.*

"Can we please get out of the rain?" Trey said between coughs. "I'm freezing."

"Of course we can." She took the umbrella from Maya and pulled her children close until they were all sheltered from the rain. Covered. Protected. Together. Just like her mother always wanted.

Maya smiled because her mother seemed happy. It had been a very long time since either felt like smiling.

Joie opened the front door of the building. She was slightly taken aback by the bulletproof glass shielding the woman behind the counter from anyone who meant her harm. Or the families who lived there. However, much to her surprise, the small entrance was inviting despite the security measures. Vibrant murals of cartoon animals graced the walls. Several comfortable chairs lined the walls of the space, and a pile of *Lighthouse* magazines were stacked neatly on an end table.

With some apprehension, she approached the counter and tapped on the bulletproof glass. The woman sitting behind the desk gestured towards a built in speaker on the wall to Joie's right. The sign above the small red button on the speaker provided the simplest instructions, *Push to Talk.*

Joie pushed the button and spoke into the speaker "Hi, my name is Joie Parker. I have an appointment with Leticia Myers."

"I need to see some kind of identification, please," the woman said. "You can place it in the drawer below."

After confirming Joie's identity against the names on the appointment calendar, the woman buzzed the door open.

"C'mon kids," Joie called to the twins. "Let's go."

All three followed the woman into an office barely the size of a walk-in closet. The name plate mounted on the door indicated this was the office of Mrs. Leticia K. Myers. Sitting behind a small desk, feverishly typing on the keyboard of an all-in-one computer, with stacks of worn manila brown folders in every conceivable empty spot, was the elderly woman Joie had encountered in that parking lot all those months ago.

"Hello," Joie said softly not wanting to interrupt the old woman.

"I remember you," said the woman upon seeing Joie. "You're the lady I met outside Starbucks. The one who liked to use all that colorful language."

"Wow, you really have a good memory." Joie blushed, ashamed for being remembered primarily due to bad behavior. She extended her hand. "Hi, my name is Joie Parker. This is my daughter, Maya, and my son, Trey."

"Good to see you again, Joie. Nice to meet you Maya and Trey. My name is Miss Lettie." She returned Joie's handshake with a surprisingly strong grip.

"Hi," the twins replied in unison.

Miss Lettie motioned to the woman who let them in. She told her, "Honey, take these kids into the dayroom and give them some fruit." She looked at the twins. "You children like fruit?"

"Yes ma'am," Trey replied for both himself and Maya. "Especially oranges and bananas."

"You are in luck young man because we have both." Miss Lettie smiled warmly. "Now you kids go on. I need to talk to your mother for a few minutes."

After the children left the room, Miss Lettie motioned to Joie. "Take a seat over there."

Joie did as she was told. A brief scan of the small office indicated that Miss Lettie ran the place. The walls were decorated with so many plaques and certificates that very little of the actual wall was visible. Going by the date on one of the certificates of recognition yellowed with age, Miss Lettie had been running the shelter for well over thirty years.

"Thanks for seeing me," Joie replied uncomfortably wringing her hands. "I never imagined I'd ever need to live in a place like this... not that this is a bad place or anything."

"No one ever does," Miss Lettie told Joie. "But sometimes your life looks better on the surface than it really is underneath."

"I guess so." Joie sighed. "Lately, my life has been nothing but a struggle. A struggle finding work, a struggle finding a safe and decent place to live, trying to keep my children in school so they'll have some kind of normalcy in their lives… Miss Lettie, I'm so tired of struggling. I need your help…" Joie's eyes filled with tears she promised herself she wouldn't shed.

"Child, if you live long enough, you will have struggles. We all do," Miss Lettie explained. "Truth is, nobody knows the struggles each of us goes through on a daily basis. People think we have it made because of how good we look; the nice clothes we wear; the beautiful house in the good neighborhood, but they don't really know the hell some of us go through every day."

"This isn't how my life was supposed to turn out."

"You want to talk about it?" she asked, giving Joie her full attention.

Joie hadn't opened up to anyone about the troubles going on in her life. Not to her father, not to Ronnie, not to anyone. But experiencing a warmth she couldn't explain coming from Miss Lettie, she decided to take a chance and finally allow someone else to share the worries plaguing her for months.

"My life started falling apart after my parents moved away. Then my mother passed…"

"My condolences…" Miss Lettie uttered.

"Thanks." Joie then began to ramble on, "After awhile, it seemed like my family couldn't catch a break. My husband got arrested for something he didn't do, lost his job, and was sent to prison. Then my job was transferred to Richmond. I couldn't get another job so when we couldn't pay the mortgage, we got evicted. I didn't have anywhere to go. My father lives in a tiny apartment in Tampa, Florida. He didn't have any money to help because he has financial problems of his own. After we were evicted from our house, me and the kids moved in with a friend. That didn't work out so we stayed at a motel for about a week. When my money ran out, we moved into the car—lived in the park for a couple of weeks."

"Sounds like you handled things on your own for as long as you could."

"I tried my best." Joie's eyes welled up with tears. "After my money ran out and we started living in the car, we showered in the YMCA when we could. We ate peanut butter sandwiches for dinner. And every now and then, we splurged on fast food. But as soon as the weather started to change, I realized we couldn't keep living in the park—in our car, sleeping in tents, pretending like we were camping… Hell, I couldn't even afford to buy gas anymore."

"I understand." Miss Lettie handed Joie a tissue.

"My son was real sick, so I took him to the doctor. But when they asked for my address, I was afraid to tell them we were homeless because I didn't want Child Protective Services to take my kids away from me."

"You had good cause for concern because CPS often steps in under these circumstances…"

"I know." She wiped her nose. "But through it all, I kept my kids in school. I didn't want their education to suffer because me and their daddy couldn't hold things together."

Miss Lettie simply nodded at the familiarity of the story. Every woman who ended up on the other side of that desk all had differing versions of the same story.

"One day I just happened to see the *The House of Ruth Ministries* van. I remembered meeting you so I searched for the card you gave me and I called. I explained our situation to the nice woman. She told me to come in… And well, you know the rest."

She smiled at Joie and said, "Listen to me. I know you probably feel like you're the only person to have gone through bad times, but you're not. I started this place to help women and children who have no other place to turn to. Honey, every single one of these women who live here have faced the same, and sometimes much worse situations."

"I never thought I'd ever wind up in a place like this…"

"Well, you *are* here," she reached across the table and took Joie's hand. "And now that you are, *how* you get out of here is up to you. We can offer you temporary shelter, but you have to do the rest."

"I can honestly say that I never gave a second thought to how woman dealt with situations like this."

"Let's get you checked in." She handed Joie a stack of forms to complete. "The state of Virginia does give us a little bit of money, because we are a non-profit agency. Unfortunately, I have to maintain records of everyone we offer assistance, just in case I am audited."

"This is just until I start working again." Joie leafed through the forms, shaking her head and making sounds of disapproval in the process. "Why do they need to know all this about my kids?"

Miss Lettie peered over her tortoise shell bifocals, pursed her lips, and smiled politely because every single woman who ended up on the opposite side of her desk always told her the same thing. "No one expects to be here very long, but just in case you are, we need you to complete the forms listing the children's school and include an emergency contact. Just in case…"

Joie reluctantly completed the forms which asked all sorts of personal information she preferred not to have answered. *Was she married? Did she or her children suffer any physical or psychological abuse? What was the name of the children(s) father? Where did she work? Was she on government assistance? Who were their nearest living relatives? Where did the children attend school? Did she or her children have HIV, AIDS or any other sexually transmitted disease?* And so on and so forth….

Miss Lettie reviewed Joie's responses. Asking questions when necessary. And about an hour after she sat down, Miss Lettie handed Joie the key to her new apartment.

"Now I need to go over a few rules which are all listed in this brochure. The most important ones to remember are no men, and no illegal drugs of any kind are permitted on these premises. Period. The staff will have access to your apartment 24/7, but most times we will try to provide you with an hour's notice before we enter. There is 10 o'clock curfew, unless you happen to be working a night shift. Your children cannot be left unattended for more than ten minutes." She smiled sweetly at Joie. "Do you have any questions?"

Joie responded by answering 'no', but she felt a little bit of the old Joie creepin' back. Inside her mind she screamed, *"You must be out of your fuckin' mind old lady if you think me and my kids are gonna live under these conditions!"*

"Good," replied Miss Lettie. "There's one more thing… We have a mandatory inspection of the apartment every fifteen days to insure it is being maintained. This place may not be much to look at, but it is a safe place for you and your children. And we fully intend to keep it that way for our next families."

"I understand," Joie humbly replied. "Thank you, Miss Lettie,"

The old woman rose from behind her desk as quickly as her arthritic knees would allow. "Follow me. We'll go get your children and I'll walk you to your new home."

Joie, Maya, and Trey followed Miss Lettie out the back door and into an unexpected courtyard filled with evergreen trees, a surprisingly still-green cover of grass, and a good-sized playground area. The building that looked to be in major need of paint job from the street was a pleasant surprise within the perimeter. The four, three story buildings that made up the apartment complex bordered a courtyard. Each building consisted of nine separate one and two-bedroom apartments—three on each level, a shared laundry room on the bottom floor, and a community dayroom with its own separate television.

Because it was a rainy Saturday afternoon, the dayrooms were filled with children. One could stand in the middle of the courtyard and listen to the cheerful banter of happy children coming from all three dayrooms.

"Mommy, this place doesn't look so bad after all," Maya said, approvingly. "This just might work."

"Wow! They even have a basketball court!" Trey added, forgetting that he wasn't feeling well.

Joie quickly admonished the twins, "We ain't staying here that long, so don't get all excited!"

Miss Lettie shot Joie a stern look but kept her comments to herself. Over the many decades of having worked in the shelter, she had dealt with all types of women in all kinds of circumstances so Joie's reaction to accepting charity was very typical.

"This is just temporary. We're only gonna be here long enough for me to get a job and our own place again."

They stopped at the lowest level of the apartment building located on the far left of the courtyard. Miss Lettie gingerly climbed one flight, taking each one step one at a time. Joie and her children followed the old woman to where she stopped in front of apartment 202. After Miss Lettie caught her breath, she said, "Okay, we're here."

Joie took a moment before fully inserting the key in the lock.

"What's wrong, sweetie?" Miss Lettie asked. "Doesn't the key fit?"

"Yes, it fits. It's just that…it's that…I don't understand how we ended up here…" Joie began shaking her head.

"Honey, just be glad you have a 'here' to come to. Now go on and open that door and get these kids out of this damp air. You already have one sick child. You don't need two."

Joie slid the key into the lock and slowly turned the doorknob. The thought of moving into an apartment reserved for battered and abused women, despite the fact that she was neither, gave her a sick feeling in the pit of her stomach. Her parents taught her to always be self-reliant and to never accept welfare no matter how bad things became. And despite how kind Miss Lettie was, or the sounds of children's happy voices streaming into the space, she knew in her heart that this is what rock bottom felt like.

Maya tugged at her mother's jacket to get her attention. She looked up with those big brown eyes of hers, which in some way made it easier for Joie to push all those troublesome thoughts aside. She pushed the door wide open only to be greeted by the smell of old chicken grease, covered up by the strong scent of *Pine-Sol*. Notwithstanding the sickening comingling of odors, the inside of the apartment was only a tad better than she imagined.

"It's kinda small, ain't it?" Joie asked, surveying the combination living, dining, and kitchen area. Her eyes traveled to the dingy carpet covering the living area and the worn linoleum in the kitchen. The walls were painted mustard yellow, or perhaps the walls were yellowed by age and several layers of grease. *Lawd help me if a damn cockroach runs across this floor.*

"I'm sorry all we have available is this one-bedroom." Miss Lettie motioned towards the sofa. "That there is a sleeper sofa. The children can sleep on the sofa, or you and your daughter can sleep in the bedroom because it sleeps two. Or you can give them the bedroom. It's up to you."

Maya walked over to the traditional style sofa, badly in need of a good slip cover to hide the ugly red and green checkered pattern. She poked it as if she expected the fabric to move under the pressure of her finger. With some trepidation, she sat down on one of the cushions, giving a slight bounce. Her dour expression reflected how they all felt.

Trey scouted the rest of the small apartment. He walked into the kitchen, which was really only a corner of the room, and peered into the tiny refrigerator. "Empty," he uttered in disappointment. Then he ran his hand over the small sink that was positioned next to a compact two-burner stove, and finally took a seat in one of the two chairs at the worn table.

Joie made her way towards the bedroom, but first she poked her head inside the only bathroom. It was tiny as well. The fixtures were dated, obviously well used, but overall the bathtub, sink, and toilet, appeared to be clean and in working condition. The door to the small bedroom had been removed, for reasons unknown to her. The bedroom contained two twin beds, covered in blankets that looked like they needed a good wash, pushed against either wall. A scratched up chest-of-drawers that was missing the second drawer sat in one corner.

A chair that could serve double duty as a dining room chair was placed near the dresser. She flipped the light switch because the only window failed to provide much light in the dark room. There was no fixture to shield the light bulb, so the light that resulted seemed way too bright.

"Well, what do you think?" Miss Lettie asked. "Is this going to work for you all?"

"Where is the TV?" Trey asked, noticing for the first time the lack of electronic devices. There was no television. No computer, not even a clock radio. They had the bare necessities and not much else.

"We don't provide televisions in the apartments, but you're welcome to visit the dayroom." Miss Lettie responded, cheerfully. "Or you may purchase your own TV, but we don't have cable."

"Trey, we can both go down there together," Maya added, trying to lighten the mood.

"This will work fine, for now, Miss Lettie." Joie sat her purse down on the table. "It's better than living in the streets. Right kids?"

The twins began to grumble under their breath. Neither one wanted to stay.

"Good, good, good," Miss Lettie said. "Well, you'll find everything you need in the closet. Sheets, towels, extra blankets. And you can come on down to the pantry to pick up a few things to get you started for the next few days. We have all kinds of goodies here because lots of good people make donations."

"Miss Lettie, I can't thank you enough for everything you've done for us. If it wasn't for your kindness, my children would probably be with CPS by now."

"You're welcome, Mrs. Parker." She walked toward the door. "Come on down whenever you're ready to stock up your pantries. We're open until six."

"Thank you, Miss Lettie. Thank you so much," Joie replied. For the first time in her life, she felt a sense of gratitude.

Joie decided to give the kids the bedroom. Anything to make this experience a little less painful. She took the sofa sleeper. While they were getting situated in the apartment, deciding what to put where, and how they could make the dreary surroundings into a semblance of a home, an unexpected knock came at the door.

Trey called out, "Mommy, somebody's at the door. Do you want me to get it?"

She dropped what she was doing in the bathroom. "That's all right, Trey. I'll get it."

Joie opened the door to find a borderline obese woman, who reminded her of Monique in the movie *Precious*, right down to a red bandana tied around her head, standing on the other side. From the impression she gave with her cross-armed impatient stance, this was not a 'welcome to the neighborhood' visit.

"Hi," Joie said.

"Are you Joie Parker?" the woman asked.

"Yes."

"Here." She thrust a plastic cup topped by a yellow lid towards Joie.

"Excuse me?" Joie asked. "Who are you?"

"My name is Linda." The woman thrust the container at Joie again. "I need you to pee in this cup."

"What for?"

"Baseline drug test," she replied, matter-of-factly.

"Nobody told me I had to take a drug test."

"Well, I'm telling you now." Linda took a step to come inside. "So let's get to it."

"Whoa! Hold up! You think I'm gonna pee in this cup?! And let you watch me?! Just because you show up at my door?!"

"Those are the rules. If you want to stay here, you have to take a baseline drug test and weekly ones after that. I'm surprised Miss Lettie didn't tell you... She must have forgotten."

Joie told Maya and Trey who stood listening intently, "You guys stay here. I'll be right back." She stepped outside with Linda. "Come on. I want to speak to Miss Lettie about this."

Linda exhaled loudly showing her annoyance. "You're just wasting your time. But go ahead. I'll follow you."

Both women marched down the stairs and across the courtyard back to Miss Lettie's office. Joie was full of righteous indignation; Linda was simply sick and tired of going through the same scenario time-after-time with these new occupants. She didn't make the rules, she just enforced them.

The elderly woman was at her desk sipping a cup of hot tea. Joie knocked on the door. Miss Lettie looked up.

"Back so soon?" she asked.

Joie responded, "Miss Lettie, this woman says I have to take a drug test. Nobody said anything about me having to take weekly drug tests."

"Oh, I see you've met Linda." She carefully set the cup on her desk and sorted through the pile of folders until she found the one she was looking for. "I must have overlooked it when we went over the rules of living here. Linda is right. Before you can live here, you need to take a drug test. You'll have one weekly and sometimes no notice. It just depends…"

Joie opened her mouth to tell both women where they could stick their mandatory drug tests. But then she thought about her kids, her situation, and knew that she had nothing left to fall back on. This was it whether she liked it or not.

"Your choice," Linda added. "But if you don't do it, you *and* your kids have to leave."

Miss Lettie chimed in apologetically, "It's really not that bad, Joie. It will only take a few minutes. Then you're done."

"Fine," Joie replied in defeat, seeing that her options were to pee in the cup or return to being homeless and living in the street. She snatched the cup from Linda's hand, walked into the nearest restroom, pulled down her panties, perched over the toilet, and peed into the cup while Linda watched. And in that moment, the realization hit Joie like a ton of bricks that she had just lost her last remaining thread of dignity, along with everything else.

Chapter Thirty-Two

The laundry room filled up quickly on Saturday mornings, which is why Joie was there late Friday night trying to get a jump on everyone else. Although each building's laundry room held six washers and six dryers, it still wasn't enough to satisfy the needs of all its occupants without having to wait for others to finish.

"You new here?" asked the woman folding clothes on the nearby table.

Joie nodded.

"Welcome to the neighborhood. I'm Ranesha Graves."

"I'm Joie. Nice to meet you," she replied. "How long have you lived here?"

"Let's see… We moved in about three months ago. Since it's the beginning of October, that means I've lived here three months longer than I ever expected." She laughed.

"That long, huh?" Joie joined in the laughter. She checked out the laundry Ranesha was folding. "I see you have a son."

"Umh huh," She pressed the t-shirt to her chest. "Got two kids. A boy and a girl."

"For real? Me too. Mine are twins. Just turned nine years old."

"Is that right? We should get together some time. My daughter is five and my son recently had his thirteenth birthday."

"Cool," Joie replied, happy to finally meet someone who was friendly. Most of the other woman she had encountered since moving in kept their distance, for whatever reason. "Well, this is my last load."

Ranesha tore a corner from a magazine she was reading and began to scribble. "Here is my cell phone number. Call me sometime when you want to get together."

Joie accepted the paper. "I don't have a phone anymore. Had to give it up after I lost my job."

"Woman, go on down to the county office and get your free phone. That's how I got mine."

"You got a free phone from the county?"

Ranesha pulled the cell phone from her back pocket and showed it to Joie. "Yeah girl. It might not be the newest model, but it works just fine." She laughed.

"Umh! I didn't know the government gave away cell phones, especially smart phones." Joie examined the phone in disbelief. "You sure?"

"Once you sign up for welfare, you can get an EBT card too."

Joie guffawed, "I ain't about to sign up for nobody's welfare. I am gonna get myself a j-o-b."

"Well, excuse me." Ranesha reached for her cell phone, offended by Joie's arrogance.

"I'm sorry, I didn't mean anything…"

"For your information, I start working next week for a temp agency."

"Congratulations!"

"It's only an entry level position, but there is potential to go full time after three months."

"Girl, you're doing good just having a job these days. I wish I could find something that paid a decent salary like the job I used to have," said Joie.

"I ain't trying to burst your bubble, but you need to let go of what you *used* to make and instead focus on what you can make now." Ranesha gestured by snatching the air with her hand for emphasis.

"You don't understand… I used to have a professional job that paid *good* money. I'm not supposed to be… here."

"Look, I was just trying to help you. That food down in the pantry only goes so far, and until you get a j-o-b, it's gonna be really hard to feed yourself and those two growing twins."

"Don't get me wrong. I appreciate you telling me about the cell phones. It's just that I'm afraid if I get on welfare, me and my kids will get used to it and end up falling into the trap so many of us black women get into. You know what I mean?"

Ranesha turned away to transfer her wet laundry from the washer to the dryer. "Just because you need a hand up, don't mean you are getting a handout, Joie. And not all of us women on welfare are good-for-nothing, lazy, welfare queens who sit around on our fat asses having babies just to get more money from the government. Some of us have just fallen on hard times. That's all."

"I know all about falling on hard times because I'm living in them right now," Joie replied. "I'll tell you what… First thing Monday morning, before my appointment at the employment office, I'm going to go down to apply for a free phone. I'm gonna need one when they start calling me about a job anyway."

"There ya go," Ranesha said. "So give me a call when you get your phone. We can split a pizza and a bottle of cheap wine while the kids are watching TV."

"I'll do that," Joie said. "See ya later, girl. By the way, it was really nice meeting you."

"Likewise," she replied. "By the way, for what it's worth, I've met lots of women since I've been living here and you're right... You don't belong here. And the sooner you get out of this place, the better your chance is of never having to return."

"What do you mean?"

"You were right about what you said earlier. Once you get used to the government taking care of you, it makes it that much harder to go out and earn a living. I've seen it too many times from women who intended to use welfare just long enough 'til they could get back on their feet. Problem is, welfare provides a better living than working a minimum wage job. Some people catch an attitude of 'why struggle when you can get what you need for nothin'?'"

"Well, I appreciate you saying that." Joie stuffed the last of her freshly washed clothing into a pillowcase she used to double as a laundry basket. "Because this will be the first and last time I ever plan on sucking on Uncle Sugar's tit. My momma and daddy didn't raise me this way and I for damn sure ain't about to raise my own like this."

~ ~ ~

The first two weeks living in the apartment rolled by fairly easily. Residing in the complex with dozens of other women and children in various precarious relationships, took some getting used to. But for the most part Joie, Maya and Trey were adapting rather well. The worst part of living in the apartments was a lack of privacy—everyone knew each other's business, including what time you left in the morning, when you got home, who stopped by for a visit and how long they stayed—but at least it was a safe environment. Although Miss Lettie was strict, she was also very generous with providing Joie with the necessities she needed to make the apartment feel more like home.

To help break the ice, Joie invited Ranesha Graves and her children over for pizza and a movie on Friday night. She hoped they could all become friends.

The pizza delivery guy stood outside her apartment door removing two large boxes from an oversized warming sleeve a half hour after Joie phoned in the order. She bought two large pizzas thanks to a two-for-one coupon she had received in the mail. Nowadays, this simple dinner was a luxury she could only afford on the rarest of occasions.

Joie had just opened the door when they all showed up.

"What's up, Joie," Ranesha remarked, inhaling the aromas of melted cheese and pepperoni. "Looks like we got here right on time."

"Hey girl," Joie said as she checked the boxes to make sure her order was correct. "Yeah, you're just in time for pizza."

"These are my kids, Rain and Bryson. Kids, say hi to Miss Joie."

"Hey, Miss Joie."

"Y'all c'mon in. Maya and Trey was just about to start watching a movie." She pulled a crumpled twenty dollar bill, along with the coupon for a free pizza, from the back pocket of her jeans and paid the pizza guy. "Keep the change," she told him because after paying for the pizza, it was only a dollar and change left.

"You two can go back to the bedroom and introduce yourselves," Ranesha told her kids.

The children rushed past their mother towards the bedroom where Maya and Trey were watching television.

The driver stuffed the money into his pocket and hurried back to his car. Even though pizza joints no longer guaranteed a thirty minute delivery or get a free pizza, the young driver discovered that people gave more generous tips when their food arrived fast.

"Let me help you with those," offered Ranesha.

"Thanks."

"Look what I brought..." Ranesha pulled two screw top bottles from her handbag. "Wine!"

"Cool!" Joie retrieved a stack of paper plates and several plastic cups from the cupboard. She reached inside the refrigerator and pulled out a milk jug, now filled with sugary grape flavored kool-aid.

"You want me to open a bottle now?"

"Stick one of those bottles in some ice for a minute so it can cool down. You can use that big bowl under the sink. And put the other one in the fridge."

Ranesha removed her jacket and draped it across one of the two kitchen chairs. She filled a large bowl with water and ice cubes and jammed the bottle into it.

"Kids!" Joie yelled into the bedroom. "C'mon and get your pizza!"

All four children rushed into the kitchen, each jockeying for a position around the small table. When each child held a plate with two slices of pizza and their cups were filled with kool-aid, Joie shooed the kids away. "Y'all can take your food back to the bedroom…"

"Mommy, you said we ain't supposed to eat in our bedrooms," Trey reminded her.

"Well, you can today." She set two plastic cups on the table and partially filled both with the lukewarm wine. "I'm making an exception today because we're celebrating."

"What are we celebrating, Miss Joie?" Rain asked.

"My first week on the job, that's what." She shooed them once again. "Now get on outta here so me and your mama can talk."

"Yes, ma'am," they replied in unison.

"Come on, guys," Maya called out. "The movie is about to start."

Ranesha picked up both cups, handed one to Joie, and then lifted hers up. "A toast. To both of us finding jobs, and to getting the hell outta this dump."

"To us!" Joie picked up her cup, tapped it to Ranesha's and took one huge gulp.

The sickeningly sweet liquid caused Joie to gag. She spit the wine back into the cup. "What kind of wine is this? Vick's cough syrup?"

Ranesha laughed out loud at Joie's reaction. "Quit trippin'. It's not that bad."

"I'll let you tell it." She picked up the bottle and read the label. "The last time I had wine this nasty was when I was a teenager shoplifting from the local drug store. Ooowee! Never been so sick in my life as when I drank that mess."

"Keep drinking. Trust me, it gets better." Ranesha downed what remained in her cup.

"The hell I will. I don't need no hangover when I got to work tomorrow. That job down at the Peninsula Town Centre might not be what I'm used to, but I don't want to lose it because I smell like rot gut wine." Joie emptied her cup into the sink. "That was some nasty shit!"

"Oh well… More for me."

Joie handed Ranesha a plate with a slice of pizza. "Eat this. I don't want you getting sick up in here. Throwing up all over the place so I have to clean it up."

"Thanks." A long string of mozzarella cheese dangled from the slice to her mouth. "So tell me about the job. How do you like it so far?"

"The people are nice... My schedule is all over the place... The pay sucks... But, hey, I'm just thankful to finally be working again. After a few months of saving up my money, I'll have enough for the deposit on a two bedroom apartment."

"I'll know you'll be glad to get out of here."

"What about you? How's your job?"

Ranesha exhaled long and hard. "At the rate I'm going, I ain't never gonna be able to get my own place with the way they been cuttin' my hours down at the call center." She took a long sip. "And, to make matters worse, I'm already coming up on my fourth month living here."

"Damn... Do you think Miss Lettie will let y'all stay longer if you need to?"

She shrugged. "I don't know. Six months is the limit."

A commotion coming from the bedroom drew both ladies attention away from the cheap wine and cold pizza. Loud shouting, mostly coming from Bryson, filled the bedroom where the children were supposed to be watching a movie.

"You want to see what's going on, or should I?"

"It's your apartment..." Ranesha replied, continuing to indulge in her cheap wine. "But since it's my child doing all the yellin' I guess we should both go."

They went to see what all the commotion was about. Joie pushed the door open to find all four kids standing opposite each other. The boys stood less than a foot apart, as if they would begin throwing blows at any moment.

Trey screamed at Bryson, "You better take it back or else!"

"I ain't taking nothin' back. Your daddy is a liar!" Bryson shouted holding his balled up fist at Trey. "He the reason why we livin' in here!"

"My daddy ain't no liar!" Maya jumped between Bryson and Trey.

"He is a liar! And he a thief, too!"

Trey moved Maya out of his way. "You better stop talkin' about my daddy."

"I ain't gonna stop talkin' about him because he stole my momma's rent money! He ain't nothin' but a liar and a thief!" Bryson stood before Maya and Trey with tears streaming down his face.

"Whoa! Wait a minute!" Joie got between the boys. "What in the world is going on here?"

None of the children said a word.

"Bryson? What's the matter?" Ranesha asked.

He scowled at a picture of Cedric sitting on the dresser. Tears of frustration streamed from his eyes. His mother didn't know that he was the one who took her rent money and he surely didn't want to tell her now.

Maya spoke up and said, "He said daddy stole their rent money."

"What?!" Joie looked from Ranesha to Bryson and back again. "Y'all know my husband?"

"No, Joie," Ranesha replied. "I didn't even know *you* until a week ago, and I don't know nothin' about your husband."

"Then what is Bryson talking about... Why is he saying Cedric stole your rent money?"

"Bryson?" She took her son by his arm. "Young man, you better start talkin'. Do you know Miss Joie's husband?"

"If that's him in that picture, yeah, I know him."

Joie's eyes went to the beautifully framed photo perched atop the dresser sitting next to the television. It was a family picture she insisted upon taking when they were remarried. They decided to dress everyone in white and purple that day.

"How do you know my husband, Bryson?"

"I know Mr. Parker from the youth center. He was one of my counselors." He used the back of his hand to wipe the tears from his face. "I used to think he was cool."

Ranesha picked up the picture for a closer look. "Oh yeah, I seen him before." She scrunched her face, making a funny expression. "I didn't know this was your husband."

"Yeah, that's my Cedric." Joie crossed her arms protectively across her chest. "He, uh, lives up north."

"Oh..." Ranesha replied uncomfortably hearing Joie's curt response. "I'm sorry, girl. I didn't know."

"That's okay. I don't like to talk about it..."

Ranesha refocused her attention on her son. She needed answers. "Bryson, why did you tell these kids that Mr. Parker stole my rent money? I thought you said you didn't know what happened to it."

The teenager turned sullen, not wanting to admit what he did to contribute to his favorite counselor getting arrested. *If only Mr. Parker had minded his own business, none of this would be happenin' to me.*

"Boy, you better tell me what the hell is going on!"

All eyes were now on Bryson waiting to hear the secrets he kept hidden for months. They were all curious about what he had to say, but none were more adamant about learning the truth than his mother. He dropped his head to stare at his feet which wanted to flee from all their questioning.

"I gotta tell you something, Mama."

"What is it, Bryson?"

"You didn't lose your rent money that day."

"Say what?" She focused all her attention on Bryson. "Keep talkin'."

"I took it." He sniffled. "…from outta your purse when you was sleeping."

"You did what?!" Ranesha reached out and impulsively slapped Bryson upside his head. "I ought to kick your little ass! Had me questioning myself like that!"

"Ranesha!" Joie shouted. "You don't have to hit the boy!" Hitting children was where she drew the line. It was one thing to punish a child, but neither she nor Cedric believed hitting them accomplished anything except resentment.

"I knew I had that money in my purse." She covered her eyes with one hand and shook her head. "Where is the money now? What did you do with it?"

Bryson took a step backwards. Out of his mother's reach. Ended up with his back pushed against the wall.

"Well?!" she asked.

"I used half the money to buy…" He dropped his voice so low it was barely above a whisper. "I bought some drugs with it."

"You did what?!"

"I'm sorry, Mama!" He pleaded, "…don't be mad. When you told me you didn't have enough to pay all the rent, I wanted to help so I bought some pills with the money you had. I was gonna give you back the rest when I sold enough to pay all the rent. Those boys said if I sold them around the neighborhood, I could make a lot of money."

"Oh my God… I never meant to burden you or your sister with my financial problems." Ranesha whispered, distressed. She had tried her best to shield her kids from the temptations of the street, but the older Bryson got, the more difficult it became. It took every ounce of will power she had to not remove the belt from Bryson's pants and beat the mess out of him.

"Mr. Parker saw me talking to Heat and 'em in the park. After he found out what I was doing, he took the drugs and the money from me. Said he would go to the bank and then give me all the money we needed for rent. He told me I could pay him back by working down at the youth center. But he didn't come back. And that's why we got evicted. Because he stole our money."

Joie's heart raced upon hearing Bryson's admission. *You have got to be fucking kidding me! This was the child Cedric helped? And now he's standing right here in my decrepit apartment confessing that those drugs were his? What are the chances of this actually happening?*

Ranesha pressed her lips tightly together and narrowed her eyes until both resembled mere slits. She hissed, "Your husband took my son's money? My rent money? Is that true?"

"Wait just one minute!" Joie took in the irony of the situation. "You don't know this, but my husband was arrested because he was carrying your son's drugs."

Ranesha blinked twice to clear the anger clouding her vision.

"That's right! My Cedric is up there in that damn prison for the next twenty years because they thought he was dealing drugs to children!"

"What? You're telling me that your husband was sent to prison over this?"

Joie nodded.

Ranesha looked at Bryson. "Did you know about this?"

"Kind of…"

"What do you mean? Kind of?"

Bryson returned his mother's stare. "We were there when the police stopped Mr. Parker. Me and Rain. He looked at us when they handcuffed him and put him in the back of their car. I thought he was gonna tell on me, but he didn't. I didn't know he was still in jail."

"Why didn't you say something?" Maya asked Bryson. "Why didn't you tell the police those were your drugs instead of letting my daddy go to jail?"

"I didn't say nothin' because I didn't want to get in trouble."

"Damn shame..." Joie exclaimed. "All this could've been avoided if Bryson had just spoken up."

"And then what, Joie?" Ranesha asked. "What do you think those police would have done to my child?"

Joie remained silent as she pondered her friend's question. Considering the state of siege on black men in America today, she knew all too well what could have happened, which is why Cedric intervened in the first place. Her husband had made taking care of fatherless boys one of his goals in life, much to the detriment of his own family.

"I'll tell you what they would have done. They would have sent his little ass to juvenile detention as quick as you could open your mouth. After that, he would be just another little niggah in juvie. Part of the penal system." She smacked her lips together and declared, "Well, you came by it honestly, because you just like your no-good daddy."

She turned to Joie and added, "This boy's daddy is a weak-assed, good-for-nothin' sonofabitch who owes me thirteen years of child support. But I ain't never gonna see a single dime because his ass is always in prison, about to go to prison, or just getting out of prison."

Joie wondered how such a God-fearing woman like Ranesha could denigrate her son's father to his face. It was bad enough to hear what she thought about the man, but to hear her actually compare Bryson to a man she held with such disregard was very troubling. Even if Joie felt her children's father was the devil himself, she could never say those ugly words about him to them.

Bryson flinched when he heard the comparison to his father. He had never met his daddy. According to his mother, he was basically just a sperm donor. Either way, he was not a part of his son's life. So hearing his mother say he was just like his daddy was more painful than getting slapped upside the head.

"Well, we got to do something because my husband don't belong in jail for protecting Bryson. It ain't right..." Joie crossed her arms tighter across her chest, trying to control her growing anger.

Bryson glanced around the room at his mother, his sister, and the Parker family. Seeing their troubled expressions, he shrugged his shoulders and said, "I'm sorry. I didn't mean to get Mr. Parker into trouble. I was just trying to help my momma."

Ranesha went to her son and draped her arm across his shoulder. She gave him a little squeeze. After all, he was still her child. "I know you weren't trying to get him into trouble. I just wish you had come to me first."

Holding unto the picture of his family, Trey asked naively, "Why is everybody so mad? Since those drugs weren't my daddy's, this means he gets to come home. Right Mommy?"

Joie exhaled slowly as her eyes scanned the contents of the miserable little apartment. She took in the bed's worn mattress covered by a threadbare blanket they found in a pile of discarded household items in the storage room. Trey discovered the small television in the apartment next door when the last family moved out a few days ago and quickly claimed it as his. She looked at her children who were both several pounds lighter than they should be. And then she studied her own reflection in the small mirror. The care she used to take in her appearance was gone. Because weaves cost more money than she could afford, she had resorted to using boxed relaxers. Her clothing budget was reduced to only what was necessary. She now lamented over how far they'd fallen.

But mostly, Joie took in the aftermath of a child's bad decision and how it had affected her family. In an instant, their entire world had changed. She couldn't hold Bryson responsible. He was just trying to help out his family without fully understanding what the consequences of his actions would be. And as for Ced... Well, Ced was doing what he did best—helping troubled kids stay out of trouble. He could have turned Bryson in to the authorities. He had every right to. Yet, he didn't.

"Mommy? Is what Trey said right?"

Joie opened and closed her mouth several times trying to figure out a way to respond to a question to which she had no answer.

"Mommy, is daddy going to come home now?" Trey and Maya asked again.

Joie's mind raced. Hearing the desperation in her children's voices, she wanted nothing more than to tell them that everything would be fine.

"Well, is he?" Maya asked desperately.

She turned to Ranesha when she responded to her children's questions. "I hope so, kids. But it's not just up to me."

While the movie the kids were so excited about droned on in the background with superheroes using their special powers to fight off terrifying villains, Ranesha played out different scenarios in her mind as she kept her arm draped protectively over Bryson's shoulder. As much as she wanted to protect her child from this, she knew that by doing so would only make it easier the next time he decided to make a quick dollar. What if he became a drug dealer? What would happen if he got into some dumb beef over territory that neither one of them could ever legally own? Or worse, what if he robbed and killed an innocent person? How far would she go to protect him from himself?

"Ranesha?" By saying her name, Joie posed an unspoken question without actually uttering it out loud.

Finally, with a heavy heart, Ranesha responded sorrowfully, "Yeah. We'll help you, Joie. We'll make this right."

Upon hearing his mother's declaration, Bryson sank to the floor. He didn't cry. He wasn't scared. He was simply relieved to have finally unloaded the heavy burdens he shouldered about stealing his mother's money, Mr. Parker getting arrested, and them getting evicted from their home.

Chapter Thirty-Three

The citizens of the Hampton Roads region awoke early Saturday morning to streets covered by four inches of heavy wet snow. The weathermen said the first snowstorm of the season had arrived late, considering it was December.

After months had passed of corresponding via letters, email, and phone calls, Joie decided the time had come to visit Cedric in prison. She was finally able to get a free weekend, hoping this would be the perfect time to take a trip. Too bad this was the weekend the snowstorm hit. Joie called the bus company to see if the buses were still running. They were delayed, but the trip was still a go.

Just as they agreed, Ranesha showed up to Joie's apartment at exactly six o'clock carrying a travel mug of steaming hot coffee and a bag of day old donuts. She knocked on the door.

"C'mon in!" Joie called out.

She let herself in with the key Joie had given her for emergencies. "Hey girl, it's just me."

"Good morning, Ranesha. Thank you so much for watching the kids. After all this time of not seeing my husband, I miss him more than I ever imagined." She looked behind Ranesha. "Where are your kids?"

"They're still asleep. Bryson is old enough to watch Rain until I get back. I'm only a few doors away if they need anything. Besides, I thought it would be easier to get all the kids together once everybody is awake."

Joie laughed. "Just wait until my kids see this snow."

"Is is alright if they play outside?" Ranesha took a sip from the canister. "My kids love playing in the snow."

"Uh huh. As long as they put on their hats, gloves, and boots. They can stay outside until their little fingers start to shrivel."

Joie stuffed a change of clothing into her backpack and used a large plastic storage bag for toiletries, filling it with a toothbrush, toothpaste and deodorant. She checked her reflection in the mirror. "I hope he likes my new look. I don't think he's ever seen me without a weave."

"I think you look beautiful."

"Thanks for saying that." She ran her hands over her short afro. "I hope he don't think I look like a boy."

"How long has it been since you last saw each other?"

"Almost three months. Ever since he was sent up north."

"That's a long time." She took another swig of coffee. "How come you're not taking the kids with you? They're always asking about their daddy."

She sighed long and wearily. "Cedric said he doesn't want the twins to see him in prison."

"I understand." Ranesha contemplated Joie's situation and the role her family had inadvertently played in it. "Well, since Bryson told that lawyer what really happened, maybe he can do something to get your husband's sentenced reduced. You never know."

"So what did old Hunter Wylie have to say when Bryson told him the drugs were his?"

"Not much. But he did mention something about y'all being behind on your payments. Said he needed more money before he would look into it."

"What an asshole! Bryson practically dumps Cedric's get outta jail card in his lap and all he can worry about is money?!"

"I'm sorry, Joie. I don't know what else to tell you. Without your attorney to plead your husband's case, you are just flailing in the wind. He said you would need a miracle to get him out without his help."

"Is that right? Well, now that I know for sure those drugs didn't belong to Cedric, there ain't no way in hell that I'm gonna sit here and do nothing while my husband is in that prison."

"For your sake, I hope your attorney changes his mind."

Thinking about Hunter Wylie caused Joie to grit her teeth.

"Bryson knows what he did was wrong. I know it too, that's why I'm not about to let his little ass think he's gonna get by without being punished. Your husband sacrificed his freedom to keep my son from turning into a drug dealer. I swear that we gonna do what we can to help y'all. Your husband will be home in no time at all."

"From your lips to God's ears," Joie mumbled.

Ranesha replied in surprise, "Joie Parker! I do believe that is the first time I have ever heard you mention The Lord. I was starting to think you were a heathen."

"I ain't no heathen, woman. I was raised in the church."

"Is that right? Then why don't you go anymore?"

"I don't know. I guess religion hasn't been that important to my life. I don't see how going to church is going to change anything."

"You just haven't found the right church. Ask Miss Lettie about the one she and I attend. Give it a chance again. It might just change your life, like it did for me."

"Well, you have got to tell me about how church changed your life another time. I'm gonna be late if I don't get the hell outta here. My bus leaves at eight and it'll probably take me an hour to get there since the roads are covered in snow."

Ranesha shrugged her shoulders. "Not much to tell. I just made the decision that my life was much better with God in it than it was without. Once I opened my heart and accepted Him as my Lord and Savior, things just started happening for me. Good things."

"If your life is so much better with God in it, why in the world are you living in this decrepit dump?"

"See that's my point exactly, Joie. I could be living on the streets. Or my kids could be in foster care. The way I see it, I am blessed to be here. At least I sleep in a nice warm bed every night. And even if it ain't all that I used to have, I believe this is not all that I'm going to have either."

"I'll let you tell it, girlfriend. But what I know is the struggle is real and if God wants to come down and reveal Himself to me, well, then maybe I'll do the religion thing again. Until that happens, I'm gonna put my faith in me, myself, and I."

"Alrighty then. I will leave that subject alone." She placed a doughnut in the microwave. "You want one?"

"Yeah, I didn't have time for breakfast." Joie wrapped the donut in a paper towel and stuffed it inside her purse.

Ranesha turned on the faucet which took a moment for the water to flow. "What's up with your water?"

"I don't know. I put in a service request. Guess it takes a while for them to get to me."

She rolled her eyes in disgust. "If our maintenance man wasn't so busy doing who knows what, he could probably have been up here already."

"Did I tell you that me and the maintenance man used to go to school together back in the day? I ran into him a couple days ago when he was working on the furnace downstairs."

"Is that right?"

"Yeah, he said that if I ever need anything fixed around the apartment that he was more than happy to stop by. He even gave me his private number."

Ranesha cleared her throat before she spoke. "You know, Joie, not everybody you run into has your best intentions at heart. Not everybody brings goodness with them."

"Huh?"

"You'll probably found this out for yourself, but when you live in a place like this, you tend to run into all kinds of people who want to take advantage of us. They think we're stupid for letting ourselves fall this far. Even if the situation that got us here is totally out of our control."

"Girlfriend, what in the world are you talking about?"

"I'm just saying to be careful who you let into your life." She grinned slyly. "Your old friend the maintenance man...? Well, he's been known to fix a lot more than backed up toilets around here."

"What? You're telling me that the maintenance man is really *a maintenance man*?" Joie laughed out loud.

"Uh huh. That man has taken more booty calls than anyone I have ever known."

"Thanks for the advice, but I was not born yesterday. I know how to deal with men."

"I'm not saying that he's a bad person. Just be aware of his real intentions." She shrugged innocently. For all I know, he's providing a valuable service here. At least these woman don't have to go far to get their swirl on."

"Damn girl. You make it sound like he's with a different woman every night."

"Probably not every night." She laughed heartily. "But for real though... I believe every person you run across touches you. And from what I've noticed, they usually either add or detract from your life."

"You sound just like my mother. She's always talking about what people bring into her life..." As soon as the words came out of her mouth, Joie realized she had temporarily forgotten her mother was no longer alive.

"Your mother sounds like a smart woman. I'd like to meet her one day."

Joie dropped her head when she responded, "She passed earlier this year..."

"I'm sorry. I didn't know…"

"Thanks. I tend to forget that she's no longer here. In fact, I find myself picking up the phone to call her when I need to talk."

Ranesha focused on her coffee while Joie busied herself with packing.

She stuffed the family picture—the one that started all the drama, into her bag for Cedric. After several minutes passed, they allowed the awkward silence to end naturally before either spoke again.

Joie planted a kiss on each of the children's foreheads as they slept. Checking the weather report once more on the little television to make sure the snowstorm had passed, she shrugged into her coat, put on her hat and gloves, and slipped her purse over one arm.

Ranesha said, "Have a safe trip and tell your husband that I look forward to meeting him one day. Tell him to stay strong. Keep the faith."

"Thanks again for watching the kids." She rushed out the door and into the cold. "My husband don't belong in that prison, Ranesha."

"I know he don't," Ranesha responded back. "And so does God."

Chapter Thirty-Four

Taking the *Express City* bus up north was exactly how Joie imagined it would be. The gruff driver was late, the bus was overcrowded, and the interior looked like it hadn't been cleaned in years. Many east coasters referred to the *Express City* bus as the ghetto line. The rickety bus often broke down somewhere along the way to New York, leaving passengers stranded for hours.

Even though the accommodations weren't the best, the cheap fare made up for Joie having to sit elbow-to-elbow next to a teenage girl with dyed purple hair, who kept nodding off on her shoulder.

The bus was scheduled to arrive in D.C. by eleven. Visiting hours at the prison were from one to three. The way she figured, she would get off the Express City bus in D.C., and then transfer to another bus which took her to northern Virginia where Cedric was held.

Considering they got a late start because of the bad weather, they made very good time. The heater sputtered out a weak stream of lukewarm air, barely warming the passengers near the back. The only toilet didn't flush. This drew loud complaints from those who had to use the bathroom, but none were louder than those that came from the unfortunate passengers seated opposite the smelly compartment.

Several hours later, the bus sputtered into the parking lot of a bus station located within the outer beltway of D.C. The driver announced loudly over the intercom, "We will be making a ten minute stop to allow passengers to disembark. Any through passengers who aren't on the bus when I close the door will be left behind."

Joie gently nudged the girl's head from her shoulder and quickly gathered her belongings. She took one last look at the teenager who couldn't have been more than sixteen, but wore enough makeup for a woman twice her age. Every instinct told her this child was a runaway, but this was not her problem. Not today.

She disembarked from the *Express City* bus and hurried to the bus station to purchase a ticket for the Greyhound bus. The exchange at the ticket window took less than ten minutes. Feeling lucky that she was able to catch an earlier bus, she found a seat near the window.

The Greyhound bus was parked alongside the *Express City* bus. She noticed the purple haired teen with her head now propped against the window as if she were still asleep. A poorly dressed middle-aged man, with bloodshot eyes and a week's growth of beard, stopped at the seat where Joie had sat minutes before. He stood over the teenager, staring down at her and then glanced around to see if the girl was alone. When the man noticed Joie staring at him, he smiled a wicked grin displaying badly discolored teeth. He took the seat next to the girl. *Poor thing,* Joie thought. *Of all the passengers for that child to sit next to for the next few hours, it's a damn pervert who found her. Those assholes must have victim radar or something...*

~ ~ ~

The taxi dropped Joie off in front of the prison. With towering concrete walls topped by rounds of razor wire, it was an imposing place to say the least. The area immediately surrounding the prison was totally devoid of trees, bushes, and any other formation that may provide coverage for an escaped prisoner. The grey sky and cold wind only made the setting seem bleaker, if that were possible. She counted at least four guard towers from where she stood; each strategically situated to allow unobstructed vantage points for the armed guards to monitor the prison. The visitor's entrance was not difficult to locate because a long line of mostly women and children stood patiently waiting for the one o'clock siren to sound.

Joie clutched her coat tight around her body to ward off the cold wind that whipped down across the open fields. She was glad she had worn her knit cap and warm boots because that hawk was no joke. After just a few minutes of waiting in line and listening to other women chit-chat like they were old friends catching up, the one o'clock siren sounded and they where let into the waiting room.

Correctional Officer Higgins, also known as CO Higgins was the guard in charge of her group. He was much nicer than she thought he would be, especially when she told him it was her first visit.

He stood before the visitors in an authoritative stance with both hands positioned at his waist. By the size of the man's biceps, it was obvious he worked out on regular basis. The bulky belt he wore was weighed down by handcuffs, a billy club, a canister of pepper spray, and of course, his weapon.

In a loud booming voice he announced, "All right, ladies and gentlemen. I need you to follow all our instructions. Anyone who deviates from the rules will be removed from the visitation area. You must remain on the opposite side of the table from the inmate. You may kiss your prisoner once at the beginning of the visit, and again at the end. Only approved items may be handed to the prisoner."

Joie tentatively raised her hand, resulting in disapproving glances from several of the other ladies. Her interruption was wasting precious visitation time, in their eyes.

"Ma'am? You have a question?"

"Yes. I brought a picture of me and my kids to give to my husband. Is that okay?" She pulled the picture from her backpack.

CO Higgins signaled towards another guard standing at the back of the room for assistance. The guard made his way to Joie.

"You may give your prisoner the photograph, but the frame and the glass remain here," instructed CO Higgins.

She handed the picture to the guard and silently watched as he removed the photo from the frame. He tossed the glass in a trash can and returned the picture to Joie.

Loud sighs came from several women, followed by comments from the others. *"Don't she know she can't give no prisoner glass? That was so stupid! Looks like somebody didn't read the rules before she came here! I hope she know she wasting our time!"*

"Thank you," she said, ignoring the rude comments from the regular visitors.

Joie chose an empty table away from the others. Whereas many of the ladies behaved like they were at a family reunion, she had no intention of making friends with them.

~ ~ ~

When Cedric first received the letter from Joie asking if it were alright for her to visit, he balked. Three months of prison had not been kind to him. The food was barely edible and since he had no money on his account to purchase anything from the prison canteen, he often went hungry. He figured he had lost at least twenty pounds.

But now that the day had finally arrived when he would see Joie, he could barely contain his excitement.

Kicks took notice of the improvement in his cellmate's mood. From his usual place of standing in the corner with a book in his hand, he asked, "Young brother, what has brought about this change in your attitude? You're usually pissed off."

"Man, my woman is coming to visit me today."

"That's cool man. It's good that she wants to see you."

"Yeah, I haven't seen her since I was moved up here months ago. This is her first visit."

Kicks peered over his spectacles and asked, "Really? Why hasn't she come before?"

"It's hard traveling all the way up here, especially with the kids."

"You do realize that this will not get any easier as time passes."

"Yeah, I know." He fingered the books recently delivered to him by his ex-wife, Lovely. "Man, would you believe my ex actually came here to bring these to me?"

"Your ex? Why in the hell would your ex-wife visit you? But the more appropriate question is, why in the hell would you *want* your ex-wife to visit?"

"Aw man, my ex really ain't that bad. She's just young. Plus, she's already moved on to someone else. She just came up here to give me my books—the ones she accidently packed up with her school shit."

"Take my advice and let that ex move on." He peered over his glasses. "You two got kids together?"

Cedric shook his head.

"Well then, like I said, let that ex move on. Ex-wives and current wives are like oil and water. They don't mix."

"You got that right. My wife took one look at Lovely and threw both her shoes at her." He laughed. "And one actually hit."

"Damn Cedric... I didn't know you was a player."

"Naw man. One woman at a time is enough for me." He stared at the pictures of Kicks and his ex-wives. "Joie is the only woman I need. Or want."

"My last wife used to visit me all the time for the first couple of years I was locked up. Right around year three the visits trickled down to mostly holidays and my birthday. After that, I would see her once a year at Christmas. I believe it was somewhere around the sixth year, she stopped visiting altogether. I got served with divorce papers soon after."

Cedric pondered the possibility of not seeing his family ever again. It hurt like hell. "Well, that's not going to happen to me. My wife is faithful to our marriage. And to me."

"Is that right?"

He replied angrily, "Look man. I'm sorry your wife checked out on you, but my girl is different."

"For your sake, I hope your wife *is* different. Ask around. Most of the brothers who were married when they got locked up in this joint have gotten divorced, especially those serving long sentences."

"That's not going to happen to me."

"If you really love this woman like I think you do, why make her suffer by being tied to this kind of a life? Release her so she can live."

A guard appeared at the door, interrupting the men's conversation.

"Inmate Parker, you have a visitor. Let's go." He placed his electronic access card against the scanner to unlock the door.

Cedric glowered at the older man, holding back his anger against Kick's presumptuous attitude about something he knew nothing about. Yet, he held his tongue. There was no way he was going to mess up this visit over an argument with an institutionalized old head prisoner who hadn't seen the outside of prison walls in over thirty years.

Kicks studied him from his corner. "Think about that I said, young brother. No wife should ever have to get used to coming inside a men's correctional facility to visit her husband."

Cedric held out his hands and allowed the guard to place the handcuffs around his wrists. Then he shuffled out the door and into the hallway to wait with a dozen other prisoners who were granted visitation privileges. They began their short walk going through several doors that clanked tightly behind each section of prison they went through. The closer he got to the visitation room, the harder his heart beat in his chest. *What if old ass Kicks was right? What if Joie decides she can't wait for me to get out? And worst of all, what if she stops believing in my innocence?*

~ ~ ~

Joie sat at one of the tables impatiently waiting for a glimpse of her husband. One by one, every prisoner who emerged through those heavy metal doors was greeted by squeals of delight from the women and children who waited on the other side. She compared those reactions to some sort of warped graduation ceremony, only there was no one graduating. There was just a semblance of happiness after months of suffering through a loved one's absence.

She glanced at the huge clock hanging on the wall over the entrance. It was already one thirty. The second hand loudly ticked away each moment of visitation at an incredible speed. Experiencing a brief moment of conspiracy theory, she imagined the clock was rigged so that visiting hours were shorter than the actual time allotted. Perhaps just another head game to mess with the prisoners, she surmised.

Joie searched the faces of the children waiting to see their fathers. Some were excited, others not so much. She was glad she had left Maya and Trey at home because they did not belong there. She secretly wondered how many of these prisoners had also been children visiting their fathers in prison. It was a vicious cycle that sucked you in and spit you out.

When she had convinced herself that Cedric had changed his mind and returned to his cell, she caught a glimpse of the man she called her husband. In spite of herself, she happily shouted out loud, just like all the other women when she spotted him.

"Ced, baby, I'm over here!" Thank goodness he smiled; otherwise she might not have recognized the thin man who stood before her. He was at least thirty pounds lighter. His skin was ashen; his eyes were sunken, his cheeks seemed more chiseled. He now sported a cleanly-shaven head whereas he used to keep his hair cut short. The mustache was also gone.

He rushed to the table, leaned over, and embraced his wife as if she were the lifeline he needed to survive.

Joie lovingly kissed her husband's face. She kissed each eye, his nose, his forehead and finally his lips. "Oh baby, I have missed you."

The guard cleared his throat loudly, a clear signal that they were pushing it with the public display of affection.

"I missed you, too." He used his rough hand to gently wipe away her tears. "How are you, Joie?"

"I'm fine," she lied.

"Yeah, me too." He smiled. "I miss seeing your face."

"That's why I brought this." She pushed the picture across the table, eyeing CO Higgins to make sure it was okay. It was. "So you can see me and the kids everyday."

"I remember this picture," he said tearing up. "We took it right after we got back together."

"That's right." She allowed her eyes to drift over his body, taking in every single inch, holding the image in her mind so she would not forget him.

"How are Trey and Maya?"

"They're fine. You know their birthday was last month."

"That's right. They turned nine." He hung his head in shame. "I forgot."

"It's okay. We baked cupcakes. I let the kids decorate them." She smiled. "They made such a mess."

"I can imagine. Tell them I said, Happy birthday."

"I will." She wrung her hands together nervously underneath the table. "They told me to tell you that they can't wait for you to come home."

"That's good. Tell them that I miss them too," he said.

She nodded.

"Your letter said that you had to move. Where are you living now?"

"Well, we moved in with Tequitta for a minute."

He leaned back in his chair and laughed softly. "You and Tequitta in the same house? I would have never imagined that."

She exhaled. "Yeah, that didn't work out too well. Who would have thought that she was obsessive-compulsive about cleaning? I may not be the cleanest person who ever lived, but I for sure ain't the messiest. Anyways, I think she's really getting serious about that Paris guy." Joie decided to leave out the part about her practically cursing the woman out.

"Good for Tequitta." He leaned forward and asked again, "So where are you living now?"

"About two months ago, we moved into an apartment complex run by a nice lady named Leticia. We call her Miss Lettie for short. Place ain't too bad, considering it's a shelter for battered women and their children."

"A shelter for battered women and children?"

"Yeah, but not all women who live there have been abused. Obviously..." She raised her eyebrows and continued. "The *House of Ruth Ministries* is there to help battered women, but also women like me—women with young children who have fallen on hard times."

"How long will you be there?" he asked with a pained expression, knowing he was the cause of his family having to live in a shelter.

"Six months is the limit. I just pay what I can afford for now, which ain't much."

"Then what?"

"In another couple of months, I should have enough money saved up to get our own place. I wasn't able to get my old job back, but I found a part-time gig in one of those specialty clothing shops near the mall. It don't pay that much, but you know me... I can stretch a dollar when I need to."

"Damn, baby..." He stared off into space. "I really fucked up our lives, didn't I?"

"It's gonna be alright, Ced." She reached for his hand but promptly withdrew it upon hearing the guard clear his throat again. "Damn, they watch you like a hawk in here, don't they?"

"Yeah, this is bad, but at least we ain't separated by a glass window. Some inmates have to use the damn phone to speak to their visitors."

Joie's tone softened upon noticing the tension creep into his face. "How are you doing in here?" she asked knowing full well that whatever response he gave would not adequately answer what she was really asking which was, *'How in hell are you going to survive living in this hellhole for years to come?'*

He shrugged and then leaned his head to the side. "You know. I'm making it. Just taking one day at a time."

Joie placed her hands atop the table and leaned forward. She started to speak, but Cedric cut her off. His eyes went to her fingers. Kicks' words about divorce reverberated in his mind.

"Where is your wedding ring?"

She withdrew her hands from the table and placed them in her lap. Lowering her head in embarrassment, not wanting her husband to know how desperate she had become, she slowly shook her head from side to side.

"Joie, where is your wedding ring?" he asked again this time with more force.

"I had to take it off."

"Why the fuck did you take off your ring? Don't you love me anymore?"

In spite of the noise within the large room generated by excited voices of people who hadn't seen each other in a long while, the ticking clock seemed to grow louder with each passing second.

She stared at Cedric's mouth, watched it move, but no sounds came out. All she could hear was the clock. Tick. Tock. Tick. Tock. With each second marked off by the hands of that clock, Joie was reminded of all the shit she had to endure over the past months. Memories of pawning their valuables, including her wedding ring, and then being propositioned by the pawn shop's owner, flooded back with a vengeance. She thought about how closely she came to prostituting her body to Amir, and the shame she felt afterwards. She could never forget being homeless and how frightened she and the kids were sleeping inside their car. The desperation she felt everyday just trying to hold it together was overwhelming.

"Joie, I'm not going to keep asking you... Where is the ring I gave you?"

All this shit I've gone through and he is asking me about a goddamn wedding ring. I should tell Cedric everything. Let him know the hell he's put me and the kids through. I want to tell him how much I love and hate him at the same time. But I can't. Just look at him. I know he is trying his best to hold it together. But so am I.

She observed the anger blazing deep within Cedric's soul. Not at her, but at his situation. So instead of laying all her woes on his shoulders when he couldn't do a damn thing about any of it, she held her tongue because no good would come from the thoughts swirling inside her head. Expressing how badly he had messed up their lives would serve no purpose other than momentarily making her feel better.

"Baby? Are you okay?" He leaned forward with concern upon seeing his wife's tearful eyes.

She stared at her husband's slender and almost unrecognizable face, knowing deep down inside that she would not tell Cedric about her meeting Bryson and his mother. She couldn't give him false hopes about getting out of prison. They had no money to pay Hunter Wylie to file an appeal. Hell, she didn't even have money to put on his account so he could buy a bag of fuckin' potato chips. He had to sit here for twenty years and serve his sentence or wait until he made parole to be free. Whichever came first.

"Joie?!" Cedric shouted. Instead of getting the attention of his wife, he got the attention of everyone else in the room. "Joie?!"

Joie heard him calling her name. As if she were outside her body, she felt incapable of responding.

"Everything okay here?" the guard casually asked. He had seen this reaction a thousand times from visitors overcome by the realization of what their loved one was facing. Thus, he was not overly concerned.

An older woman who was there visiting her son looked on with concern. This wasn't the first time she saw a wife break down when visiting her husband for the first time. Being an old pro at this because her husband, and now her son, was behind bars, she left her son at the table and went to Joie's side.

"It's gonna be alright, precious." The woman stroked Joie's face tenderly. "You just a bit overwhelmed, that's all."

"Joie, are you okay?" Cedric asked from across the table. As much as he wanted to be the one who comforted his wife, he knew that if he crossed the table, he would be removed from the area.

The older woman spoke soothingly when she addressed Cedric. "She's gonna be fine. This happens to a lot of us the first visit."

Joie came around as if she were coming out of a thick fog. She used the sleeve of her coat to wipe away the tears streaming down her face. She told the helpful woman, "Thanks. I'm alright now. I just got a little overwhelmed like you said."

Cedric abruptly stood up on his side of the table. With one finger, he pushed the family picture back to Joie's side. "Baby, I am not going to do this to you. Or to the kids. And I do not want you to fight me on this either."

"What are you saying?"

"I don't want you coming back here. When you get home, I want you to file for a divorce."

"What?" she asked stunned.

"I don't want you putting your life on hold for me. I don't want you coming up here to visit me in prison. I want you to file for a divorce and move on with your life." He swept his arm across the room. "Look around, baby. I'm going to be in here for at least ten years and that's if I meet my parole requirements. This ain't no way for us to be married. This ain't no way to live."

"I love you, Ced. I don't want a divorce."

"If you don't file. I will." And with that he called for the guard to take him back to his cell. "I love you, Joie. I always will. But I will not drag you down any further than I already have. And don't try coming up here again because I'm taking your name off my visitor list."

"Cedric?! Don't you walk out of here! We are not through talkin' about this! Damn it, Ced, come back here!" she yelled. But it was no use. She watched him go through those double doors without so much as taking a second glance back.

But what Joie didn't see were the tears streaming down Cedric's face. Walking away from Joie, Maya, and Trey was one of the most difficult decisions he ever had to make. As much as it hurt to see her pained expression when he mentioned divorce, it was better than watching her love turn into a sense of obligation with the passing of each year. In his previous line of work, he saw the after effects of children whose fathers were in prison. He knew what the wives and girlfriends dealt with trying to remain faithful to a convict. There was no way he wanted to deal with that, nor put his family through years of pain. Kicks' was right. A correctional facility was no place for women and children.

Chapter Thirty-Five

The driver of the taxi who dropped her off at the prison just a couple hours earlier was also the driver who picked her up. "Where to ma'am?" he asked when she shut the door.

"The Budget Inn Motel. I think it's just a few miles from here."

"Ten miles to be exact. I drive this route every Saturday. Back and forth shuttling visitors from the prison to the town." He took a look in the rear view mirror at his passenger. He noted her red puffy eyes and tear stained face. "First time?"

Joie nodded. "Yeah, it was. How did you know?"

"Lucky guess." He took another look in the mirror. "Good thing you're leaving early. Only one motel in town. Rooms fill up quickly after visiting hours are over, unless you have a reservation."

"Guess it's a good thing then…" Not wanting to engage in further conversation, she moved out of the driver's line of sight. Her head hurt with the pounding of extreme heartache settling in her temples. She wanted to go home, but the bus didn't leave until the next morning. Thus, she was stuck in the middle of nowhere in a backwoods town with nothing but time to think about divorcing the man she had just remarried less than a year earlier.

The driver took Joie's silence as her cue of wanting to be left alone. He tuned the radio to a station that played hits from the 1980's. The first few notes of Phil Collins', *In the Air Tonight*, played on in the background.

Joie perched her chin on her hand as she stared out the window at the barren countryside. The fields that were usually overgrown with tobacco, soy, or cotton, were now covered in a blanket of snow. The trees were weighted down with melting snow that would refreeze and later turn to ice. It was truly a beautiful sight.

"Can you please turn that up?" she asked the driver. "My husband loves this song…"

"No problem," the driver replied and then obliged.

Up until now, Joie's thoughts were all over the place. *So you want us to get a divorce, huh? You want me to walk away and let your ass rot in prison when I know you don't belong there. Ain't that some shit? You're just gonna decide how my life is going to be from here out because you think I can't handle it. You got the nerve to tell me to divorce your ass like it ain't nothing? Like I can just turn off my emotions with the flip of a switch? What the hell, Ced?*

Riding in the backseat of a taxi in what was basically the middle of nowhere, Virginia. Three little words kept reverberating in her mind… "*Let it go. Let it go. Let it go…* " as if someone was whispering in her ear.

Her thoughts replied to the silent voice inside her head, "I can't let it go. What if this is it? Ced is all I have left beside the kids. If I let go of him, then I'm really gonna be lost…"

"*Let it go…* "

So right then and there, in the backseat of that taxi, she made a decision to let go of the angst, let go of the worries and frustration, let go of anything she couldn't control. She pushed all her problems aside and allowed herself to get lost in the offbeat of the haunting melody and ethereal lyrics courtesy of Phil Collins' soulful voice.

Listening to the strum of the guitars and the rhythmic beat of the drums, suddenly, and out of nowhere, an overwhelming sense of calm washed over her. She finally understood what Ronnie had tried to get her to hear for all those years. It wasn't some crazy new age mumbo-jumbo that Ronnie made up! It was real! She had finally found the offbeat! An imperceptible blip of a moment between the beats of each note. More so than a tangible object she could see and touch, the offbeat was a state of mind—a quiet place where peace, love, contentment and, yes, even joy resides. Upon that realization, she smiled.

The driver drove on in silence. The winding country road took them by vast snow covered fields through a forested road lined by tall pine trees on either side. He took a glance in the rear view mirror at his passenger. With eyes glazed over by too much thinking, she appeared to be lost in the music. So instead of filling the space with meaningless chatter, he continued on without saying a word, preferring to let the words of the song fill the space.

Less that fifteen minutes after he picked Joie up from the entrance to the prison, he pulled underneath the awning of a three story stucco building. He turned down the radio to a more reasonable level to allow for conversation. "We're here."

Joie took a long hard look at the building. From the outside, though very sparse with the outside decoration, it didn't look too bad. "I thought this was a motel. Why aren't there any outside entrances?"

"Everybody has to come through this main entrance. It's to protect the guests in case there is a prison break. They can lock down the doors here as quickly as that siren at the prison sounds."

"Oh. I see." Joie paid the driver what she owed. Keeping close tabs on her meager budget, she gave him a dollar tip as she exited the warmth of the car. "Thanks. And actually, I think the more correct description would be to call this the Budget Inn Hotel, instead of Budget Inn Motel."

"Wait 'til you get inside," he responded with a chuckle. "It is definitely a motel."

Joie shrugged nonchalantly. "Actually, it don't matter either way what it is. I'm leaving first thing tomorrow morning."

The taxi's radio buzzed to life with a female dispatcher's voice. "That's probably another pickup at the prison. You take care now." The driver gave a quick wave and pulled off.

The small town that existed primarily off of visitors to the correctional facility was the epitome of a one stoplight town. Main street consisted of a convenience store which also housed a small café, a gas station, a laundry mat that also served beers, and of course, the hotel motel. From the few houses she had seen, there were maybe less than a hundred full time residents.

She checked into the motel and located her room. The growling in her stomach served as a reminder that all she'd eaten today was the donut Ranesha gave her earlier. She took a quick shower and made her way across the street to the café. She was the only customer.

"Where is everybody?" Joie asked waitress.

The middle-aged woman, dressed in a white and yellow checkered dress adorned with a stiff white apron, was about as cliché as a small town waitress could be. Bad skin covered up by a thick layer of pancake makeup gave her the appearance of a mannequin. Apparently no one told her that the overly teased hairstyle from the 70's was no longer in vogue. Her saving grace was the lovely smile she was quick to give to her customers. The blue stitching on the white oval nametag below her lapel spelled out, Rosie.

Rosie placed two piping hot pies she had just removed from the oven into the display case and did a quick check of the time. She retrieved the pencil from behind her ear and pulled out a pad. "In about thirty minutes, we're gonna be standing room only. Once visiting hours are over, they all come here for a bite to eat. Now what can I get you, honey?"

Joie ordered the special; a hearty bowl of soup, a grilled cheese sandwich, and a slice of cherry pie. She had to be careful with her money because she still had to buy her return bus ticket home.

Just as Rosie had predicted, the small café quickly filled up with dozens of women and children who made their way back from the prison. For some of these women, the Saturday visits had become a family ritual.

Joie was finishing up her dessert when someone tapped her on the shoulder. She looked up. It was the woman who had comforted her in the prison. "So we meet again."

"Yeah, I come here all the time." The woman gave Joie the once over before asking," How you doing?"

"Much better," Joie responded. She had no intention of telling this stranger what had really happened.

"That's good to hear." The woman pointed to the empty stool. "Mind if I join you?"

"No. Please. Take a seat." Joie didn't feel like talking to anyone, especially someone who was visiting another inmate, but since the woman had helped her out, she decided politeness was in order. "Thanks again for your help. I kinda zoned out for a minute."

"Like I said up there, it happens to all of us first time visitors. I've seen women break down a whole lotta times." She maneuvered her heavy body on the stool next to Joie.

"How long *have* you been coming up here?"

The woman shook her head and replied, "Too long. At first I used to come here to visit my husband, but now I'm visiting my son."

"Damn. Both your husband *and* son are incarcerated?"

"Used to both be here." The woman paused to place her order with the waitress. "My husband was sentenced to life shortly after we were married. It was a drug deal that went bad and he ended up killing two men."

Joie didn't say a word, but the thoughts in her mind were running a thousand miles a minute.

"I got three kids. Two boys and a girl. For about fifteen years, I used to bring both my sons up here to visit their daddy. I told him that even though he was in jail, he was still their daddy. I wanted my kids to know him."

"Fifteen years, huh?" Joie glanced at the woman's reflection in the mirror behind the counter. Now that she saw her face more clearly, she realized the woman probably wasn't much older than she was. "So you didn't take your daughter?"

"Naw, she got a different daddy. I had her after my husband was locked up. Thank the Lord *her* daddy always kept a decent job so he sent us money on a regular basis."

Joie tried to not stare at the woman as she studied her more closely. She was overweight, probably hypertensive, and had bad teeth. The darkened skin under her eyes and around her neck had diabetes written all over her. The ill fitting coat she wore looked second hand or had been worn for years. She probably did menial labor from the condition of her calloused hands which were covered in dry, ashy skin. Joie guessed her age to be fortyish, despite her looking as if she were pushing sixty.

"Once my sons were teenagers, they didn't want to come up here no more. But I forced them. I thought I was doing the right thing."

"Is your husband still here?"

"Naw, he died a couple years ago after spending damn near twenty years of his life in prison. Complications from hepatitis finally took him."

"I'm sorry." Joie slowly sipped her water. The wheels continued to turn as she listened to the woman's cautionary tale. "How long has your son been in?"

"Going on five years next month." She shook her head in disbelief. Or perhaps it was disgust. "Would you believe he got locked up for breaking into a shoe store he used to work at? Apparently he was stealing from the store for a while before he was caught."

"That's a shame." She glanced at the other younger children happily eating dinner with their mothers.

"Can I ask you a question?"

She nodded.

"Do you think you made a mistake by bringing your sons to visit their father? I'm only asking because my husband told me not to bring our kids with me." She didn't mention that now he had also excluded her from the list of visitors.

"Yes. I know I did, but what choice did I have? He wanted to see his kids and they needed to see their daddy. My sons, especially the one who eventually got locked up, started getting a little too comfortable with the entire situation. In his eyes, he foolishly started thinking that prison wasn't so bad."

"Who gave him that impression?"

"My husband did. The man was institutionalized. Prison culture was all he knew because he had been in prison for most of his life. Plus, every time he did get out, he did something that got his ass locked up again. His criminal record prevented him from finding or keeping a decent job. He used to joke that he had it better inside than out. *'Three hots and a cot is better than sleeping on the street'*, is what he used to tell me. Said at least in prison, he knew what to expect."

"Damn…" Joie knew what she said was true. Cedric used to tell her that was the prevalent attitude from the kids he helped. "What happened to your other son?"

"I took his little ass down to the Army recruiter as soon as he graduated from high school. I couldn't chance losing him to the streets or to prison. He's doing wonderful now. Married and living in Germany."

"Good for him." Joie placed ten dollars on the counter to pay her bill. "Sounds like you've been through a lot. Did you ever feel like giving up? You know… Stop visiting your son?"

"I'd be lying if I said I didn't feel like quitting. But he's my child. I refuse to give up on him. But one thing I have refused to do is bring his two-year old son to visit and I don't let that knucklehead girl bring him either. It's time for this chain of incarceration to be broken. And with God's help, we are both gonna do it."

Joie was onboard with the woman until she mentioned God. "Can I ask you another question?"

"Sure."

"I'm curious, and I don't mean no disrespect, but how is God supposed to help your son?" Joie asked in all sincerity. "If God was looking over y'all, don't you think he would have kept him out of jail in the first place?"

The woman stared at Joie as if she were an alien. No one she knew had ever doubted God's grace. At least not openly. "That's not how God works."

Joie smirked at the woman. One thing she couldn't stand was a Bible thumper.

She turned her hefty body towards Joie. "Do you ever pray?"

"I used to when I was younger, but I haven't lately. Why do you ask?"

"How is your life? Are things going the way you planned?"

"Obviously my life ain't going the way I expected. If it was, I for damn sure wouldn't be up here in the middle of nowhere visiting my husband in prison."

"I never knew anybody who climbed a hill starting at the top. Everybody has to start at the bottom." The woman grinned. "Maybe this visit to your husband is your bottom."

"It sure as hell ain't the top." Joie smiled back. "How do you keep your strength in all this? You seem so...so filled with contentment."

"Well, at first I started meditating a few years back. Then I started praying. Now I pray at least twice a day. Even started reading my Bible. You should try it."

"How is *that* working for you?" Joie asked skeptically.

"My life is getting better by the day. I even lost fifty pounds last year. Got a little bit more to go, obviously, but I'm getting there."

"Good for you."

Rosie the waitress interrupted their conversation when she placed the woman's food on the counter. After a brief prayer, she began digging into a house salad topped off with a healthy heaping of tuna. And took a sip of water flavored by freshly squeezed lemon slices.

The waitress brought Joie her change from which she folded a one dollar bill in half and left it on the counter for a tip. Before putting the rest of the change in her purse, she paused. *On second thought, since I'm feeling generous and the service was excellent, I'm gonna leave Rosie two dollars instead of one.*

Joie hopped down from the barstool with a better outlook than she had when she first walked in. She told her, "Sister, I want to say thank you again for your kindness and your words. You don't know it, but you've given me a lot to think about when I get home. My late mother used to say that God places people in your life when you need them most, and I guess that is why I ran into you today. I needed to hear your testimony."

The woman smiled warmly at Joie. "Before you make any difficult life changing decisions, why don't you try praying over it first? You'll be surprised what happens when you open your heart to His Grace and Mercy."

"Thanks for the advice. I can't say whether I'll take it, but I appreciate it all the same. Well, time for me to go. I'm going to try and get some rest before my bus leaves tomorrow." Joie shrugged into her coat. As she slipped her hands into the warm gloves, she exclaimed,

"This is our second conversation and I just realized I don't know your name."

The woman wiped her mouth with a napkin and extended her hand. "I'm sorry. Where are my manners? I meant to introduce myself when we were back at the prison. My name is Joy."

"What?! Your name is *Joy*? You must be joking."

"No, I'm not kidding. My name is Joy."

"For real? That's your name?"

"Yes." The woman's expression shifted from friendly, to verging on being slightly annoyed, and then to confusion. "Why? Is something wrong?"

Joie burst out in happy laughter. Talk about coincidence! If she didn't know better, she would swear her mother had a hand in placing this woman in her path. She accepted the woman's warm hand in hers. With the most sincere smile she could muster, she replied. "Nothing is wrong, Joy. My name is also Joie."

"What?" the woman asked in genuine surprise. "Your name is Joy too?"

"Yep. But I spell my name with an ie."

"Well, Joie, spelled with an ie. It is so nice to meet you."

"It is nice to meet you as well, Joy." Joie grinned up at the ceiling, but really at the sky above, smiling at the angel who sent this woman into her life. At a time when she needed it most. In the offbeat of her life. In this little town in the middle of nowhere Virginia, she had literally and figuratively encountered Joy in the offbeat.

~ ~ ~

Later that night, Joie dreamt that she Cedric were out taking a leisurely stroll when they inadvertently ended up lost inside the Hampton Roads Bridge Tunnel. The further they walked, the darker it became until the darkness was absolute. Somehow, they became separated. As she felt her way around in the darkness, she heard Cedric calling for her. As the sound of her husband's voice grew fainter and she no longer heard him, she fell into a deep despair, resigned to her fate of remaining forever lost in the darkness. Terrified and alone.

Still in the dream, Joie morphed into a childlike version of herself, huddled in a corner, sobbing uncontrollably, and calling out for Cedric. Though she remained in impenetrable darkness, she felt the warmth presence of her mother's spirit enveloping her, telling her to not be afraid. She told her that she was not alone. All she needed to find her freedom was to open her eyes and see what was in front of her.

The child version of Joie disappeared and was replaced by the adult Joie. Her spirit mother pressed a small card in her daughter's hand before guiding her towards a white man smoking a smokeless cigarette. Joie didn't want to go towards the man. She wanted to search for Cedric. Although she couldn't see Cedric, she knew he remained in the darkness looking for her.

Joie's spirit mother proceeded to nudge her towards the white man. She placed Joie's hand in his. And instead of going back to find her husband, and upon her spirit mother's insistence, she reluctantly allowed the man to guide her out of the tunnel. Into the light. Towards a solution.

Chapter Thirty-Six

Cedric reluctantly returned to his cell trying to convince himself that the cramped quarters he shared with Kicks wasn't so bad. Some had it much worse with three inmates to a cell. For all of Kicks' quirks, at least he didn't smear feces around the cell like some of the other inmates. Nor was he a raving lunatic with a chip on his shoulder ready to explode in an instant. On the contrary, he was a self-educated man and always had his nose in some book.

He recalled the countless conversations he had with teens about staying out of prison. A few had been in just once; but just as many had returned time after time as if life on the outside was the exception and not the rule.

Those teens who had graduated into habitual criminals often spoke about prison as if it were some perverted version of home. They said that when they were incarcerated, they didn't have to struggle with fitting in, having somewhere to live, finding a way to make a living. The correctional facility provided them with three meals a day, a warm shower, and a relatively safe place to lay their heads. They knew what to expect because despite what the prison guards said, it was the criminals who ran the prison and set the rules about the hierarchy of prison life.

On the outside, these men were labeled as criminals, felons, ex-cons and were always looking over their shoulders for signs of trouble. Like attracts like, so they tended to gravitate towards each other; which was a problem in itself because the terms of probation prohibited association with known criminals.

In many cases, their families had all but forgotten about them as they moved on with their own lives. Practically speaking, no one had time to listen to their pitiful stories about how "the man" wouldn't allow them to get a job, nor would family members provide more than minimal support during what may have been an extended probation period. All this led to feelings of isolation, which often resulted in these men falling back into criminal activities in order to return "home". The rates of recidivism were astonishing. This behavior was certainly pathological, unfortunately, it was also reality.

He had heard those stories from so many brothers over the years. Listening to them in the past, he felt not one iota of sympathy. The way he figured, going to jail once was a mistake. Anything more than that was a choice. However, after spending time with these inmates, he realized how wrongly his assumptions had been. Many of those who were incarnated really didn't belong behind bars.

He almost laughed at the irony of his situation. Never in a million years did he imagine he would be on the wrong side of these walls looking out. He climbed up on the top bunk and laid on his back staring at the peeling paint on the ceiling. *I can survive this. Hell, I must survive.*

Kicks took notice of his cellmate's demeanor when he returned from visitation. He could tell by Cedric's defeated gait that the visit did not go well. The loud, long, heavy sighs coming from the top bunk confirmed his suspicions. After several minutes passed, he figured that would be enough time to let the man gather his composure, he asked, "How did it go?"

"Fine."

"Did you take my advice and cut her loose?"

"Yeah, I did."

"That's rough man, but trust me when I tell you that its better this way. Keeping your woman on this leash of coming to visit you every weekend is a kind of punishment she does not deserve. No sense in having your woman serving the same sentence as you. She wasn't the one sent to jail…"

In his mind, Cedric knew he had done the right thing by releasing Joie, but his heart told him a different story. He had no idea how he would survive without seeing his family again. For most inmates, those weekend visits were the only thing keeping them sane. And after observing inmates who had been incarcerated for long periods of time, he realized there were two routes he could take. He could lose his grip on reality and revert to playing with his own shit like so many other inmates did, or he could make the best of his situation. In that very moment, he chose the latter.

~ ~ ~

Suffering through a fitful night's sleep, courtesy of a crying baby in the next room, Joie awoke early Sunday morning with remnants of the cryptic dream still lingering in her mind. With a new unexplained sense of urgency, she showered and packed her bag. Joie was not one to place faith in a prophetic dream. But this did not feel like a dream. Superstition was for the weak-minded is what she always said. Yet, she believed that somehow her mother had visited and gave her the answers she so desperately sought.

The Greyhound bus departed the terminal right on time, placing her in D.C. ahead of schedule. This time the *Express City* bus lived up to its reputation of being unreliable. Twenty miles on the other side of Richmond, the bus broke down, stranding its passengers on the side of the road for four hours. Eventually a mechanic came out and attempted to fix the problem, but soon gave up. The driver finally relayed their status back to the company and they sent out a replacement. Turns out the engine had thrown a rod because of a persistent oil leak.

By the time Joie arrived home, it was almost two in the morning. When she pushed open the door to her apartment, a blast of cold air rushed inside the warmth of the living room rousing Ranesha out of a deep sleep.

"Hey girl," Joie whispered.

"Hey yourself," Ranesha said pushing herself to an upright position. She picked up the remote and silenced the television. "I expected you back a long time ago."

"I'm sorry. The damn bus broke down."

"What time is it?"

"A little after two."

Ranesha stood up rubbing out the crick in her neck from sleeping on the uncomfortable couch. "How did it go?"

Joie released a long sigh and then shook her head. "I'll tell you about it tomorrow. You need to get home to your own kids."

"Yeah, I guess you're right. I gotta get them up and ready for school in a few hours."

"Thanks for watching the twins." Joie slipped out of her coat. She bent over and removed the boots from her feet, massaging the warmth back into her toes. "I owe you one."

"No you don't. Your kids ain't no problem to watch." She slipped both arms into her coat. "Now mine are a different story. When I was over here with your kids, my son decided he wanted to cook something to eat. That hard-headed boy of mine damn near burned down the apartment trying to cook some French fries."

"Oh no! Is everything alright?"

"Yeah, thankfully Rain had the sense to come and get me before the fire jumped out of the pan."

"Thank goodness for that." She walked Ranesha to the door. "I'll tell you all about my trip tomorrow. For now, I just need to get some rest."

"Okay, I'll see you later."

Joie quietly tiptoed into the bedroom trying her best to not wake her sleeping children. She smiled down at her daughter noticing that she had actually listened when she told her to wrap her hair in a silk scarf before going to bed. Though the scarf was now more off than on, at least she had tried. Trey was sound asleep in the other twin bed.

The door to the closet creaked loudly when she pulled it open and peered inside using the flashlight on her cell phone to see.

"Mommy? When did you get home?" Maya said sleepily, rubbing her eyes.

"Just a few minutes ago." Joie continued rummaging through the bags of clothing piled on top of each other.

"Did you see Daddy?"

"Sure did. He told me to tell you he misses you."

"I miss him too," she replied in a sleepy voice.

Joie continued her search. The light from her cell phone helped, but not by much. What she did see reminded her that she needed to make a visit to the Goodwill. Miss Lettie was generous with giving them bags of clothing, but most of it was so out of style that she refused to inflict those fashion mistakes on herself, much less her children.

"What are you looking for?"

"Shhhh," Joie whispered. "Go back to sleep."

"You're making too much noise," Maya replied.

"I'm sorry. I'm looking for my old purse. I think I tossed it in here somewhere."

Maya sat up in her bed. She leaned over and switched on the small bedside lamp Trey had also acquired from the empty apartment next door. He was such a resourceful young man. "You mean that big black purse you used to carry around all the time?"

Joie stopped rifling through the jumble of odds and ends piled on the closet floor. "Yeah... My big black bag with the gold-plated emblem on the front. Have you seen it?"

"Uh huh." She pointed to the far corner. "I put it over there. I was using it for my hair products."

"Yep, that's it." Joie retrieved the handbag from the corner, flipped it upside down, and gave it a good shake, dumping the contents unto the bed. A cascade of ribbons, hair clips, sponge rollers, combs, and hair brushes spilled from the bag. "Shoot... It's not there."

"What are you looking for?"

Joie sighed in frustration before giving the bag another once over. "A business card."

"Those little cards with writing on them?"

"Umh huh," she replied, distracted. She unzipped all the outside compartments and then sat down on the small bed. "I used to carry this purse all the time. I thought I put it inside here."

Maya reached under her mattress and pulled out a stack of cards she had gathered from around the apartment complex. Most were reward cards from grocery stores that people had haphazardly tossed. A few were preapproved credit cards that weren't any good unless the person actually completed the finance application. And others were business cards from local businesses that people took and casually discarded.

"What's all that?" Joie asked.

"I use them for debit and credit cards when we're playing store."

Joie shook her head and laughed. "Whatever happened to using pretend money?"

Maya informed her matter-of-factly, "Mommy, nobody carries cash anymore."

"True," she said. "Let me see those."

Maya handed over the stack. "Don't get mad. You left a whole lotta cards in that purse. I didn't think you needed them anymore."

Joie smiled reassuringly. "I won't get mad." She went through the stack of cards one-by-one, becoming more impressed with Maya as she did. The stack was arranged in order by color and store of issuance. When she reached the business cards, she smiled. "Found it!"

"I'm glad, Mommy." Maya rested her head back on the pillow. "Can I go back to sleep now?"

Joie reached across Maya and switched off the light. She planted a gentle kiss on her forehead. "Yes, you can go back to sleep. I'll see you in the morning."

"Do I have to go to school tomorrow?"

"Yes, you're going to school because I have to go to work."

"I'm glad you're home, Mommy."

"Me too, baby. Me too."

Joie stared at the business card. It read, *Lawrence K. Robicheaux. Aerodynamic Engineer, NASA Langley Research Center, Hampton, Virginia.* His work address, phone number and email address were also inscribed on the card. She flipped it over in her hand several times trying to recall their conversation that day they were stopped in the tunnel.

"He told me his name was Larry. I do remember that. And I know he mentioned something really important, but I cannot recall what it was." She took a seat in the kitchen and continued to stare at the business card. "I was hungover and claustrophobic. That's probably why I can't remember much. Well, only one way to find out why my mother's spirit wanted me to get in touch with this man. I'll call him first thing tomorrow morning."

~ ~ ~

Joie dropped the kids off to school on her way to work. After getting less than four hours of sleep, she was fueled by caffeine and adrenaline when she pulled into the parking lot of the mall. She checked the time. It was ten minutes to nine, giving her exactly eight minutes to make the call.

Before she could change her mind, she pulled the cell phone and business card from her jacket, and dialed the number. After several rings, a man's voice answered on the other end.

"Larry," he answered, curtly.

Joie paused, unsure what she was going to say to the man.

"Hello?" he asked. "Is someone there?"

She gathered her courage and said, "Hi Larry. This is Joie."

"Joie?"

"Yes, Joie Parker." She inhaled and continued. "We met while we were stuck inside the HRBT a couple months ago. I was the crazy woman you let sit inside your car."

"Joie! Yes, I remember you now. How are you?"

"Better, now that I'm out of that tunnel."

"That's good." He recalled their last conversation where she had practically called him a racist. "What can I do for you, Joie?"

"First of all I need to apologize for how badly I behaved that day. I was damn near out of my mind because of all the stress I was under. I should never have said those things to you, especially considering how nice you were to me."

"I appreciate you saying that. Apology accepted." He pulled the phone away from his face to address a question from a colleague. "So Joie... You probably didn't just call me out of the blue to apologize. What's going on?"

"You're right. I didn't." It took every ounce of courage to continue. "Before I drove off, you told me to call you if I ever needed anything. Well, I need to know if you were just saying that or if you actually meant it? Because lots of people say stuff without meaning it. You know, like when they ask you how you're doing, they don't really want to know. It's just conversation..."

Larry quickly responded, "I don't just make casual statements like that for conversation." He pulled the phone away again to speak so someone in the background. "Joie, I don't want to be rude, but I have a very important meeting in a couple of minutes..."

"I understand. I didn't mean to waste your time. I'll let you go," Joie said. She was sorry she had called. This man was not going to help her.

"Wait a minute," he said. "Don't hang up. I was going to see if you wanted to bring your children by the center later on. It will give us a chance to talk. I think you mentioned how excited they would be for a tour."

"Don't you even want to know what I want?"

"Of course, I'm curious. But I don't have the time right now to properly speak with you because of my meeting. And I'll be tied up the remainder of the morning. What do you think about stopping by later this afternoon?"

"I have to work until two. And my kids don't get out of school until three."

"How about three-thirty. My assistant will be happy to give your children a quick tour of the building while we talk. Will that work for you?"

It took only a few seconds for Joie to respond, "Three-thirty is fine."

"Perfect. I'll leave your name on the visitor's list. And bring your husband with you. I'd like to meet him."

"My husband won't be able to make it. It'll just be me and the kids, but thanks for inviting him."

"I've got to run. I'll be looking forward to seeing you again, Joie. And meeting your children. What did you say their names are?"

"Maya and Trey."

"Maya and Trey?" He paused while he scribbled their names on a post-it note. "Got it…"

"Thanks Larry. I'll see you later today."

Chapter Thirty-Seven

Later that afternoon, instead of going home and before picking up the twins from school, Joie drove to Buckroe Beach. The sky was overcast with hints of an early Nor'easter or possibly a late season hurricane brewing somewhere in the Atlantic. The strong wind whipped the cold air across the water until it reached the shore. The temperature was in the thirties, but the wind chill made it feel like it was at least twenty degrees colder.

With total disregard of the frigid temperature, Joie left the warm comfort of her car to take a walk. Watching the ocean always helped her think more clearly. She often told anyone who would listen that she couldn't imagine ever living away from the water. The ocean was in her blood.

Normally, the Chesapeake Bay was gentle. But not today. Today, the sea delivered wave after foamy wave unto the shore as if some angry monster were churning away below the surface. She imagined that further out, miles away from the shoreline, furious, violent waves would grow so big that they'd toss ships about like nothing. Seasoned seafarers would refer to this as an angry sea.

She needed time alone to think clearly about Cedric's request for a divorce. Ponder whether it was better to end her marriage and simply move on, because in some ways, getting divorced would be easier to handle than remaining together. Her mind tossed around different scenarios. *Dealing with Cedric's life in prison and all that mess that goes with it is going to be more than a notion. Maybe me and the kids can move to Florida with my father. The only reason to stick around Hampton now is because the kids are in school. As much as I love this town, without Cedric, this don't feel like home...*

Thinking about her father made her miss him all the more. She pulled out her cell phone and scrolled down to his number, still labeled *Mom and Daddy.* She dialed his number.

"Hi Daddy," she said when he picked up.

"Joie?"

"Yeah, Daddy, it's me."

"I almost didn't answer because I didn't recognize the number. Thought it was a telemarketer or one of those pesky bill collectors." He chuckled in the background.

"No, it's just me."

"It's about time you called your old man. I've been trying to call you but the message said your number was no longer available."

"Sorry about that. I switched carriers. They gave me a new number." She didn't mention that her phone was part of a government handout because her father would totally disapprove.

"So how are you and my grandchildren doing?"

The lump developing in her throat made providing a cheerful response difficult. Her father could always tell when something wasn't quite right with his child. It was as if he had some sort of paternalistic sixth sense. She swallowed hard and squeaked out, "We're doing okay. How about you?"

"Got no complaints. I'm really enjoying living in this senior citizen community, but I sure do miss you. And that's why I was trying to contact you because I was thinking about coming up for a visit to see you and the kids. If you and Cedric can make room for your old man…"

"Daddy, I've got something to tell you."

"What is it, angel? Are Maya and Trey okay? What's the matter?"

"The kids are okay." She used her sleeve to wipe the tears from her face before they froze. "But things have changed a lot since the last time we spoke…"

Bit by bit, Joie relayed the recent events of her life to her father, after which she felt some of the weight had been lifted. Even though she was a grown woman, married and with children, when it came down to it, she was still daddy's little girl. Just the sound of his voice made her feel better.

"Why didn't you tell me all this sooner? I could have given you some money so you wouldn't have lost your home."

"Daddy, you had so much to deal with after mommy passed. You were trying to get back on your feet. I didn't want to be another burden."

"Burden? You are my only child, Joie. You will never be a burden to me." He sighed in frustration on the other end. "Lord, if Slim knew you and the kids was living in a homeless shelter… She would lose her mind."

"It's not really a homeless shelter…"

"And you say Cedric was sent to prison for selling drugs?!" He reacted as if someone had slapped him. "I don't believe he is guilty for one second. Not my son-in-law!"

"That's not all." She decided to come clean and put all her cards on the table. "Cedric told me that he's going to file for a divorce if I don't file first. He said he was removing my name from his visitor's list so I can't visit him no more. I don't know what to do, Daddy. Do I abandon my husband when I know he's innocent? How do I just move on knowing he's in prison for a crime he didn't commit? We were having some problems before he was arrested, but none that would make me want to turn my back on him. I still love him… But being married to a convict is more than I can bear. I am so confused."

"Sounds like Cedric is trying to do right by you and the kids. I know that you want this mess to end, but I am not going to tell you to divorce your husband since it is obvious you still love him." He paused before stating, "I sure wish Slim was here. She'd know what to tell you."

Upon hearing that her father wasn't able to fix this particular problem, she allowed the tears to fall freely. This was one situation she had to handle on her own. Resigned to her fate, she said, "That's okay, Daddy. I just needed you to know what was happening up here. I don't want you to worry. Me and the kids are going to be just fine."

"I am going to wire you a little money. It's not much, just a few hundred dollars, but at least you can buy the kids some warm clothes and treat them to *Chucky Cheese* or something…"

"Thanks, Daddy." She stared at the grey clouds hanging low in the sky. They matched her mood perfectly. "I gotta go. It's time to pick up the kids from school."

"I love you, angel. You keep your chin up. Everything is going to turn out fine. One way or the other. And now that I have your number, I'm going to keep closer tabs on you."

Not trusting her voice to remain strong, she nodded on the other end. The last thing she needed was her father to be worried about her. Even though he had every reason to be.

"Maybe I'll come up for a visit when you get situated."

"The twins and I would love that. We really miss you," she managed to say.

"I miss you too, sugah. You give my grandkids a hug and kiss from me. I love you."

"I love you, too. I'll talk to you later." She placed the phone in her pocket, wiped her eyes, and made a promise to herself that she would never again allow her fate to be placed in the hands of someone else.

Despite the bone-chilling air entering her nostrils, causing beads of snot to drip unto her upper lip, she continued to walk. Her tear-filled eyes were drawn to the sky searching for an answer.

"God, if you're up there, I need you to give me a sign. Anything to help me make this decision. It's been awhile—since I was a child—that I felt the need to pray. Lately though, it seems every time I turn around, somebody is telling me about You helping them in their time of need. All these people been tellin' me to give it to the Lord. Lay my burdens down at Your feet. Well, here I go. I'm going to give it all to You."

Joie dropped down to her knees on the cold, wet sand. Looking up at the sky, she shouted, "God! Help me! Please! Help me! I am so lost! Lord, I can't tell up from down, or right from left. I've done a lot of bad things in my life that I am probably paying for now, but I have learned my lesson. So Lord, if you're really out there, please, please, please help me!"

She remained on her knees, motionless, staring up at the sky and then down at the water, waiting for a miraculous sign to present itself. She wondered how the sign would appear. Would it be a white dove clutching an olive branch that landed at her feet? Perhaps an affluent citizen would approach her with an amazing opportunity that would take care of all their financial problems. Possibly her phone would ring with news about Cedric's arrest being one huge mistake.

But after waiting for several minutes, the only thing she felt was the numbness of her fingers and toes setting in. Disappointed, discouraged, and now totally convinced that she was really alone, she stood to her feet and returned to her car.

"Nothing. Absolutely nothing..." she whispered to herself, drying all remaining tears. "Just as I thought."

Chapter Thirty-Eight

"I'm here to see Mr. Larry Robicheaux," Joie told the gate guard posted at the entrance to the NASA Langley Research Center. She glanced in her rearview mirror at the long line of cars waiting behind hers. "He invited us over for a tour."

"You'll need to get a visitor's pass before I can let you thru," the guard replied in a no nonsense voice after checking the list of visitor requests. He glanced in the backseat at the twins and then said, "Park in that lot. Go inside that building. Pickup your pass and then come back."

She did as she was instructed. Once inside the small structure, they noticed signs were posted everywhere telling you what you could or could not do while on the NASA center. The very first sign instructed her to sign in. Another said to 'turn off your cell phone' before approaching the counter. She also saw a large sign warning that concealed weapons were not allowed and that once you had access to the center, your vehicle could be searched at any time.

The woman who was perched on a chair behind the counter checked Joie's driver's license, verified her proof of registration and current insurance before issuing a temporary pass granting access to the center. Luckily, she had just renewed her insurance policy, as it had lapsed for several months.

"Good afternoon children," said an elderly gentleman sitting at a desk behind the counter. His vest was so adorned with hundreds of NASA lapel pins that you could barely tell what color it was originally.

"Hello," Trey answered for himself and Maya. "Do you work here?"

"I sure do. Going on thirty years," the old man replied.

"That's a long time," Maya said, fascinated by his full head of extraordinarily white hair.

"It sure is. Been here longer than some folks have been living." He studied the twins. "Let me see... I'm going to guess that you are ten years old and your sister is nine."

"Close. We just turned nine years old," Trey answered proudly.

"Both of you?" the man asked amused.

"Yes sir. We're twins," Trey explained. "Our birthday was last month."

"You don't say?" the man replied. He bent down to retrieve a box from underneath his desk. "How would you and your sister like a couple of NASA stickers as birthday presents?"

"Is it okay, Mommy?" Maya asked excitedly hopping from one foot to the other.

"Yes. But be sure you tell the nice man, 'thank you'."

The man leaned over the counter and handed the stickers to the children. The pins covering his vest made a clinking sound. "Here you go. Three for each of you. This one here has the NASA logo and the other two are of the International Space Station and the Space Shuttle Atlantis."

"Wow! These stickers are so cool!" exclaimed Trey. "Thanks!"

"They sure are!" Maya added. "Thank you so much!"

"You are very welcome." The old man smiled. "I love it when children are interested in science. Means there is hope for us after all."

"Thank you," Joie said to the man.

She piled the kids in the car. The guard checked the visitor pass and waived her through the gate. The directions on the map, provided by the lady at the visitor center, made finding the building where Larry worked easy. It sat directly next to a massive wind tunnel.

At precisely three-thirty, Joie was greeted by a young African-American woman who introduced herself as Larry's assistant. While she escorted the trio to Larry's office, she explained that she was an intern working part-time to gain experience to help write the thesis for her degree. She was only twenty years old, but was already working on her doctorate.

Whereas Joie was impressed by the young woman's academic achievements, the young lady actually sang Larry's praise. Apparently, he had invested hundreds of hours of his personal time in the local schools encouraging minority students to pursue an education in STEM.

She said a motivational speech given by Mr. Robicheaux was what helped her decide to become a nuclear scientist. And his involvement in the community didn't stop there. He and his wife had started a scholarship fund to offer partial scholarships to minority students majoring in one of the STEM programs.

"This is Mr. Robicheaux's office. He had to run across the street to check on a project, but told me to show you in. Make yourself comfortable." She pulled a plush leather chair from behind the conference table and motioned for Joie to take a seat.

"Thank you," Joie told the young woman. "I must say... You sound like you like really working here."

"Now that you mention it. I suppose I do," she replied cheerfully. She turned to the twins and said, "I can show you guys around the building if it's okay with your mom."

"Mommy, is it okay with you? Please, please, please?" they begged.

"I think that'll be alright." She looked at the twins. "But we need to wait for Mr. Robicheaux first. I want you both to meet him before you take off."

"Well, let's not keep the kids from their private tour," Larry uttered in a loud booming voice as entered his office.

"Hi Larry," Joie said when she saw the familiar face. Although she didn't really know him, it felt like she was meeting an old friend. "Good to see you again."

Larry was slightly taken aback by Joie's appearance. She was at least twenty pounds lighter. The luxurious flowing locks—courtesy of an expensive weave—were no more. And she was dressed in plain clothing covered by a simple blue smock. A work uniform.

"Joie Parker. How are you?" he asked in all sincerity. His hand rested on her shoulder with a fatherly touch.

"I've been better; could be much worse."

"These are your children?" He turned his attention to the kids.

"Yes, these are my kids, Maya and Trey." She smiled proudly because despite the number of ways she had messed up her life, her children were awesome. "Kids say hi to Mr. Robicheaux."

"Hi Mr. Robicheaux," they replied in perfect unison.

Larry motioned to his assistant. "Why don't you take the children on that tour now so Mrs. Parker and I can talk? And if you have time, you can walk over to the Space Shuttle mockup."

"I can barely wait to tell my class what I did today!" Trey said. "They'll never believe that I had a private tour of NASA."

"I think your classmates will believe it when you show them an autographed picture of a real astronaut." Larry pulled two autographed pictures from a folder on his desk and handed it to each child. "We just happened to have a couple of astronauts touring the campus today. I had them signed earlier."

"Cool! Thank you!"

The twins skipped happily after the young woman, eager to begin their tour. In their excitement, neither twin noticed the look of desperation on their mother's face.

"Well, well, well, Mr. Lawrence Robicheaux," Joie said. "It seems you are a man of many talents. After hearing your assistant gush about all that you've done for the community, I guess I shouldn't be surprised that you gave me your card and told me to call if I needed anything."

"I do what I can," he replied, humbly while rummaging through his desk drawer. "Ah... There it is..."

"And you're modest, too." She watched him pop one of those vapor cigarettes into his mouth. A fragrant wispy trail of white vapor spilled from one end. He inhaled the vapor as if it were magical. *The white man in my dream smoked that type of cigarette... Maybe there is more to this than coincidence...*

He sat back in his chair and exhaled. "Sorry. Hope you don't mind. At my wife's insistence, I'm trying to give up smoking. These vapor cigarettes are the only things that seems to work."

"No, I don't mind at all."

"So tell me, Joie. What brings you here today?"

"You were so kind to me while I was stuck inside that tunnel. And when you gave me your card and said to call you..." She dropped her head and began picking at the frayed cuticles on her fingertips. "Actually, this may sound really strange, but I had a weird dream the other night. Some people call it a premonition, but I'm not sure what it was. Anyway, I was sort of *told* to contact you..."

"Really? Why don't you tell me about it?" He checked his calendar, noting his schedule was clear for the remainder of the day. "The twins are in good hands with my assistant, so we have plenty of time to talk."

"Okay, but you may think twice about helping me after you hear my story." She paused before continuing. "...I don't want you to get the wrong impression about me."

"I'm not here to judge you."

"Okay. Here goes..."

Joie leaned forward in the comfortable chair and propped her elbows on the table. Her reflection in the highly polished wood stared back.

Larry left his desk and joined her at the table. Though he was technically a stranger, for some reason Joie decided she could trust this man. Maybe it was because her mother's spirit guided her to him in the dream. Whatever the reason, for the next hour, Joie told Larry her story beginning with the day her mother died. She told him about Cedric being arrested. And also how she had lost her job, her home, and was now living in a shelter. Well, she didn't tell him every gritty detail about her life because some things just ain't meant to be shared with a stranger friend.

Larry listened while Joie spoke, interrupting only to ask questions when necessary. He was used to letting others speak uninterrupted. As a mentor, he had discovered that the more people talked, the more they revealed of themselves. So that is what he did. And boy did she reveal quite a lot about herself.

"Joie, your situation looks bleak to you because you are so deeply in it. But from the outside looking in, I don't think it's that bad. You managed to find a job and a place to live. Both may not be ideal, but from what you've told me, it is an improvement over where you were."

"Larry, I don't think you were listening to me. I am this close to being homeless again. In a couple of months, Miss Lettie is going to tell me that we have to move. And unless I relocate to Florida to live with my father, I don't have anywhere else to go."

"All you need is a better job to help you get back on your feet." He pulled his blackberry from his pocket and scrolled through his email contacts. "I think we may have a few openings in our budget department. If you'd like, I can put you in touch with a friend down in human resources."

Joie's eyes bucked wide open. "What? A job here at NASA?"

"Sure. Why not? From what you've told me, you have the right credentials. It sounds like you're more than qualified. I'm sure they can find a position for you somewhere."

She tried not to become overly excited. After all, until she had actually spoken to a real live hiring official, it was all just conversation.

He scribbled a name and number down on the back of a post-it note. Then he punched several keys of his blackberry while they spoke. "I'm sending my friend an email letting her know to expect a call from you first thing tomorrow."

"Thank you, Larry." Her eyes threatened to tear up, but she willed them away. "I can't tell you how much this means to me."

"Don't mention it."

"What about my husband?"

"Yes, I was just thinking about that…"

"My husband is innocent, but that lawyer won't touch his case until I pay him thousands of dollars."

Larry dropped his head and began to laugh.

"What is so funny?" she asked, becoming angry that he thought this was a laughing matter.

"Do you remember the day we met?"

"Of course, I remember." She clutched her chest protectively. "That was the last time I felt like I was having a panic attack because of my claustrophobia."

"Well, after I arrived at work, I discovered why the traffic had stopped."

Joie looked at him hoping he would get to the point quickly.

"You won't believe what happened…"

"So tell me!"

"A flock of geese accidently found their way into the HRBT. The DOT shut down traffic to remove the geese before some foolish, but well-intentioned person attempted to rescue the birds and cause a major pile up inside the tunnel. So instead of letting those geese run amok, they stopped traffic resulting in a 10 mile backup."

"That's an interesting *and* very funny story Larry, but what does that have to do with getting my husband out of prison?"

"Don't you see? Had it not been for those geese becoming lost inside that tunnel, traffic would not have stopped. And had you not become claustrophobic, you wouldn't have reached out to me. Our paths might never have crossed. Bottom line is, had we not met, I wouldn't be able to tell you that my daughter, Erica, is an attorney who works pro-bono to free inmates wrongly accused of crimes. Her success rate is one hundred percent."

"What?" Joie couldn't believe her good fortune. "You're telling me that your daughter might be able to get my husband released?"

"It's worth a shot, especially since that young man… What's his name?"

"Bryson."

"…especially since Bryson is willing to admit those drugs were his."

Joie pushed back from the table. She rushed towards Larry and threw her arms around his neck. "Thank you! Thank you so much!"

"You're welcome." He laughed again. "First things first. Let's get you that job so you won't have to worry about being thrown out into the street. In the meantime, I'll arrange a meeting between you and Erica. You can bring her up to speed on your husband's case."

"This seems almost too good to be true."

"Of course Erica will need to speak with your husband as well, but if what you tell me is true, he has a pretty good chance."

"Once Cedric finds out that someone is willing to help him, he'll be more than happy to meet with your daughter."

~ ~ ~

Joie stopped by the Western Union located in the *Food Lion* to pick up the money her father had wired. From the two hundred dollars he sent, she used twenty to treat the kids to Chick-fil-A, put aside a hundred to buy them all new shoes, and the rest would be used for food and gas. It was enough to hold them over until payday. However, if her conversation with Larry was any indication, her days of worrying about money would soon be over.

She dropped the kids off at their apartment and then went to knock on Ranesha's door to share the good news. No one answered.

Joie returned to her apartment, opened a bottle of cheap red wine, partially filled a disposable plastic cup with the ruby-colored liquid, and took a seat on the worn sofa.

"Can we go outside to show our friends what we got from NASA?"

"Yeah, go ahead."

Maya and Trey ran out to the courtyard to brag to the other children about their trip to the wind tunnel. They would probably be outside for at least another couple of hours showing off their NASA swag. She smiled at their excitement.

She picked up her cell and punched in Ronnie's number, also wanting to share her good news with a friend. The call went through before she remembered how badly their last conversation ended.

"Hello?" answered Ronnie.

At first, Joie considered hanging up. After all, she had a new number so there was no way Ronnie could know it was her.

"Hellooo?" Ronnie sang out again.

"Hey Ronnie. It's me, Joie."

She was greeted by an angry silence.

"Please don't hang up!" Joie quickly added, "I want to apologize for everything I said the last time we spoke."

Several more seconds passed with no response.

"Hello? Ronnie? Are you still there?"

"Yeah, I'm here," Ronnie responded in a tightly controlled voice. "What do you want?"

"I called to apologize."

The sounds of silence came through so loudly on the other end, Joie wondered if Ronnie had hung up. Finally she heard a long sigh on the other end.

"I am so sorry what I said to you the last time we spoke. I was going through some things and feeling some kinda way, but that's no excuse. I was acting like a straight up bitch. I apologize."

"You said some pretty crazy stuff to me."

Luis sat next to Ronnie on the sofa, cuddling baby Isabella while Luis Jr. slept between them. He whispered quietly, "Who is that?"

Ronnie pulled the phone away from her ear. She mouthed to Luis that it was Joie.

Upon hearing it was Joie on the other line he tried to take the phone from Ronnie. She shook her head, "no". She indicated she wanted to hear what Joie had to say.

"Girlfriend, please listen. I want to ask for your forgiveness." Joie knew she needed to say more, but begging was not in her repertoire. At least it wasn't until today.

Ronnie carefully got up from the sofa, stepped over the twins toys strewn all over the living room floor, and headed into another room to avoid waking the babies. When she was out of earshot, she whisper-shouted into the phone, "Why should I forgive you, Joie? Just because you call me months later with some lame-ass apology?"

Joie decided she would put her repertoire aside and try some good old fashioned begging. "Ronnie, please... I don't want our friendship to end over my bullshit. I was acting like a child trying to make you feel bad for what you and Luis worked so hard for. Please forgive me, girlfriend. Pleeeaseee..."

"Okay. I will forgive you on two conditions."

"Shoot."

She settled in the plush window seat of the kitchen nook and poured a glass of Dominican rum. "You need to apologize to Tomas."

"Apologize to Tomas for what? He's the one who left me a fuckin' dear Jane letter in that hotel room."

"Joie, Tomas told me and Luis what happened in that hotel room. He didn't want to, but we kinda twisted his arm after he wouldn't say why you left."

"What did he tell you?"

"Apparently, you went all freaky-deaky on Tomas' ass. You called him all kinds of names when he wouldn't have sex with you. Even threw your stuff all up in his face."

Joie became uncharacteristically quiet. Try as she might, she couldn't remember what had happened in that hotel suite. She just remembered how confused she was by the note Tomas left the next morning. "Tomas said I did all that?"

"Yes, and he didn't have a reason to lie."

"I must have been really out of it." She frowned in deep concentration trying to remember. Little by little, the conversation with Tomas started to come back. "Oh my goodness... I thought I had dreamt all that."

"You remember now?"

"Yeah. I guess I do owe him an apology. I think I said some really nasty things to him."

"Um huh. Tomas didn't tell us everything that went down, but I could only imagine what he left out."

For the first time in many years, Joie was embarrassed by her actions. She knew Tomas wouldn't go into the intimate details about their sexual encounter with his cousin and his wife, but just the thought of him mentioning how skanky she behaved was bad enough. "I'll write Tomas an apology letter just as soon as we get off the phone. I don't have his address so I'll mail it to you, if you don't mind."

"That's fine. I'll make sure he gets it."

"You said there were two things. What's the second?"

"I want you to stop being so damn mean. Everyone is not your enemy, Joie. Some of us are here to help you. If you would let us."

"Know what? I'm starting to believe that is true." She thought about all the strangers who had entered her life recently, wanting from her nothing more than she was able to give. "Ronnie, we have been friends for a long time. I know I've done some awful lowdown shit to you. But I never wanted to alienate you. After my mother passed, it felt like my world had fallen apart."

"You did sound really strange the last time we spoke." She wanted Joie to keep talking so she could get to the bottom of it. "I didn't want to say anything about how you were acting until you explained what was going on. But when you cursed me out, I said 'fuck it' and made the decision that our friendship wasn't worth the drama it brought."

"Ouch! That really stings."

"It's the truth..."

"I'll accept that... Even if it hurts." Joie closed her eyes and reflected on the past few months. "Ronnie, I need to tell you something."

"Okay..."

"My life has been a living hell since the last time I saw you."

"What's going on, Joie?"

"I didn't know how good a life me and Cedric had until it all started to fall apart. If only I could take back some of the shit I dished out..."

"You sound different. Where is all this self-reflection coming from?"

"Let's just say that it's time for me to make amends to whole lot of people."

"What's wrong? Are you sick or something?" She took a deep breath and uttered, "Oh my God! Are you...dying?"

Ronnie's unexpected questions regarding the status of her health made Joie laugh so hard, she snorted wine through her nose and on the floor. "Naw, girl, I ain't sick!"

"That's a relief." She exhaled and took a long swig of wine. "So what is *really* going on with you?"

"If you have time to talk, I guess I may as well tell you everything..."

Ronnie did have the time, so that is exactly what Joie did for the next hour.

"Daaaaaaamn, Joie... I can see why you were trippin'. You were dealing with some over-the-top mess. Even though me and Cedric had our moments, I don't for a minute believe he was selling drugs to kids. And to think that you been dealing with this all the while living in a homeless shelter..."

"Things had gotten pretty bad, but I don't want you feeling sorry for me." Joie blew her nose again. She used her foot to brush the used tissues from the sofa cushion to join the pile on the floor.

"I'm not feeling sorry for you, Joie." Ronnie replied in frustration. "But if you and the kids needed money, all you had to do was ask. After all, those are my godchildren."

"I appreciate you saying that, but I think I got this." Joie felt good for finally being able to make that declaration. "All I need from you is your friendship. I've lost a lot of things in my lifetime. I don't want to lose my only true friend."

"Joie, I'm glad you told me what's going on. I was starting to think you were losing your mind." She laughed.

"I never said I was sane to begin with." Joie joined in the laughter. "You know, life can be a bitch and if you don't roll with it, it can knock you flat on your ass."

"I hear ya."

"Well, I gotta go. I hear the kids coming up the stairs and with all the boo-hooing I've done, I know I must look a hot mess."

"All right, I'll let you go." Ronnie wanted to say more, to chastise Joie for not clueing her in on the situation earlier, but she knew Joie already had enough on her plate. "Just promise to keep in touch and call me if you need anything."

"I promise." Joie smiled again, content in the knowledge that their friendship remained intact. "And tell that husband of yours that I'm sorry for being such a bitch. He is so lucky to have you."

"Thanks, girlfriend."

"I love you, Veronica Indigo Duarte."

"I love you too, Joie Marissa Parker."

After she ended her conversation with Ronnie, Joie pulled out a pad and wrote the most heartfelt apology letter to Tomas de la Cruz she could muster. She apologized for bringing him into her drama-filled life years ago, and trying to hold onto a relationship that was doomed from the start because she was in love with her husband. She told him that any woman should be lucky to be with him because he was a wonderful man. And finally she apologized for her shameful, behavior in his hotel suite. The letter wasn't very long—only a few short paragraphs—but it was long overdue. Tomas was many things, but an asshole was not one of them.

Chapter Thirty-Nine

Joie made arrangements to meet Erica Robicheaux in the downtown branch of the Hampton library to discuss Cedric's case. She chose the library so she could bring the twins along, instead of leaving them alone in the apartment, which was against Miss Lettie's rules anyway. While the children sat in the children's section engrossed in their books, the adults found a quiet area away from prying ears.

"Now, tell me again what this boy…um, Bryson Graves, told you about that day in the park," Erica said to Joie.

Joie relayed the entire conversation being sure to not leave out any important details.

"You say his mother was there when he told you this?"

"Yes. It was me, my kids, Bryson, his sister and his mother." Joie peered down at the yellow notepad where Erica was scribbling notes. "Ranesha Graves is his mother's name."

Erica tapped the pencil against her forehead. "And you say that your husband was arrested, went to trial, and sentenced—all in less than ninety days?"

"Pretty quick, huh?"

"That's the understatement of the year. I have never heard of anyone being sent to prison so quickly. Even hardened criminals are given more latitude than what your poor husband received."

"I don't believe Cedric received a fair trial because that judge was trying to make an example out of him. His lawyer even said the same thing."

"What was the name of his previous attorney?"

"Hunter Wylie." Joie pulled his card from her wallet and handed it to Erica. "Will you need to speak to him?"

"Yes, since he's already done all the leg work."

"The last time I talked to Mr. Wylie, he told me that he wouldn't touch Cedric's case until I paid him thousands of dollars. Will I still have to pay all that money so he can give you Cedric's files?"

"Probably not. Anyway, I will confer with him. See what he's willing to give up for free. Maybe we can cut him a check out of our fund to cover his expenses."

"So you think we have a chance of getting Cedric released?"

"I need to do a bit more research before I can give you a definitive answer, but based on what I know so far, chances do look very good."

"Thank you, Erica."

"Of course, I will need to speak directly to your husband." She poised the pencil over the pad. "Have you been able to contact him?"

"I mailed him another letter a few days ago. I'm hoping to hear back from him pretty soon."

"Do you happen to have his address at the penitentiary on you? Sometimes the mail gets through quicker when it comes directly from an attorney's office."

"Yeah, here it is." Joie placed an envelope stamped "*Return To Sender*" in large red letters across the front. "I'm hoping the last letter I mailed to him don't get sent back unopened. Like this one and the ones before."

"Joie, you do realize that I can't work on your husband's case without his written consent allowing me to represent him."

"I know. I'm gonna keep trying to reach him. The last letter I sent, I made the return address like it was from his family, so maybe he'll open it."

"Well, keep me posted. I want to meet with him as soon as possible so I can determine where we stand." Erica gathered her things and shoved the paperwork into a satchel, not unlike the one Hunter Wylie carried.

"I will definitely do that, Erica."

"Joie, it was a pleasure to meet you. My dad speaks very highly of you."

"It was nice meeting you, too. You father is a very good man." Joie rose to walk Erica to the entrance. "In fact, I got that job at NASA because of him."

"Actually, you got the job because of your credentials. My father just put you in touch with the right people who could make it happen." She reached out and shook Joie's hand. "Making things happen is all about connections. And who you know…"

"Want to hear something funny?" Joie asked.

"What's that?"

"While we were trapped down in the HRBT, Larry told me that I reminded him of you."

"Did he?" She smiled slightly. "How so?"

"He said I was tough as nails on the outside, but like a marshmallow on the inside."

Erica softened upon hearing her father's favorite description of her. This wasn't the first time he made that observation, but usually those comments were only directed to her. "My father is partially correct. I do have a soft core, otherwise, I wouldn't be able to do the type of work that I do. But he is also right about me being tough as nails. There is a reason my success rate is one hundred percent, and that has absolutely nothing to do with me being all soft and mushy on the inside."

Joie watched Erica walk to her car with a confident gait that she herself no longer possessed. Now that had met the woman, she could see a slight resemblance in their personalities. But whereas Erica was keenly focused on her tasks at hand, Joie had no focus. She vowed to fix that that character flaw in no time flat.

Chapter Forty

Within a matter of weeks of meeting with Larry, Joie sat in the NASA human resources office completing a thick packet of new employee forms. The telephone interview she participated in was flawless. She possessed the education, experience, and this time—the right attitude. Joie was offered the position within an hour of her interview.

Maya and Trey were beside themselves once she told them about her new job. Joie thought the twins would be ecstatic because they were leaving the shelter and moving into their own place. But that wasn't the case at all. They were more excited because of *where* she would be working. They imagined they would be the coolest kids in their school after informing their classmates that their mom worked at NASA.

The HR clerk walked Joie to her office. After getting settled in, she asked a friendly coworker to escort her to Larry's building on their way to the cafeteria. So during their lunch break, while she received a brief history of the NASA Langley Research Center, they meandered around historic buildings surrounded by massive oak trees, whose leaves would provide a canopy of shade in the summer months.

As they rounded the corner to the main street, she was amazed upon seeing several structures that appeared to be gigantic golf balls. Though most of the buildings were built soon after WWII—many displaying a triangular orange symbol from a bygone era designating them as nuclear fallout shelters—the center was well-maintained.

"Are you sure this is the right building?" Joie glanced upwards at the five story building, marveling at the architectural design that made it so unlike other buildings on the center. At first sight, she thought it resembled something out of a futuristic movie. The oddly shaped building's top three floors were layered in shimmering, reflective glass designed to represent NASA's entry into the 21st century.

"Yes, this is the right place. This building is part of our New Town project. Tenants only moved in here a few months ago." Her coworker scanned his badge to gain entrance. "After you…"

"Cool…" Joie uttered, impressed by the sleek design.

They quickly found Larry's office. He was sitting behind his desk furiously typing away on his ergo-dynamically shaped keyboard with a focused intensity indicating he did not want to be disturbed.

"Sure looks like somebody's busy," Joie called out, amused.

Larry looked up with an annoyed expression which was quickly replaced with a pleasant smile. "Joie! What a nice surprise. I heard they hired you."

"No one is more surprised than I am."

He got up from behind his desk and greeted her with a quick hug. "Congratulations!"

"Thank you," she said. "I just wanted to stop by to say thank you for all your help. With the job. Introducing me to Erica..."

"You're very welcome." He smiled again. "How do you like this place so far?"

"I think I'm going to really like working here. Everyone has been so helpful."

"That's good to hear." He pushed his glasses upwards using his forefinger. "And speaking of Erica... How are things going with that...*situation?*"

"As well as can be expected," she replied, conscious of her coworker waiting outside in the hallway. The last thing she needed was for her husband's whereabouts to become a source of gossip.

"Good," he replied. An awkward silence ensued because there was nothing more to be said on the matter.

"Well, I'll let you get back to it."

"Joie, once this mess gets cleared up, the wife and I would love to have you both over for dinner."

"Thanks, I appreciate the offer."

"It's not an offer; it is an invitation."

"Well then... Thank you for the invitation." She smiled warmly. "I will keep in touch and let you know when we can make it."

He checked his watch, furrowing his brow. "I don't mean to cut you off, Joie, but I have five minutes to get this report out."

"I understand." She backed out into the hallway. "I just wanted stop by for a quick visit."

"It was good seeing you," he called out and gave a wave. "And stop by anytime. My door is always open."

Joie knew that Larry Robicheaux was sincere with his dinner invitation because he was not the kind of man who spoke simply to hear his own voice. So when he said he would invite them over to dinner; that is exactly what he meant.

~ ~ ~

Ironically, the place she decided to lease was one street over from Tequitta's. She discovered this fact only after taking a drive to scope out the area after seeing the townhome on a rental website. The pictures posted on the website piqued her interest because they showcased the home beautifully. The townhouse was fairly new, was located within the twins' current school district, and with three bedrooms, it was the perfect size. And at the price the owners were asking, well, it all seemed too good to be true. So before she called for the details, she decided to do a drive by. Wanted to make sure it wasn't a bait and switch scheme.

It was Trey who first realized the direction they were headed seemed very familiar. "Mommy?" he said, staring out the window as they drove through the neighborhood.

"Yes," Joie responded.

"Are we going to move back in with Auntie T?" he asked.

"No, sweetie." She continued to follow the turn-by-turn directions printed on the sheet of paper she held in her hand. "Why do you ask?"

"Because this is the same way we used to go to Auntie T's house."

Joie pulled to the side of the street and followed the detailed MapQuest directions with her finger to their destination point. Trey was right. They would be going right past Tequitta's house.

"Maybe we can stop by and say 'hi'," suggested Maya. "We haven't seen Laila and baby Derek in a long time."

"Um, I don't know if that is such a good idea." She paused to gather her thoughts and arrange them into a proper frame of reference. "The last conversation I had with Auntie T did not end well."

"Mommy," Trey sided with Maya and asked nicely, "Can we please stop by for just a few minutes? We're almost over there anyway..."

Since Joie had made a promise to herself to try to be a better person, she figured it was time to swallow her pride and make amends with Tequitta. In a cheerful voice, she sang out, "Know what? I think it would be a great idea to drop by Auntie T's. She'll probably be thrilled to see us." Knowing full well that Joie was probably the last person she wanted to see.

"Yay!" the twins cheered. "We get to see our sister and little brother again!"

Joie drove several more blocks before reaching Tequitta's house. She pulled up to the curb and parked, contemplating her next move. *What am I gonna say to fix the damage I've caused? Does Tequitta even want to see me? What if…?* But before she could complete her thoughts, the twins hopped out of the car and bounded up the driveway. Reluctantly, she followed.

Laila flung the door wide open when she saw the twins on the other side. From all the kids' reactions, you would have thought they hadn't seen each other in years, instead of months. Laila called out inside, "Mama, Miss Joie and the twins are here!"

Tequitta walked into the foyer with a drying towel in her hands and a cute little apron tied around her waist. She leaned over and greeted the twins with nothing but affection. "Hey guys! What a nice surprise!"

"Hi Auntie T!" the twins replied, giving her a great big hug.

Joie put on a cheesy grin and said cheerily, "Hey Tequitta, we were just in the neighborhood. Thought we'd drop in to say hello."

The look Tequitta gave Joie was so cold it could have frozen the air in the space between them.

"Maybe see what you're cooking for dinner…" Joie stammered out a feeble attempt at humor. It didn't go over very well.

"Can we go play in my room?!" Laila asked.

"Yeah, y'all can go play." Tequitta answered, still staring at Joie.

"Just for a few minutes! Joie shouted after them.

After the kids were out of sight, Tequitta placed both hands on her hips, smacked her lips together and shouted, "You got a hell-a-lota nerve coming to my house considering how you last spoke to me!"

"You're right." Joie raised her hands in surrender. "I acted like a total bitch the last time I saw you. I'm sorry for the things I said to you."

Tequitta had prepared herself for a fight, but was instead presented with an apology. Still, she wasn't going to crumble that easily. Not based on a few half-hearted words of Joie's regret. She crossed her arms and leaned against the wall. If Joie wanted her forgiveness, damn it, she was going to have to work for it.

"I cannot help who I am, but I was wrong for treating you so badly when I should have been grateful for your help. You took us in when we didn't have anywhere else to go and instead of me being grateful for your kindness, I acted like an asshole. I know my words may not be enough, but I am truly sorry." She tried to give her a puppy dog sad look.

It was beginning to work because Tequitta uncrossed her arms.

"They love their brother and sister. The kids love you. And I gotta admit, you've really started to grow on me." She smiled warmly. "You have been so good to us and I have been so mean to you. I don't want to mess up their relationship with you over my foolishness."

Tequitta rested her hand over her chin and stared at Joie trying to determine if her words were sincere, or if she was just trying to pull another fast one. "What do you want, Joie?"

"Nothing. Just your forgiveness."

"That's it?" Tequitta asked, still suspicious of Joie's motives.

"Yes, that's it."

"Okay." She crossed her arms again. "Why now?"

"Me and the kids have been through a whole mess of drama over the past six months. Things are finally looking up for us. I got myself a very good job and now I'm looking for a place to live."

Tequitta threw both hands in the air and cried out, "Hell no! Y'all cannot move back in with us!" She shook her head so furiously a hair clip fell out of her hair.

"Woman, ain't nobody tryin' to move back up in here with y'all. We both know that didn't work the first time. I'm trying to get my own place. Look." She pulled the sheet of paper containing details of the rental from her purse. "I was thinking about leasing this townhouse. It's just right around the corner from you."

Tequitta took the paper from Joie's hands. She scanned the description of the townhome. "You for real?"

"I was on my way there now to check out the exterior. If it looks nice, I'm going to make an appointment to see the inside."

"I know this place. It's right around the corner. I've seen it on my jogging route." She handed the paper back to Joie. "It's legit."

"The pictures posted online were really nice." She tucked the paper back inside her purse. "Me and the kids need to get out of that shelter."

"You've been living in a *shelter?*"

"We really didn't have many options." Joie shrugged nonchalantly. "It wasn't a typical homeless shelter and it wasn't so bad, but I am ready to move on."

"What about Cedric?"

"Taking that one day at a time," was all she said because they had yet to graduate to that degree of friendship where you discussed your husband.

Tequitta's tone softened the more they talked. "So you're really doing okay?"

"Yeah. Thanks to people like you, I'm gonna be just fine. Me *and* my children."

Tequitta finally stepped around Joie and shut the front door. "You guys hungry? I made a huge pot of spaghetti."

"So you accept my apology?" Joie asked sheepishly.

"Yes, I accept your apology." Tequitta reached out and gave Joie a quick hug. "C'mon in. Let's eat so you can go check out that house."

After dinner, they took a walk to see the townhouse up close and personal. From the outside, it was perfect so she called and made an appointment to see the interior.

Joie completed the rental application and was handed the keys to the townhome the very next day.

~~~

It was a welcome relief to finally move out of the shelter and into their own place again. There wasn't much furniture to move after selling most of their possessions. And thanks to the procrastination of the storage unit's owner, they hadn't gotten around to auctioning off her household items. Once she paid the balance at the storage unit, she was able to retrieve what was left of their belongings.

Her cell phone, propped on the hood of Cedric's hoopty, rang just as the movers were placing the last of the boxes into the townhome.

"Hello?" Joie shouted into the phone, out of breath from running over to answer before the caller hung up.

"Joie?" asked the caller.

"Yeah, this is Joie." She pulled the phone from her face and checked the number. "Who is this?"

"Hi Joie. It's Erica."

"Hey Erica!" Joie pulled out several hundred dollar bills from her back pocket and paid the movers. She jokingly referred to them as the "cash money brothers" because they operated on a cash only basis which probably meant they didn't file any taxes. She held her breath when she said, "I hope you have some good news for me…"

After what felt like an eternity, Erica finally spoke. "I spoke with Ms. Graves and I also interviewed her son, Bryson. I'm sorry to have to tell you this Joie, but he changed his mind. Bryson doesn't want to speak to the police."

"What?!" Joie closed her eyes tightly hoping that by doing so, it would make the pain less intense. "Why?! The last time I spoke to Ranesha, she said they were going to do the right thing."

"I'm sorry, Joie. But unfortunately, this is very common." Erica breathed out her mounting frustration. "He's afraid of getting himself into trouble with the police. And his mother is scared the authorities are going to take Bryson from her if he talks."

"Isn't there something you can do? Can't you force him to confess?"

"I'll keep trying, but until Bryson goes to the authorities, there isn't much else I can do. And as much as I want to force him to talk, I really can't because he is a minor."

"Damn..." Joie stared at the twins happily playing in front of the two-story townhome they would now call home. "Everything is going so well in my life. I got a new job. We have a place to call home. Now all I need is my husband back..."

"I am sorry, Joie. I hoped to be able to deliver happier news."

"It's not your fault, Erica." She wiped the tears from her eyes. "Thanks for trying."

"I will look at some other avenues and be in touch if anything changes. Until then, try to stay positive."

"I'll try." Joie hung up. She still hadn't spoken to Ced since visiting him at the prison. And unless he called her, she had no way of reaching him.

Maya happily skipped over to where Joie had plopped down on the front stoop. She sat next to her mother, rested her head on her arm and grinned. "Mommy, I am so happy to have my very own bedroom again."

"That's good, baby. I'm happy too." Joie tried to contain her feelings. The last thing she needed was for her kids to find out their daddy wasn't coming home after all. They were so happy that she didn't want to spoil their day with the news.

"Can I invite Laila for a sleepover?"

"Of course you can."

"Can she spend the night tonight?"

"Your bed isn't even put together." Joie patted Maya's Afro puffs down. They sprung right back to where they were before she touched them. "...and your room is a total mess. Where is Laila going to sleep?"

Maya tilted her head to the side as if she were in deep thought. "We can both sleep on the floor."

"Maybe next week would be better. That way we will have the house setup."

"Okay," Maya replied, reluctantly. She couldn't wait to show off her new room.

"Do you need something else?"

"Can me and Trey go to Auntie T's house?"

"Yes, you can go, but be back in an hour for dinner." She buttoned both twins' coats before allowing them to leave. Although it was now in the fifties, by the time they returned home, the sun would be setting, causing the temperature to quickly drop.

Joie was glad that she had apologized to Tequitta and cleared the air. After all, it wasn't Tequitta's fault that she had fallen on hard times. Besides, Laila and Derek Jr. were the only family her kids had locally. No sense in penalizing the children because she couldn't keep her big mouth shut.

After the twins turned the corner and were no longer in view, she walked into the house, ran her hands over the surface of each and every wall, upstairs and down, declaring to any malevolent spirits which may have remained from the previous occupants that this was her home. *She* was now the queen of this castle and wasn't about to deal with no mess from no one—and no thing.

One of the movers had inadvertently left a package of cigarettes on the kitchen counter. Though she didn't normally smoke, Joie needed something to take the edge off the stress building in her neck since the phone call from Erica. She glanced around the kitchen hoping to locate a lighter or even a book of matches, but there was nothing. Thank goodness the stove was gas!

She turned the cigarette package upside down and gently tapped it into her hand until one cigarette came through the opening. She pulled it free. The click-click-click of the pilot light met with the gas coming from the burner, produced a pretty blue flame. She leaned over and lit the cigarette, inhaling the menthol smoke into her lungs. Almost immediately, she felt light-headed.

Taking the lit cigarette in her hand, her walk-thru ended downstairs in the living room. She took a seat on the fireplace hearth and pulled out her cell phone.

With one quick swipe of her finger, she hit the speed-dial. The phone rang several times on the other end before anyone picked up. Joie hated calling Ronnie only when she needed to discuss her problems, because lately that seemed to be all she had to talk about. Gone were the days when she called just to shoot the breeze.

"What up, Joie?" Ronnie answered.

"Hey girl." Joie took a deep hit off the cigarette watching the orange glow of the tip become brighter. "You told me to call when I had an update. Well, I've got good news and bad news. Which one do you want to hear first?"

"The good news of course."

"Okay, the good news is I got a job at NASA."

"What?! Did you say NASA?! The location bordering Poquoson?!"

"Yep, I started this week working there as an accountant. I think I'm really going to like it. The atmosphere is different than what I'm used to. All those hippie researchers and scientists... But the twins are beside themselves to have their mom working at NASA."

"Congratulations! That is great news."

"Yes, it is. And we also moved into a townhouse. After the owner found out I was working at NASA, he let us move in without a deposit."

"That is wonderful! I am so happy for you." Ronnie took a deep breath and braced herself for whatever was about to come. She knew that whatever else Joie had to say would be a doozie. "Okay...so give me the bad news."

"Hold on. Before I do, tell me about you guys. How are you, Luis and the twins?" She made a conscious decision to no longer be a "one way friend" who only talked about her life, as if the other person did not have their own issues to deal with.

"We're doing fine. Luis is working and I'm taking care of the babies... You know, same ol', same ol'."

"Uh oh, I hear a little something extra in your voice..."

"You know I love my children and I love being home with them. These kids mean the world to me, but I need to do something else. I feel like my brain is turning into mush. To tell you the truth, I haven't been feeling much like myself lately."

"Ronnie, what's going on?"

"I'm thinking about opening up a little boutique next to Luis's office. Do something I have always wanted to do."

"For real? I thought all you wanted to do was raise those cute little babies and write books. And speaking of writing, how is your first novel coming along?"

"Girl, I have written the first paragraph of the first chapter and that is it. My writing room is being used for storage space for baby stuff. Little Luis and Isabella have sucked the creativity right out of me. Along with the fullness of my breasts."

"I understand. Raising twins ain't no joke. I was glad my parents were around to help babysit Maya and Trey so I could keep working." Joie misted up at the memory of her late mother. "So tell me about this boutique."

"It's just a thought for now. I've been looking at my options of business ventures. Opening a store is one of them. Me and Luis have a lot more to discuss before it actually takes form, though." Ronnie let the idea of actually going into business take root. Mentioning it to Joie made it feel just a bit more real. "That's enough about me. What is the rest of your news?"

"It's about Cedric."

"Is he okay?"

"I honestly don't know. I haven't spoken to him since the last visit." Joie sighed wearily. "But his attorney just called and said that little boy ain't gonna tell the truth about those drugs. He changed his mind."

"What does that mean?"

"It means that my husband is going to remain locked up in prison for a very long time. And he wants me to file for a divorce because he doesn't want me waiting around for him to get out."

"Damn... Joie, I am so sorry."

"Me too." She inhaled the last of the cigarette before stubbing it out in the fireplace. "Guess it's time for me to start planning out the rest of my life without Cedric in it."

"That's a damn shame that his attorney can't fix this. What the hell are you paying her for?"

"I'm *not* paying her. She took on his case pro-bono because I couldn't afford his other attorney." Joie felt lightheaded and queasy from smoking the cigarette. "Erica takes on the cases of inmates who are wrongly accused."

"That's cool. Since she does this for a living, maybe she can come up with another plan to free Cedric."

"Ronnie, I still love my husband. He is the love of my life, but I have to move on."

"Are you sure that's what you want to do?"

"When me and Ced remarried, I thought that was it. It was going to be me and him forever. Through thick and thin. For richer or for poorer. Sickness and in health... I just never expected his going to prison to be in the equation."

"There aren't any guarantees in life, Joie. No matter how good we think things are going... Shit happens. Why do you think there are so many divorces?"

"Yeah, I know shit happens. But check this out. Cedric was the one who told me he didn't want me to wait for him. He said if I don't file for a divorce, he would. Those words are from his mouth, not mine."

"Damn." Ronnie could only shake her head. "I don't know what to say."

"Ain't nothing to say. I guess the time has finally come for me to stop being *lost* in the offbeat and start living in the offbeat..."

"Lost in the offbeat, huh?" Ronnie said. "I don't mean to diminish your situation, but I guess we are both feeling a little bit lost right now."

"Really? I thought you would be the last person to say she felt lost. You have everything you ever wanted."

"I'm not saying that I'm unhappy, because I do have a great life. I'm just saying that I need to do more with it. Rediscover my purpose...You know what I mean?"

Joie sat in her rented townhome amidst stacks of unpacked boxes and furniture made dusty by months of sitting in a storage unit. She thought about the last few months living in that shelter-apartment with barely enough money to feed her kids. And before that, being homeless and living out of their car. Her head swam from smoking a cigarette on an empty stomach. She had just gotten off the phone with her husband's attorney who had basically told her that Cedric was fucked. And after paying the moving guys, she had enough barely money in her wallet to buy food and gas for the car. Yet, despite her issues, she took the time to listen to Ronnie vent.

"Luis has his business. Kiara has her life in California...The twins will always be well taken care of... Plus, I'm not even talking about working full time. I just need something to keep my mind busy."

As she listened to Ronnie lament over her privileged life, she pushed away thoughts that the old Joie would have had to tell Ronnie to *shut the fuck up and stop bitchin' because she was feeling a little bored.* Instead of doing this, she chose to support her friend and offer some advice, "Remember a few years ago when you left Virginia and everything behind to start a new life in California?"

"Yes, I remember."

"When you first told me what you were up to, I thought you were crazy. I thought you were chasing ghosts from the past when you said you were going to meet your daughter, but you didn't let anything or anyone dissuade you. Making that trip was part of your purpose. You started talking about living in the offbeat... Remember? Hell, you were the one who used to encourage me to live in the offbeat, so if anyone can discover that thing that makes them feel more fulfilled—rediscover your purpose, it is you."

"You're right." Ronnie replied gratefully. "I guess I just needed to hear someone else put my life in perspective for me."

"It's always easier to analyze someone else's life because you're on the outside looking in. I just wish I had a better grasp on my own situation."

"Well, like I said earlier, maybe that attorney still has a few tricks up her sleeve."

"I sure do hope so." Joie noted the time. She had been on the phone for almost an hour, which was longer than she had planned. Soon the twins would be running through the door with empty bellies and dirty bodies. She still needed to fix dinner and also locate that box of bath towels.

"If there is anything you need, please call me." Ronnie added, "I mean it. Anything. Me and Luis have got your back."

"Thanks, girlfriend. Well, I've gotta run. Tomorrow is Monday and I haven't even found sheets for the beds yet."

"You're going to work tomorrow?"

"Yeah, I don't have any time saved up to take off."

Ronnie smirked on the other end. "Since when does a minor technicality stop you from taking care of business? If you need the time off, work it out with your supervisor. You just moved into your place, I'm sure they'll understand."

"You do have a point." Her eyes scanned the contents of the living room and the kitchen. Nothing was in its proper place. "I can probably make up the time by going in early and staying late."

"Woman, take care of your business and get your house in order. After that, everything else will quickly fall into place."

"I think I'm going to take your advice." Joie found the delivery flyer for Chinese food because she really didn't feel like going to the grocery store or cooking dinner. "I'll catch up with you later. Tell Luis I said hi."

"Sure will."

Joie hung up the phone. Still feeling queasy, she ran upstairs to the bathroom and hung her head over the toilet. Her stomach involuntarily lurched, bringing up what little remained of her breakfast. Feeling much better after releasing the contents of her stomach, she rinsed her mouth several times, but the disgusting taste of nicotine and vomit remained.

Voices coming from downstairs caught her attention. It was the twins, but they were not alone.

"I'll be right down!" she called out. She swished her mouth with more tap water before drying her face with her t-shirt. It didn't get rid of the lingering cigarette taste, but at least the aftertaste of vomit was gone. She made a vow right then and there to never smoke again.

"Hey Tequitta," Joie said from her place on the upstairs landing. "What are you doing here?"

"It was getting dark so I walked the kids home."

"You didn't have to do that, but thank you." Joie continued down the stairs and went to a box marked 'bathroom'. "Where are your kids?"

"My parents are in town visiting, so they took them to dinner."

"Oh. That's nice." She sliced through the packing tape with a box cutter and pulled out two towels and then handed one to each twin. "You kids get cleaned up. You smell like outside."

Both Maya and Trey pulled off their coats and tossed them on the floor. Joie didn't get upset with them because there was nowhere else to place their coats.

Tequitta glanced around the cluttered living room. "This is a very nice place."

"Thanks. We have a lot of unpacking to do, but we'll get there."

"I didn't think you'd have time to cook dinner so I brought some food with me." She handed Joie a paper bag containing a covered casserole dish. "It's nothing fancy. Just a little something I threw together. There are also paper plates and plastic utensils inside and I snuck in a bottle of wine for you to drink later on."

"Tequitta, you didn't have to go through all this trouble. I was going to order Chinese delivery."

"It's no trouble. I just wanted to do something nice for you."

Joie studied the woman standing before her. She looked like a million dollars. Her shoulder length hair was blown silky straight. It was tucked underneath a red beret that topped her perfectly made-up face. The coat she wore fit her body as if it was custom made. The thigh high leather boots that graced her long legs certainly did not come from any stores off-the-rack shelf. In all actuality, she looked like she had stepped off the cover of a magazine.

Though they were not at the point of being best friends like she and Ronnie were, she was thankful for the kind gesture of a homemade meal.

In spite of Tequitta's newly moneyed look, Joie noticed something was off. Tequitta's eyes seemed to continue moving when her head didn't. The slight, almost imperceptible slurring of her words, confirmed what Joie had suspected all along. Tequitta was drunk off her ass. Some things never changed.

"The food is a traditional chicken and rice dish my mom used to make for my dad... I thought you'd like it."

"Well, thanks again." Joie took the bag into the kitchen and placed it on the counter.

Tequitta followed her. "Joie, the twins told me you won't take them up to visit Cedric. I hope they didn't do anything wrong by telling me."

Joie wrung her hands in frustration. "No, its fine. Prison is not a place I want my kids to become used to."

"I understand." Tequitta measured her words carefully before continuing so as to not upset their fragile relationship. "Maya also said that Cedric might be coming home soon because a big-time attorney is working on his case to get him freed. Is that true?"

She had no intention of discussing Cedric's status, especially considering her earlier conversation with Erica. Yet, despite her drunkenness, Tequitta's concern was endearing.

"Yeah, his attorney is doing all she can to get him out. I'm hoping he'll be home soon."

"I sure do hope she is successful."

"Thanks, Tequitta. I'll let you know how things turn out." Joie wanted to end this conversation sooner rather than later. But then again, from the way Tequitta slurred her words, chances were she wouldn't remember much of their conversation anyway.

"If there is anything I can do to help… Maybe offer some legal advice or something. You'll let me know?"

"I will. Thanks."

She displayed a toothy grin and announced, "Well, I have some news myself."

"You do? What is it?" Joie continued cutting open boxes. She didn't mean to be rude, but Tequitta's visit was not expected.

"I'm getting married!" She raised her left hand towards Joie's face. The exquisite diamond engagement ring shone brightly under the recessed lighting. "Paris proposed to me a couple days ago."

Looking at Tequitta's engagement ring brought back a memory she would just as soon forget about her own pawned wedding ring. She wondered if that slimy pawn shop owner had displayed her ring alongside all the others. Or if it was even still there. "What? You're getting married? Congratulations."

"Thank you." She stretched her hand out to admire how the light bounced off the intricate cut. The wedding rings Derek gave her now rested on the middle finger of her right hand.

"Didn't you guys just meet?" She thought to herself, *that explains the nouveau rich look. Her new man must be loaded.*

"We've been dating for over six months now." She guffawed. "That's long enough to realize we want to spend the rest of our lives together."

"Six months? Has it really been that long?" Joie frowned as she tried to reconcile the fact that while her life with Cedric was probably over, Tequitta was beginning life anew with husband number two.

"I wanted to let you know because after we get married, me and the kids will be moving to northern Virginia."

"You're moving?"

"Yeah. In a couple of months. His family owns land up there. We were thinking of staying in Hampton, but since he recently gained custody of his son, he wants to live near his family."

"Did you tell Maya and Trey about your plans? That you guys were moving?"

"Yes, I did. They were upset, but I told them that y'all can visit anytime."

"Thanks," Joie said. That ought to make it easier... Hey, can I ask you something?"

"Sure."

"I hope I don't offend you with my question, but what about the race issue? You have two beautiful Black children and this man is white. I assume his son is white also... Is he ready to raise your children? Are you ready to raise his?"

Tequitta seemed to sober right up. The smile she wore earlier withdrew into a scowl before she spoke. "I understand what you're asking Joie, but what should race have to do with us getting married and raising our children? I love Paris. He loves me *and* my kids. I adore his son. We aren't being naïve by thinking we won't have problems, but we'll handle it. Together. Anyway, if either of us had reservations about marrying outside our race then we would never have gotten engaged."

"I'm sorry. I didn't mean anything by it," Joie apologized. "I only asked because of what's been happening lately... All the police shootings, rioting, racists coming out of the woodwork... Seems to me that it would be easier to just stick with your own."

"You see, Joie, its people with attitudes like yours who keep this whole racism issue alive. Why can't we just be two people who meet and fall in love? My parents aren't the same race and they are still together. And yes, his son is white, but that's not an issue. Paris and I have discussed this *race issue* and decided that it won't be the center of our lives. And if other people have a problem with us being married... Well, I guess that is just too damn bad."

"I hear ya. Life is too short to be worrying about what other people think." Joie walked over and embraced Tequitta affectionately. "I truly am happy for you. I wish you both all the best. Forget everybody else."

"Right on!" Tequitta gave her a fist bump.

"There is something to be said about letting go of people and situations that bring nothin' but problems to your life. My mother used to always tell me that some people come into our lives for a minute, some for longer, and others for a lifetime. Trouble starts when you try to make those temporary people permanent. I guess I'm just now figuring out who is who."

"Well, which am I Joie?" She crossed her arms protectively across her heart in case the answer was not the one she expected. In spite of what she had always told herself, for some reason, she wanted Joie to like her.

"I think that you are actually a good person. Plus, since our kids are related, you are someone who will be in my life for a lifetime. And you know what, Tequitta? I am perfectly fine with that because I truly do like you."

"Know what Joie? I like you too." Tequitta shrugged out of her coat and tossed it on the kitchen counter. She removed her beret from her head and placed it on top of her coat. Pushing up the sleeves of her cashmere sweater, she offered, "How about I help you get these boxes unpacked."

Joie laughed. "Don't think I'm gonna turn you down because I sure could use the help."

"Then let's get to it."

"You know what Tequitta?"

"Hmmm, what's up?"

"I had you figured all wrong. You are really cool. I can see why Derek chose you over me."

"Is that right?"

"Umh huh, because I used to be a real bitch," Joie said before bursting out in laughter when she saw the shock register on Tequitta's face. "Now don't pretend like I wasn't."

"You got no argument from me there sister," she replied and joined in the laughter. "I just never imagined you would admit it."

For the rest of the evening, Joie and Tequitta opened the remaining boxes and put away as much as they could in between sips of red wine. The twins also worked diligently to get their rooms in order before turning in for bed. By the time midnight rolled around, both women were exhausted, collapsing on the floor in a heap of tired muscles.

The way Joie figured, she might as well embrace Tequitta as a friend. Though each woman was flawed in her own unique way, Tequitta with her drinking and Joie with her wild and loose ways, they understood it was better for all concerned that they maintain a good relationship, if for no other reason than for the sake of their children.

Chapter Forty-One

The noise from the recycling truck's mechanical arm, scooping up the flattened cardboard boxes from the sidewalk and loading the debris into its open bay, woke Joie with a start. It was Tequitta's idea to break down the boxes and put them out late last night. If it was up to Joie, the boxes would have remained stacked in the garage until she finally got around to throwing them away.

She opened one eye and scanned the dark bedroom momentarily forgetting where she was. Gradually, the realization of being in her new townhome sank in. She rolled over to check the time. It was six o'clock; only fifteen minutes remained before the alarm would go off blasting the morning news.

The moment her feet hit the floor, she knew it was going to be a rough day. She stood up ever so slowly arousing every sore muscle in her body from a deep sleep. "Damn! Why did I let Tequitta talk me into unpacking all those boxes last night? And I shouldn't have drank so much wine... Ugh, I feel like I've been run over by a truck."

The trip to the bathroom was an uncomfortable ordeal of carefully maneuvering her arms into a position that caused the least amount of agonizing pain. She proceeded to use her battery operated toothbrush to remove the furry coating caused by too much wine and not enough sleep.

"Mommy, do we have to go to school today?" Trey asked from outside the bathroom door.

"Yes, baby. But go back to bed. You still have an hour before you have to get up."

"Okay."

Joie returned to her bed, which was really only a box spring and mattress at this point because the bed frame was missing several screws.

"It's a good thing I told my supervisor that I was moving this weekend. This way asking for another day off won't be a total surprise," she whispered to herself, justifying her action, before calling her supervisor. She left a brief message informing him that she wasn't coming in. It was risky requesting a day off within her first few weeks of working, but the way her body felt at the moment, there was no way she could go anywhere.

Despite being thoroughly fatigued, she wasn't really sleepy. So she laid in bed and listened to the radio until it was time to wake the twins. In between listening to the radio talk show hosts chattering about foolish and unimportant topics, she went through the laundry list of things to do.

I got a lot on my mind, but the first thing I need to do is call a lawyer to discuss my options for divorcing Cedric. From what Erica told me, and since I still haven't heard from him, I guess it's time to do this. No use in putting it off any longer because if I'm going to make a fresh start, it might as well begin today.

Maya ran into her bedroom carrying two new outfits in her hands. "Mommy, what should I wear to school today?"

Joie stared at the pretty outfits, not recognizing either set of clothing. "What are you doing up so early."

"The trash man woke me up."

"Where did you get those clothes?"

"Auntie T gave them to me last night. She said Laila's new grandmother has sent her so many new clothes that she won't miss them at all."

"That was nice of Tequitta to give them to you." Joie noted the designer labels and shook her head. "Those clothes cost a lot of money, Maya. Are you sure Laila's new grandmother won't mind?"

"Auntie T says Mr. Paris's mother owns a boo…a boo…"

"Boutique?" Joie jumped in to help.

"Yes. His mother owns a boutique so she gets new clothes all the time." She held both outfits up to her petite body. "Aren't they pretty?"

"Yes, they are both very pretty." She pushed herself up and leaned against the wall trying to not wince at the pain shooting up her arms, across the sides of her back, and continuing down the muscles of each leg. "I think you will look nice in either one."

"I think I'm going to wear the purple set today."

"Good choice," Joie said, and then added, "Maya, wake your brother and tell him to get ready. I'm going to drive you to school this morning."

"Do you have to?" she responded back. "I wanted to ride on the bus with Laila and her friends."

"That's fine, but you have to include your brother. I don't want him being left behind by you and your friends the first day riding the bus."

"He won't be alone. Trey met some boys his age when we were walking to Auntie T's house yesterday. They already told him they'd see him this morning on the bus."

"All right, but I'm still going to walk you to the bus stop."

Maya noticed her mother was still wearing her pajamas. "Are you going to work today?"

"No, I'm staying home. I have a lot of things I need to take care of while you kids are in school."

"Oh. Okay." Maya grinned mischievously at her mother. "I can stay home and play hooky with you if you want me to."

"No, that's alright, baby. What mommy has to do today is not going to be fun."

~ ~ ~

Two weeks later...

Maya and Trey sat at the kitchen table doing their homework while Joie stepped out on the back deck to use the phone. They were both so engrossed in multiplying fractions and correcting misspelled words she didn't want to disturb either of them.

"Girlfriend, you will never believe what happened!" Joie blurted out as soon as Ronnie answered.

"What's wrong, Joie? Are you and the kids all right?"

"Yeah girl, we're fine." Joie waved off her concern as if it were unwarranted.

"That's a relief." Ronnie realized she had been holding her breath. "So what's up?

"I got something to tell you. Do you have time to talk?"

"Sure. I just put the twins down for their nap. What's up?"

"Last night after me and Tequitta finished hanging some shelves..."

"Wait just a minute! Did you say you and Tequitta?"

"Yeah, didn't I tell you? We're cool now. She stopped by yesterday and helped me hang shelves in the bathroom. Even offered to hang some pictures."

Ronnie pulled the phone away from her face and stared at the image of Joie's caller ID. The voice on the other end sounded like Joie, but this was not the Joie she knew.

"You still there?"

"Yeah, I'm still here. I'm still getting over the shock that you and Tequitta are now hanging out."

"Girl, it ain't that serious, but anyway I haven't told anyone else what I'm about to tell you."

"Joie, will you please get to the point? The twins are going to be awake before you finish telling me whatever it is you have to say."

"Okayyyy…. Don't be so damn impatient." Joie took a deep breath and began to relay the chain of events. "Last night, I turned off all the lights as I prepared to go to sleep. But before I got into bed, I had the urge to do something I haven't done in a long time."

Ronnie began to laugh just imaging what her friend was up to. "I know it's been a long time since you had sex, but please don't tell me you went and brought some stranger home. Not with the kids in the house."

"Girl, puhleezeeee! That ain't even close to what I did…"

"That's a relief."

"Will you please stop interrupting me so I can continue? I'm trying to tell you something important."

"Fine. Go ahead."

"Anyway… Before I got in my bed, I dropped down to my knees, clasped my hands together and prayed like I did when I was a child. I asked the Lord for help because I was seriously considering divorcing Cedric." Joie took another deep breath before she continued speaking. "Last night I asked God to give me something to help me make a decision on what I should do."

"Joie? Did you say you were *praying?*"

"Hold on… I'm not finished… So this morning, while I lay in bed listening to the radio—one of those radio hosts was giving his morning inspiration, I decided I wasn't going to work. I chose to stay home and get my house in order because right now there are still boxes all over the place."

"Well, you did just move. It takes time to get settled. So what does this have to do with you making a decision about Cedric?"

"I'm not finished… My supervisor called me back to find out if I was okay since I had called in sick."

"Okay…."

"Well, after I got off the phone with my supervisor, the phone rang. It was Cedric! He called to tell me that Erica, his new attorney, had stopped by to see him this morning. Turns out that Bryson—that boy Cedric helped—went down to the police station last night and admitted those drugs were his. He told them all about how Cedric took those drugs from him to keep his little butt out of trouble. Told them my man didn't have nothin' to do with those damn pills."

"What?! Joie, that is incredible!"

"I know!" she exclaimed. "But that ain't all there is to my story."

"I'm listening..."

"Not only am I happy because my husband is coming home, but I think I had a prophetic vision."

Ronnie chuckled on the other end, thinking Joie was fooling around. She asked in a sarcastic tone, "Are you smokin' weed again?"

"No. I am straight sober."

"You're telling me that Cedric is getting released because you prayed about it?"

"Yeah, I think so."

"In that case, if you believe He answered your prayers, then He did. Then again... Maybe He answered Cedric's prayer. Or it could have been Maya and Trey's."

"Could be."

"Joie, it sounds like you found your religion. Good for you."

"I'm not religious, but I do believe in God."

"I recall you talking about your upbringing. And I know that your parents were good Christians, but you never talked about God. Plus, it's just your entire persona is so....so...not religious."

"I'm not talking about *religion*. I'm talking about God."

"I see..."

"I got sick of my parents forcing me to go to church. I started questioning the whole religious thing and stopped going when I turned eighteen. Except for the odd Sunday here and there, I haven't been back since."

"I understand why you stopped going. I was also turned off by religion. All those fake greedy preachers starting churches for the wrong reasons. All you have to do is turn on the television to see what I mean. Damn shame."

"You know what, Ronnie? I can deal with those greedy preachers as long as they deliver the Word. I stopped going because of the politics involved in the church. Seemed like way too many self-proclaimed Christians are hypocrites from Monday through Saturday. But let Sunday roll around and they suddenly become holier-than-thou.

Quick to judge others and declare those who don't believe what they believe as heathens. I saw how they treated people outside the church when they thought nobody was watching. Those people called themselves good Christians, but their behavior said something totally different…"

"I totally get it. Me and Luis haven't been in awhile, but when the twins are older, we plan to start taking them. They need a foundation. And we need to fellowship with others. I do miss that."

"I finally understand that going to church don't have a thing to do with my loving the Lord. He resides in me. No matter if I am sitting on a church pew or standing in a field of flowers."

Ronnie listened to Joie, feeling her metamorphosis come through the phone line. Her heart was touched.

Joie began to cry. "Maybe that's what's wrong with our marriage." she sniffled. "We neglected to put Him at the center of our lives and look what's happened to us."

"Okay, so you strayed. But you can find your way back."

"You think so?" Joie used her shirt to dry her eyes. "I have been feeling lost for so long…"

"Why are you crying?" Ronnie asked with concern. Although she had known Joie for decades, the sudden change in her attitude was slightly disconcerting, as well as exhilarating.

"I'm crying because I think I saw God today."

"What?! Where?! How?!"

"After I hung up with Cedric, I needed to take a walk to clear my mind. I was feeling confused about our conversation."

"What were you confused about?"

"I'm not exactly sure why I was feeling confused. I just know I was feeling some kinda way. First he tells me to divorce him, the next thing I know is he's telling me he's coming home."

"You must feel like you've been riding a roller coaster of emotions."

"Right. So anyway, it was about eight-thirty when he called. It was still early so I decided to take a walk in the neighborhood park. It was really windy, but sorta nice with the temperature in the upper fifties. I remember thinking that it looked like rain was on its way because the sky was really cloudy. There weren't many people on the jogging path. Just a few older ladies walking their dogs. I didn't know so many people were home during the day…"

"Joie, will you please get to the part about seeing God?! I'm dying of suspense!"

"Okay, stop trying to rush a sistah." She closed her eyes so as to not forget any detail. "I was basically walking and having a conversation with myself. Asking what should I do? Should I stay with Cedric and see this through? Should I go ahead with the divorce since my life is going so well now? I mean, I love Cedric and all, but we were having problems before all this happened. I don't know if this whole 'prison' thing was my opportunity to move on. Maybe he would come home we would end up going through the same ol' mess. All over again."

Ronnie exhaled loudly on the other end of the phone. "I thought you wanted to be with Cedric. Do everything possible to get him out. Isn't that what you've been trying to accomplish since he got locked up?"

"Yes, but for the past couple of weeks, I had accepted that I could make it on my own. I was taking care of the twins just fine without him. I made peace with my decision to divorce him. At least, I thought I did."

"Okay. I can understand why you were feeling a little confused. But you guys love each other. Right?"

"Yeah, but you and I both know that love don't have nothin' to do with it."

"That is so true." Ronnie agreed. "Being in love can bring you nothing but heartache if you're not careful."

"Right. So I basically said out loud, not really expecting an answer, that if I was supposed to stay with Cedric, I needed a definite sign."

"What happened?"

"Like I was saying, it was very cloudy. Well, I just happened to look up at the clouds when I saw something very strange hanging low in the sky. I thought it was the moon because it was a perfectly round, white circle. This thing was huge! But then I remembered that I saw the moon last night and it was just a crescent. I kept staring at the object thinking how odd it looked. The clouds kept passing over the object but it didn't move."

"That does sound strange. Then what?"

"At first I just stared at the white disc trying to process what I was seeing. My eyes told me 'moon', but of course it wasn't the moon. I turned around to see if anyone else was nearby so I could ask them if they were seeing what I saw. Finally, the clouds fully parted and I realized I was staring at the sun. Only this time I had to look away because it was so bright."

"That sounds really weird, Joie."

"I know, right? Then the clouds rolled back and there it was again. A pure white, perfectly round disc hanging low on the horizon. It stayed that way for a good minute before the clouds again parted. In all my years on this earth, I have never witnessed such a sight."

"You can't look directly at the sun, Joie. It'll blind you." Ronnie explained. "Didn't you learn that in school?"

"I know you can't look at the sun directly, Ronnie," she replied slightly perturbed. "But I did today. For several minutes. While I was on that path asking for help with coming to terms on my marriage, I believe He was telling me that I was making the right decision by staying with Cedric."

"Wow! You received all that from taking a simple walk?"

"In my logical mind, I understand it was probably just a coincidence that I happened to be standing on that path at the very moment those clouds passed in front of the sun. This probably happens all the time. I just never looked up to witness this phenomenon. But in my heart, in my soul, I have to believe it was something more…"

"I don't know, Joie. With all the uncertainty going on in your life, I don't doubt for a moment what you observed was Heavenly. If you told this to someone else, they'd probably have some sort of scientific explanation. But I like your explanation about seeing God much more."

"I do too. I know people claim to see God in the most bizarre objects. Toast. A block of government cheese. Dryer lint… I just never imagined I would be one of those people I once thought were crazy."

"Wow!" Ronnie exclaimed again. "Joie, you continue to amaze me. One day you're cursing me to high heaven and the next you receive a vision from God. Whatever you are doing in your life, you need to keep on doing it."

"Girl, I'm just finally trying to live right. One day at a time…"

Chapter Forty-Two

"Hey Miss Lettie," Joie said upon seeing the older woman manning the front desk of the *House of Ruth Ministries*. She pressed the talk button and said in the speaker, "I stopped by to drop off the key to my old apartment."

"Hello, Miss Parker," Miss Lettie replied in a cheerful voice. "You sure do look pretty in that dress."

"Thank you. I was on my way home from work and even though I'm a couple weeks late, I decided to swing by to return the apartment key."

Miss Lettie buzzed her in. "Oh you don't have to worry about that key. We always rekey the locks before the next family moves in."

Joie removed the key from her keychain and placed it on the desk. "Well, this also gave me an excuse to stop by to say hi."

"I am so proud of you," Miss Lettie said. "I knew when I met you that you wouldn't be here for long."

"Really? How did you know that?"

"When you've been in this business for as long as I have, you gain a certain knack for knowing which women will overcome their situations and those who won't. You just had that extra something in you..."

"Miss Lettie, I want to thank you for everything you've done for me and my family. Without your help, I don't know how we would have survived. If there is anything I can do to repay your kindness..."

"Actually, there is something you can do. Since you've got that job over at NASA, maybe you can arrange it so the children who live here can get a tour."

"That's a good idea. I'll ask around to see what we need to do."

"That will be wonderful. Your children were so excited when they came back. They told everyone here about their special NASA tour and how exciting it was. I think it would be fantastic for the other children to have a similar experience."

Joie handed her a check written out for two hundred dollars.

"What's this?" She took the paper and read it. "You don't have to do that..."

"I know it's not much. Since I've only worked at NASA for a month, that's what I had left over after I placed the deposit down to get my utilities turned on. I want you to accept it as a token of my gratitude to you and the House of Ruth Ministries."

"Thank you," Miss Lettie replied. "You know we never turn down donations."

"You're welcome." Joie peered through the window behind Miss Lettie out into the courtyard. "I wanted to stop by to see Ranesha, do you know if she's around?"

"You just missed her. Coincidentally, she turned in her key just a few hours ago."

"Did she say where she was moving?"

"She said she was moving in with some family members in Newport News, up near the Patrick Henry Mall until she can get on her feet. She was offered a permanent job with one of the contractors on the Langley Air Force Base. Told me she's making more money than she could have imagined."

"That is very good news." Joie scribbled on a piece of paper. "I have a new cell phone so I'm going to give you my new number in case you see Ranesha again."

"I'll make sure she gets this."

"What about Bryson?" Joie prepared herself, hoping the news wouldn't be all bad. "Did she say how he's doing?"

"Now that you mention it, she did tell me that her son was sent to juvie. Didn't say why though or for how long, only that he needed to learn his lesson now while he was still young enough to change." She shook her head. "I always thought he was a good kid."

"I hope Bryson turns out okay, not only for his sake, but for Ranesha's. I know how difficult it is being a single mother of a boy. They look to the closest male role model they can find and don't care if he is a drug dealer or a high school teacher."

"And that is why I opened this shelter all those years ago. As adults, we need to do more to raise, nurture and encourage our kids to do the right thing so they don't grow up to be criminals. What you said about these young boys—and girls, being raised by single mothers is too often where the problem lies. I don't care how good of a mother you are. These kids need two loving parents, a mother and a father to raise them. And I'm not talking about the weekend here and there. I'm talking about two parents in the home."

"Miss Lettie, both you and I know that does not reflect the true reality of today's world. Whether we like it or not, way too many kids in our community are being born out of wedlock. These little girls wind up having babies from multiple men who have babies with multiple women. My husband told me that on more than one occasion, several of those kids who attended the youth center found out by accident that they were half siblings."

"Doggone shame what's going on with these young people today…" Miss Lettie sighed wearily while shaking her head. "I keep up on the news. I've been watching how these policemen keep slaughtering these young Black men… Some in broad daylight, like it ain't nothing. Reminds me of the way they used to lynch Black folks back in the day. Only this time the killing is legal because those racist police have the system on their side."

Joie thought about her two children and the world they were growing up in. The Black community had hoped with the election of President Barak Obama, that their lives would get better, and the world would embrace the young Senator from Illinois. No one could have ever imagined that a Black man leading the most powerful nation in the world would result in setting race relations back fifty years.

Truth be told, a whole lot of hate groups were emboldened by the disrespect of President Obama by our elected officials. It was almost vogue to come out of the woodwork to proudly share a racist rhetoric with the world. Instead of coming together as one nation, indivisible under God, the United States of America was slowly morphing into the Divided States of America.

"I didn't mean to get started, but this subject burns my hide. And you want to know what's even worse than police officers killing our young men in the street?"

Joie shook her head.

"Black-on-black crime. It is as commonplace as the day is long and has become such a normal part of our lives, that murders don't even make the front page of the paper."

"You're right, Miss Lettie. Things have gotten really bad."

"All we need to do is look in our own neighborhoods to see how quickly we are killing ourselves. The crime rate in our communities is abysmal!" Miss Lettie balled up her fist and smacked it hard on the desk.

Joie nodded her agreement. "You're right. But if those bad-assed kids want to go out and commit crimes, what am I supposed to do?"

"Get involved, that's what you can do. You mentioned your husband works with children…"

"Yeah, he used to work with lots of young men. He unfortunately also considered many to be lost souls because they were so far gone."

"But he cared enough to do something to make a difference in the lives of some of those children. And that's where it all begins, with caring."

"You know Miss Lettie, I am so grateful for people like you—folks who use their lives to make a difference in others. If it wasn't for the House of Ruth Ministries, and I know I speak for many of the ladies who have lived here, I don't know what I would have done."

"If you really want to make a difference, don't let what you have received from the House of Ruth end with you. Because I think Joie Parker has a lot to offer this world. Don't you let nobody tell you any differently."

She listened to the woman's words and let them take root. *Maybe there is something I can offer to the world to make this a better place. But what?*

The anger slowly dissipated from Miss Lettie's face. "I was part of the civil rights movement, and I am well aware of what this generation is facing." She declared, "As long as I have a breath in my body, I will continue to help my people and my community any way that I can."

Chapter Forty-Three

Joie sat at her desk completing an online financial management course when her cell phone rang. Caller ID indicated a private number. Because the office was quiet enough to hear a pin drop, she stepped outside to answer the unexpected call. When she whispered, "Hello", she was greeted by one of those annoying robotic female voices.

"Hello. You have a collect call from Cedric Parker, an inmate at the Virginia State Correctional Facility. If you wish to accept charges, please press one. Otherwise, you may end this call now by hanging up."

Joie's heartbeat quickened upon hearing that the call was from Cedric. She quickly accepted the charges by pressing 'one' on the keypad.

The robotic female voice continued, *"This phone call is being recorded. If you do not wish for your conversation to be recorded, press two to disconnect now. Otherwise you may remain on the line."*

She waited patiently as the call went through several rounds of clicking noises before being connected. Finally, she heard Cedric's voice on the other end.

"Joie?" he said.

"Hey baby, I'm here."

"It is so good to hear your voice again."

"Yours too." She wiped away a tear. "How are you holding up?"

"Much better now that I know I'll be released soon." He chuckled on the other end.

"I told the twins that you're coming home. They are so excited! We decorated the house and everything."

"That's good, baby." He paused and then said, "Joie, I need to ask you a very important question?"

"Okay. What is it?"

After a long weary sigh, he asked in a nervous, squeaky voice, "Baby, are... are we... are we still married?"

Joie broke into happy laughter at his question. "Yes, of course we're still married."

"Thank God," he replied. "I know I told you to divorce me. I'm just so glad you didn't."

"I couldn't. I love you too much. And you know how much I hate to be told what to do."

"Baby, baby, baby! Those words are music to my ears. Whew!"

The smile she wore could have lit an entire neighborhood as she listened to the sexy timbre of her husband's voice.

"So tell me. What did you do to convince young Bryson to come forth? I hope he isn't going to get into much trouble."

Joie closed her eyes and looked upwards in gratitude. She replied, "I didn't do anything. He did it all... and I'm sure Bryson is going to be fine."

"He?" Cedric asked in confusion. "Who is *he?*"

Joie laughed out loud and explained, "It's not what you think, sweetheart. I'll tell you all about it when you get home. So, when *are* you getting out?"

"That's why I'm calling. Erica told me that I'm going to be released tomorrow afternoon."

"Tomorrow?!" Joie squealed in delight. "For real?"

"Uh huh. They're transporting me back down there tomorrow morning. So I need you to pick me up from the Hampton Municipal Court building."

"Ced! I am so happy!" she yelled as quietly as she could. "The twins are going to be so excited you'll be home in time for Christmas."

"Baby, I'm happy too. Thank goodness this mess is finally going to be over."

One of Joie's coworkers who sat nearest to the entrance overheard the commotion coming from the hallway. He poked his head through the door to see what was going on. "Is everything all right, Joie?" he asked.

She covered the phone with one hand and told him, "Yeah, everything is fine. I just got a little bit excited, that's all."

"Who was that?" Cedric asked upon hearing a man's muffled voice.

"Nobody. One of my coworkers."

"Did you get your old job back? Was that Rufus? Why is..."

The robotic voice chimed in and cut off Cedric's question. "*This call will automatically disconnect in one minute. I repeat, this call will automatically disconnect in one minute.*"

Joie suddenly realized that since she hadn't spoken to Cedric, nor had he read any of her letters, he was totally out of the loop with all that had transpired in her life over the past several months. He had no idea she was now working at NASA, nor that she and the twins had moved into a townhome. Since she hadn't spoken to him for more than a few minutes since their first *and* last jail visit, she was at a loss at where to begin explaining. So instead of trying to fit everything she needed to tell him in a five minute phone call, she begged off and said, "No, that wasn't Rufus."

"Who was it?"

"Cedric my love. You have nothing to worry about. I got a new job and that was one of my coworkers."

"What? You got another job? That's great, baby."

"I can't wait to see you. I have so much to tell you."

"I got a lot to tell you too." Cedric heard the click signifying the call was about to end. "I'll call you tomorrow with an update, but you can expect to get a call before three."

"Okay, Ced. I love you."

"I love..." Click. The call was disconnected before Cedric could finish saying goodbye.

Cedric replaced the phone on the receiver and walked past the line of inmates queued up to make their weekly phone calls. What he knew now, that he didn't know before he became an inmate, was the importance of those weekly phone calls. Just a few minutes of hearing a loved one's voice was enough to make even the most hardened criminals weep. The people on the outside did not know this, but it was a well known fact that many inmates were heartbroken if they happened to miss out on their weekly call. For them, those five minutes of speaking with a loved one, were worth more than all the gold in the world.

The daily routine of prison life was easier if one quickly adapted to the jailhouse culture. Cedric had to learn which prisoners were cool; which ones were crazy; and the ones to avoid at all costs in order—in order to just survive.

New inmates were the worst because they often entered prison believing their street credentials would see them through, but they soon discovered differently. Cedric had one advantage though. Because he had counseled so many of the young men, or their brothers, fathers or sons, he had a different type of credibility called *respect*. The knuckleheads knew to leave Mr. Parker alone because he was 'cool'. Also, the word had spread that he had not turned in the kid he had taken those drugs from. He could only assume those other boys on the basketball court had somehow made this fact known.

After that first visit from Joie, Cedric knew that in order to survive being imprisoned, he had to put thoughts of being released far from his mind. He saw how dudes who thought they were getting out lived on edge, waiting for the CO to pull them out of their cells when their attorney visited and the disappointment they went through when it didn't happen. Those guys jumped out of their skin whenever mail call rolled around as they waited for updates on their cases. And the longer they waited, the more anxious they became often becoming so tightly wound that they ended up committing minor infractions that ultimately prevented their release. Yeah, those were the guys who were doing real hard time.

Cedric had accepted his fate of spending decades behind bars— that is until the day Erica Robicheaux unexpectedly entered his life and lifted his hopes. For a minute, he became one of those anxious dudes. But ever since Erica's visit two weeks ago, when she told him that Bryson had changed his mind about going to the police, he went into a deep funk and had momentarily considered suicide. Thankfully, Kicks was there to help put his head back on straight. After that fiasco, he made a vow to himself to never let himself get caught up in that situation again.

And then this morning, totally out of the blue, Erica arrived with news that he was being released. Bryson had done the right thing and come through after all.

~ ~ ~

Joie stepped outside her building into the cold crisp air to steady her nerves. With each breath, she felt her heartbeat quicken with the realization that her husband was indeed coming home. In less than twenty-four hours, she would once again be Mrs. Cedric Parker, experiencing all the delights that came with that title.

The anticipation of seeing Cedric again left Joie with a strange combination of excitement mixed with trepidation. She wasn't sure what to expect. Cedric was the one who had filled her head with stories about how men were changed by prison life. Husbands who used to be mild-mannered would lash out at their wives and children because they had become accustomed to living in an atmosphere where violence could erupt at any moment. He likened their reactions to the Post Traumatic Stress Disorder experienced by soldiers returning home from war. Those outside the prison system didn't know it, but inmates were also susceptible to PTSD. And the results could be just as traumatic *and* just as deadly.

Chapter Forty-Four

Joie arrived at the Hampton Municipal Court building at precisely three o'clock. She parked in the same lot from six months earlier. Although Cedric wasn't able to call with the details of his release, Erica had. If everything went as planned, she would be with her husband in less than an hour.

The courthouse was fairly empty. As the majority of court cases tended to be held in the morning, most people were finished with their business and preparing to head home for the day.

She tried waiting outside the courtroom where Erica told her to wait, but her nerves would only allow her to sit still for two or three minutes at a time. So rather than jumping up whenever a door opened, she paced the hallway eyeing the holiday decorations to pass the time.

"Joie?" called out a man's voice. "Hey, Joie. Over here!"

She stopped pacing the hallway and turned upon hearing her name. Rufus, her ex coworker and friend, stood at the far end of the building clutching a small stack of papers on one hand.

"Rufus!" she called out as she walked towards him. "What a nice surprise!"

"Well, look at you looking all beautiful!" he exclaimed before enveloping her in a friendly embrace. "I missed talking to you, girlfriend."

"I've missed you too," she replied. "What are you doing here?"

"Trying to beat the deadline for this property tax reevaluation. I have until the end of the year to file, but everyone knows what happens during the last two weeks of December down here at city hall."

"Nothing!" they simultaneously declared before breaking out into laughter.

"You really do look amazing, Joie. I love the natural look. Very becoming." Rufus gave her the once over. "And I see you lost those few pounds you been tryin' to get rid of."

"Thank you," she replied, not wanting to explain the reason for her weight loss. "How have you been? How is it working up in Richmond?"

He put one hand on his hip, smacked his lips together, and rolled his eyes upwards in an unabashed display of gayness. "Gurlllll, you would not believe the mess going on since the office moved up there. Headquarters fired our old boss and put that African dude in charge."

"Really? Why?"

"They conducted an audit and discovered that sucker was embezzling money from several accounts and also taking kickbacks from some of our clients. He stole almost three-hundred thousand dollars over the past few years. First they fired him and then they pressed charges."

"I knew something wasn't right about him." Reflecting back on her boss's behavior over the years, she was not surprised by the news. "So they put Amir in charge of the entire office?"

"Uh huh. Sure did." Rufus checked the hallway to make sure no one was eavesdropping. He leaned in close and whispered, "And guess what else?"

"What?" she asked wide-eyed, drawn in by his drama.

"Amir said he wished they had brought you up there because you had the best results after the audit. He told everyone that they made a mistake letting you go because all your accounts were on point. He wanted to give you your job back."

Joie opened and then closed her mouth, recalling the last encounter with Amir. In her mind, it had not ended on a high note. "Amir said that about me? When?"

"He said it a few times. Most recently just a couple of weeks ago. We tried to reach you. Your voicemail said your phone was disconnected. I even drove past your house a few times, but I forgot you had sold it. Seems like you just dropped off the face of the earth."

"Rufus? Are you sure Amir said he wanted to rehire me?"

"Yes, I'm sure. He also told me he has a lot of respect for you because you refused to be bought." Rufus looked at Joie sideways. "I'm sure there is more to *that* story, but you can tell me another day. So what do you want me to tell him now that I've found you? And what is your new phone number?"

Joie felt as if a huge weight had been lifted from her shoulders. There had been numerous occasions over the past several months where she wanted to reach out to Amir to set things right. But due to great embarrassment over her behavior in that hotel room, she felt it was best to just let the situation settle down on its own. "Tell Amir that I appreciate his consideration, but I'm good."

"Oh. Okay," Rufus was surprised. "So you *don't* want your old job back?"

"That's right." She slapped her forehead as if she had forgotten an important point. "You don't know…"

"Know what?"

"I'm working over at NASA now. And I'm making almost twice what I made on the old job."

"Good for you!" He gave her a high five. "You go girl!"

"It was pretty rough for awhile not having a job, but I'm on my way back."

"I hear ya," Rufus took notice of Joie's empty hands while juggling his own loose papers. "So what brings you to the court building at this hour?"

She considered telling Rufus about her situation, after all, there was a time when she considered him as her dear friend. Yet, as she ruminated over the details of her life, she suddenly realized that it was okay to move on. There was no purpose in telling this man about her troubles because now they were mostly behind her. So she simply said, "I'm meeting my husband here."

"Oh. Okay." He checked the time on his watch. "You know, I'd love to stay and meet him, but the tax office closes in fifteen minutes. If I don't get this taken care of today, Lord knows when I will."

"That's okay, Rufus. We can get together some other time." Although Joie had said those words in sincerity, in her heart she knew the more appropriate words should be 'Good-bye'. Because just like her mother told her some people come into your lives for a just a moment.

"Well, you take care of yourself, Joie." Rufus also knew this was good-bye. "I'm happy you're doing so well. You deserve it."

"Thanks." She turned on her heels and made it back to the designated waiting spot outside Court Room number 3. Now that she knew Amir had let bygones be bygones, she was all too willing to put that business in the past and leave it there forever.

Joie sat outside the courtroom patiently awaiting Erica's arrival, passing the time by watching other people and playing a guessing game writing the script of their lives. She noted there was a lack of smiling faces in this section of the courthouse because this is where lives were coming to an end. She wondered how many young people had traded in their youth for a life behind bars. By the look of the women and children streaming through the court's doors, it was way too many.

The wooden bench seemed to grow harder with each passing moment. After running into Rufus, she decided to stay put, lest she unexpectedly come across another acquaintance. She opened her purse looking for her cell phone before remembering it was locked inside the glove compartment of Cedric's car.

In the midst of people watching, Joie noticed a young woman who was barely twenty pushing a baby stroller from the courtroom. Her gaze settled upon the face of the precious baby sleeping underneath the covers. She smiled before glancing up at the baby's mother.

"What the fuck you lookin' at?" asked an angry young man glaring directly at her.

Joie looked up, startled by the booming voice aimed in her direction. A young man of barely legal age, stood with his legs slightly parted to hold up the pants that hung way below his rear. He wore a Yankees baseball cap with the rim squared off atop his head. The anger coming from him was palpable, though misplaced.

"I said what the fuck you lookin' at bitch?!"

"I-I-I was just thinking how pretty your baby is, that's all."

"Don't be lookin at my muthafuckin' baby!" the young man shouted.

The baby's mother giggled as if her man insulting a woman for smiling at her baby was somehow appropriate. She pulled the blanket over the child's face and rolled her eyes in Joie's direction.

Instead of responding like she normally would have, Joie turned her head. If that young man was angry enough to get pissed because someone said his child was pretty, then Lord help the child because it wouldn't have a chance with parents like that.

The clock struck four at precisely the moment Erica Robicheaux exited through the court room doors.

"Hello Joie" She extended her hand. "It's good to see you again."

"Hi Erica." Joie gripped the woman's slender hand. "I can't thank you enough for what you've done for my family. I couldn't believe it when Cedric called and said he was getting out today."

"Don't thank me. You can thank Bryson Graves for finally stepping forward. Without his confession, none of this would have happened."

Joie thought about Ranesha and what she must be going through sending her son off to Juvenile Detention. However, as much as she sympathized with Bryson, he had to learn from his mistakes now or risk much worse as he grew older.

"How much longer before Cedric is released?"

"Actually, that's why I'm here..."

"Oh no..." Joie felt her heart sink. "What's wrong?"

"Nothing is wrong. I came to walk you down to where Cedric is. He's completing the paperwork as we speak."

Joie clutched her chest and sighed out loud in relief. "I'm sorry. It's just that I still can't believe this is finally almost over. I keep thinking somebody is going to walk up to me and say there's been another mistake."

"Well, that isn't going to happen. Once your husband is released, his record will be expunged and you all can go home to begin putting your lives back together.

"That sounds good to me."

"Alrighty then. Let's go get your husband."

Joie passed by the young couple who continued to glare at her.

"Bitch!" the young man said.

"What was that about?" Erica said.

"Sadly, that is our future generation," she answered.

Both ladies continued to the lower level and headed towards an office enclosed by glass walls. When she caught sight of Cedric's gaunt body sitting across the desk from the court clerk, she gasped in surprise.

"What happened to him?" Joie asked, covering her mouth to hide her shock. "He's so thin."

"Some men in prison are too stressed to eat. I guess Cedric was one of them." Erica reached out and gently lowered Joie's hand from her face. "No matter how shocked you are at his appearance, he's coming home with you."

Apprehension crept into her bones as she wondered if her husband's physical appearance was any indication of his mental state.

"Honey, you can work on fattening your husband up when you get home."

"You're right." Joie's eyes welled up with tears. "I guess it's true. I am finally getting my husband back."

Cedric glanced to his right at the two women standing outside the office staring at him. At first he didn't recognize his wife because Joie had lost so much weight. She also sported a new hairstyle. The false eyelashes were gone, as well as the overly made-up face. She was dressed in a simple pullover sweater, a pair of nice slacks, and boots. All-in-all, she was a beautiful sight for sore eyes.

"Can I go inside now?" Joie asked.

"Sure. I think they are just about finished with the paperwork," Erica remarked.

Joie thought she had taken several steps towards the entrance, but in reality, her feet remained planted squarely on the floor. In the hallway. She felt a gentle nudge at her back.

"Go on…" Erica encouraged.

Cedric rose to his feet upon seeing that Joie was headed towards him. He ran his hands over his face and tried to smooth out the wrinkles of the now baggy jogging suit he wore when he was first imprisoned. The gesture was meant to make himself more presentable. It did not work.

Instead of experiencing feelings of relief at finally seeing Cedric again, ugly irrational thoughts crept into Joie's mind about what may have happened to her husband during his short prison stint. She silently cursed herself for having watched all those crazy movies about prison life because now she wondered if her husband might have gotten caught up in it. She closed her eyes and pushed the unimaginable away. There was no way in hell that Cedric could be turned out by a bunch of thugs. She hoped.

He noticed the hesitation on her part, but chose to overlook it because his own imagination was also working overtime. He knew that his wife got things done using whatever means necessary. Joie's resourcefulness had caused issues between them more than once, but this time he appreciated her ingenuity. He pushed away his own ugly thoughts about what he imagined his wife had to do to keep the family together, because as everyone loves to say about situations they have no control over, 'it is what it is'.

A tear slid from Joie's eye. She gave him a reticent smile. It was so unlike her.

"I missed you," was all he could manage to say.

"I missed you more," she whispered in return. "Are you okay?"

"Come here." He pulled his wife into his open arms. "It's the same ol' me. Ain't nothing changed, baby. I am still your man. All man."

At the sound of her husband's voice confirming what she already knew deep inside her heart, she felt everything was going to be okay.

All the uncertainties about why she remarried her husband were gone. The drama with her vacillating between Tomas and Cedric had been laid to rest. She had lost almost everything that mattered, was pushed into the lowest valley of her life, yet she had survived in spite of it all. At the end of the day, all that mattered was her children needed their daddy and she needed her man.

"Welcome home, Cedric. Welcome home..."

Chapter Forty-Five

Several months later...

"Ronnie, I cannot believe how good you look!" Joie exclaimed. "Even better than the last time I saw you."

"Girl, it took every ounce of will power I could find to lose the rest of that weight I gained from being pregnant. As soon as the twins were able to walk, I started working on me."

"Well, you look great!"

"Thanks. You're looking pretty good yourself." She glanced over at Cedric who stood admiring a colorful bauble imported from Indonesia. "You two look really happy."

Joie grinned from ear to ear. "We are. In fact, ever since he was released, Cedric seems to have made making me happy his mission in life."

"That explains your glow." She leaned in closer and asked, "Are you doing the same for him?"

"Let me put it this way... I lost him once because of my own selfishness and stupidity, and the second time because of a fluke. That man is the best thing that ever happened to me and I am not about to mess up again."

"I heard that..."

"How about you? Are you and Luis all right?"

"Better than ever."

"That's good to hear."

"So how long are you guys visiting this time?" Ronnie rearranged the window display consisting of various sized intricately woven bamboo baskets.

"Just five nights, this time. When we came down here for your wedding last year, Cedric insisted we make this our annual vacation. We both love Santo Domingo so it's not a difficult decision." She snickered. "Might even decide to move down here like you guys did."

"I understand. I love this city and cannot imagine living anywhere else."

"In all seriousness Ronnie, I'm just happy to have my husband back home. I learned a whole lot about myself during that time. I also discovered that being a prisoner's wife ain't no joke."

"I'm just happy everything worked out for Cedric. And for your family."

"Yeah, and thanks to Erica, with the money he received from that fund established to assist the "wrongly accused", we decided to splurge part of it on this much needed vacation."

"You ain't the only one needing a vacation. Now that both me and Luis are working full time, we hardly ever see each other at home."

"I hope you're not leaving my godchildren with a babysitter."

"Naw girl, Luis' mother helps out with the twins."

Joie raised her eyebrows. "The way you talk about those babies, I can't imagine you ever wanting to be away from them."

"Oh, don't get me wrong. I see the twins throughout the day. Their *abuela* brings them over quite often." She laughed.

"What about Luis? What does he think about you working?"

"Girl, he was the one who encouraged me to open this shop down the street from his store. He loves the idea that his wife is an entrepreneur."

"Ooooh good! You guys probably hook-up in the back room to get your groove on, huh?"

Ronnie laughed out loud. "And you know we do. Every chance we get!"

"That's my girl." Joie glanced at Cedric hanging out near the back of the store. "Umph! That man shops more than some women I know."

"Hey, leave him alone. If your husband wants to buy a few gifts, let him. I'll even give you the friend's ten percent discount."

"Ten percent? Is that all?"

"Okay. Fifteen." Ronnie enjoyed the banter.

Joie selected a vase from the shelf. "This is pretty."

"Funny you would choose that particular piece. Tomas found that vase in a little village in Sierra Leone."

"Tomas de la Cruz picked this out?"

"The one and only."

"So...uh... How is *Señor* de la Cruz?"

"Girl, you know Tomas. Nothing ever gets him down for long."

"You guys still keep in touch?"

"Well, he *is* Luis' cousin. And he visits so often, you might as well say he lives with us part time."

"Is that right?" She checked on Cedric before whispering, "Did he get my letter."

"Yeah, he got it. He seemed cool with whatever you wrote."

"That's good."

"Yeah, he's been traveling a lot lately. He brings back funky little finds. Sometimes he'll even take Kiara with him if she's here visiting with us."

"Speaking of Kiara, how is she?"

"She's fine. Even bought a nice little condo in Santa Elena near Travis, and she is working full-time at Luis's old company."

"That's wonderful..." Joie glanced over to see where Cedric was. "Soooo... It sounds like Tomas is doing pretty good for himself. Is he working for you?"

"He does okay." Ronnie did not like discussing the status of her cousin with Joie, considering their history. "As a matter-of-fact, Tomas is part owner of this shop. He only does the traveling because I can't."

"Good for him..."

Ronnie hoped mentioning Tomas would not stir up any feelings in her friend. She also hoped for Joie's sake that she was totally over him.

On Joie's part, as far as she was concerned, she did not want to continue discussing Tomas, or recall any part of her previous relationship with him. She was remarried to Cedric now and that was the way she wanted things to remain. She abruptly changed the subject.

"Ronnie, I absolutely love the name of your boutique."

"It is kinda catchy, ain't it?" Ronnie gushed proudly.

"I should have known you would name your store *In the Offbeat*."

"I thought it was an appropriate name because it is my philosophy about life."

"Know what? At first I thought that living in the offbeat sounded like some new age shit. But I have to admit that I finally understand what you mean. I even felt it for a minute. Funny thing is, instead of me living in the offbeat, I was lost between the beats of my life. Things were pretty messed up for awhile."

"Joie, when you live a life you're not meant to live, you will never be able to discover your joy. Your peace. Infinite love. Plus, if you have a life filled with drama, you may temporarily discover the offbeat, but you won't remain there for long."

"I have turned over a new leaf," Joie declared. "I have put all that drama aside to live a normal life with the love of my life."

Ronnie smirked at her friend. She knew better.

"Okay… At least I will never be bored." Joie smiled inwardly at the secret she had yet to share.

"As long as it works for you…"

"So exactly why did you name your shop *In the Offbeat?*"

"First of all I like the phrase. People see *In the Offbeat* and want to know what it means."

"Makes sense…"

"And just look around." She swept her arm across the eclectic, yet cozy space. "No two items are alike. All the products we sell are unique and made by people who live their lives on their own terms."

"Do you sell anything made in China?"

"Not if it's mass produced. We are very selective who we buy from." Ronnie continued, "Take that vase you're holding, for instance. While Tomas was visiting Sierra Leone, one of his friends introduced him to a woman who owned literally nothing more than the dress she wore on her back. By our definition, you would probably think she was living a miserable existence."

"Was she?"

"Just the opposite. This woman spent her days making beautiful vases from bits and pieces of things people tossed away. Tomas asked her why she put so much attention into fashioning items that were basically useless."

"What did she say?"

"She told Tomas that making those vases was her contribution to the world. That it gave her joy to produce something beautiful from what others considered as trash. She made these vases and gave them away because it made her feel good. Well, Tomas agreed to purchase her entire inventory."

"What will happen when you run out?" asked Joie, carefully returning the vase to its place on the shelf.

"Nothing. We will just sell something else."

"You have a lot of nice pieces here. And very expensive." Joie peeked at several price tags. Very few items were within her affordable price range. "People pay good money for this stuff?"

"You would be surprised at what tourists pay for one-of-a-kind artwork. Luis knows this guy who works over at that resort where you're staying. They agreed to bring a tourist bus by the store every Saturday and Sunday in exchange for a small commission. Most of the tourists like the items so much that they contact me when they return home asking about other items I have in stock. I've even started selling items online through my website."

"Sounds like you are doing pretty good for yourself, girlfriend."

The phone behind the counter rang. Ronnie rushed over to answer.

Cedric had intentionally given the women their privacy to chat. When he saw Ronnie break free to answer the phone, he made his way to the front of the store. He plopped his shopping basket on the counter.

"Did you tell her?" he whispered into Joie's ear.

"No, not yet. Give us a minute to catch up first."

"Okay, but don't let it go too long."

"I will tell her in my own way." She glanced at the shopping basket. "What's all that?"

"Gifts for the kids and your father. They always say we never bring back anything for them."

"Maya and Trey always say that even though we *always* bring them something back from our trips."

"I know, but since they're in Florida visiting your father for spring break, I thought these little figurines of jazz musicians standing under palm trees would be nice. The saxophonist is for your dad. The bass player for Maya, and the drummer for Trey. "

"Baby, you are so thoughtful." Joie poked around the basket. "I hope you didn't pick up anything too expensive."

"We're on vacation. Don't worry. I got this covered."

"You know the lease payment for our building is due when we get back. And don't forget about payroll…"

"I have not forgotten, sweetheart."

"The boss can't afford to not be on top of things." She gingerly rested her hand on his forearm.

"Yeah, yeah, yeah… I know we have to pay our employee's salaries. Don't you worry your pretty little head about it."

Ronnie hung up the phone and returned to where Joie and Cedric stood.

"That was Luis' mother. She's on her way over with Isabella and little Luis. She'll be here in an hour. Can you guys stick around?"

Cedric answered, "I'm sorry, Ronnie. But we have to check into our room by three. Joie just wanted to stop by to see the store since it's on the way."

"I understand." She hugged her friend. "Okay, I'll let you guys go if you promise to drop by the house for dinner before you leave."

"Don't you worry about that. I am not leaving this country without seeing my beautiful little godchildren. And Luis, too," Joie added.

"Well, all right. Let me ring you up so you guys can get going."

"And don't forget to throw in the really good friend *and* godmother discount."

"I'll hook you guys up, Joie."

While Ronnie wrapped the figurines in bubble wrap and placed the items inside protective cardboard boxes, Joie proceeded to stare at Ronnie with a sly grin on her face.

"You look like you are up to something. In fact, I know you are..." Ronnie laughed. "...because you look like the cat who swallowed the canary."

Joie smacked her lips together and tried to pout. "Lawd have mercy. It's scary how well you know me."

Ronnie went over to the door and flipped the sign around to 'Closed'. "Okay, Joie. What the hell is going on? Why are you being so mysterious?"

Joie glanced backwards at Cedric. He nodded. "Well, we have some good news!"

"Would you stop being so dramatic and just tell me already?!"

Joie clapped her hands together and jumped up and down. She shouted, "I'm pregnant, Ronnie! We're going to have a baby!"

"What? Did you just say you were pregnant?"

Cedric joined the two women. A look of gratitude spread across his face. "Surprise!"

"Really? You're pregnant for real?!"

Joie nodded.

"Noooo." Ronnie clamped her hands over her mouth and then embraced her dear friend. "You're joking!"

"Nope. I'm really pregnant."

"How far along?" She pulled back to look at Joie's waistline.

"According to my last checkup, I'm about four months."

"Oh my God! Joie! Cedric!" Ronnie burst into happy tears because she knew how much they both wanted this. "What a blessing!"

"Thank you, girlfriend. I didn't think it was possible."

Ronnie's hands went to her face as she tried to quell the tears that sprang forth. She was so happy for her friend who seemed to finally be experiencing the joy she had searched for so long. She no longer seemed lost.

As for Cedric, he smiled in contentment because they were living the life they both so much wanted. While in prison, he had spent his time taking classes on becoming an entrepreneur. Upon his release, he drafted a business plan, obtained a small business loan, and opened a learning center for middle school students right smack dab in the middle of Hampton. With a strong focus on tutoring, self-development, and providing teens a safe place to hang out, the *Young Intelligent Teens* place, or YIT as the kids coined it, had proven to be more profitable than anyone had expected.

With the collaboration of several influential educators in the area, including the support of Larry Robicheaux and also Miss Lettie, throwing their support behind Cedric's idea, in the three months since opening the YIT, they were inundated with requests to join, resulting in a six month waiting period.

Cedric chimed in with joyful tears clouding his vision. He looked at Joie and declared, "Veronica, this woman right here has made me the happiest man on earth. I love her with all my heart."

"I love you, baby," Joie whispered in his ear and kissed his tears away. To Ronnie she said, "I think I finally discovered my purpose."

"Raising your children?" Ronnie asked.

"Raising my children is part of my purpose of. But more importantly, my purpose is standing by my man and supporting him while he does his part to make this world just a little bit better than when we got here. One child at a time."

Ronnie shot Joie a questioning look. "What are you talking about, Joie? I thought we were discussing your new baby."

"It's all good, girlfriend. Cedric and I will tell you and Luis all about it over dinner."

~~~ The End ~~~

About the Author

PATRICIA HOPKINS is the author of three other novels, *MORE THAN A NOTION, LIVING IN THE OFFBEAT*, and *LOVING IN THE OFFBEAT*. She has also written a collection of short stories to include I AM THE SHADOWMAN, and OLD GRACIOLA YOUNG. A native of St. Louis, Missouri, she now resides in Texas.

Visit her website www.wanderlustbooksllc.com for more information on upcoming releases.

www.ingramcontent.com/pod-product-compliance
Lightning Source LLC
Chambersburg PA
CBHW060416260626
47161CB00013B/215